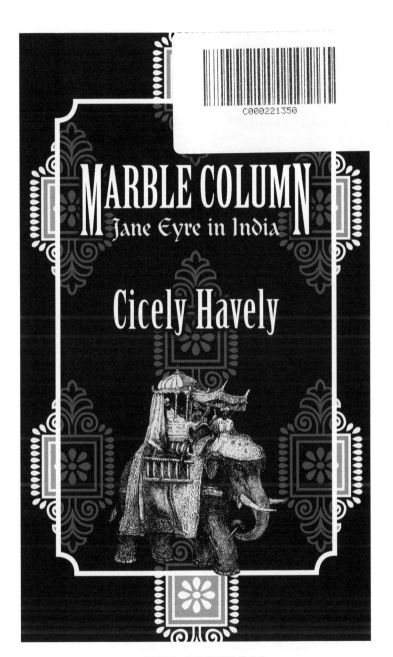

# MARBLE COLUMN
## Jane Eyre in India

## Cicely Havely

*EER FICTION*
Edward Everett Root, Publishers, Brighton, 2022.

***EER FICTION***

Edward Everett Root, Publishers, Co. Ltd., Atlas Chambers, 33 West Street, Brighton, Sussex, BN1 2RE, England.

*Full details of our overseas agents in America, Australia, Canada, China, Europe, and Japan and how to order our books are given on our website.*

www.eerpublishing.com

edwardeverettroot@yahoo.co.uk

Cicely Havely, *A Marble Column. Jane Eyre In India.*

Hardback ISBN 9781913087845

eBook ISBN 9781913087852

First published in England 2022.
Cover by Pageset Limited, High Wycombe.

Book production by Andrew Chapman, PrepareToPublish.Com.

# THE AUTHOR

**Cicely Havely** was born in Yorkshire, grew up in Clifton, Bristol, and went to Oxford. After completing degrees in English, she joined the Open University, where her writing and broadcasts ranged from the medieval to the post-colonial. She has lived in the USA, and for over 30 years has travelled extensively in India and S.E. Asia.

*For Nick*

# CHAPTER 1

**It is a relief to be out on the road again,** now two years have passed. Time not for the grief to be done with, but time for a man to take charge of life once more. Edinburgh will do it. But it is stuffy inside the carriage, even though a pelting rain drives against the windows with each squally gust. A faint catch of breath in his daughter's nose tells him she is asleep – a snore, one would call it, if Adèle were not such a very refined young lady. And dutiful too, trying her best to describe the passing scenery for her blind papa: *There are sheep…And now there are turnips*. It has to be said that she lacks his wife's once keen eye for the natural world. It is high-time for Jane to turn back to the living.

His daughter has her own gifts. Adèle can sing an elaborate new song after half-an-hour's study, and he has been told that no-one trims a new bonnet more cleverly. Like her mother. And no doubt there are other talents that she has inherited from her French *maman*. He shifts a little, because it would be unwise to recall Céline's particular accomplishments; but he thinks that their daughter ought soon to be married.

The night of her eighteenth birthday, after an hour's dancing, panting a little, her breath on his cheek sweet with some nearly harmless punch. The candlelight catches a gleam of sweat on her neck, and when she squeezes his hand, her glove is damp. Then Lady Ingram's sour whisper, behind her fan: *a husband is needed for that one, fast. But who would have her?*

As matters stand now, Adèle will be a stupendous heiress. Could

I

any suitor be indifferent to both her prospects and her tainted blood? She will be easy prey. Any young creature would be fretting after two years' mourning. Soft rustles and creaks tell him she is waking up. 'Are we nearly at the inn, Papa?'

For her, this journey is to be a holiday. She deserves it. He bangs his cane on the carriage roof and Tug stirs at his feet as the hatch opens, letting a few drops of accumulated rain fall cold on his head. 'How far till we stop?'

The shaft of dull light dims further as Harry bends to answer. 'Five miles by the last post, Mr Rochester. We should be there within the hour.'

A sudden gust, stronger than before, rocks the whole carriage and a quick stream of water patters to the floor, rousing Tug completely now.

'Poor boy!' says Adèle, tousling his fur. 'Does oo want a walk then?'

This language that women use for pets – and babies. He wonders if she is even half-conscious of her needs. She must want to stretch her limbs as much as the dog does. 'Tug must be content with a turn round the stable-yard tonight. Harry can see to it.'

'Oh Papa!' says Adèle. 'Harry will be helping Robert bed down the horses, after this drenching. Let me take Tug, do Papa!'

'And have you drenched too? Not a bit of it. I will take the fellow.' He knows what stable lads are like.

'You will get your shoes dirty. Papa.' She is teasing him now. Tug, on a leash, will lead him safely past large obstacles, but feels no need to avoid dung. Quite the contrary.

'The boot-boy will take care of them. I need you to find our next instalment.' Among their boxes is a year's worth of back numbers. Reading the periodicals together is another pleasant habit that seems irretrievably lost.

The inn at Richmond knows him of old. 'Aye, we heard' says the landlady. 'The strangling sickness. To lose all three. The little ones – they're always a worry. But the big lad too –.' She sighs. 'And how's your poor wife bearing up? Not with you, I see. 'Tis understandable.' He is glad when she is summoned to the kitchen, where the smell of roasting meat promises a good dinner.

A lively fire burns in a snug private room. He will drink in company, but he prefers to eat in private. The wine is more than passable, for an inn.

'This will interest you, Papa' says Adèle when she joins him. 'It is

Mr Lockhart, in Blackwood's.' He can tell, from the altered sound as she sits, that she has changed her dress. A waft of her light cologne swells in the fire's heat. *'Our very footmen compose tragedies, and there is scarcely a superannuated governess in the island that does not leave a roll of lyrics behind her in her band-box...'.* She stops and gives a haughty sniff. 'Huh! We do not care to hear governesses referred to so slightingly, do we papa?'

She wants him to laugh, and he does, though the sensation is unfamiliar. 'No indeed! I have always maintained that your stepmother should write a novel.' He remembers how she would say *And where will I find the time?*

'Shall I bring in your dinner?' The landlady's voice breaks in on his thoughts. 'And who is this fine young lady?'

Surely she cannot suspect −? 'My daughter' he insists. 'From a previous − '

'Ah!' She interrupts, as if no more need be said.

*Bertha* he thinks. *She supposes I refer to the mad-woman.* He does not choose to correct her, thinking that the world has shifted while they mourned, and he is impatient to catch up.

**The new house is what has brought him to Edinburgh** − or so he has given it out. Grief has made the house at Ferndean as uninhabitable as the Thornfield ruins. Every slight acquaintance tells him that what his wife needs is a change of scene, and so he has engaged an Edinburgh architect. James Mackenzie, the coming man, has promised to build him the finest house in —shire, though as a remedy Rochester fears it will be no more effective than a quack's bolus.

The coming man is flirting with his patron's daughter. It is unnecessary to ask for Adèle's raptures over every last detail of the plan − which she is familiar with already because she has written letters at her father's dictation and read out Mackenzie's replies.

'Comfort and convenience, expressed with elegance' the young man declares. 'These are my watchwords! Could anything better convey the spirit of our times, Miss Rochester?'

'I'm sure the new house will be all those things' she replies. 'But I have to admit some small regret for the loss of mystery in modern buildings. Where are the secret passages, the concealed chambers?'

The young puppy expects no more than simpering agreement, her father thinks with some admiration. But despite that, he must side with his architect. 'There will be no mystery in *this* house.' He has spoken too sharply. 'In my experience, romance in a house means no better than gloom and bad drains.'

Mackenzie springs to his feet and turns a page in his portfolio. 'Light and good drainage are guaranteed, but romance is an option readily available. Indeed, I have anticipated Miss Rochester's wishes, as you can see.' And with a shiny silver pencil he points to the new diagram.

A draughtsman has heavily inked-in the outline of the ground-plan, so that the patron can make it out; but now, at some distance from the frontage, something else is indicated: an irregular, jagged shape.

'What's this? Do you have in mind some folly? A grotto, perhaps? Am I to add a hermit to my household?'

Mr Mackenzie is positively dancing. 'A grotto? Oh, very good! But better still – a ruin! The remains of the old hall. *Nothing* could be more exquisitely picturesque.'

In Adèle's raptures he hears escaping all her pent-up self-restraint. He picks up the architect's magnifying glass, ostensibly to peer at the plans laid out in front of him, but actually to withdraw a little from these wild transports and Mackenzie's lavish plans for his money. At her age, and with her mother's blood, how could she not want to be in the fashion? Is it any wonder that after being mured up for so long she should have a taste for tales of nuns locked in their silent cells, while all the currents of life beat up against their cloistered walls? He had thought to pull down the blackened ruins of that ill-fated house, but if it will please her, then let the ruins stay. He himself will hardly see more than a blur in the distance.

And what of Jane? All he can feel sure of is her indifference.

'Can we go, dear Papa? Oh, *please* let us go!'

Bewildered, he thinks for a moment that the architect must have made bold in some oafish way; but instead Adèle is imploring him to accept an invitation.

'It is an assembly, Papa! There will be music, and dancing – and – Papa! – the author of Waverley himself is promised!'

He is being invited to an assembly.

'There will be many learned gentlemen for you to meet, Papa.'

'And learned ladies' adds the coming man. 'Miss Rochester will be an ornament –'

Even Tug is pawing at his leg. 'The great Scott himself, eh? He has another book out, I believe.' His daughter has not forgotten how to twine him round her little finger. Like her mother.

**In the carriage, as they return to their lodgings**, he senses the particular fidgets of a young woman who wants a new dress – though she says not a word. And why deny her? After so long in black she must surely be allowed to primp again. It is good to have one woman in the world that he can make happy. She shall have the Thornfield ruin, and she shall have her dress. Some light colour. Something that he can see.

'Et maintenant. Un petit cadeau pour ma trés chère petite fille. Une nouvelle robe, peut-être?'

Already she knows the names of the best dressmakers in town, though when she had the opportunity to find them out, he cannot think. In a hushed, velvet-soft boutique he fingers the muslin. 'It seems very flimsy. You will catch cold. Remember, this is *proxima Thule*.'

Adèle pirouettes; a pale shimmer, a gleam in the mirror. 'O Papa! It is the fashion! One never catches cold when one is in fashion.'

'A shawl, perhaps?' hints Madame. 'We have some very fine Indian shawls just come in.' A demure assistant shakes out the folds – soft green, amethyst – and in that small movement of air he catches a distant scent of sandalwood. The dog, bored until now, stirs and sniffs.

**Next morning, the carriage is ordered early.** It is still dark when the wheels roll over the cobbles: *rurr-attle-attle-at-at-at*. Adèle will sleep till midday after the excitement of the assembly. In a while the city is behind him, and as the first light breaks, he catches the smell of cattle on the move. Twice the carriage is halted as beasts are herded across the road. 'Gerroff, you daft buggers' shouts Robert, flicking his whip to keep their horns off the varnish.

Beyond the low farms there are few buildings, until the broad green pastures disappear and a high wall suggests that his destination must be close. A gatehouse of some kind. 'Mr Rochester, to see the Superintendent.' Not all are free to come and go here. Gravel under the wheels, and square lawns to either side. The sun is well up now, and when the carriage halts and he alights, the dog jumping down ahead of him, he can see that he is facing a modern building with a pediment over its central section. Low arcades join the centre to smaller, identical wings, and he wonders whether the disorderly minds which the building houses are soothed by its regularity. Out in the country here, the smoke has had no chance yet to dim the yellow sandstone, which glows happily in the early sun.

Robert secures Tug's harness, gives him the loop, and the dog takes off after new smells, nearly unfooting him. A figure in black introduces himself as the Superintendent's assistant. Dr Buchanan is making his morning rounds, but if Mr Rochester will follow, he will not have long to wait.

The doctor's library is well lit by two tall windows. Books line the walls and are piled high on the floor. The air is thick with the smell of paper, new and old, of pipe tobacco, and something else which has Tug as worked up as if he were investigating a rabbit warren. Trying to calm the dog distracts him from nervous anticipation of the interview to come, but Tug tangles his leash in the legs of some kind of cabinet, which topples and sends books, papers, a metal apparatus and a glass tumbler by the sound of it crashing to the floor. When Dr Buchanan arrives, he finds his visitor hardly more in charge of himself than he is of his dog.

'Good God, man, what do you have buried here?'

'My shrunken heads!' says the doctor. 'Newly arrived from the South Seas!' A whiff of sawdust suggests that he is delving in a packing-case.

Tug pulls enough to wrench his master's arm out of its socket. Rochester cuffs him and the dog sinks to the floor, apparently resigned – unlike his master, who is now very conscious that he does not present the composed, rational figure that he would wish, given that he is consulting the superintendent of a celebrated lunatic asylum. There is enough light for him to see that the doctor is a burly figure. His coat appears to be made of some rough mustard-coloured tweed, while his waistcoat is bright yellow. A vagueness below suggests that his breeches and stockings must be dark in colour. But chaotic though his personal habits would seem to be, Dr Buchanan's brisk opening words announce a man whose constant professional aim is to restore calm. 'A fine dog you have there. I gather you have trained him to lead you about. A most ingenious idea. What do you call the fellow?'

He knows that he is being put at his ease. A familiar medical procedure. 'Tug. His sire was called Pilot, which would have been a better match for the function.'

'But the name serves ed-mirably! Are ye not familiar with the new

6

tug-boats that bring ships into harbour? Steam-driven – as I think this eager chap must be.'

The doctor's accent seems curiously refined for a large man – a slight pursing of the vowels. 'Tug because from a puppy he would rather choke than submit to the leash.' He suspects that Dr Buchanan may think he is describing himself. It is time to take charge. 'Doctor. I am here not on my own account but for the sake of my wife.'

'And does she know that you are here? Is she aware of the implications of this consultation?'

'She knows that I am deeply troubled by her persistent melancholia.' He would like the doctor to know that he has some expertise.

Dr Buchanan is searching among the papers on his desk. He swears under his breath as something falls to the floor. 'Your letter. You use an *amanuensis*. This is a lady's hand?'

'My daughter. Naturally I could not set out the exact nature of my concern.' Adèle should not know that he fears his wife is half-way to being driven mad by her loss. Now is the moment to be explicit, but something holds him back.

'Your daughter? So you have a surviving child – from a previous marriage?'

'From an ancient liaison. She is the only thing about it that I do not regret.'

'But your wife has lost all her children. Such wounds do not heal fast.'

He bursts out. 'Good God, man! Do you not think –' Tug lifts his head, gives a short, subdued bark. 'It is not her grief, but the manner of it. Her silence. Her lack of response. My wife is a woman unusually adept in expressing her feelings. Her powers of description were incomparable. For ten years she was not just my eyes upon the material world, but my eyes into the darkest corners of my understanding –'

'Whoa there Mr Rochester! There are men who would welcome a degree of silence in such a wife! But are her powers of description all that you are missing? Are you not saying that it is some greater loss you are suffering? You had a wife as your companion and help-meet – your bed-fellow too. A man such as yourself –'

The doctor is probing too close to the nerve. Besides, he has not come here to talk about himself. 'She appears to be dead to all feeling – and yet I know from the turmoil in my own soul –' He breaks off, and becomes aware that his own silence has been noted, though surely in a man, silence regarding the state of his inmost feelings must be the proper course.

After a while Dr Buchanan resumes. 'It could be said that your wife's previous compulsion to find expression for every fleeting sensation was a form of nervous excess, and that her present reticence is more normal in a female. However, you would not have written had you not some reason to think that her silence was morbid. Has the lady exhibited any tendency to self-destruction?'

'For my wife, that would be a sin. It is quite unthinkable.'

'She is religious? An excess of religion is a well-known cause of melancholy.'

'She was not formerly a zealot. Nor an enthusiast. But she believes that our lives – and thus our children's deaths – are ordered by God.'

'Does she think those deaths were a punishment? For what sin?'

He drops his head, holds out his arms – as if, for a moment, he is crucified. 'What indeed? For being more content than most of the world?' With an effort he pulls himself together. 'I have tried to reason with her. A loving God does not punish the innocent. My wife was until recently a woman of such animation that I was always aware of her inner thoughts at work, like a vibration. Now that inner life seems to have dwindled – to nothing.'

The doctor scribbles a while, then leans back. 'Believe me, her inner thoughts are still circling – though she may not understand them and you cannot read them.' Rochester recognises the gesture of a fat man trying to dig his watch out of his waistcoat pocket. 'But I must be in the Old Town by noon and I need to consult my assistant beforehand. May I beg a seat in your carriage? We can continue our conversation as we ride.'

**Nose down, the dog pulls him over the gravel.** What he is after, God knows. What he himself is after is just as compelling, just as elusive. The doctor's measured deliberations have only stoked his frustrations.

Tug stops to cock his leg. When Dr Buchanan has gathered his papers, Rochester must be ready with a better account of why he is here. Jane is not mad as the world knows madness. That he must make plain. She is not violent, like Bertha; she does not rave. Tug plunges on again, making it impossible to keep track of his thoughts. He yanks crossly at the leash. Surely Buchanan is ready to be off by now. His wife is not a lunatic. She does not bay at the moon – only stares at it, hour after hour. A spasm of fear runs along his veins. She must be cured. That is why he is here. This fellow Buchanan is reputed to have worked miracles.

He hauls Tug round until he can see the bulk that is his carriage in the distance, and the smaller, human blur with a yellow waistcoat, waiting. The dog sets off at a run.


**The doctor still seems more interested in Tug** than the plight of his wife. 'You put a deal of trust in the beast, I see. To run with him like that. Have you no fear of an obstacle?'

He ignores the question. 'Where am I to take you? Be good enough to give my coachman your instructions.' Surely in his own conveyance he will have some authority. 'I fear I have not given you an adequate description of my wife's condition.'

'To Liberton's Wynd if you please. So, tell me – your wife.'

But he does not know how to begin. 'My wife is not mad, but her mind is disordered. She does not see what is not there, nor does she hear voices. But –'

Buchanan interrupts. 'As before, you tell me only what she is not, or what she is no longer. And even of that – with respect, Mr Rochester – I doubt you can be sure. Blindness must hamper your observations, and I cannot believe that you – a rational Englishman – have actually asked the lady whether she is seeing what is not there.'

Is he being laughed at? In the silence that follows he wonders how much Robert is hearing, from the coachman's seat.

Buchanan starts afresh. 'You and I, Mr Rochester, were raised to believe that reasoning will supply every answer. But this modern age is telling us that reason is not enough. To men of science – like ourselves – your wife's conviction that these deaths are a punishment is not reasonable. We blame foul waters or a pestilential vapour.'

He attempts to curb his impatience. 'No act she might have committed deserves such a sentence.'

The doctor gives a short laugh. 'Few men would be so confident of their wives' unblemished virtue, Mr Rochester. And there are sins of omission as well as commission. She has neglected some charitable duty, perhaps? Failed to support some indigent relative? These little things can loom large in the female conscience.'

'There can be nothing that would require the deaths of three children.'

'By your arithmetic, Mr Rochester. Not hers.'

The carriage rolls on towards Edinburgh for several minutes before Rochester speaks again. 'But she is still young – and I am not yet –'. He gropes for a word. 'Not yet enfeebled. Naturally I wish to help her recover her spirits.'

'A pilgrimage was once considered a reliable remedy.'

Yes, he is definitely being laughed at, and yet this notion finds a toehold in his brain. He recollects the dog, rousing himself when the dressmaker shook out her shawls. That whiff of sandalwood. It takes a moment to hear what Buchanan is saying.

'And it has become quite popular since the war. Combines all the advantages of a change of scene – sea air and all that – with a penitential degree of discomfort and a religious expiation. Eh?'

Temptation rushes towards him. To leave all this behind him; to flee – as he would once have fled from Thornfield and Bertha. But almost before he can register the thought, Buchanan has recalled his attention. 'Mr Rochester. You may not be aware that I know something of your history. Of your previous wife and the circumstances of her death.'

'What the devil has that got to do with you? Or with our present business?'

'Only that you may have more cause than most to dread a sickness of the mind.'

Unwillingly, he concedes the doctor's point. 'Beyond that, my history is no concern of yours. My present wife's condition is totally different.' Quite the opposite he thinks, grimly. Bertha was insatiable.

Buchanan laughs again. 'I'm afraid there's no one fonder of gossip than a medical man. The operation which restored some sight to your eye is justly famous, and with it something of the circumstances in which you were blinded in the first place.'

'And what is it that is said of – those *circumstances*?' If the villain does not take care, he will have Robert haul him out of the carriage.

'That you sustained your injuries in the course of trying to save a deranged arsonist from self-destruction.'

'Nothing more?'

'That she was – in law – your spouse. Good God man, why did you not have her kept secure in an asylum? The Retreat at York would have saved your trouble – and the risk of being burnt alive in your bed.'

Because Bertha would still be alive, he thinks. Her existence would be known. And Jane would not have married me. But what he tries to say has a little truth in it. 'For better or worse, she was mine. That place is run by Quakers, is it not? I fear that my late wife's predispositions –.' He stops, once again unsure of his words.

'Her nymphomania?'

The term is unfamiliar but he can guess at its meaning and he nods.

'You thought such God-fearing folk would be outraged? Tush, you will find few better acquainted with depravity. They send their women into the foulest prisons. But if you are thinking of putting your present wife away –'

Now it is his turn to interrupt. 'Never! Quite the reverse. I want her with me – but as she was.'

Buchanan carries on calmly. 'I think such a regimen might suit her well. The Quakers are expert in the borderlands between unreason and the voice of God. Or bring her to me. I am sure that your wife is not at present insane, Mr Rochester, though your concern does you credit. But without her, I can do little.'

*Not at present.* The words re-kindle a fear that was abating. 'And how would you treat her?' He has heard of horrors.

'We would talk, Mr Rochester. Only talk. My methods – which are being spoken of as revolutionary – are really very simple. Talk. Peace. A little kindness.'

'She barely talks to me.'

'A-ha!'

'You think that is specially significant? And that she might speak with you?' He can feel the doctor's eyes upon him. As the silence persists, Rochester finds a need to respond building irresistibly within him. He fights it down, thinking *This is how the man works.* God knows what nonsense I might spew if I give way. 'I do not think I could allow that. Nor do I believe that Jane herself would wish it.'

Buchanan bangs on the roof of the carriage. 'My destination, I am afraid. But I would like to continue our conversation – in a different setting.'

The fellow wants to prod my skull, he thinks. He feels that he has been taking part in an argument that he has yet to win, though he could not say what the dispute is about. Perhaps it is simply too long since his intellect enjoyed any exercise. 'I would be honoured to hear more of your work.'

'Then join me at my club. The Beggar's Blessing, in the Old Town.'

'A curious name.'

'With a curious history – which will be explained in due course. Shall we say nine?

**By eleven, Edward Fairfax Rochester is roundly drunk.** Drunker than he has been for a dozen years, and mighty pleased to be so, though now the stink of congealing mutton fat and the ammoniac reek of old cheese are warning him of the splitting head that awaits him tomorrow. Whole groves of empty bottles glint in the candlelight.

And yet he feels curiously invigorated, as if he were on the edge of some discovery. He looks round for his host but the doctor has left to relieve himself. It might be wise to ask to be shown to a chamber pot himself, before the evening becomes any more helpless.

The yellow waistcoat heaves into view and the legs of a chair screech on the stone floor as the doctor re-settles himself. 'Well, Rochester! How d'ye find our select gathering?'

Some ragged singing gathers volume at the other end of the table.

*Oh laddie! she cried and sighed, he's deid ma' puir eel!*
*He's knockit oot his brains 'gainst the bottom o' ma creel!*

Every word that can be stretched to imply something lewd is greeted with a coarse roar, and the banging of fists, tankards and the handles of knives. While he is aware that he is not renowned for his sense of humour, he wonders how any sane man can be amused by such idiocy.

Dr Buchanan grunts. 'To feel superior to this low wit is to be aware of the wisdom one has gained with one's years. Do ye no' agree?'

He could not have expressed himself better, but before he can muster a reply which would demonstrate his own superior wit, a lanky figure (half the bulk of the doctor) hoves into view.

'Well, Rochester! A good deal more to a man's liking than yester-night's prim dealings, would ye not say?'

He recognises the fellow now, who clearly thinks that his every word deserves the largest possible audience. At the assembly, he scrabbled for the Bard's attention. Popinjay, Adèle called him. A Marquis or some such. Among the introductions at the start of this evening he remembers other titles, a judge, two venerable advocates and a Professor of Greek who might also have been present on the more refined occasion. The popinjay brays along with the singing.

*Piper, quo Meg, hae ye your bags,*
*Or is your drone in order?*
*If ye be Rob, I've heard o' you;*
*Live you upo' the Border?*
*The lasses a', baith far and near,*
*Have heard o' Rob the Ranter;*
*I'll shake my foot wi' richt gude will,*
*Gif ye'll blaw up your chanter.*

More banging, whistles and trumpeting farts. Buchanan bellows over the din. Perhaps his great bulk preserves him from the worst effects of the drink. 'Explain the origins of our society to our guest, my Lord.'

With a wave of his arm the popinjay calls for a chair, and more wine. 'My ancestor' he announces; and as he seems to expect, the very word seems to command silence, save for a few snores. 'My ancestor, King James —'

'On the wrong side of the blanket' a voice interrupts.

'My *lusty* ancestor' continues the popinjay, much gratified by this acknowledgement of his ancestral bastardy, 'when traversing his domains in the guise of a bagpiper, once found himself stranded on the verge of a raging torrent.'

'Get to the point, my lord!'

My lord switches to an outrageous dialect. 'A buxom, gaberlunzie lass came to his rescue, hoiked up her petticoats' — much mighty roaring — 'and elevated her sovereign across her hurdies. He repaid her kindness wi' a gaud coin' — the roar grows to a crescendo, with more farts and whistles — 'an she gies him her blessing: *May prick nae purse nae fail ye!'*

'*May prick nae purse nae fail ye!'* chants the company.

He senses that all eyes are upon him. Leaning forward to reach his glass, he disturbs the dog, who has been sleeping under his chair, and now — possibly fuddled himself by the room's boozy fumes — wakes and barks loudly, like a guilty sentry aroused from a nap. But if this is a warning, his master pays no heed. Amid raucous laughter, Edward Fairfax Rochester pronounces a toast. 'A sentiment with which every man must concur: May prick nor purse ever fail us!' He is a long way from Ferndean.

Amid the general hubbub he finds the popinjay addressing him directly once again. 'The pretty creature hanging on your arm, last night. Not your wife, I'd wager.' He snorts with laughter.

The scoundrel means Adèle. 'My daughter, sir.' The wretch deserves to have his words knocked down his throat, and yet it is not disagreeable to have a pretty young woman in a fine new dress mistaken for his mistress. He is instantly mawkish. For too long he has been without the embraces that a mistress – or a wife – should provide. Once warm and ready limbs slumbered at his side. Now there is only emptiness.

Dr Buchanan has heaved himself to his feet. 'The singers have need of your fine baritone, my lord. And I have matters to talk over with our guest.' He hauls the lanky nobleman to his feet and gives him a shove towards a slurred reveller who has embarked on another ribald rigmarole: *Our bald-headed hermit, on ent'ring his cell.* He thinks it is the judge.

But if Buchanan is about to assert that this club of his is providing some kind of therapeutic parable, Rochester must prove that he is ahead of the game. 'I assume that what you observe here has some bearing on your understanding of your patients.'

'Say rather that it helps me to understand that there is a deal of madness in the sanest of men.'

'Which is better relieved here, where it will go no further, than in circumstances where it may break out dangerously.'

'Go no further?' The doctor pushes a flagon along the table. 'Of that I can hardly be sure. A recent resurgence in religion and respectability' (he is almost growling) 'has forced our wee brotherhood into the shadows. But – as I am sure you are aware – there are impulses which cannot be entirely suppressed and must find an outlet.'

Rochester sniffs the fumes that rise from the unstoppered neck then pours himself a large tot. There is something piquantly worldly about this conversation. His domestic circle at Ferndean has lacked any opportunities to talk of such matters, man to man. 'And so this society expresses the rebellious spirit of Caledonia?' He feels that the whisky has sharpened his wits.

The more raucous revellers have formed a line, which begins to circle the table. When one stumbles, the whole line threatens to crash on top of them, but with exaggerated cries of apology and concern they right themselves and the procession continues. Tug wakes up again, and pulls at his chain.

The doctor laughs. 'Pah! This is no better than a grog shop for rich hooligans. A salutary spectacle, do you not think?'

'And a ghastly warning.' The revellers are now grouped by the hearth, where there is enough life in the fire to outline a tottering huddle. Light gleams on pewter and on glass, and from a fumbled beginning a low chant arises.

'Lord Kelly's toast' the doctor informs him. 'A tradition of ours. *Rum holes in Jamaica.* Though its origins are obscure, the general meaning will be plain, I think. You married a plantation fortune yourself, did you not?'

Unconsciously, he has been expecting some personal application to emerge from this experience. But he is damned if he is going to be unsettled by the doctor's impertinence. 'I think I have paid the price for my error.' He unpins his sleeve, pushes it back, and holds up the stump of his arm.

His gesture coincides with a rare slump in the hubbub, which now dies away to a silence – broken, after a yawning moment, by a yelp of glee: *it's our bald-headed hermit – come again!* Under the uproar he hears the doctor's level tones: 'So you are after all a moral economist. What debt then does your wife think she owes, that she must pay with her children?'


**A servant is summoned to show him to his lodgings** – a servant plainly familiar with taking the weight of his drunken betters. 'Dinna let the hussies catch yuir ee, if ye value yuir purse.' Not ten paces out he picks up a scent that was once well known to him, a blend of frowsy finery, sweat and cunt, topped with patchouli. The darkness undulates with preening whores – the porch of the Beggar's Blessing is a prime site for trade. The servant clicks his tongue. 'A' wouldna, sarr. If yae dinna wan' ae dose' but he adds (rubbing thumb and fingers together) that there is better and cleaner to be had, for a consideration.

Pride will prevent him taking a whore – but by God, he wants a woman. The evening's entertainment has stirred a consciousness in his groin that something – perhaps the cold air – has turned to an ache. When a sleepy maid opens the door to his lodgings, Tug jumps at her. At her squeals, Harry his manservant emerges from the basement stairs, hauls off the dog and steers him by the elbow. Any man who returns to a respectable lodging at three in the morning must be expected to be the worse for wear, his master supposes, but Harry seems to assume that he is about to make a grab for the wench. As if he guesses what company that master has been keeping. The thought disgusts him. The lesson of the night is surely that he must be a better man.

'Down, sir! My dog is no gentleman, I fear.' He smiles at the maid, attempting to appear harmless and benevolent, but knows that his words are slurred.

'Is there anything I can do for you, sir?' The girl's voice trembles.

'You can get to bed. To your own bed. I'll fend for myself.' Dammit, a salacious shadow seems to cling to every word he utters.

She scurries off. 'Shall I take Tug to the gardens, sir?' Harry enquires. 'He'll need to lift his leg, and take a run before he settles.'

And so do I, he thinks. *A run. A ride. A rut.* The evening's cackles are still running in his head. Passing Adèle's chamber he stumbles over the turned edge of a mat, curses, then hushes himself noisily, loud enough to wake the dead. In his own room, he flings himself into a chair, closes his eyes – and the darkness lurches beneath him. Impossible to lie down until the worst effects have worn off. He should have gone out with the dog. For a moment, he thinks longingly of the night air, but as his adjusting sight makes out a tray, with bottles and glasses on a table by the fire, only one course of action seems feasible. He pours himself another drink, despite knowing full well the price he will pay for many hours to come.

*Pay. Pay.* What is this monstrous debt that his blameless wife believes is due? Whisky burns on his tongue. His sight. His hand. He has paid the price for his own misdeeds. Once he sought to escape the thrashing his conscience deserved by plunging into just such oafish excess as he has witnessed this evening. And worse. The sots he has kept company with tonight are mere windbags in comparison with the brawlers of his youth. A scathing contempt curdles his thoughts. Even now they will lie snoring and farting alongside their grimly patient wives. They lack the true bravado.

And again, he is thinking of Céline and the luxury of those perfumed hours with her dressmaker, watching her spend his West Indian gold. Bertha's fortune. How apt it seemed, to squander her dowry on a courtesan. A coal collapses in the grate, and a sudden bright tongue of flame illuminates the room for a moment. He is no better than the company he has left.

Scorn drives him to his feet. He crosses the room – aware, from the first step, that a scalding headache has taken hold – and pushes the curtains aside to find that the first light is touching the roof-tops. He strides back across the room and yanks on the bell. Orders strong tea and dry toast. Harry returns with a tray. 'Shall I let Miss Adèle know you'll be keeping to your room?' He shakes his head. Winces. The architect is expecting them. A new house. An old ruin.

With the first draught of tea he realises how parched he is. The toast is harder to face, but he must get something down. *The Retreat at York would have saved your trouble.* For twenty years he has laid the blame for his shameless adulteries at Bertha's door but never his own. She was his: she belonged in his house – the shameful, uncontrollable parts of himself, locked in the house he could not bear to inhabit until Jane came to live there. And now he has agreed that its burnt-out shell should be left to stand, to satisfy his daughter's romantic whim.

If he could, he would take the dog and leave. Have Harry bring a bag. Head for Glasgow and a ship. Flee the pother of the new house before its foundation stone is laid. But he cannot. It is not moral obligation that holds him back; more a fuddled sense that without an object, he is lost. He pulls at the neck of his shirt, suddenly in need of air to his throat. Rage has given way to something more like fear. As he forces himself to breathe deeply a sudden deathly weariness overcomes him. Bending to unfasten his shoes reminds him that he is still far from sober and he falls back onto the bed with his stockings tumbled about his ankles, and his breeches agape.

He dreams that he is clinging to the sides of an alarmingly frail boat that rises and falls as the waves pass beneath it. A hooded oarsman will not allow the tide to carry them forward and somehow he understands that they must wait for a wave larger than all the rest to carry them over some reef or sandbar. Each time the small craft rises and tilts he sees ahead of him a barrier of heaving waters and clotted foam – and is that sandalwood he smells? With all his strength he bawls for his wife – *Jane! Jane! Jane!* – but knows he has raised no more than a whimper. The wave that he has been waiting for, gathers beneath him. His own strangled snore wakes him. The sea still heaves.

# CHAPTER 2

**Diana, my cousin,** is come to keep me company while Mr Rochester travels to Scotland. Though she is a dear and familiar visitor, I would prefer to be alone, and so as I watch a cold sun flash on the window of my husband's departing carriage, my relief is marred a little by knowing that she is anxiously waiting for me within.

She calls from the hall. 'Come to the fire, Jane. It is starting to rain! You will catch a chill.'

No, I will not. Neither typhoid fever nor the strangling disease has laid a finger on me. Sometimes I fancy that I cannot die.

The tea things are set out on a low table by the hearth. Diana busies herself with hot water, with milk. Her sewing lies on a cushion. The long curls of her youth are tidied under a neat cap. So many times we have been together like this, ready to amplify the news that has already passed between us in the brief letters that are all a busy mother has time for. We have shared the small goods of our lives – have the white foxgloves flowered, how goes the curate's romance – by the fire with our sewing, once the children were asleep.

I must ask. It is always my first query. 'So how are the children?' My children are asleep. They will never wake again.

She sips her tea, and I know that for her too this moment is fraught with the change that has come between us. 'They are well' she says – cautiously, as if she thinks it might be kinder to report that they are ailing. Then she dares to look at me – her eyes as blue as her brother's – and perhaps relieved to discover that my expression is unaltered, she continues. 'George grows daily more like his father. He cut his finger quite badly, shaping the keel of his new boat, but he stood the stitching without a whimper.'

Diana's husband was a captain in the navy, now unwillingly retired: a fine man, used to command, struck down not by war, but by the peace. 'And is Captain Fitzjames more content?' This sequence is perfectly familiar, yet my voice seems strange to me.

She picks up her sewing. 'He rubs along' she says, as if she feels that she must make light of her troubles, because they are dwarfed by my calamity.

This is heavy work. I would like to say that I have a headache, that I must lie down, but it is not true and I could not stand the fuss. 'I hope it was not the knife that Mr Rochester gave him – that cut George's finger. I worried that it might be too sharp for a little boy.'

A slight shift in her posture tells me that Diana is more comfortable. I have given her a sign that we may talk about her children. They are staying with Diana's sister Mary and her brood, at the parsonage at Morton, out in all weathers. Mary is well. Her husband Mr Wharton is well. Lady Granby has presented both the boys' and the girls' school with new primers. She is well. Lady Granby's father – Mr Oliver – is not hale, but he too is well. 'Perhaps it is fortunate that Lady Granby was widowed so young. The marriage was never happy. But she will be lonely when the old squire dies.'

We fall silent at this. Diana sorts through her wools and rethreads her needle. The purpose of her work is not to refurbish her dining-room chairs, but to fill our silences. She smooths the canvas across her lap to check her pattern, but we are both thinking of her brother.

Diana believes that Rosamond Oliver – the unhappy Lady Granby – might have married her brother St John, who has been gone from England for a dozen years now. But I know that, kind and sweet-tempered though she was, Miss Oliver was then even less suited to be the wife of a missionary in India than I was. 'She is very much changed' I say. The lady's dissolute husband lived just long enough to inherit his father's baronetcy and a fortune that barely matched his debts, and when the widow Lady Granby returned to her childhood home, she was not just visibly tempered by bitter experience but touched with a new seriousness of purpose. 'She is almost become the wife that St John needed.' *Sin-jun.* When did I last speak his name aloud? Is it the sound which prompts the thought: *you are the wife he needed – you who preferred the love of man to the work of God –* ? I am caught up once again in the torrent of St John's will. The thought is not new to me.

'Lady Granby asked Mary if she should send money to St John's mission.' Firelight glints on Diana's scissors as she clips loose threads from the back of her tapestry. 'Mary told her that the bishop in Calcutta is not well disposed to missionaries, and that there are heathen in Millcote in as much need of salvation. With old Mr Oliver's fortune at his disposal, my brother could have achieved at least as much good at home as he hoped for among the Hindoos.'

We pursue the shadows of what might have been most tirelessly when that which is becomes unbearable. There has been no news of St John for so long that I think both Diana and Mary have almost lost hope. As for myself, though I cannot say I hope, I find myself tempted to imagine some other story unfolding. Surely a soul so adamant is not easily brought to dust.

Something about me must have alerted Diana, because she looks up. 'Are you well, Jane? Is the fire too hot?'

I must guard my thoughts more closely. But in the last few months I have become a little more skilled at diverting attention from myself. 'You have still heard nothing from the Archdeacon in Madras?'

'St John has had precious little support from that quarter in the past.'

'But if any ill has befallen him – even if there have been disagreements –'

'Do you not think I would have told you, if there had been any news?'

'You might have thought that news of another death would be too much for me to bear.' There – I have said it; the only news of St John that we really expect to receive.

Diana stares at me for a moment, and then peers at her work. It seems that she has made a mistake, for she unpicks a few stitches before speaking again. 'We don't know for certain that he is dead. Only that when he last wrote, he felt death to be close. Do we not often feel the same, when we are downcast?'

She is inviting me to say something about my own feelings, but I put that aside. The St John Rivers we all remember was a man of unalterable convictions, of fiery ambition and remorseless will. A man of marble. A man who would have scorned despair. When the zeal of his early correspondence was first tinged with frustration, my firstborn was still a toddler and I was too busy – and too content – to pay much heed.

Diana holds up her work to check that her pattern is in order again. 'If he were a woman, one would have advised him to busy himself with household tasks. There is nothing like a spring clean.' I hear her chatting on about how restorative it is, to beat a carpet, but I am remembering how St John's letters told of endless squabbles among the clergy and the pettiness of the European congregations. *The fellow takes himself too seriously* said my husband, and I was inclined to agree. 'Why did God send him to India?' Diana's sudden cry rouses me. She stabs her needle into her work, raises her hands to her head and stares into the fire as if it were Daniel's fiery furnace. 'What was His purpose? Why has He allowed him to fail?'

'Does anyone have more cause to question God's purposes than I?' Now it is I who cry out, and I must close my eyes for a moment until my pulse has steadied. 'St John has his faith' I say more calmly; 'and so must we. God has His reasons, even if we cannot understand them.'

'And does that comfort you, Jane?' She too is calmer now.

We have both been taken aback by our outbursts, but I think she attributes my momentary unrestraint to pent-up agony. If the dam were to burst, she would rush to embrace me, and welcome my tears. What she does not understand is that my grief is no flood, but a deep, unfailing well. Comfort? No. 'It lends me patience' I say.

'Forgive me, Jane' she responds, and I can see that she means to rise and touch me – until I put up my hand and she sinks back into her seat. 'So many times I have wished my brother were here. His faith might have supported you.'

I think that he would have no more compassion for my feelings now than he once had of my refusal to marry him, but I can find no words, so I stand up to put more wood on the fire. Under the weight of the new logs, a half-consumed brand collapses, and a portion falls and rolls towards the edge of the hearth. I pick up my skirts and nudge it out of harm's way with my foot, but a few sparks fly out and light on the front of my gown. As I brush them off, I am aware that Diana is reassured by how briskly I deal with them. She continues to watch me between her stitches – stitch, glance; stitch, glance.

My loss is certain. Hers and Mary's loss of their brother is as yet no more than a silence. Everything they say of him, everything they think, must be provisional. When the truth is made plain, it will be necessary to revisit every present conjecture. I smile a little, thinking how oddly the uncertainty St John Rivers has created sits with the certainties of the man I remember; a man who presumed he was speaking for God Himself when he demanded to marry me.

Diana catches my smile, and perhaps she thinks I am imagining the words of comfort her brother might supply, because she lets me sit quietly for a while. Before either of us speaks again our housekeeper comes to tell us that our meal is ready. Tonight, with the master away, I ask her to join us. With Mrs Fairfax at our table, Diana and I will not sit silent.

At first, it is all of my husband and Adèle: have they managed to reach the inn at Richmond in this rain? Will the beds be sufficiently aired? I change the subject. 'Has Bessie boiled up the strawberry jam?' Last summer's preserves have developed a mould.

'The master's favourite! I was always uncertain that we had a good set.'

'Are there lemons to be got in Millcote?' asks Diana. 'Or rhubarb? A little tartness helps.'

'Gooseberry does well too' I say, and I see them exchange a look; there are no gooseberries in March. There is more talk of jams, but I am in another place, like those strange lop-sided crabs that hide in an alien shell. One hardened claw ventures out, to eat, to shift myself, to go through all the necessary motions of life; but inside I am misshapen, disproportionate and fragile as tissue-paper. Civility I can manage, even efficiency; but all capacity for those larger acts and feelings that give pain as well as joy have left me completely. My very being is suspended. I have forgotten anger, hope, and love.

**Diana begs weariness after her journey**, but she will not go to her room until she is assured that I will go to mine and so – to please her – I take my candle too. I sleep, but when I wake something in the nature of the silence and darkness tells me that it is still many hours till dawn. This is the familiar pattern of my nights, and I know that sleep will not easily reclaim me; but what is unfamiliar about this moment is the absence of my husband. My bedfellow.

Blindness has sharpened his other senses, and he wakes whenever I wake. At first, he would take me in his arms, to comfort me; but I lay there uncomforted, and gradually his embrace has dwindled to a mere touch of his hand on my arm – an almost timid enquiry, to which I cannot find it in me to respond. On such nights it is a relief when his breathing slows and he sleeps again, and now – God help me – it is a relief that he is gone, and I think – I wish – for a moment that he will never return.

My heart beats faster as this unbidden impulse becomes a conscious thought. Horrified, I push away the coverings and cross the room to the window. Behind the heavy curtains is a window-seat, and from it, in a sudden interval of moonlight, I can see the churchyard where my children lie. Time, friends have told me, will blunt the keen edge of my pain. But I have found a strange, settled security in my grief; I am the rock in the stream, unmoved by what sweeps past. It is for such endurance that I preserve myself: brush the sparks from my skirt, eat, drink, and now fetch a shawl – not because I fear a chill, but because the cold is distracting me. I protect myself from the lesser pains of cold or hunger so that I can fix an undistracted mind on my enduring.

**A few days pass**. I catch Diana and Mrs Fairfax a-whispering – they are pleased by my progress. We inspect the rest of last year's preserves for mould. Another look is exchanged: *she is taking an interest – a good sign*. They mistake the shell for the woman within.

A package comes from Edinburgh. *We are safely arrived*, writes Adèle, *and settled in the best lodgings in the new part of town*. It is like tidings from the moon. I pass it to Diana while I glance at the plans for the house that is supposed to become our new home. The outlines have been heavily inked, presumably so that Edward can make out the design, though I doubt that he has been able to decipher the little figures, faintly sketched in pencil, with which the imaginary gardens are peopled. A woman who points out the pigeons circling the dovecot to the child holding her hand; a couple strolling arm in arm through the *parterre*; a lad bowling his hoop in the yard.

'*Papa has given me a new pink gown and we are to attend an assembly where it is expected that the author of* Waverley *will be present*.' I hardly hear Diana's gasp. 'Our hero! Imagine! Do you remember, Jane, reading *Marmion* at Marsh End, that Christmas? St John was still with us.'

But Edward was not. He was lost to me. My children unborn. I had fled from grief. To read a brand new book was to hear the call of the young century, far from its noise.

Diana is merrily reciting:

> *Heap on more wood! – the wind is chill;*
> *But let it whistle as it will,*

*We'll keep our Christmas merry still.*

She stops abruptly, as if uncomfortably remembering that pleasant memories are forbidden in a house of sorrow.

I must come to her aid. 'St John gave me the book.' A tale of a battle lost and honour preserved; of nuns walled up and superstition routed. There was a wild, romantic streak in him which perhaps only ever revealed itself to me: *I burn for the more active life of the world* he once confessed; *the uniform duties of the ministry weary me to death.* Did he understand that I too had longed to escape from the humdrum confines of my lot? At Thornfield, in the early days, I would climb up to the roof and gaze at the skyline, and yearn for what lay beyond. St John found his India; and I – I married Mr Rochester. And was a mother, for a while.

I pass Diana the plans. 'Our house to be.' A new shell for the hermit crab.

'How light!' she cries. 'How airy! Shall I call Mrs Fairfax to look over how the kitchens are set out?'

Should I worry about how the housekeeper of the old place will feel about the new? Mrs Fairfax is quickly in raptures. She summons Bessie and Hannah from the kitchen, to tell them how comfortable and convenient we shall be. The system of underground pipes amazes them both. 'Oh Miss, what a good husband you have!' says Bessie.

'But what's this?' asks Diana. 'I cannot make it out.' She points to the outline of another building, facing the new house from a distance. Some central parts have been inked, others left more faintly indicated.

'That looks like the old hall' says Mrs Fairfax. She was far away when it burned.

I quickly scan the notes that the architect has attached to his plan. Yes, those marks are Thornfield; what remains of it. 'Much of it is to be razed' I read. 'But the central tower is to stay, and some parts of the East wing. It says here *These remnants will draw the eye from the front aspect of the new house, and add picturesque detail to the surrounding landscape.*' My voice is unsteady.

Mrs Fairfax says nothing.

'I believe every gentleman's estate must have a ruin nowadays' says Diana, after a silence. 'It is the fashion.'

**It is a fine afternoon** and Diana persuades me to take a walk through the shrubbery. 'How do you like the plans?' She is still wild about the new house's conveniences, its spacious rooms, and I think how good she is, not to envy me, when she and Captain Fitzjames must live in the narrow confines of Moor House. Then I remember that she has four healthy children.

She takes my arm. 'I see you do not care for the ruin. And I am surprised that Mr Rochester should want it retained. I doubt he will even be able to see it.'

My carapace, it seems, is still imperfect. 'From the new house, no. But closer, he will be able to make out its shape.' Its remaining battlements, from where his late wife fell.

'If you do not like it, Jane, you must ask him to pull it down. You know he can refuse you nothing.'

While I refuse him everything.

'And the rubble will be useful' she continues. 'Even if the old stone is not suitable for the new facade, I am certain it could be used for the outbuildings, or for the foundations. You might save a great deal of money.'

Am I to have the ruins of Thornfield under my feet? Or do I prefer to have them in plain view from my drawing room? 'How practical you are, dear Diana' I say. 'Where did you learn such things?'

'If you remember, Captain Fitzjames advised Lady Granby over her new almshouses. A man who runs a tight ship at sea has many talents that can be put to use on dry land.' She sighs. 'Lady Granby has promised to use her influence to secure him more employment, but there is little building around Morton. Money has dried up since the war.' Then suddenly she brightens. Her fingers tighten on my wrist, she turns and looks into my face, her eyes bright and animated by a sudden excitement. 'Jane, Jane, do you not think that my husband might be of assistance with your new house? Mr Rochester will need an overseer he can trust, someone whose taste and judgement he can rely on —'

I put up a hand. 'You must speak to him when he returns. But I believe the architect will have his own views in the matter.'

My lack of any enthusiasm plainly dismays her. 'Oh, Jane! Write today, please!'

Why can I not say yes? Then I have it. 'You must write yourself. After all, you can best describe what Captain Fitzjames has achieved for Lady Granby. Mr Rochester may not be hard to persuade.'

She looks at me very carefully, trying to find in my face some trace of the misgivings she suspects. But I have no doubts of her husband's capabilities. It is the new house itself that is the source of my indifference, and I can no more find in myself any keenness to spur on the project than I can find the will to resist it. 'Really, there is no one I would be happier to see at the task.' That at least is true.

She turns me round at once. Excitement has whetted all her senses, and as she hurries me back to the house, she points out a clump of early daffodils, the first soft green shoots of the honeysuckle, a bright wren flicking his tail as he tugs moss from a sun-warmed stone – and I know that in these things she sees hope, and a glowing future, as if the season were changing for her sake. I too once believed that joy and hope were qualities that Nature herself exuded and that I could absorb, like scent from a rose, but for me that connection is broken.

We are in sight of the house when she stops me. 'There is other news. With yours from Scotland another letter came, for me. From my sister.' The glory I have lost is playing in her eyes, and I dread the words that hover on her lips. 'Mary is with child again.'

I am young enough to have other children; to replace my first clutch. Though it is not spoken I know it is expected, in due course. This is what the new house is about: a new nest; a brighter, healthier nest. What I murmur I hardly know, but it seems to suffice and she is so distracted by plans and possibilities that she hardly notices. I watch her run in-doors to write her letter.

**Tonight, the sky is cloudless** and the moon is full. It is cold enough for a frost. When I wake as usual, deep in the darkness, I take myself to the window-seat and stare up at the familiar white face. It was she who exhorted me to flee from Thornfield when I discovered that he whom I loved had a wife still living, and now it is her pure light that lays bare an awful revelation. I should be in India with St John Rivers.

Now the madness that I know my husband fears is almost upon me. I push aside the heavy curtains and return to the room to escape the moon's beams, but a little of her radiance pursues me and bathes the chamber's familiar furnishings in an unfamiliar, searching light. The oak panelling, once comfortably old-fashioned, the worn turkey carpet, my unremarkable brushes and mirrors – all suddenly reproach me with luxury and indulgence. The bed, which my restless sleep has tumbled, the bed which for so long cradled our tenderest bliss, now accuses me of debauchery.

And I am guilty. Against the wall an upright chair stands in a patch of light, and I stumble towards it as if I have been ordered to face a questioning. My confession is ready. When I defied St John and answered my master's call to return, one glimpse, one touch would have been enough, the moment I found my beloved unaltered in his love for me. No matter that Bertha was still alive, I would have thrown my conscience to the winds, forgotten my pride, my dignity, all my resolve and gladly – eagerly – fallen into my master's embrace.

Closing my eyes, breathing rapidly, I examine my conscience – a familiar landscape. Must I be punished for the sin I might have committed – but did not? In the turmoil and elation of discovering that my master still loved me, that he was free, and that now I could be truly of use to him, I lost sight of a more solemn destiny. Instead, I babbled like snowmelt in springtime and represented St John as no more than a rival, to tease Edward as he had once teased me. For my husband, then and since, St John has been the rejected suitor and no more, a solemn, zealous relative he is relieved not to have to entertain in our house. I do not think he has ever guessed how nearly St John won me to his cause and while our children lived, I never considered that I should have accepted him. But I should have gone to India. For months this thought has possessed me, but tonight remorse turns into revelation. I can follow St John at last.

I panic for a moment, then run to the window again, seeking the moon's affirmation, but this is beyond her scope. This is not my God speaking, who once unstintingly poured out the quiet blessings of domestic happiness. This is St John's God; an angry, demanding God, telling me that the hour is come when I must be the instrument of His will. This is why I have been stripped of comforts. I throw open the casement and the chill night air strikes straight to the bone, as if like metal that has been beaten on the blacksmith's anvil, my soul is being hardened in deep, cold water. This is why my children have been taken from me, so that I can be free. God's ruthlessness appalls me, even as I begin to understand how relentlessly He will command in order that His purpose be fulfilled.

This madness leaves me as quickly as it came, but not the conviction. Yes, I must go to St John. Exhausted by my emotions, I can almost smile when I remember the kindly souls who have recommended a change of scene. When I also remember that long ago it was only St John's insistence on marriage that deterred me, I can almost laugh aloud. He cannot expect to marry me now. I am married already. His God has taken care of every detail. He has spared me from deadly diseases for this venture; tested my powers of endurance – even supplied the financial means to reduce those dangers and discomforts that are unavoidable on such an arduous journey.

I hurry to my table, find paper, ink and pen. *I am coming* I write – and then I halt. From nowhere, an unexpected shyness overcomes me. To convey what is burning in my breast, I must pour out my soul, as intimately as if I were writing to a lover. My hand trembles, and as I put down my pen a sudden sobriety creeps into my heightened feelings and I feel a kind of shame, as if I had been found out in some reckless infidelity. There will be resistance, I know. Edward already suspects that grief has affected my mind – and this will confirm his forebodings. But as I am, I cannot be much of a loss to him. Though I know that the arguments I shall face will not be easily answered, my conviction only strengthens. A heart that I thought was dead is quickening. If St John is alive, I can assist him. If he is dead, I can discover how he met his end and set his sisters' minds at rest. And if I die in the attempt – well, it will be better than the living that I have here. Too eager for any sleep, I wrap myself in my shawl and return to the window seat. The moon continues on her steady, silent path and when she gives way to the dawn, I rebuke myself for hoping that she will instruct me. The calling I hear now comes from a greater voice than hers.

**Do I expect the new day to be transfigured by my vision?** Instead, I am sullen and irritated by the need to explain myself.

'Poor Jane!' says Diana. 'How wan you look! Bessie, how can we tempt her appetite?'

When I was a child, Bessie was my nurse-maid – and my only friend. She still likes to coddle me, but the pastry she sets before me is dry in my mouth. I eat, but I have nothing to say. My certainty is enough and I chafe at the prospect of trying to convey what no-one will be willing to accept. I try to resume my letter to St John, but even that frustrates me, while as for explaining to my husband – really, I think that I should not need to explain myself at all. The call is too imperative, its source too unquestionable for any mere explanation of it to be necessary.

And then – a miracle!

Diana and Bessie are busy setting some linen to air when Mrs Fairfax brings the day's post to my desk. A pile of torn papers is all I have to show for my own attempts at correspondence, and so – thinking that some temporary distraction might unlock my words – I sort through what has arrived and discover another packet from Cousin Mary. Inside, the first words I read are *St John lives!*

Is this an answer to my prayer? No, because in truth I hardly need it. So powerfully am I possessed that all doubts have fallen aside. I know already that St John must be alive. I could not be so compelled if he were dead. God may be stern, He may even be cruel, but He is not malicious. I am prepared for my cousin to be worn down by his task, because that is why this strength has been vouchsafed to me, so that I can serve him. But he cannot be dead. My spirits soar as I run to the kitchen to find Diana.

Her reaction does not surprise me; her head has always been cooler than mine or her sister's. But I had hoped for better. When the joy which the whole kitchen shares has died down, she takes me to a quiet spot where she can read the rest of Mary's missive without distraction. I pace up and down fretting for the moment when I can crown this good news with my own resolve. When she sets down the last of several pages, her expression is subdued.

'I think perhaps my sister has let the new baby cloud her judgement. There is no news of St John directly. No certainty that he lives. The letter she refers to is from the Archdeacon, who says that St John has left Madras.'

Her reserve is unbearable. 'And no wonder!' I cry. 'A place where his work was impeded, where the congregation lacked all seriousness and his fellow clergy treated him with contempt! He is gone where he can be of more use.'

Diana interrupts me. 'You are right up to a point. I fear there may have been a quarrel. The Archdeacon writes of –' she looks for the page – *a continued refusal to defer to his Bishop's authority.* But that aside, his fate is still uncertain. He is believed to have set up a small school in Mysore, but he has had no communication with the Bishop's office.'

'Mysore is near the hills, is it not? He has gone there to repair his health.'

She is sorting through the pages again. 'Jane, this letter is dated last November. It says that he left Madras some time ago – and in India, where a man may eat his breakfast in good health and be dead by night-fall! We know my brother has been in a weakened state for a long while. Mary is more hopeful than I can be. Why has there been no message of comfort for your loss – *in two years*, Jane? Even if our letters have miscarried, I cannot believe that he would not have let us have news, were he still…'

Do her words tail off, or do I cut across them? 'I shall go to him' I say. 'I will find him.' 'Jane!' she cries. 'Are you out of your mind?' She leaps from her chair, as if that very minute she must restrain me. The pages of her letter scatter across the floor.

# CHAPTER 3

**A man stares at the road ahead of him**. Only when the driver rouses himself to slap the bullock's haunch with his cane does the cart roll forward any faster than its two occupants might have walked. Its wheels raise hardly a smudge of dust.

The young driver is slight, dark-complexioned and dark haired, a South Indian like most of those in the constant streams of people moving along the road. The other passenger is different, and all but the weariest turn to stare. Though his face and his bare forearms are the brown of a worn leather sandal, the locks that hang lankly over his brow are the colour of half-ripe corn. Once, he might have tried to outface this relentless curiosity; now he endures it, like the sun. Occasionally he mops his forehead with the back of a thin, work-worn hand, but for the most part he sits motionless, staring into a distance that he does not see, gripping the rails of the cart as if he fears that a sudden jolt might send him flying. But it is no fault in the road that suddenly flings the driver from his perch and throws his passenger onto the sacks and bundles piled in the well of the cart.

Dread rather than any injury makes him stagger as he clambers to the ground. His man is squatting in the roadway, investigating the damage. A wheel's iron rim has burst, and the freed end has smashed through one spoke and cracked two others. Already a crowd is gathering. Some of the footsloggers have turned back, while those who were heading in his direction have speeded up and children are running from the fields. The incident will be all the more irresistible once a *firinghee* is known to be involved. A woman carrying a pot on

31

her head steadies it with one hand whilst drawing her veil across her face with the other. She stares at him, motionless and unreadable.

His tribe would expect him not to let the crowd see how helpless he feels. Reaching into the cart, he finds his black coat and pulls it on over his sweat-sodden shirt, as if this might improve his standing. But he has rolled up his sleeves earlier, and shrug and twitch as he may, he cannot settle the garment comfortably. If he hears the merest hint of the laughter that must be building, he will be seized by a futile but murderous fury. He steadies himself on the side of cart, and bends at the knee as if to inspect the damage. What he is really doing is trying to pray, though God seems unlikely to come his aid over something so mundane, when it is so long since He previously vouchsafed much sign of His support. But perhaps some other kindly spirit responds to his plea because when he straightens up and turns to face the crowd again, what he sees is something like condolence. They are concerned for his plight, and though he is still anxious for his dignity, he is no longer in quite as much danger of losing his temper. 'Kamil!' he calls warily. 'Ask them how to find someone who can repair the wheel.'

What Kamil calls out in his own language is far lengthier than his master's few words, as if he has added some gloss of his own, and a morbid suspicion re-kindles St John's vexation, even though he knows he is being unreasonable. There is a renewed murmur, and a few of the men push through the crowd for a noisy conference. Small boys cluster eagerly around them, hopping from foot to foot, all hoping to be sent on some errand that would earn them a few *pice*.

'Sin-jun-sa'b, they say it is too late. It will be dark soon. We must stay here.' The crowd stares and nods.

Though the light is harsh, the heavens are overcast and the trees that line the road have no shadows. He peers through the branches, trying to find where the sky is brightest, to measure how many hours of daylight are left. Their day began before dawn, allowing ample time to reach Pisgah before nightfall. 'Get me a blacksmith and a carpenter. Tell them I will pay a fair price.' Money, he thinks peevishly. Always money. He sways slightly and shivers, then gathers himself. 'The cracked spokes can be lashed. The road is good enough.' The signs are unmistakable now: this frantic, uncontrollable irritation tells him that he is coming down with fever.

Kamil confers again. St John has never learnt how to be sure of what that side-ways movement of the head means: at best, he believes, only some kind of half-willing concession.

Annoyance flares again and a wave of heat inflames his face, but

Kamil is returning with a smile. 'They will fetch men from the village, sahib; but they still say you must make camp for the night. A tiger has been seen near the road.' The men on the verge pick up what he is saying. *Baagh* one calls helpfully. Another gives a ferocious growl.

If it's not a tiger it would be thugs or dacoits, he thinks. They may not be actively hostile but they like us to be fearful. To admit that he is sick would be to lose the last of his control over the situation, make himself helpless. He cannot even unpack his precious supply of cinchona bark because nothing escapes the curious eyes that surround him, and Kamil is too guileless not to answer the questions that would follow. He clenches his fists to still the trembling that must be imminent, and prays for strength to endure the indignities he will be half conscious of before he slides into delirium.

Kamil releases the patient bullock from its yoke and tethers it to a tree. Another small group gathers round, to assess its finer points. Suddenly anxious again, he starts forward as he sees that two of the men unloading the cart are carrying a sack of rice away from the heap they are building on the edge of the road. But they are simply making a place for him to sit in comfort under a tree, out of the dust, and a little shame mingles with his other racing emotions. He raises a heavy hand to wave his thanks, but the men are too busy to notice. A boy skitters towards him, drops a satchel at his feet and hares away as if St John might be dangerous.

When he bends to pick up the bag, dizziness swamps him. He hauls himself upright and sees that the woman with the pot on her head is nearby. He beckons her towards him and mimes drinking. The cinchona is in the satchel. How he might prepare it without attracting more attention is utterly beyond him, but he slides his hand into the bag to reassure himself of its presence and finds himself touching a packet of letters he would prefer to forget – not because their unread contents might contain bad news, but because he has no answers for them. He would leave the packet among the tangled roots of the tree that shades him, but inevitably some child would come running after him, expecting to be rewarded for an unwanted good deed. The woman is at his side now, and when she releases the veil that has been covering her face to take her pot in both hands, he sees that pale glossy scars patch large areas of her neck and jaw. His consciousness wavers, and he sees something he never saw – another woman, far away, falling, falling. A sudden catch of flame ignites her garments and she tumbles like a burning leaf. Such flaring glimpses of other worlds are familiar symptoms, and even though the real woman in his presence is bending close enough for him to catch the smell of her – sweat, dust, and the faint trace of some perfumed oil – she seems no more than a creature in a dream. As he takes the water she is offering, the insects that he sees hovering round her head are like flaws in his vision.

In the tunnel of the tree-lined roadway the air is hot and still, and he dozes, only half aware of the shifting bustle around the cart. The noise rises as boulders are brought from the fields to prop up the axle so that the damaged wheel is clear of the ground. Then the spectators withdraw to the verge and squat there, waiting almost silently. One man rolls a few shreds of tobacco in a couple of leaves, another eats a small mess of rice from a coconut shell he holds under his chin.

Then the boys are back, noisy and skipping with excitement, leading a small procession. One man carries a smoking brazier, another a basket of charcoal. The blacksmith, in a leather vest and a grimy dhoti, swings a vast hammer in one hand and pincers in the other. A carpenter carries a reeking pot of glue. The crowd rearranges itself around itself around a makeshift forge. Through half-closed eyes – the light is making his head throb – he peers for the woman with the burnt face, and finds her offering her water pot to the circle of spectators. As each one swigs, she holds out a hand and receives a few small coins which she tucks into the blouse of her sari. He finds a little space in his dulled thoughts to be glad that she is deriving a benefit from his misfortune, and to regret that he did not think to give her something himself.

The huddle is too dense for him to see much more than a few sparks and a thin black smoke rising. The dull, rhythmic clatter of palm-leaf fans whipping the coals red-hot is a sound he knows from the hearth in his own kitchen. It is some comfort that he is outside this circle. The effort of will that it always takes to tolerate the silent, appraising crowds that seem to emerge from nowhere is beyond him now. More than mere bystanders, they seem essential to any activity, as if nothing can happen without this ring of intense attention. He remembers stopping to tie his shoe the first Sunday after his landing at Fort St George. The lace broke as he tightened it, and he found a place to sit at the foot of one of the black columns that fronted some official building. When he looked up from knotting a repair, he was already surrounded by just such a wall of intensely staring faces as those encircling his cart now. *These people are what I have come for*, he reminds himself. *It is for their sake that I am here.* But not a trace of energy can his thoughts rouse in him. Only a childish helplessness. He never knew that they would be so many. Or that they would be so unconcerned by the chance that he offers, to escape from their sin.

He is unaware that he has been sleeping until he feels Kamil's hand on his shoulder. The crowd has parted now so that he can inspect the completed repair. Each one of them is beaming, as if they had all shared in the work. He gets to his feet and is nearly overcome with giddiness, but he manages the few strides steadily enough. The wheel looks better than he expected. The iron rim has been nailed back in place, and the two cracked spokes have been glued and bound. An ingenious arrangement of new wood and iron rods replaces the spoke that was shattered. It should get him home, but a patch of brightness too intense to look at in the otherwise opaque white sky tells him that the broken wheel has cost about three hours. They cannot reach Pisgah by nightfall.

**The road ahead disappears into a shimmering miasma** and the air is so parched that it is an effort to breathe. His thoughts have lost all coherency, but as they stream past him like litter in a whirlwind, he feels compelled to catch those he can, to pin them down and wrestle till they explain themselves. The pattern of the continuous over-arching trees torments him. *Full thirty feet long! I swear it!* He remembers an English woman's emphatic voice. Fanning herself furiously. Her quivering bosom.

A rush of contempt sharpens his thoughts. In an instant – in this climate – they might be called to face their Maker, and yet they waste their time in idleness. The woman – Mrs Porter; the name has come to him – bragging about her *cabinet of curiosities...the skeleton of a hamadryad, full thirty feet long!* Her talk only of the vendors that tried to cheat her, the earthly treasures she has laid up – and he sees them all as the dust they will become: her silks a shadow, her ivories splintered and all her pickled specimens no more than a mess of broken glass and oozing putrefaction.

He looks up, as if he might see Mrs Porter leading her baggage train with all its rotten freight towards the golden gates, where a stern angel forbids her entrance. But what he sees is the boughs that over-arch his own small wagon – and how they enclose him, one after another, an endless, inescapable vortex dragging him towards a vanishing point where he will be disgorged into some Godless chaos.

He fixes his gaze on the bullock's hindquarters and the moment passes. Athwart its spine, above its tail, its rounded hip-bones lurch and swagger and the silvery hide darkens where the skin rolls over the bone beneath. Then the edges of his vision blur and he sees a line of women heading up the bank from the river where they have bathed, and the twitch and sway of their hips under their damp drapery. One pulls the edge of her garment over her wet hair, her eyes downcast as she picks her way carefully up the slope, watching her footing. He closes his eyes, too weary for the effort of actively banishing her from his thoughts, and she persists, as firmly as she is placing her feet in the sandy soil.

A jerk in his groin brings him back to his senses. Shocked, he tries to focus on the animal's steady plod, but now the creature has hoisted its tail. Its anus winks and gapes, and expels a loose chunk of yellow dung. As the turds flop and the stench reaches his nostrils, he knows that God has pointed out the filthiness of his unbidden thoughts.

'Are you alright, sahib?' Kamil sounds anxious. He flicks the beast's backside with his cane and it picks up speed.

'Not too fast. The wheel may not hold.'

Kamil touches his arm, offers water, and he gulps it down. Then, steadying himself on his servant's shoulder, he clambers into the back of the cart and lies down among the bundles. Though every fibre of the sacks scratches like a hog's bristles, for a while he sleeps, mercifully dreamless.

**The dusk and the unencumbered sky above him** tell him that he is safe. But when he pushes himself upright (and it takes all his strength) he sees a forest clearing, and that Kamil is nowhere. He can hear the panic in his voice as he calls, and the night grows perceptibly darker as he waits for an answer. A spotted deer is watching him warily from the edge of the trees. The herd is cropping the taller grass along the clearing's bushy margin, tails twitching nervously – and then, at the crack of a twig, all heads are up, and they flee.

Relieved, he sees Kamil bringing wood. A circle of ash near the cart tells him that this is a camp site that has been used by other benighted travellers, or herders tending their goats. His own bullock is grazing close by, tethered to a rope that runs between two stout pegs. From the temperature he guesses that they have already climbed some way into the hills and at the same time he registers a similar mildness and calm in his being. The fever has retreated, and he sends up a quick prayer of thanks for his delivery. But while his brain is clear, he is still weak, and though he knows he should help his servant gather more firewood, he stumbles when he tries to get down from the cart. Kamil, bent to blow on the flame he is nursing, looks up, obviously startled, thinking of tigers.

And then he hears voices, and the creak of harness. A mahout's distinctive jabber as he steers his beast into the clearing. It is dark now, and the elephant's rocking outline against the star-smudged sky, piled and sagging with bundles, is monstrous; but its arrival is reassuring. Behind come two ox-carts, larger and more heavily laden than his own, one drawn by a pair, the other by four. A gold-tipped horn glints with Kamil's small fire.

He sinks to the ground and leans against the wheel of his cart to watch his servant approach the newcomers, conscious that his racial superiority is useless here. Not for the first time he reflects on how fragile that superiority is, beyond the fort, the pillared offices, the few small white-washed churches. Only his God makes him the better of these men, who are setting camp with a speed and efficiency which speak of an expertise that he totally lacks. They have brought their own firewood. When he picks out Kamil's voice, at ease among his fellows, he feels childishly lonely. God has called him to be solitary. Has not allowed him the solace of a wife. His mind drifts and he feels under his hand the trim head of the woman he once chose for his helpmeet. Now he sees God's will in the choice she made. Better that she should have deserted him back in England, than come to India and failed him. The Lord dispenses His mercies with a stern and exact measure and has granted him energy enough, but none to spare. A wife who could not cope with the trials of his lot would have undone him.

He stares at the distant fire, and finds himself once again thinking of the woman emerging from the river. She has a name; she is Jaya, Kamil's elder sister, and her coiled hair hangs like a snake down her back. An early convert, though there is still a baffling stubbornness in her that he cannot reach. At night she puts out an earthenware saucer of milk for the cobra that is supposed to guard the kitchen hearth. If there is a snake, it should be driven out and killed, but Jaya puts down her saucer of milk, and every morning it is empty. Rats, most likely, or a mongoose. Or the striped squirrels.

The men's voices have risen now and he suspects that toddy or something worse is circling, but when Kamil, unusually jovial, calls him closer to the fire he feels absurdly grateful. He moves into the space that has been made for him knowing that none of the travellers are interested in his company: they simply think he is too foolish to watch for the tiger that might snatch him. One man wags a finger, like a parent warning a child to stay out of trouble, and as if he were a child, they make no further effort to include him in their conversation. In any case his grasp of their language is inadequate. Tamil, Telegu, Kannada – anyone of them might have been of more use to him than the Hindustani he taught himself in England. That God should have sent him to a place where he is so little understood he now counts as the first of many lessons in humility. It is a bitter irony that a large British army in the area means that most of his business can be conducted in some form of the English language.

Yet if he had the local tongue, what would he be hearing? Coarse jests, no doubt, and the kind of commonplace observations which would only have set him further apart. During his years in India has he ever done something as simple as asking a stranger to come close to the fire, so that for a moment at least that man might have known that the two of them were kin? The benefits he has to bestow are far more than a passing kindness, but he is not as comforted as he should be. He tugs a bale into place, folds his coat round his satchel for a pillow and lets his gaze wander. God may have many purposes, simultaneously. Infinite purposes, indeed. A burst of laughter on the far side of the fire recaptures his attention and it comes to him that the cruel and licentious Indian deities that once inflamed his zeal, often seem to be no more tyrannical in their effects than the God of Abraham in an English village.

The moon is risen fully now, its white disc almost complete, the rash of its barren craters clearly visible. Effortlessly, it lights the whole clearing and the surrounding forests, and the men fall silent, as if admonished. He shifts, and feels the edge of something hard pressing against his shoulder: the package of letters he collected in Mysore. It is too bulky to contain only the Archdeacon's familiar reproaches; the rest of it will be news from his sisters and his cousin in England, all addressed to Fort St George, and forwarded from there. When he calculates how many months – no, years – it has been since he left Madras, the impossibility of now excusing his failure to keep them informed courses through his being like a new wave of fever. When he rips open the packet, it is more to punish himself for his omissions than any wish to learn of his family's doings.

A single folded sheet is tucked into the tape which holds together a bundle of sealed letters. The moon gives light enough to read by. *Kindly inform your correspondents in England of your current whereabouts. The Archdeacon's office can no longer redirect your letters.* He closes his eyes for a moment to get the better of his irritation, then looks deep into the forest for further solace. The trees, spindly and insignificant in a harsher light, are now outlined in moonlight. Their slender silver columns rise from a shimmer of pale grasses. Fireflies flit in the darkness above a tangle of undergrowth and he thinks that if he fixes his gaze on those silent traces, sleep must surely claim him. As he drifts into unconsciousness the bundle of letters slips from his hands and falls among the bales – and is returned by a watchful Kamil.

There can be no doubt about what Providence intends. With a sigh he unpacks three separate letters, all addressed in his sister Diana's hand. He has no idea what letter of his they might be answering. So many of his attempts he has torn up, frustrated by the impossibility of explaining himself clearly without stirring a pointless concern. There is nothing to be gained by revisiting his old battles, as if one day the outcome of episodes long since concluded might somehow be changed. He despises himself for stoking his own righteousness, and yet how eagerly he reaches for his bitterest memories: *The Bishop fears there would be trouble* – that maddening, chilly calm. Then himself, unable to hold back: What business has a Christian, being afraid of *trouble? Remember, Rivers: the vows you made at your ordination – to obey your Bishop.* But to be so faint-hearted, long after the Company has at last seen the light? When Wilberforce himself has told Parliament that converting India is the *greatest of all causes?* Because who dares doubt that freeing a man's mind from the slavery of an abominable religion is of far greater merit than freeing his body of its shackles?

Now the last of his peace is gone and what comes roaring down upon him is a rage that he had thought was exhausted. Maybe his sister's letters will send him to sleep: her small domestic dramas and her children's doings have come to seem as unreal as a bed-time story. Two – not unusually – are water-stained. Coming ashore at Madras is a risky business. He opens the most damaged of the letters first, and finds that its date is more than a year since. As always, the first close-written paragraphs can be skimmed: Diana's concern for the state of his health is always at least half a year out of date, and will be no more irrelevant after a longer delay. *Do not, I implore you, go out of the house with your head uncovered. Lady Granby has heard from a gentleman lately returned from the Indies that an undershirt of fine flannel, worn close at neck and wrist, is a proven remedy against the fever.*

It would be better if no more news from home ever reached him. The man that his sisters and his cousin write to barely exists any longer, and in their letters he comes back as a stranger to himself. It is a relief that most of the lower half of this page has been spoilt. The next seems to be an account of a ball, of who led the dance, who wore the most becoming gown, what food was served and who flirted with – Good God! Such froth makes him wonder for a moment whether marriage and children have softened her brain. But it is not Diana who has changed – and how can she possibly know what his life is like when all she knows of India comes from exotic sagas or catalogues of horror? His own colourless letters could have done little to set her right. He reads on, a little more ready to forgive. The ball, it seems, was given by cousin Jane to mark the eighteenth birthday of her husband's bastard daughter – his *ward* as Diana delicately calls her, though she knows the truth of the matter.

*The dowager Lady Ingram was there, and I could tell she thought it was a poor affair. But for us it was a rare treat. Lady Granby (you remember – Rosamond Oliver, that was) lent me a gown and I wore Mama's garnet brooch. Adèle is a credit to cousin Jane's steadying influence, spirited, but not at all flighty, as one might half-expect from her beginnings.*

A woman he once believed was marked out by God for His service, and now the best that can be said of her is that she is a *steadying influence*. A dull crash rouses him as a branch collapses into the heart of the fire, scattering red-hot embers. And another, with gowns to spare, whom he once loved wildly, though now his recollections seem more like a romantic tale from long ago than an episode from his own life.

Gradually the fire dies down to a red glow in a ring of grey ash, and as dawn and its birdcalls replace the silent moonlight the other travellers begin to rouse themselves. As he picks up his discarded letters, he sees for the first time that many of his companions are old men, no more than skin and bone, with scant clothing and nothing to protect their feet. Preparing their beasts for departure, they hoist loads which even in good health he could not have lifted.

**The bullock breaks into a steady trot** as soon as they regain the road and when the sun is fully risen St John returns to his sister's messages. He wants the feelings they will rouse to be quietened before he reaches his own gates. Then he turns a page – and suddenly Diana's familiar writing turns large and uneven.

*I fear this account of our pastimes will soon rebuke us that we did not know sufficiently how happy we once were, nor thank God for his bounty before – as now – we have occasion to seek his mercy. News is come today that all of our dear cousin's children are taken sick with the diphtheria. Let us hear soon of your prayers, dear brother, that the worst may not befall her. Your loving sister, Diana.*

So that is why there is no letter from Jane in this bundle. Even as his heart contracts in his chest, he thinks how strange it is, that in the urgency of her fear, his sister should imagine that her words might reach him as quickly as a letter sent from Morton to Milltown by the mail-coach. There are two more letters and good or bad, what they contain will long ago have grown familiar to their sender. As he picks away the wax on what looks like the older of the two, the marks of the sea look like the stain of tears. It turns out to be dated a mere seven months since, presumably the latest of the three, not the second, but he continues reading. The handwriting is calm again.

*Dearest Brother*

*I had thought that by now we should hear from you some words of comfort for our darling Jane, and I fear lest your silence should conceal a new sorrow. If you are sick, or if – God forbid! – you have joined her children in heaven, then I beg any stranger who reads this letter to send us news. But I must write as if I were certain that you are still living and that by some chance you do not know what has happened.*

He reads quickly. Jane has lost all three of her children. That, he supposes, is the message of the remaining letter. For a moment he drops his head to his hands and the stiff pages rasp against his unshaven cheek. Then he reads on.

*Many months have passed since her bereavement, and yet neither I nor sister Mary can detect any sign of her recovering. She spurns all consolation – not weeping or languishing, but stern and untouchable. How can a merciful Father inflict so much suffering on one so good and so generous?*

He will pray for his cousin of course; pray that her darkness may be illuminated by understanding and her anguish calmed by resignation. And he will write to her. He must. It is time to break his silence, though he does not know what he will say. Somewhere on the edge of his conscious thought hovers an uncomfortable resentment. He does not want these deaths here.

Market traffic is joining the road, raising a yellow dust. They reach the river, wide, shallow and divided into several streams after its descent from the hills, and he remembers how his sisters once conjured out of their youthful admiration a vision of him like St John the Baptist on the banks of the Jordan, preaching to vast crowds who could not fail to see the light his eloquence revealed. In India he was to be the Protestant Francis Xavier. Now all that he shares is the Jesuit's frustration. Like him, Xavier was ordered to set aside his mission and revive the faith of his own countrymen, whose conduct did nothing to set a good example to the natives they lived among. But at least he has Pisgah. His share of cousin Jane's inheritance has paid for the place that is his haven, his stronghold – and his hiding place. A swerve rouses him. They have turned off the main road and Kamil is unwrapping the scarf that has covered his face. A wave from the hillside tells them that they have been spotted. The boys will run down the lane to greet the cart while the girls line up in clean pinafores. He knows that he is too austere and alien to be loved, but this welcome always touches him. Someone – Jaya, he thinks – will alert the cook: it is customary for a fowl to be sacrificed, to greet his safe return. The dust of the road is behind them now, and the bright lane is patched with the shadows of full-grown mango trees.

**He bathes, then gathers the household for prayers.** Under his surplice he wears black cotton trousers and a loose muslin shirt, with well-worn chappals on his feet. The older boys report on their progress in arithmetic and the girls present their needlework. After lunch (the chicken) he sleeps for an hour, then returns to the school-room, which also serves as the chapel. He shows the children the new books he has brought from Mysore, and hears their lessons. In a corner, the widow Poonam, who has been his servant since the beginning, recites Bible-stories as the girls sew. Towards the end of the afternoon, Kamil supervises the class while he makes the inspection that is his custom after any absence.

He has called this place after the mountain from which Moses glimpsed the promised land he never reached. Its buildings are arranged in a rough circle on the flat summit of a small hill. Three large and ancient trees stand in the centre of the grassy *maidan* that they enclose – a space for the children's exercise. A broad veranda runs from room to room, broken only by the entrance from the lane and a further gate on the opposite side which leads down to the fields.

For safety's sake the kitchen and its fire occupy a separate building, reached by a short path from this second gate. St John's own rooms are close to the same segment of the circle, with outward-facing windows that allow him to look down on the cultivated terraces below. The whole effect is simple and harmonious, and as he completes his circuit a sense of well-being displaces all but the shadow of his more troublesome thoughts.

He takes the path to the fields by the river, where he finds the labourers slumbering in the shade of a tree; what is ripe has been harvested, the rows have been weeded and a breeze is coaxing a hollow melody from the bamboo bird-scarers. At this time of year in this location, nature is kind and generous. It is pleasantly cool as he climbs the rocky track to the terraces where the hardier crops are growing – maize and millet, and an experimental sorghum crop fenced off to protect it from the goats whose bells he can hear in the distance. All are doing well, and he allows himself to sit for a while and absorb the beauty of his surroundings.

Though the higher peaks of these western mountains form an almost unbroken spine, their eastern foothills are a complex tangle. A tributary of the river that runs along the Mysore road here forms a wide bend bordering the level mile or so that includes his fields. A series of rapids upstream and down have isolated the spot, and the deep forest that fringes the cleared ground have added to an illusion of remoteness, though a path along the river bank leads to several populous villages not far away. A lively breeze is rattling a stand of bamboo and whispering among the reeds, but otherwise the whole vista is at peace.

Not now the man who views it. A moment's leisure has re-awoken both guilt and resentment. Any letter from the country he once called home reminds him of the difference between the ghost that lingers there and what he has become. Of the mere dozen adult converts he brought with him on his exodus from the bondage of Madras, all that remain are Kamil and his sister Jaya, her child and the ever-loyal and now very needy widow Poonam. The others have returned to Fort St George, where English-speaking Christian servants can command wages that he cannot afford. All the servants and field-workers he has hired locally have resisted his efforts, and it is heathen labour that now feeds the dozen orphans he has rescued from exposure or beggary. Perhaps because of the news they contain, the letters he has just received have stirred a deeper than usual sense of failure. Though he tells himself that his farm and school are not a worthless achievement, the devil at his shoulder reminds him that this is not what was expected of him – nor what he thought God had planned for him. Such thoughts occupy a permanent space at the back of his mind, overwhelming him only when he has time to reflect – time that he does not permit himself very often. Now the lengthening shadows tell him that he should be supervising the children's evening meal.

He finds them queuing with their bowls along the veranda. There has been no sign of Jaya since his return, and though this is not unusual his general mood tinges her absence with a creeping anxiety. After supper he looks for her brother and spots him sitting on a root of the big trees, where the children's mats are spread. The day's final bible story is usually Jaya's task, and well before Kamil has finished, St John is imagining the worst.

'I have not seen your sister' he manages at last.

Kamil makes a hapless, embarrassed gesture for which neither man has a word. St John understands. For five days every month Jaya retires to a small hut somewhere beyond the kitchen. He has attempted to explain that this practice is not necessary for a Christian woman, but she has not changed her ways. Like feeding the snake, this once annoyed him. Now he suspects that it is less an incompleteness in her faith, more a rather daunting determination not to be too ready to please. Still, he is relieved.

He eats the last of the chicken alone in his study, trying to plan his letter to Jane. The first three attempts he tears up before he has covered the first sheet. There is nothing he can say that the rector of her own church cannot supply. His sister Mary is married to a clergyman and they are on the spot. He abandons his desk and steps out onto the veranda, still parched after his journey. A thin cotton cloth covers the earthenware water-pot and he tosses it onto the rail, dips a beaker, drinks and dips again. The water runs through his body like rain sinking into dry sand. Small stirrings in the nearby trees tell him that the night wind is coming, and he leans forward, face up-turned, waiting for refreshment. He does not notice that the cloth has blown down until he hears a small movement behind him. Jaya is covering the jar. The thick plait of her hair is twined with a fresh garland of jasmine, and a breath of its soft murky scent reaches him on an eddy of the breeze. She bows slightly over the tips of her fingers, palms together. '*Namaste Sinjun-sahib*. We have all prayed for your safe return.' He has noticed before how particularly serene she always seems when she emerges from her seclusion.

'As you see, your prayers were answered.' So absorbed has he been in his thoughts that the sound of his own voice is odd to him.

'My brother tells me that you met other travellers on the road, and shared their camp.'

'We did indeed.' He can think of nothing more to say.

She waits. 'Perhaps some *chai? Masala chai?* It will help you sleep.'

He manages to speak at last. 'That would be good.' Her feet pad along the length of the veranda, trip quickly down the steps and onto the path. After a few moments he hears a murmur of voices from the kitchen, then sees a low bloom of orange light in the distance as someone fans the fire. He returns to his study and another blank sheet of paper. Could there be a greater difference in the lives of two women than there is between his cousin Jane and his Indian servant? One is educated, wealthy and pampered, free to marry where a selfish heart has led her. Yet now that a great but not unusual misfortune has come about, her spirit is broken – as if she expected that perfect and abiding content was her birthright.

Perhaps he should tell her of Jaya's life. Sometimes in the past the physical act of writing has set his ideas flowing. *Her parents were of the untouchable castes – her father a tanner and a drunkard. She was married as a mere child, widowed before the marriage could be consummated, and abandoned by her family.* Already he is certain that this is something he will never send, but he continues. *When she caught the eye of an Englishwoman, she was scouring chamber pots behind the officers' mess in Fort St George.* He feels his lip twitch with contempt. Mrs Porter collects her Indian entourage as if they were specimens for her wretched cabinet of curiosities. Jaya, she claimed, had been snatched from the widow's pyre: her true fate was not sensational enough for a woman who expects her India to be highly flavoured.

He picks up his pen again. *This lady took on Jaya to assist her children's ayah, then set off on her famous travels. On her return she found a not un-rare curiosity in her own compound – a brown infant with blue eyes: Captain Porter had seduced her nursemaid.* No, he can never send this. Even in happier times any story of a servant led astray by her employer would hardly strike the right note with Cousin Jane, so nearly led astray herself. He slams down his pen and pushes the paper away. A small noise alerts him to Jaya's return, with a brass tray in her hands. She bends to arrange a cup, a covered pitcher and a small bowl of jaggery – cautious, as if she has caught sight of his irritability. 'How is your boy? I did not see him in class.' He needs her to leave him, but he speaks to keep her there.

She stiffens, a little defensively. 'He says the other children are too slow.'

It is possible. The lad is bright, but unruly. 'Perhaps I could give him more advanced lessons.' Anything, to please his mother. He cannot read her silent response. Only when the last of her footfall can no longer be heard does he move to sit on the edge of the charpoy and pour the chai – sweet and fragrant with ginger and cardamom. When he attempts to return the empty cup to the tray, he finds that the hard edge of his seat has numbed his legs. He staggers – and finds her reaching out to steady him.

'What is the matter, sahib? My brother says you had fever.'

'Nothing. Nothing.' He did not hear her return and feels vaguely humiliated.

She helps him to his bed with all the composure of one used to dealing firmly with small children. 'You are tired, sahib. You must sleep.' She crouches again, to remove his sandals. 'I came to take these things away. The sugar. Ants come.'

The last of the moonlight strikes the rim of the brass tray. It silvers her pale robes and the flowers twined in the plait of her hair. The skin of her neck is the colour of the chai he has drunk. It shimmers with the same milky sheen, and he longs more than anything in this world to bury his face deep in its warmth. More than his hope of heaven.

# CHAPTER 4

**When Kamil approaches him,** St John cannot at first make out what the young man is after. Then it dawns on him: Kamil wants to be married.

It is a reasonable request, only to be expected. Men and women marry young in these climes. Kamil, somewhere around twenty, has shown restraint by holding out for so long. But he seems to want the sahib to arrange the matter. St John racks his brains for memories of how such things were managed in Morton but can recall nothing of use. There are precious few Christian converts within a hundred miles for Kamil to choose from, and the oldest of the female orphans is no more than eight, but if the search for a bride were to take him away, Pisgah would be very hard to sustain. Kamil assists with the older boys, organising their exercise and their share of work on the land; soon he will be a competent teacher. He also takes the products of the fields to market and deals with local officials, whose language he shares; recently he has taken charge of dealings with the garrison at Mysore. And if his sister Jaya were to follow him – for a moment St John experiences something like panic. Then he steadies himself. It is the bride who leaves her family behind. And the Lord will surely provide.

'There is a girls' school in Pondicherry, I understand. I will write to the headmistress.' A convent school – but he is braced for compromise.

Kamil bobs up and down in front of him, so impatient he can hardly speak. 'Sahib, I have a girl. She is ready.' And then, with all the abandon of a man who has already taken the plunge he adds 'But she is not a Christian.'

She – Asha – is a young woman who sells onions in the market. St John has himself often noticed the modesty which sets her apart from the other women selling their produce. She sits cross-legged and upright with her sari-pallu drawn across her face, and her glossy brown onions arranged neatly on a tidy piece of indigo-dyed cloth at her feet. The other market women, long past any chance that their beauty will entice a customer, bawl out their wares bare-faced, even brazenly tug at the lower garments of anyone who pauses.

'You have spoken to her? And her parents? Do you have an understanding?'

'Her mother is a widow, Sahib. They rent just one small field. She has a brother who –' Kamil gestures at his temples and pulls a face. 'Who is –.' He gives up.

'She has no dowry, I suppose.' St John does not wait for an answer. Dowry will be part of the cause that left another baby girl at his gate just a week ago. 'And you would want to make a home for all three? Here? With me and your sister? Jaya depends on your support.' He knows he has his thumb in the scale.


**Kamil inclines his head once, twice, three times.** 'Sahib, I would never leave you. And I have hopes that she will become a Christian.'

St John stops him. It is not because Kamil aspires to bring more souls to the Lord that he wants to marry this girl. When she lets go of her veil to weigh her onions, her brown cheeks are as sleek and flawless as her vegetables. But nevertheless, he is pleased as well as relieved. It is a good man who is willing to take on a widowed mother and a simpleton. Later, God willing, he will baptize her, and maybe the mother as well. 'You have told her that she must work, help with the children? Her mother too?'

Sensing that consent is close, Kamil nods even more eagerly, and St John holds up his hand. 'Then you have my blessing.'

The immediate change in Kamil's demeanour is enough to make plain to St John how long the poor fellow has been moping. He buys new clothes, oils his hair and sports a fine moustache. His high spirits enliven the whole household, save for his master, who finds himself strangely saddened by various arrangements for the wedding that discreetly exclude him. All the same, he must make his position plain, and when lessons are finished for the day, he invites Kamil to join him for a stroll by the river.

'I shall be very happy to administer the sacrament of marriage' he begins. 'Afterwards, your bride is very welcome to invite any friends from the village to join us at a simple wedding breakfast.'

Kamil fingers his new moustache in some embarrassment. Although he is dutifully committed to the Christian ceremony, it is the festivities in the village that excite him. He asks if he can use the bullock cart to take his new family to the temple. 'I shall ride a white horse.'

St John knows that he must remonstrate. 'You have put your old ways behind you.' But Kamil's crestfallen air softens his resolve. All he insists on is that his own ceremony should be held first. 'Because you must be married by a Christian priest before you take your wife to your bed.'

They are passing a stretch of the river where the village women come to bathe. Although a tall stand of papyrus screens them from view, their voices are audible and perhaps that is why neither man speaks until they are safely past. 'First for the Lord Jesus. Then temple. Afterwards, bed' Kamil mutters.

They step to one side as a child drives a small herd of high-trotting goats towards the village, while St John debates whether to explain that provided the Christian ceremony takes place first, there is no need to wait until after the temple. Indeed, an irritable part of him wants to insist that consummation must take place before the temple ceremony, as a way of acknowledging that it is both invalid and redundant, but the thought is absurd and, in any case, Kamil puts an end to his deliberations with an unexpected question. 'Will you come to the temple, sahib?'

It would not be seemly for a Christian minister to attend a pagan wedding, yet there is some regret in his response. 'Thank you. But that is for your wife's people. For the village.' Regret deepens as he sees Kamil's inadequately concealed relief.


**As the wedding approaches**, far more troublesome feelings beset him. Though a cold bath is more of a relief than a penance in this climate, hearty exercise has usually been enough to free him from sinful thoughts and distracting sensations. But the peculiar excitement of a wedding is harder to restrain, and a consciousness of what cannot be spoken about drifts on the air like a heavy scent. Poonam takes a sly delight in finding ways of making Kamil blush, and the high spirits with which Jaya helps her brother re-furbish his quarters seem to betray an alertness to matters a good Christian woman should prefer to conceal. But when St John asks himself whether he should try and arrange a marriage for her, perhaps with some well-disposed native Christian who would not object to her illegitimate son, his reaction tells him at least half of what he does not want to admit: that it is he who needs the sanctioned outlets of marriage. For a mad hour he even considers writing to Rosamond Oliver back in Morton. Like Jaya, she too is now a widow.

Yet the message his body conveys, his mind insists on refining. It tells him that it cannot be Jaya herself who is responsible for the suffusion of desire that has possessed him since his return from Mysore. That is no more than the last effect of a transient fever, a consequence of exhaustion as meaningless as a rash. His new awareness of her comeliness is no more than the contagion of her brother's pre-nuptial excitement. Considerable discipline is required to prevent his thoughts straying under the regime of long walks and strenuous gardening that he imposes on himself, but physical weariness at least ensures that his sleep is undisturbed by any dreams. However, it also precludes any letter-writing and as the day of Kamil's wedding draws closer, it is not only improper thoughts that come unbidden to his moments of inattention, but guilty reminders of his continued failure to write to his cousin.

St John is used to introspection; self-examination is essential to spiritual discipline, and he allows himself a day's solitude to investigate why this particular sin of omission weighs so heavily on his conscience. He packs a knapsack with food and water and sets off for the hills, armed with a stout stick. At first, he encounters a steady procession of villagers making their way down the hillside with their produce – women mostly, from the hill-tribes, who stare at him openly and seldom return his greeting. Then, as the morning wears on, he finds himself alone. Sharp ridges spread down from wooded summits blue as smoke, like headlands dividing an endless series of terraced bays, and each bay is bisected by a dark and tangled cleft, where the streams are still running. He can see the occasional flash of sunlight on falling water, where soon there will be nothing but dry stones. Higher still, the forest covering is broken by flanks of sheer rock, glinting like an old mirror where the sun strikes its surface. Although the women have disappeared from the path, the landscape is dotted with distant figures. Every nook that can be levelled is under cultivation. Far below him he sees a man ploughing a boulder-edged field that is hardly bigger than his school-room. The air is so still that he can hear him urge the straining bullock. Here above the plain the soil is pinkish, and as the clods fall from the share, they glow like a blush rising in a woman's cheek.

He reminds himself that it would be useful to make notes on what crops are faring well. The last monsoon was less than generous and already the heat is building, but providing the hills are not afflicted with any of the insect pests and mildews that plague the region, his own yields should be sufficient. If his share of cousin Jane's inheritance had not allowed him to farm good land close to the river, his household could not have prospered. This recollection brings him at last to what he has been avoiding all morning – even though it was why he has allowed himself this holiday.

How much selfishness is involved in his willingness to allow his family in England to believe he must be dead? He is certain that he will never return. To keep silent would merely anticipate a death that must come in due course and probably soon. His father did not make old bones; in this climate a white man seldom achieves anything like the Bible's allotted span. Let us leave aside condolences too late to soothe Jane's bereavement, he tells himself. News that I am alive would pointlessly revive a hope that should by now have turned to acceptance of my loss – for I must be lost to them, whether I live or die. Is it not better that they should learn to forget me, when who I now am is not the man they remember? Yet will I not add hurt and bewilderment to their grief, if they eventually learn that I have lived but kept silent?

He is crossing a skimpy bridge when he hears purposeful footsteps gaining on him from behind. Though thugs are supposed to have been eradicated from this area and he has nothing worth stealing about him, he grips his stick a little tighter. But the figure that falls in step beside him is a sadhu, naked except for the felted cape of his own hair and a beard not quite long enough to conceal his genitals. '*Namaste*' he greets him.

The sadhu nods. He is tall and upright, thin but not starved. The yellow dust that coats his body is uneven, crusted like mud in places, elsewhere a mere film. Where his skin is visible it shines like old polished wood. A smile twists St John's lips as he remembers the shock that ran around the fashionable Madras congregation when he suggested that some of the early fathers of their own church must have been just as grubby and extravagantly eccentric.

'D'ye find mi funny, heh?'

The accent is Scottish. St John stops in his tracks. 'You speak English?' The question is ridiculous.

'Ooch' says the sadhu. 'I was a sepoy in Colonel Morrison's regiment until ma eye gi' oot. His paymaster for five years.'

St John looks more closely. One of the man's pupils is thickened with white. Odd that he should have been thinking of thugs when it was this unlikely person's commanding officer who rounded up so many of them. A man respected by the Mysore court as well as the common people, and – by all accounts – largely unconcerned by racial distinctions. 'I should like to have met him.' After forty years in India the colonel retired to Scotland a few months before St John's arrival. Unwillingly, according to Mysore gossip. Some disagreement with new Company policies.

The sadhu points at his knapsack. 'Any grub in there?'

The two of them find a patch of shade and sit down. The sadhu eats slowly, reflectively, peering around him. He follows each belch with a *pardon*.

Though he cannot give any credence to gods who prompt their followers to grow their fingernails through their palms or stand on one leg for a lifetime, St John has some kind of respect for these pilgrims. Not the respect he extends to purposeful forms of service, but in its ideal form he can admire the austerity of the sadhu's calling. His own religion teaches him that only a man who has forsaken home, brethren and sisters, father and mother, wife and children shall inherit everlasting life, yet it is only in the service of false gods that countless thousands seem willing to submit to such a harsh injunction. For a moment he examines the idea that declining to write a letter might be a sign of his own forsaking, but the Lord will not let him off the hook that easily. Still, such thoughts have stirred his curiosity. 'Did the regiment not provide you with a pension?'

The sadhu wipes his mouth with his beard. 'Aye. The Colonel was guid to his men. But I left it to ma wife and bairns.'

'Would it not have been better to have stayed and supported them?' The wife and bairns will have no more idea of this man's fate than Cousin Jane and his sisters in England will have of his.

The sadhu has his mouth full of rice and chapati. He shrugs and points vaguely to the heavens, as if it is nothing to abandon everything and step out onto the endless road naked and alone. 'A calling. Like yuirself' he says eventually.

'You know who I am then?'

The sadhu is tearing another chapati. 'They say yuir mad.'

He laughs. 'I often think the same.' They are silent for a while. The sadhu lies back and scratches the parts that an Englishman would deem private. St John notices that his body hair is alive with lice and edges away. His own preferred forms of asceticism tend towards the clean, the cold and the discreet. His compatriots insist that all sadhus are rogues and charlatans; perhaps this individual is at best no better than a sturdy beggar of the kind he has often seen on the road to Mysore – or the road to Morton, come to that. Then it strikes him. 'You are close to home. You have not yet travelled far?'

'From Kannyakumari to Puri, to Amarnath.' The length and breadth of the country – if the man is not lying.

'Amarnath. The cold – surely –?'

The sadhu pushes back his mass of yellow-grey hair. Where his ear should have been a rim of gristle edges a seeping hole. 'Many lose fingers, feet to the ice. Even –' Another rich scratch. 'The monks gie' me a wee blanket.'

The pilgrims who climb for days through the harsh mountain passes to Amarnath worship a phallic icicle. But St John does not want to dwell on the lingam. Instead he asks himself why more Hindus cannot be persuaded to convert to a faith which is not only more rational but also less physically demanding. 'So now you are returning home?' Does he expect to be well-received by the family who have known nothing of his fate all this time?

The man sits up, heaves his legs stiffly across. 'It's ma time.' He is looking almost sheepish. 'Mebbe not *home*. But I'd like to be close.'

The true sadhu will die on the road. This one has been drawn by the very ties he renounced. 'But you are strong. You have many years...' Should he write that letter to his kin – or follow his own road, alone?

'Soon. Not today.' The sadhu rubs his belly. 'But mebbe tomorrow.' He inhales and closes his eyes. 'Or next week. Soon.'

St John looks at him, and something like a breath from the distant ice cave passes over him. The God who has declined to speak to him for so long seems at last to be offering some insight into His purposes, but His message is hard to read. Apart from the almost indiscernible rise and fall of his chest, the sadhu might be dead already, and he gives no sign of awareness as St John gets to his feet. Unsure of anything, he leaves the last of his food and water at the pilgrim's side and bows his head, but the only prayer that comes to mind is as much for himself as the sadhu: *Lighten our darkness, we beseech thee, O Lord.* His hands are joined. *'Namaste'* he adds.

**As he makes his way down the mountainside,** he thinks that at Morton he would have assisted the fellow to either the infirmary or the workhouse. Whatever the day has brought him, it has not solved the dilemma he set out with. It is something of a relief when he finds he has reached the main road where he must give his mind to the ruts underfoot and the hectic aftermath of the daily market.

A woman yells as she scoops a chicken from out of the path of a plodding elephant. On the bridge, two over-laden wagons are refusing to give way, and other carts are backing up behind them in both directions. In the heart of the noise, perilously close to the creaking wheels, the nervous hooves and even the massive, unstoppable legs of the elephant a group of market women are crouched, loudly inviting the furious carters to buy the last of their goods. A few glossy, purple and white brinjals gleam among the dust. Wizened limes on a platter of limp banana leaves. A bangled arm piles a heap of lumpy yellow-green mozambi.

Suddenly all the women are clamouring at him. He waves them aside – he has his own produce – but they only shout more loudly, pointing him towards Pisgah, urging him to hurry. *Asha*, he hears. *Asha* and much more which he cannot understand. He struggles between two wagons that will not give an inch. Where is Asha? What has happened to Asha? But his heart is saying another woman's name as he shoves and ducks through the throng on the bridge, and when at one point he is forced to take to the parapet, high above the rubbish-strewn gully, it is his fear for her that keeps his feet from slipping.

He hears the wailing from Pisgah as he staggers breathless round the last bend in the lane, but when he sees Jaya soothing a huddle of sobbing children, the thanks he sends to God have never been more heartfelt. When she leads him aside, leaving the children to Poonam, it is an effort to adjust to the bad news she has for him. Asha's mother is dead. Kamil is with his betrothed and her simpleton brother in the village, where the woman's remains will be cremated tonight.

'How did she die?' He remembers the woman by the road-side on the way from Mysore, the woman with the scarred face who gave him water. So many women's lives ruined or lost so senselessly. Is it any wonder that he cannot save their souls when they will not take the simplest steps to save their lives? He will insist that Jaya put aside her veil when she is in the kitchen. The simple hygienic cap of an English kitchen-maid would be just as modest – but he knows she will ignore him.

He has hardly heard what she is saying. Not a fire. Some other sudden visitation. He tries to berate himself for his indifference, but feels helpless and uninvolved. 'I am filthy from the road. Let me bathe, then we will pray.' As he sponges away the day's dust, he thinks of the nursery tales he will tell his small congregation. Only the youngest will accept that Asha's mother is already in heaven, herding lambs with Jesus.

**When the household is quiet** at last, he retreats to his study and attempts to study the Psalms: most are a cry for help. Then towards midnight his far from perfect concentration is disturbed by further sounds of distress. Kamil comes supporting a wailing Asha; the simpleton brother trails after them, stumbling and moaning. He can smell the pyre on their clothes. No sandalwood for Asha's mother, just common kitchen firewood. The hapless, uncomprehending lad who is now gazing open-mouthed at his books, must have held the torch to the ghee-drenched bundle who fed him this very morning. It is only after Jaya takes his weeping sweetheart to wash her face that Kamil crumples, and it is some time before he can explain that Asha and her brother are homeless. Their landlord has reclaimed the hovel that was their home and the field which provided their livelihood. Somewhere in his incoherent distress is a hint that the mother's death may be no accident.

He has learned to distance himself from the passions and irregularities of local life, and Kamil's assumption that he is the man to uncover the truth chafes at his spirit. The boy is tugging at the hem of his kurta, dribble running from his slack, confiding smile. St John shrinks involuntarily, shamefully aware that his compassion has its limits. Only when Jaya returns, with a subdued but still trembling Asha, does the child leave him to bury his head at his sister's waist – and with St John's thankfulness comes a wave of inspiration. 'Kamil. Let me marry you tonight. Then Asha and her brother can stay here, and you can comfort them.'

If he suspects that he is passing on an uncomfortable responsibility, Kamil's electric smile absolves him. Quickly St John reviews and dismisses the legality of the thing. What does it matter if the banns have not been read for the third time? Jaya and Poonam will bear witness.

When the dazed young bride has been led away to be decked in a more festive sari, he finds himself oddly embarrassed. 'What is the boy's name?' he asks at last.

'Bhanu' says Kamil. His voice is hoarse and he clears his throat. 'Bhanu. *Sun.*' He points to the sky.

'Bhanu' repeats St John. The boy recognises his name and rewards him with a look so trusting that St John's heart sinks again, re-loaded with responsibility. Then a sudden movement catches the child's eye as a mongoose darts across the grass. Instantly he is away – off the veranda, yelling, clapping, stamping his feet.

'He can be useful' says Kamil anxiously. 'He scares birds. He kept the deer out of his mother's onion field.'

'We will find him a rattle' says St John. 'I think he would like that.' He almost wishes he had strong drink in the house, for the occasion.

He dons his threadbare surplice and arranges the bands round his neck, thinking that what the bride needs tonight may be more like the comfort of a sister than the embrace of a husband, but the ceremony undeceives him. As she clings close to Kamil so that he can whisper a translation of sorts, her slight form is already molding itself to his side. She looks down at her new ring with the same satisfaction that St John has seen on the face of many a Morton bride as he pronounces them man and wife, but when she raises her eyes to her bridegroom, he finds that he must quickly look away.

**His struggle grows more terrible** as the heat builds towards the monsoon. While the public behaviour of the newly-weds is perfectly seemly, the very air that occupies the gap between their hands shudders with the history of their caresses. St John tries to convert his agitation into useful activity. Regular exercise sessions are added to the children's routine. He seeks out drums and whistles to form a makeshift band – and is incidentally rewarded when percussion seems to sop up the excesses of energy that overflow in Jaya's boy, Jivaj. But the idiot is another matter. While it is only to be expected that a bridegroom's concentration will sometimes lapse, he must brace himself to speak to Kamil: the boy Bhanu should be his charge now.

At first the lad seems happy enough. He lopes around on the edge of other children's games, apparently curious and absorbed until something else catches his eye. While there is little that education can do for him, he makes a useful scarecrow. His agitation brings the dozing mali running with his dogs to save the beans when elephants wander close to the vegetable fields. But before long Poonam comes to confide. When the boy left his crib on the night of the wedding and crept into her bed, she was glad to be able to comfort the poor child. But her joints ache and she does not sleep well in the heat, and Bhanu's once timid pleas have turned aggressive and demanding. She holds up her clasped hands in appeal. Irritated, St John dismisses her; this is for others to solve.

Poonam's moans become ever more heart-rending. Each morning finds her standing in the sunlight, ostentatiously kneading her arched back. And worse comes to light. Asha now feels that Bhanu has displeased the sahib, and that she and her brother have brought trouble to the household. It is all rather feverish. St John knows that a general unease is building, and though he would be relieved if the sultry post-nuptial mood were to be dispersed, he does not wish it to be replaced with suspicion and mistrust. He orders a bed in the dormitory for Bhanu, and instructs Jaya's son to take care of him. But Jivaj's dignity is compromised by the sad figure who now trails at his heels like an affectionate cur. St John uses the day's homily to remind all the children that Jesus befriended the halt and the lame and those possessed by devils; but the boys courteously remind him that Jesus did not have to share His quarters with a child who gibbers in his sleep.

Yet the vegetables swell and fetch a good price in the market, the chickens lay and a troublesome leopard turns its attention to someone else's goats. Slowly, the situation seems to be righting itself. Bhanu's sleep calms. Even the fever in his own blood seems to abate. Then one evening when the household is gathered for prayers Bhanu attempts to take hold of his hand and as the boy's shaggy, rolling head nuzzles his side, he instinctively starts back. It means nothing. He has never liked being touched.

However, the moment has been observed by the children, and their dismay tells him that they think he is harsh and uncaring. Perhaps this is what Bhanu senses too, for he wails and clings to his sister, who shrinks with renewed fear of the sahib's disapproval. With an effort, he tries to remind his congregation that he has always discouraged sentimental attachments and molly-coddling. From their incomprehension he learns that Bhanu has become a general pet now he no longer keeps the other boys from sleep – but it is hard to find adults and children alike staring at him so beseechingly, as if he alone is lacking any kindness. Desperately he looks around for Jaya and her good sense – then remembers that it is her time to withdraw herself. Asha is all but trembling and Kamil is as far out of his depth as St John is himself. As for Poonam – well, her mournful, adoring gaze tells him how much she fears his displeasure. If she were one of his Morton parishioners, he would suggest she finds herself a cat. *Surely this is not why I was called to India?* he thinks later that night as he strips for his own solitary bed.

What he asks for when he kneels in prayer is clarity of purpose – to be freed not only from the desires of the flesh, but the claims of feeling. Yet what he truly yearns for is some kind of spiritual housekeeping – some power that would sweep and tidy away the petty distractions that obscure his purpose, scour his life of sticky emotions and polish his resolve. He has aspired to be a servant of the Lord, but he finds himself reduced to His drudge, who must attend to the meanest of chores before the way can be made plain. Reduced? He stops himself. Was the purity of his original vision no better than arrogance and disdain? Is this the message that the boy Bhanu has been sent to convey? Does he back away from the boy's touch because he fears that he might be contaminated by an affection no more complicated than a cat twining round a man's legs?

The night is stifling. He dips a beaker into the sweating earthenware pot, drinks half and slowly pours the rest over his up-turned face, soaking the front of his nightshirt. When he pulls the wet fabric away from his skin, he feels a moment's relief. Then from across the compound he hears a sudden piercing cry, then a gasp, a murmur and finally a giggle.

**After this he becomes unnaturally alert** to the slightest physical contact. When he bends over a child's lessons, the merest breath on his cheek or hand affects him like danger. His attempts at self-examination are garbled and incomplete. If the practice were not so tainted by popery he might even experiment with self-flagellation.

The sullen, merciless heat compounds the fury in his blood and focuses it like a magnifying glass setting paper aflame. When a dead palm frond rattles to the ground during morning prayers its look of scorched ribs seems like a warning. Fire becomes his constant obsession. He orders all dry grasses near the buildings to be scythed, fraying banana leaves cut back and ditches cleared of dead leaves. After lessons, he sets the boys to lashing bamboo canes into simple ladders and the girls to knotting twigs into brooms to beat out any sparks that might ignite the thatched roofs of the compound. Though there is little for a fire to grow fat on in the recently harvested fields, he orders his labourers to strip the last crisp tatters and uproot the powder-dry stalks – and finds he has a rebellion on his hands. It is too hot for such unnecessary work, and there is more than enough to do, watering crops not yet ready for market.

In the depth of his being St John knows that this obsession is only the outward manifestation of how little control he has over the shameful, secret fires within. He tells himself that the disturbance that Jaya has innocently visited upon him is really no more than a tropical malady, part of that general flaw in nature which renders white men susceptible to the charms of brown women, and the males of a superior race liable to be tempted by those of a lower order. When nights too hot for sleep relieve him of his dreams he paces endlessly, grinding tumult into reason. It frustrates him to the point of madness that his sensible precautions against fire should be met with ridicule. Why will these people not save themselves? Their recalcitrance is as baffling as their failure to understand that Christianity is not only the supreme revelation of divine purpose, but a more humane, practical, fruitful and even convenient way of living. For the Hindu peasant, the advantages of a simpler contract with the Godhead should surely be as manifest as the benefits of safeguarding one's home against domestic catastrophe. To any Yorkshireman, that would be as plain as the eyes in one's head.

An insect is whining round his shoulders. He smacks it against his arm in a splatter of what is most likely his own blood. It is unthinkable to let petty hindrances deter him. What he is doing is for these people's own good. Tomorrow he will inspect the kitchen. The cook is deft enough, and the dhoti that he wears as he squats over his pots could instantly be discarded if it should happen to catch fire. But women frequently visit the kitchen as well, to help and to gossip, or to wheedle for some special dainty – he can see their veils dangling over the flames. He flings himself angrily onto his bed and falls at last into a sleep that is tormented by visions of Jaya, combing her hair with scented oil.

**Cook patiently explains that no dangerous processes are involved** when rice is steamed in a clay pot lined with banana leaves, or spices tossed in an iron pan that has been heated over a steady fire.

As meat (chicken or goat) is only a rare element in the household diet, a fierce blaze is seldom called for. But when St John discovers that a jeroboam of oil always stands close to the hearth, he orders that it should be removed to a distance, with enough for the day's needs decanted to a smaller vessel.

This interference is not appreciated. Cook relays his annoyance to his brother, head of the field workers, who is of the opinion that this bodes ill. Stripping the fields was bad enough but this kind of meddling means only one thing: the sahib suspects pilfering. Cook sulks; meals become haphazard. The children cannot concentrate on empty stomachs and discipline suffers. When Bhanu spots a green snake sliding into the chicken-run, his alarm sparks a hullabaloo. But the more St John becomes conscious of how order is slipping out of his grasp, the more powerless he feels to correct the course of things. He girds up his loins and makes a special effort to reassure cook that he is under no suspicion. The new instructions are merely an attempt to avoid unnecessary dangers. But cook has had a taste of power, and he is not ready to be obliging. As a consequence, St John finds that he has brought about precisely what he was most anxious to avoid. If Poonam craves a little treat or Asha wants to please her husband with some titbit, it is no use asking cook; they must take to the kitchen themselves.

Then Jaya's boy falls ill. His symptoms – vomiting and watery motions – are like as not the consequence of too many mangoes, but the end of the third day finds the boy with a raging appetite, and no one to cook his favourite foods but his mother. For weeks St John has self-consciously kept at a distance; now he feels compelled to watch over her.

'I am glad that Jivaji is better. We have missed him at lessons.'

She is slapping chapati dough between her long-fingered hands. The sound reminds him of a stream, slipping over rounded pebbles. 'He will be well enough soon, God willing.' She tosses her head sharply, to flick her plait out of her way.

His presence must be annoying her. 'You do not need to do this. You could be with Jivaj.'

She leans forward and spits on the pan atop the fire. The plait slides back across her shoulder and the curl at its tip dangles close to the glowing charcoal. A frown puckers her forehead as she whips up the coals with a fan, holding her other palm a bare sliver above the iron surface. He can hardly resist the temptation to warn her.

She spits again, and this time she appears to be satisfied, because she slaps a circle of dough onto the hot metal then pats and rotates it with swift, deft movements that he cannot keep his eyes off. When she winces and flicks a finger-tip across her tongue, he is guiltily aware that his attention may have made her clumsy. She flips the cooked chapati into a leaf-lined basket and takes up another. 'Poonam is with him. I am glad to do this.' Her forehead is smooth again now.

'Leave this to others. Give Jivaj your prayers.'

She smiles – is that scorn which curls those lips? 'Trouble God for a belly-ache?' Her plait falls forward again as she reaches for a pair of tongs.

St John knows he should leave. He feels awkward standing over her while she squats by the fire, and painfully aware that he half-wants some small accident to happen, so that he can step in. The low roofed building, always dingy with smoke and soot, grows darker still as dusk gathers outside. Peering round for some place to sit he bumps into the small shrine at the corner of the hearth and upsets the saucer of milk over his foot. He should remind her how dangerous it is, encouraging reptiles to visit a dimly-lit kitchen, but he fears to annoy her further; instead he looks round to find the pitcher. She nods at a shelf in the corner, and he gropes in the darkness at his feet for the empty saucer, takes it and fills it – overfills it, so that it is likely to slop as he carries it back. Without thinking he raises it to his mouth and drinks. The rank, goatish taste reminds him that this is a saucer that a snake may have sipped from.

She is reaching for a pinch of salt. This is another moment when he might leave her, but there is something so beguiling about how the meagre light catches the rim of her figure, a fold or two of her skirts and the moisture between her parted lips, that he finds himself staring his fill. Her knees are spread and bent, her draperies carefully distributed so that her modesty is impeccably protected and yet her movements are unhampered. Perfectly balanced, she leans forward over a simmering pot. A dusting of earth shadows her instep. When she sips from her spoon her small grunt of satisfaction relieves his tension. She is safely finished, thank God. He will see her get to her feet, then help her carry the food to Jivaj. He would like to reassure himself that the boy is on the mend.

But instead, to his dismay, she puts the pot to keep warm and reaches for the basket of chapatis. Taking one in the tongs, she holds it close to the uncovered scarlet coals, raising scorched blisters in the pallid dough. Then, to his even greater alarm he sees her pull close a covered jar, dip in a spoon and dribble a thin stream of ghee. A few drops fall into the fire, and a bright yellow flame spurts and breaks into a shower of drifting sparks. She looks up when she hears his gasp, anxious perhaps that he will rebuke her extravagance and in the second when her concentration falters, the fire licks her hand. She starts, blows on her fingers – and he sees that among the rising sparks a wisp of flame is wandering. Paralyzed by the inevitable, he watches it drift slowly for a moment, then sink to settle on her hair.

In the instant it takes him to rise to his feet, a tendril of smoke rises from the back of her head. He lurches forward. Alarmed, she staggers to her feet. The chapati falls from her hand onto the coals where it curls and blackens and bursts into a flame that writhes and clutches at her hem. He bends, reaches out, slaps with his bare hands – and in his haste he knocks over the jar of melted ghee. Drops patter over his legs and splash his bent face but he hardly notices. All he is aware of is her face, aghast and shimmering beyond the spiralling veil of flame that divides them like life from death. On he plunges, conscious only that this is the hour he was made for, and the brilliance that explodes around him seems like the divine light of revelation until he hears her scream and discovers that it is his garments that are ablaze, that flames are wrapping themselves round his legs, clambering up his arms and grasping at his hair. For a moment he feels nothing, then pain screeches across his flesh and he faints.

# CHAPTER 5

**When he recovers consciousness,** he is lying on a tousled sheet. Asha and Poonam are fanning him. For a terrible numb instant he fears that Jaya has perished, then he hears the sound of her footfall, and he weeps, not because pain has caught up with him again but because it is infinitely less than the pain he would have suffered had she been harmed.

'You have been ill for a week' she tells him sternly – and yes, he knows now that time has passed, in jagged flashes of anguish and a delirium that has ripped him to pieces. Something has survived the wreckage, but it is wan and feeble. He tries to read the women's faces, to tell what his chances might be, but Jaya's fingers are busy with the bandages that wrap his legs. Her face seems unscarred. It is enough that he has lived till this moment.

As she eases away the dressing he tries not to cry out, but clenching his teeth seems to reignite the fire that caught the side of his face, and what had been a dull, steady roar of pain turns incandescent. He lifts a bandaged hand to assess the damage. His eyes are unharmed, thank God, and his nose and mouth seem to be intact, but the size of the wadding and the stinging tenderness underneath tells him that his right cheek, his jaw and neck, and a portion of his scalp must be badly scarred. Let me not be hideous, he prays, then corrects himself. Give me the patience to accept the disfigurement that I have brought upon myself.

He struggles to lift his head, to see what he can of his legs. Poonam pushes him back, but it is too late, and what he has glimpsed is enough to make him swoon with nausea. His shin is a long rip of flayed meat, rimmed with charred rind. Surely he must die of such a wound. Jaya is leaning over him, tucking her plait out of the way, and he knows that a single hair, brushing that wound, would be an intolerable agony – and an unbearable delight.

'You saved my life.'

She sniffs – a rebuke for making that saving necessary? He can hear in the background the sound of the children reciting their lessons, and closer the sudden whirr of Bhanu's rattle. The boy is staring in from the veranda. He counts – in – out, in – out, and the steady rhythm of his breath is drawing him towards calm when a tug in the flesh of his leg rouses him again.

'Keep still' she commands, as if he were a wriggling child. In her hand is a small pair of brass tweezers. She leans forward, biting her lip a little. Something white wriggles between the tweezer's points. He hears the very faintest of thuds as the maggot drops into a dish. Bile rises in his throat and his belly spasms and contracts so that he thinks for a moment that he must vomit. She mops the sweat from his face with a wet rag, then bends to his leg again. He manages to lift his head, and discovers that she is sniffing the length of his wound. The profound intimacy of her action overwhelms him as he yields to unconsciousness.


**Not for some days does it come to him** that like Jane's husband, he has been injured in a fire – trying to save a woman. For an hour or so as he drifts in and out of a doze, he toys with the similarities and the contrasts. There are symmetries in the unwinding of God's endless plan, and there is apparent randomness. Eventually, he gives up. At the last day, the pattern will be plain. He wonders what it may mean to Jane, to learn of this odd coincidence if she ever receives the news of his death.

When he wakes in the night, Poonam is his nurse, snoring soundly with Bhanu curled at her feet. He wakes her and despite her protests insists on pencil and paper: he must write to the Archdeacon. *I have recently sustained injuries from which I cannot expect to recover. Please convey to my sisters that I died content in the faith of the Lord.* His words are barely legible. Too weak to write more or even to tear up the paper he has written on, he slips back into sleep. Next morning, he summons Kamil to take down a letter. But even as he begins to frame the first words, he is aware of some alteration in himself – a faint tingling in his deepest wound, as if some slow, deadly process has been halted, and life is returning at last. The sensation is too slight for much confidence, but if he lives, he will not have to emerge from his silence. That thought in itself is reviving.

**He wants to ask her *Am I hideous?*** but he fears she will deny it out of deference. His hair has been cut very short – by her? – and he longs to be shaved. When the bandages are removed from his arms, he supposes that the still-covered scars on his face and neck must be worse than the shiny, puckered streaks of inflammation that run up to his elbows. Miraculously, his hands have been spared much damage. His hands and his sight: a sign that there is still work for him to do. He watches carefully when Jaya changes his dressings, to detect any sign that she finds her tasks or his person repulsive. But as she picks off the maggots – fewer with each day – she hardly blinks. When she has finished, her lashes flicker like swallows over a pool.

Now he is fully conscious, it is Kamil who bathes him and assists with his bodily functions. Was it the women who have been privy to such needs while he was unaware? The question begins to torment him. One morning he wakes to find himself in a state of throbbing arousal which prayer cannot subdue. These feelings should have been consumed in the fire, he tells himself. The heavy, lifeless air seems to rekindle his burns, as if the flames that licked him were now pegged beneath his scars.

**He takes his first steps a month after the accident** – weak and wobbling as a new-born kid. Seated in a chair on the veranda he conducts a shortened form of the customary evening prayers. Stinging insects are so bothersome on these hot nights that no lamps have been lit, but a half-moon swims in the soupy sky and as he looks at the kneeling children's up-turned faces he feels his calling stir again: battered, but still alive.

Afterwards, Kamil helps him prepare for bed. 'It is good to resume the holy offices. My injuries must have caused much to be neglected.'

At first, he is not sure what the man replies. 'We said prayers every night. On Sundays I read the services' Kamil mumbles, sponging his master's back.

He thinks he has overstepped the mark, St John realises. But this man would make as good a priest as me. Better, indeed. Kamil has both love and compassion. He is not tormented by bitterness and failed ambition. How petty it is that my church is so unwilling to ordain any of the few it converts, he thinks, as if their faith and practice were unacceptable in the eyes of the Lord. If his strength is restored, he must challenge such narrow-minded orthodoxies. 'Thank you' he says. 'From now on, let us take turns – apart from the Eucharist, that is.' He knows that he might welcome just sufficient weakness to keep him out of the fray.

**If he could draw, he would paint a portrait of Jaya,** as she bends over his wounds. He has studied her long enough: the curve of her neck, the slight fleshiness beneath her chin, the gleam of a tooth as she bites her lip in concentration. Her unflustered manner of dealing with his injuries must be the capability of a mother. It is less comforting to remember that she must have acquired a strong stomach when she earned a pitiful living in the latrines of the Madras cantonments, but he smooths over such thoughts. Nothing can be disgusting to the truly compassionate mind.

'I am admiring your skill' he pretends. 'Where did you learn these things?'

She is unrolling a strip of newly-washed cotton. He can smell the sunlight that dried it.

'The Dewan sent his doctor.' She holds up the brass tweezers. 'These are his.'

The Dewan is the next best thing to Prime Minister in this state. 'How did he know of my accident?'

She does not pause in her work. 'Kamil went to the palace straight away. We know the Dewan is your friend.'

The man will hardly remember me, he thinks. It is years since we spoke. He remembers a few brief hours of engrossing conversation, in which the Dewan tried to persuade him that all the world's religions strive for the same truth. 'Kamil went that night?' *Braving the tiger?*

She nods. 'The doctor brought the – .' She hesitates, not knowing the word, and makes a wriggling, nibbling motion with her fingertips, ' – in a small box. They eat the dead skin. Clean up.'

'Maggots.' He had assumed that they had bred spontaneously in the wound, and that she was picking them away.

'Maggots.' She looks at him – far longer than her usual quick glances to check whether he is in pain as she works – then nods again, as if she has made a judgement. 'Now you can see.' She bends. 'I will help you to sit up.' She slips an arm behind his head – he can feel her palm on his shoulder – the ripe curve of her breast brushes his chest – her breath skims his cheek – and it is this that makes his head swim and takes his breath away, not the full sight of his injured leg. What that tells him is that he is fit for nothing. He could join the beggars along the bridge.

'No, no! It is good' Jaya insists.

He cannot believe her. What the maggots have left is a gnarled stick of gristle, partially coated in what looks like half-dried slime. Just below his knee a red-raw crater is still oozing a yellowish gum. But his foot is hardly damaged, and though the tissues of his ankle have shrunk and movement is limited, he will be able to walk again. It is childish not to be thankful for this.

If she senses his self-pity, she takes no notice. He watches her spread a dark paste on the strip of cotton and bind it to the unhealed portion of his leg. He forces himself to speak. 'The poultice – is that the Dewan's doctor too?' There is still an infantile tremor in his voice.

'Yes. He is very clever, I think.' Then she hesitates; bites her lip. 'He is a Muslim.'

He laughs – feebly. 'Did you think I would reject his expertise?' Something of the sort seems to have crossed her mind and he reflects on just how little of that mind is known to him.

She presses her knuckles to his forehead. How her hand can be cool when the air must be as hot as his blood he cannot imagine. He wants it to lie there forever.

But she takes it away. 'I think you must rest today.'

It is the shock, he supposes. The shock of seeing. He still has not seen his face. 'Will you find me a mirror?'

'Later' she says. She brings him a basin of something thick and sweet.

He can smell orange peel and cloves. 'Another of the hakim's potions?' She nods, then looks away quickly, so that he only catches the edge of a smile. Some ingredient she does not want me to know about, he thinks. An opiate, masked by the spices. Not that he minds. What potion could be sweeter than the down on her arm as she smooths his pillow? He is asleep before he can reproach himself.

**When he wakes, it is dark.** The compound is silent, but sounds carry long distances on such heat-laden air, and he hears from afar the ululating howl of some animal – a jackal perhaps. When he senses a stirring nearby, alarm brings him fully awake. 'Poonam?' Really, there is no need for her to keep watch any longer.

But it is Jaya. 'You asked for a mirror.' She helps him out of bed and hands him a stick to lean on.

Though he is afraid, and even trembling, something about her calm arrangements gives him the strength to walk. She leads him to the veranda, and there, on a table, he finds a wide-mouthed bowl full of water, standing in the moonlight. He has only to look down and he will see his reflection. But first she must remove the last bandages from his face, and wipe away the ointment. He cannot tell whether the touch of her fingers is giving him courage or making him helpless. She frowns a little as she dabs at his cheek with a sponge, but she has only the moonlight to work by, and perhaps she cannot see as well as she would like. Then she steps back.

He leans over the motionless water – and laughs. What he sees is a brigand. The last of the parson has gone. He hears a movement behind him, but puts out a hand to stay her concern as he takes a longer look. No doubt a silvered mirror in a harsher light would tell a less kindly story, but no-one could have managed a better introduction to the new self that stares up at him. He turns his head so that the moon can reflect the areas of taut new skin. Compared with the rest of his features, these patches seem anonymous and alien. Perhaps the shadows exaggerate how gaunt he has become. That roughly trimmed beard makes him look like some wild man of the woods. But it is not as terrible as he had feared. The beard will go – never again will hair grow more than patchily across half his jaw and much of the cheek above it – and once he eats properly his eyes will not be sunk beneath his brows. Gingerly he begins to explore his scalp and among the tender ridges he finds a few bristles sprouting. Well, a hat will cover it.

Then over his shoulder he sees Jaya's reflection join his, and an unbearable gratitude sweeps over him – not just for her thoughtfulness, but because her face has been spared – the face he loves. Admitting this fully at last, the marvel of how long he has kept this knowledge from himself mingles with all the amazement of his adoration. He knows that he must take her in his arms, but as he gathers his strength, he takes one last look at the image of himself and his courage fails. With a groan, he plunges his hand into the water and breaks the reflection. What he sees on her face when he turns, he cannot read. Clumsily, he manages to thank her, then sends her away.

He climbs back onto his bed unaided, but the jackal keeps him awake for the rest of the night.

**At least the children do not run away shrieking** when they see his scars. He suspects that they have been instructed, but they soon get used to him and he begins to take heart. Is it utterly impossible that she should love him in return? Naturally, she has given no sign – modest, unassuming woman that she is. As long as his uncontrollable feelings seemed no better than lust, he dared not allow her to occupy his mind. Now he has discovered that it is not lust but love that possesses him – love of course for her virtues as much as her grace – he can think of her freely, and very soon it comes to him that he must marry her. She is devout and dignified, and works hard without complaining. A good mother to her own child and an excellent guardian for the orphans; a skilful cook and a deft nurse – the ideal help-meet. Everything he has needed to relieve him of all the small claims that pester a man without a wife. It is easier to think rationally about all this because she has withdrawn to her regular seclusion. If she were his wife, she would surely abandon this unnecessary ritual.

Fastidiousness has always prevented him dwelling on the practice. Now – somewhat fearfully – he begins to think about it. Perhaps it is the regular encounter with her own blood that fits a woman to deal with the incontinence of children and the senile. Maybe that is why women have such an instinct for nursing the sick. This is not an aspect of Providential dispensation that he has ever needed to consider before and now, to his alarm, he finds himself unprepared for the earthier aspects of marriage. He knows the sensations of arousal and release well enough, but never unaccompanied by shame. Somehow the sacrament of marriage will purify these feelings, and love will transfigure disgust, but quite how this is to be achieved remains obscure. He has always previously imagined the marriage relationship in two very distinct aspects: as a practical partnership and a mystic union. He turns to the Bible and discovers that *The Song of Solomon* is not a reliable *vade mecum* – though its tropes (which previously seemed extravagant to the point of absurdity) – are now disconcertingly stirring: *Thy navel is like a rounded goblet, which wanteth not liquor...thy belly is like an heap of wheat set about with lilies...thy two breasts are like two young roes that are twins.*

Still forced to be idle for much of the day, an agony of indecision about how to proceed makes him tetchy and restless. He watches Poonam stretch a clean sheet tight over his charpoy and sprinkle it with water, and his irritation soars close to breaking point because she is not Jaya and nothing else will cool the fever in his blood. Sensing his displeasure, Poonam's look is heartrending, and as she pads down the veranda, he thinks he hears her sob. In the course of another sleepless night he resolves to set aside his dignity and confide in Kamil, who may be younger and in several obvious ways his inferior, but who has the benefit of experience.

**Kamil cannot disguise his unease.** Constrained by delicacy, St John bungles his confession, and learns not only that his feelings have been all too obvious to the young man for a very long time, but that he and Asha have debated whether to warn Jaya of the sahib's – presumably – dishonourable intentions.

St John is distraught. 'But Kamil! I wish to *marry* your sister.'

Kamil's expression is unconvinced. 'Marry. Then you go back to England –'

'I shall never return to England. My home is here, with you at Pisgah. With the school. The farm.'

The young man looks at him more shrewdly and for longer than he has ever looked before, until St John feels helpless under his gaze. What he must be seeing in his master is someone who will promise anything to get his way.

'You will marry her until an English woman comes.'

'No, Kamil, no! I will keep my vows – the same vows you made – *till death us do part.*'

Kamil inclines his head, and is silent for a while. He is right to be suspicious, thinks St John, though he is disappointed that a servant he trusts should regard him as no better than the blackguard who seduced his sister in Madras. This is how men of my race behave in India.

At last Kamil sighs. 'When my sister comes out of purdah, I will tell her what you say.'

'And if she wants nothing to do with me, I promise that will be the end of it.' A promise he knows he will break – which he thinks Kamil knows too.

More sleepless nights follow. He should have anticipated Kamil's concerns. Now the poor fellow will probably be worrying for his own future, if the sahib does not get his way. Asha is already too liable to fear his displeasure. While he still fears that Jaya might not be able to return his love, not for one moment has he previously imagined that she might question his integrity. But as he wrestles with a sweat-sodden sheet, thinking that no man who has ever seen a woman like Jaya returning from her bath at dusk could ever prefer a pallid, be-ribboned English miss, he knows that he is not wholly innocent of offence.

**The next time he sees her,** she seems to be specially luminous, as if her whole being were reflecting his hopes. Foolishly, he has failed to agree any signal with Kamil, but her demeanour can only mean that her brother has spoken – and naturally she is too modest to have any plain way of letting him know her feelings. He will write straightway to the chaplain of the garrison at Mysore asking him to publish the banns and conduct the wedding ceremony. The chaplain is not allowed to marry British troops to native women – a regulation that only increases the number of irregular liaisons – but St John is a civilian, and marriage with a woman of the country was formerly not uncommon. Nowadays in Madras his choice would be the subject of widespread disapproval and distaste – not to say ridicule – but that matters little. What he cannot stomach is the thought that the chaplain will apply to the Archdeacon for permission. He might as well write directly himself – and since it is he, and not the army or the Company or the Church who will be taking full responsibility for his wife, there can be no valid objection to his choice. But perhaps he does not need to indicate what kind of woman he has chosen. After several attempts he completes a letter that is bare of all save the most necessary information and ready to send whenever he is fully assured of Jaya's consent. That she should not consent now seems an impossibility; he can see no future beyond it.

**That evening when the household gathers for prayers,** he is sure that Kamil will confirm his hopes, but in Jaya herself he can detect nothing – except that she is lovelier than ever. Sundown has brought no relief from the day's heat, and the children fidget and whimper as Kamil reads the gospel for the day, but she sits cross-legged and unperturbed, even though Bhanu lolls in her lap, flapping at the flies that try to sip from his eye-rims. Poonam is nowhere to be seen.

When the children have been sent to bed, Kamil takes him aside. He seems eager to confide, but St John cannot bear to ask him outright.

'Poonam? She is tired, I think. The heat.'

'You have news for me?'

Kamil looks suddenly bashful – but what he finally comes out with is not what his master expects. 'Asha is with child.'

'Splendid!' St John pushes this aside and rushes on. 'But does Jaya know of my hopes –?'

The young man is so disjointed with bliss that other matters have probably been wiped from his mind. 'She is very pleased for us.'

Deflated, St John does not press him further. In silence he lets Kamil help him settle, then waves him away. Night finds him with a surplus of unused energy. His sole lamp is positioned far enough from his bed to keep the circling insects from his face, but at that distance its light is insufficient for reading, even if he could concentrate. The insects seem particularly peevish tonight. A circlet of mosquitoes rings the guarded flame. He can hear another whining close to his head. Beyond the circle of light, a huge cockchafer lumbers through the darkness, halts for a moment, then laboriously takes off again. He smears his face and throat with a mixture of citronella and eucalyptus oils that Poonam has prepared for him, knowing that he will have sweated it off long before morning, when another half dozen angry bites will probably have joined the rash that peppers every un-bandaged part of his body.

He does not hear her approach, but suddenly Jaya is there, in the lamplight – not her face, but her shadowed feet, the column of her draped limbs and her folded hands.

'Come closer. I am awake.' Perhaps he should have pretended to be asleep.

The lamplight catches the shine of her eye as she steps forward. He wonders what has brought her. All his needs have been attended to, and he can douse the light for himself.

'It is very hot' she says – and she closes her eyes, rolls back her head and stretches her spine. A fold of flesh curls over the edge of her skirt.

He has never seen her so unguarded. Has Kamil spoken to her at last? 'The lamp makes it hotter. Why not put it out?' To be alone with her, in the darkness – the blood drains from his head, from his arms and shoulders, leading his body to what it most desires.

A wisp of smoke lingers behind her as she carries the lamp towards the far corner of the veranda. All that he can see of her is her face and the swell of her bosom, and her hands – one transparent as she shields the flame from the small draught made by her movement. He sees the bone within, outlined in crimson when she bends to make some adjustment to the wick. The cloud of insects which has followed her is so dense that her outline seems to tremble as if she were a mirage, and as she returns, she melts into the darkness that the lamp has left behind.

'Sit here, beside me.'

Perfectly composed, she lowers herself to the frame of the charpoy. His nostrils pick up the sweet scent of eucalyptus; of cotton garments, dried in the sun; of lingering dust and sweat. The heat of her body throbs like his pulse. When he reaches for her hand, he discovers that hers is close, open and welcoming. Its imperfections surprise him – the thickened skin at the base of her thumb, a gnarling of her knuckles – but as their fingers entwine, the moment is fractured by the rush of stumbling footsteps, by a helpless, formless wail. Bhanu flings himself on Jaya, pulls at her arms, shrieks, implores.

Jivaj, Jaya's boy, is following. 'Mama, come quickly! Poonam is hurt! She will die!'

**No, she is not dying. Jivaj is an adventurous lad,** who climbs trees and scrumps mangoes, and likes to exaggerate. But it is no wonder that Bhanu is so alarmed. Poonam has fallen and cut her head, and the shallow wound is bleeding copiously. She clutches at her gore-streaked locks and raises her bloody palms to heaven – a sight that causes Bhanu to fling himself into her lap and clutch her round the waist while his sister Asha tries to pull him away.

Suddenly weakened, St John totters. This is the furthest he has walked since he was burned, and he has covered the ground between his own quarters and Poonam's small room at a speed that would have exhausted a fit man, in this heat. Kamil catches him and leads him out onto the porch, where the air is just perceptibly cooler. But there seems to be no goodness in it, and he must heave it into his lungs time and again before the dizziness passes. Around Poonam, the emotional riot continues. Not that her sufferings aren't genuine, he dutifully reminds himself; both as daughter and as wife she was beaten, and her constant aches and pains must be real enough; but he wishes that she could show a little more stoicism, and set a better example to the children. He spots Jaya steadily crossing the grass towards Poonam's room, with a basin in her hands and a pitcher on her head, and loves her self-containment.

'Cannot Asha take her brother away? The boy needs to be calmed.'

Jaya shakes his head. 'Bhanu will not leave. Poonam is like his mother now.'

His mother, whose pyre the boy ignited, thinks St John. He had imagined that the child's weak brain had mercifully failed to record his loss, but it seems to have left him with an expanded fear of disaster. 'Can you or Asha not get across to him that there is no real danger? He has been alarmed by the sight of blood, no doubt.'

'After a shock, someone as weak as Poonam will not always recover.'

'Is she weak? She is well fed –'

'She says it is too hot to eat. She gives her food to Bhanu, I think.'

If Jaya had not been spending so much of her time seeing to his injuries, she would not have allowed this to happen. If he had not been incapacitated – he pulls himself together. 'I should go back to her.'

What confronts him is a tableau of the responsibilities he has neglected. Poonam is quiet now and her head is bandaged, but she can only suck like a hand-reared kid at the edge of the cup that Asha is holding to her lips. Her bed is crowded by anxious orphans, all silently beseeching him to do – What? Before he can find an answer, Bhanu suddenly takes fright and howls – a cry that some law of nature seems to have matched precisely to the most receptive extremes of St John's nerves, and quite without meaning to, he moans – a long, shuddering groan of weariness and frustration. The stuffy, crowded cell fills with a heavy silence as Bhanu breaks off. St John hears the flame gutter in the clay diya, an insect whining, some small creature rustling in the thatch over their heads – and a sob as the boy hurls himself forward and flings his arms around his neck.

The impact sends a shaft of pain shuddering throughout his still tender wounds, and for a moment he is unaware of Bhanu's heaving sobs against his chest; then he smells the dust in the child's hair, feels the thin, clammy kurta under his hands, hears the congested snuffle in the boy's streaming nose – and as that limp and ungainly body clamps to his own, all the stern instincts that have armoured him for forty years desert him, and a life-time of unused tenderness overwhelms him. He cannot even wipe away the tears that are running down his cheeks because his arms are pinioned.

**He sends Kamil to Mysore with his letter.** A few rupees in the right hands will have it sent to Madras with the military mail. A week passes. Another creeps by.

Her voice drifts across the compound. 'Then the crow found more stones and dropped them into the pot, until at last the water rose and he could drink his fill.'

He puts his own book aside to fetch a drink and as he swallows the heat of his body seems to be flushed through for a precious moment with something richer than water. The feelings that have been a torment for so long have become a blessing. He drinks again. The well, thank God, is still flowing, but the river is very low. Every afternoon clouds mass in the West, and the odd rumble of thunder is heard, but there has been no rain. In class, the children are listless. Chalk turns to mush between their fingers and their bright young voices fall into a mumble as they trudge through their tables. They are drowsing under the trees as Jaya reads to them. He tries to remember his native land, as if its chill might refresh him, but it is beyond his imagining. It is heat he has chosen, this molten sweetness. Even the effort to read is beyond him. Some insect has eaten his book's glue, and its binding has fallen to pieces. Instead, he watches Jaya – no, drinks her in. It is all he can do. She is aware of him now, he is certain, and of how he feels. She seems willing to absorb his gaze.

A boy comes plodding from the village with a letter. Nothing can be done until he supplies the name of his intended spouse and her place of residence. Later, he thinks. Later. A movement catches his eye. It is Bhanu, come from wherever he has been wandering to reassure himself that Poonam is still alive. Nothing else moves. Not the air.

**The moon is full once more.** It hangs heavily in a whitened sky, circled in a dense wrapping of mist, a pearl swathed in gauze.

He sits by the lamp in his room, hoping that Jaya will come, but she has not returned since the night Poonam was taken ill. She cannot be sleeping. No one can sleep in this heat. The children's beds, topped with dampened rush mats, have been laid out on the bare sandy earth under the three great trees, but he can see them toss and turn, hear the murmur of their voices.

He must speak, but her composure still daunts him. If he could detect the smallest sign of need in her, he could be bolder. Dejected, he blows out the small flame, but as he readies himself to pray the darkness makes him more conscious of the moon. Under its insistent, searching light the compound presents itself like an emphatic statement, demanding that he act. Nervous and uncertain, he leaves the shadows and makes his way across the worn and dusty grass.

He finds Jaya trying to persuade the children to close their eyes. 'They are telling of wild animals.'

'Have they heard anything?'

'No. But they like to be frightened sometimes.'

And is there not something delicious in the fear that is tightening his belly as her voice fingers his skin? 'I heard a tiger yesterday. Sound travels a long way, on nights like this.'

'They come to the river. The watchmen have seen them.' Satisfied that the children are settling now, she begins to walk away.

He walks alongside and a wild thought breaks out in him. 'Who is on watch tonight? I should make sure that the fences are all intact.' They have reached a point where their ways will part, if she is to go to her own bed and he down to the water. He holds his course – and she stays beside him.

They reach the gate to the fields below, the river, the forest. He tries to rein back his heart. 'You are not afraid?'

'I like the moon. There is little danger, I think.'

Oh, there is danger – unspeakable danger, but still he leads her on. The path drops steeply here, and the parched soil has crumbled. He takes her hand and her downcast eyes as she watches her footing allow him to pore over a face which at last seems ready to reveal its secrets in this strange, forensic light. As they cross the bare fields, puffs of dust rise under their feet and linger behind them like a wake in the sea. They reach the first few trees of the forest, then the river bank where the rushes droop silenced and motionless, and there, beyond a stretch of pale sand, is what remains of the river itself: a narrow, unruffled ribbon of black water, twining between a cluster of pools, each one reflecting a moon.

A shout greets them from the watchman taking his turn in the shack on stilts that guards St John's precious vegetables. These are the weeks when the grass fails, when the forest undergrowth turns to brittle wires and leaves rattle like shards – weeks when hunger lures browsing animals out of the forest glades and makes them reckless. Together they inspect the barricades and then the beans and small marrows that grow quickly in the rich soil of the exposed river banks. The light is good enough. The smell of damp cools the sultry air. Nothing is urgent. If the watchman is surprised to see Jaya with his master, he gives nothing away – and this adds another element to the night, a sense of things falling into place, of rightness.

Yet he must say something. 'Any sign of gaur?'

The watchman points out a maze of hoof-prints in the sand, then shoots an imaginary gun in the air. 'Beng! All go!' An old army weapon, loaded with buckshot, is stored in the shack.

'And elephant?'

This is greeted with a laugh and a mighty spit, and St John realises that he has been mimicking a more manly man than himself. Suddenly he feels fraudulent, bashful and inexperienced. He is not practiced as a lover. He has never known a woman – and Jaya has known Captain Porter. Was her boy the offspring of a single, brutal encounter – or was she his petted, skilful concubine? He panics, wants to flee. The moon stares disdainfully at his weakness and a million buzzing crickets rasp at his nerves. He turns, half-frantic now – and finds that in his confusion he has missed the watchman's departure. The man is heading away with the light step of one who has been relieved. Does he think that his master has taken over his watch? Dignity demands that he call him back – and yet would not that make him an object of ridicule? It is too late now. He wonders helplessly how many times history might have changed its direction because a man cannot bear the thought of being laughed at.

And how many times has the world altered its course because a woman took a single step? Could Jaya herself have dismissed the watchman? She is making for the watchman's shack and he can only follow. He watches her hitch her sari to climb the ladder. Moonlight briefly casts the shadow of her hem across her ankles and then she disappears into the darkness below the thatch.

He hears rather than sees her arrange herself – hears the rustle of her garments, the creaks of the rattan slats as they shift under her. Though the hut is open on all sides, it is stuffy under the covering of reeds, and the heat-thickened air is clouded with smoke from the smudge-fire that the mali has built to keep the insects at bay. In front of him lies a scene of such motionless perfection that it seems that all of nature is waiting for him to move.

He does not need to look at Jaya to be sure that she is gazing too.

The landscape before them could be embossed on a silver plate. Its colours have sunk away. The impartial moon shines equally on every detail that her rays can reach, and leaves the rest to darkness. Rows of beans nearby climb up their bamboo stakes, their topmost shoots like slender fingers reaching for the light. Metallic reeds fringe the water's edge and the only movement is an eddy in the river's surface, ripples of faintly pulsing white.

St John swallows, clears his throat. The noise is shocking. Though he can hardly see her, he finds that Jaya is handing him water – warm, a little muddy, probably fetched by the watchman from the river. He wonders if he should be kneeling – senses that like the moon, Jaya is waiting. 'Will you be my wife?' A second's relief that he has managed to speak at all is followed by a wave of regret for his clumsiness, and then a worse agony of suspense, in which he hears her breathe once, twice.

'I did not think I should be married again.'

Her words free his voice. 'But you were a child! You have never been married as I want to marry you, Jaya! A contract you were too young to understand. Then widowed before... Then.... Your child.' For a while he can say no more. 'I want you to be my wife, my help-meet, my equal before God.'

She is silent again – indeed, she has stiffened. He makes to speak again but her finger bars his lips. With her other hand, she is pointing out into the darkness. A tiger is crossing the sandbank.

For a moment, the stillness of the night turns to paralysis, the quiet to the silence of eternity; the moon seems to hold her breath and the tiger walks steadily on. It pauses, sniffs almost daintily at the base of a clump of reeds, squats and spurts urine. Moonlight catches the spray. Then it strolls on, towards them – tall as a pony. He wonders whether he should find the gun, but the idea seems petty, the moment too laden with fate – and Jaya's hand is on his arm. Even now, her composure does not waver, and he feels it pass between them and seep into his bloodstream. The tiger comes close and must have scented their presence, for it lifts and turns its mighty head, and he can see the moisture in its expanding nostrils as it tastes the air – can see too that its muzzle and chest are clogged and darkened with the blood of a recent kill. Blood gleaming like tar.

He is hardly breathing, unblinking, transfixed. Around him he can smell dust and smoke, his own sweat and Jaya's, lingering traces of the mali's evening dhal – what the tiger is smelling. And now he catches a waft of the beast itself – a deep, astringent, feline tang, plus the warm, sweet note of blood. The creature stops again, and stares towards them. They are in shadow, but the tiger must know they are there. It lowers itself slightly and swings its tail from side to side, tip quivering, ready for whatever signal is forming behind its huge fixed gaze. Then satisfied, perhaps contemptuous, it stretches, and he can hear the rasp of its spread claws raking the sand. There is something like a swagger in the movement of its haunches as it heads for the river. Moonlight picks out the white patches on the backs of its ears, each crowned with a tuft of silvered bristles. Its whiskers glitter like fine wire, and as its markings shift and slide over its massively muscled frame, St John feels newly blessed, as if he has been given a privileged glimpse of the power and ingenuity of the tiger's maker. Now he dares to turn to Jaya, and finds that she is as rapt as he. He knows he might kiss her now, but instead he is content to enjoy the sweetness of waiting. The tiger steps slowly into the water, perfectly sure-footed, as if it too is prolonging the moment, and he seems himself to feel the soft wet sand yielding beneath his feet, the water rising inch by inch about his legs, lapping his loins, his belly, his chest, his throat – until his feet must clear the melting earth beneath them and he can only surrender to the river's current, swimming in a new element, trailing streams of light.

Her body is as deep and yielding as the dark waters. As his whole being gathers for its climax, he calls out *I am, I am.* The sentence is incomplete. What he is, he does not know; only that he is transformed. Along the jagged horizon, lightning flickers. A smell of rain begins to steal through the air.

# CHAPTER 6

**We have crossed the Tropic of Cancer** and a fair wind drives us on. Around is nothing but ocean: a restless landscape of dark valleys and foam-fringed mountain peaks stretching towards the indistinct line where water meets air.

Captain Benwick spotted my partiality for this vantage point a few days out of Lisbon, and has kindly arranged for a fender to be lashed in place as a step, so that I can climb to the foremost point of our vessel where only the narrow plank beneath my feet and the varnished rails beneath my hands separate me from the elements. I do not forget what I have left behind me, but when I glance down at the sharp furrow our prow cuts through the deep, I sometimes feel that I am out-pacing my shadow.

Some would say that I should have looked for my peace in resignation, but peace is not what I seek. There are still faculties within me which need their exercise. Others will quietly endure their doom, but some long to find some outlet for their suffering, so that out of their sorrow some benefits may spring. Among them, I count myself blessed, for I have the strength and means for whatever task is demanded of me. All that I lack is my husband's understanding.

But Providence has at least allowed me his company. I can hear his voice behind me now. Though I first insisted that I would travel alone, common-sense told me that the presence of a husband, his wealth and above all his authority as an English gentleman would protect me from the scrapes that even the most intrepid woman will encounter – often not a mile from her home. Travelling itself, Edward would have welcomed: that change of scene that everyone recommended: the villa we had loved, in the South of France – or why not Egypt, to see the Sphinx? These were the quieter passages of our struggle. It was St John that he refused to countenance. The months of deathly antagonism, the laden silences, the spasms of violent rage – these things are behind us now, best forgotten.

Then news came from Jamaica that Mr Mason, the brother of Mr Rochester's unhappy first wife, had succumbed to nervous instability, and his entire estate was passed by default to Edward. Like a gambler staking all on one last throw of the dice, my husband announced that if I were still hell-bent on India, he would sail for the Indies.

Where he would take a mistress. The shock and certainty of my reaction at the time overcomes me again – I am back at Ferndean, reeling, appalled – until a voice calls me back. 'Maman, maman, where is your bonnet? Have Emily fetch your bonnet! You will be brown as an Indian.' Adèle is standing a little below me, safe on the deck, shading her eyes against the sun. The wind has been too much for the dainty parasol that Edward bought her in Lisbon, and it dangles from her wrist, its ribs broken.

'It will be good to be a little hardened' I reply, but I climb down from my perch and make my way to the awning which has been rigged up for us. It was Adèle who unwittingly brought about this compromise: Edward refused to leave her behind, lest she fall prey to a fortune-hunter, but how could I allow her to go to Jamaica? Since the end of the trade in slaves, the sugar islands are become even more dangerous and debauched. And so it was at last agreed that we should all travel together, and that when I have satisfied myself about my cousin's fate in India, we shall turn about for the Cape once more, then head for the Indies. And once that business is concluded, we shall head home, to the new house which cousin Diana's husband is building for us, to look for a worthy husband for Adèle, who will have absorbed many educational benefits from the journey.

That, it is to be supposed, is what is happening now, as she giggles with Emily over some new poet. I did not think Bessie would want her daughter to come with us, nor did I think a lady's maid would be needed, but Edward's man had to come, and as Bessie acknowledged with a sigh, the girl is that sweet on Harry, she would follow him to the ends of the earth.

Our airy drawing room lacks all but the most basic amenities – a few crates and canvas chairs – but the company we have there could hardly be improved on. Bishop Fisher is to be the new Bishop of Calcutta – a see which extends to New Zealand! He was a sportsman in his youth and no doubt his robust physique was an element in his selection, for he will need great reserves of vigour to face the demands of his appointment. Ill-health is at least the official reason for his predecessor's premature retirement. His intellect is as robust as his person, and though many of his ideas disconcert me a little, his readiness to argue a fine point has provided Mr Rochester with hours of welcome diversion.

Not that I am averse to unfamiliar ideas. My acquaintance – my friendship, I think I may say – with the Bishop's lady has been as invigorating as any exercise that can be enjoyed on our cramped decks. Mrs Fisher – Alice – is a striking woman, uncommonly tall for our sex. Though long engaged, they are but recently married as she has been obliged to keep house for her ailing and disobliging father. This, says Alice, is one of those duties to which women may not be as naturally adapted as many gentlemen prefer to think.

Today the Bishop has been reading from an ancient Sanskrit text, translating for us as he goes.

'I cannot think that you will find much enthusiasm for our parables among your heathen congregations' says my husband. Tug lies at his feet 'They are thin gruel, compared with this. Where in our scriptures will you find a monkey commanding an army?'

The Bishop puts down his book, happy to spar. 'Our story begins with a talking snake. We have Daniel and his lions. The fiery furnace. A giant felled by a lad with a sling. Shall I go on?'

'Tush, man. That is the old dispensation. What about the new? The labourers who arrive in the vineyard when the day's work is nearly over, yet are paid as much as those who have laboured since dawn? How will you defend *that* to your Hindoo? No British workman would stand for it.'

I have often been unable to resist stepping in when perhaps I would have been better advised to stay silent. 'Come, Edward! The lesson is that God makes no difference between a soul born into our faith and even a death-bed conversion. It is the very parable that justifies the work of our missions.' No one responds. Perhaps I am at fault for presuming to interpret scripture when we have a Bishop on hand, or perhaps it is simply unwise for a woman to think she can join a conversation among men. I look for guidance to the Bishop's lady, who is not normally reluctant to add her voice to any debate, and find that for once she is dozing. For her this voyage is a holiday before the hard work begins. For me it is a time of preparation.

The Bishop stretches himself. 'You are right, Mrs Rochester. I cannot help wishing that our Lord had found another way of expressing that part of His wisdom. For simpler souls, the metaphor somewhat obscures the message.'

'You will find your Hindoo only too pleased to hear that Christianity allows him to get away with so little.' Captain Sharp approaches carrying two long-necked bottles, still dripping from their immersion in the sea. The Captain is another *habitué* of our improvised drawing room and the only one of us who is not a griffin – as I believe a newcomer to India is familiarly termed. He could be said to 'know the ropes' – though I must confess that I find his condescension to our ignorance a little irritating. His sun-burnt arms and the front of his white shirt are wet from hauling the wine on board – an effect that is not lost on Adèle.

'I doubt they will be familiar with vineyards in India.' Mrs Fisher is suddenly alert. She does not care for the Captain. 'My husband will substitute some more familiar crop.'

The Captain corrects her. 'They produce a very acceptable tipple in Goa.'

'That is Portuguese' says Alice Fisher stoutly. 'Catholics. I doubt we shall mix.'

'And it is the wine I purchased in Lisbon that we are to drink now' returns the Bishop. 'If you would be so good, Captain Sharp, before the chill is lost.'

Thus we pass our idle hours.

'The mughal emperors enjoyed their wine' says my husband, after a lazy silence. 'Though it is forbidden to the Mussulman. How was that?' The Bishop merely raises his eyebrows and Edward continues. 'I once owned paintings: little glasses of crimson wine; houris in the prince's pleasure gardens.' He sounds wistful. Those paintings were destroyed when Thornfield burned.

'Half-clad houris, no doubt' says Alice Fisher. 'Who smoke a hookah and hunt with cheetahs.' I wonder quite what her husband's colleagues will make of her in Calcutta.

'With cheetahs!' Adèle pipes up. 'How thrilling!' She peeps at Captain Sharp from under the wide brim of her straw hat.

'Moments of release in lives of utter futility' says Alice. 'I hope to penetrate a zenana at the earliest opportunity. To expose the degrading reality behind the superficial glamour.'

There is another silence. The men all look rather sheepish, including the Bishop.

The rushing breeze, the scatter of diamond water-drops thrown back by the cleaving prow, our square of blessed shade and the bright sun beyond lend some savour to a lunch that has in truth become monotonous: salt pork and pickled greens. Afterwards, the Bishop and his wife withdraw to their cabin; drowsy, they say. Adèle summons Emily to unlace her stays and the two of them retreat to giggle over another romance. Captain Sharp scans the empty horizon. I can see Harry amidships, smoking a pipe with a couple of the sailors. At this hour and in these conditions the crew are often idle. The sails are set, the winds are fair, we are out of sight of any land or reefs.

Only I am restless. My husband is lolling in his chair, his feet elevated on a crate, his hat pulled over his eyes, his hand on his dog's neck. I cannot tell whether he is sleeping. 'Would you like to go to our cabin?' I whisper. 'You will be more comfortable there.' He stirs, and Tug looks up. The poor creature is sadly confined. 'Or shall I read to you?'

He reaches out. 'Sit by me, Jane. Take my hand.'

I lower myself to the deck's warm planks and lean against his knee. His hand grips mine so tightly that I think for a moment this is the grip of a drowning man who would pull me down rather than let me go.


**Today we are to cross the equator.** The sea will not change colour, no obelisk will mark the spot, but I feel curiously agitated, as if I am approaching some crucial junction in this strange journey. It is dawn. On our left – to port I should say – the first rays of the sun are gilding the watery horizon, but the ship behind me is still shadowed by its sails, and it is a sound that tells me I am not alone. Some mariner, I think, with too much liquor taken – and I must confess that compassion is not my immediate response. Then I see that it is the Bishop's lady; she is bent double over the side of the ship and her whole frame is heaving.

I rush to her side. 'Alice! Mrs Fisher! Have a care – you will fall overboard!'

'That would be a merciful release' she manages to gasp, before heaving again.

'Are you sea-sick?' I take her hand and lead her to a deck-chair. In the growing light I can see that her face is as green as the sea itself, and a clammy sweat coats her brow. A moment of dread seizes me. In these fiery zones, who knows what deathly fevers might engulf our ship? I think of Mr Coleridge's ballad and of myself *alone, alone, all all alone, alone on a wide, wide sea* – and then I hear her voice.

'I think I must be with child.'

It is my turn to feel faint. I grip the rail and stare overboard. Sunlight has not yet reached the waves around us, and the inky deeps below look solid and impenetrable, like molten glass. She knows the outline of my story but I cannot expect her to be aware of the pang her news inflicts on my heart.

'What can I get you – to ease the nausea?' I was never so afflicted myself, so I do not know what to do.

'Sit beside me. Talk. It will pass soon.' She breathes deeply between each utterance, to steady herself.

'I am often here, to watch the dawn, but I have not seen you here before. How long – when did you discover your condition?'

She groans. 'I thought it was the pork, but I have avoided it since and still I am sick. And I have missed my courses.' She pushes herself a little more upright. 'There! It is passing. How strange, that one's body should seem to want to expel its own buried treasure.' She turns her head, and the sun – now safely delivered above the horizon – bathes her with gold. 'I feel like an oyster, growing a pearl.' A radiant smile breaks across her face.

I have felt the same. Three times. 'Perhaps some hot tea? I am sure cook must be stirring.'

She nods, absently, and I know that she is intent on what is within her – not just the child, but the future. A first faint odour of frying bacon reaches my nostrils as I make my way towards the galley and I see that other figures are emerging, including Adèle. She stands yawning at the foot of the ladder that will bring her up on deck, still muffled in her wrapper. A whiff of tobacco nearby tells me that it is not the sunrise that she has risen to greet.

'Good morning, Captain Sharp!' He should know I am about.

Our Chinese cook – a perfect replica of the comic peasant one finds tucked amongst the swarming detail of a porcelain landscape – is busy searing meat, and a bloodied black and white pelt on the floor has me looking round for Tug in alarm – until he makes a goat's horns with his fingers at his temples. I ask for sweet tea with ginger. A remedy for sea-sickness, I explain. 'For Mrs Fisher.' His face breaks into a rather improper grin. I make my own face a severe blank, but confined as we are, we can hardly hope to have secrets.

Over breakfast Captain Benwick warns us that the ceremony as we cross the line may be too indecorous for our tastes. If we would like to avoid it, he will arrange for screens to divide our bower from the hurly-burly on the main deck. But Mrs Fisher – fully restored by the tea – declines. 'After all,' she says 'we shall no doubt be called upon to witness countless bizarre and colourful ceremonies in India. And if what I have read of nautch-girls is correct, some are bound to be indecorous. This is an opportunity to steel ourselves, for what is to come. Will you join us, Mrs Rochester? And Mr Rochester too?'

I still feel unsettled and so muted by her news that I can only turn to Edward.

'To the man of science, no corner of human behaviour is without interest, no matter how outlandish' he says. 'Though I fear the details will be lost on my poor eye-sight.'

I suspect that Captain Sharp does not recognise the element of irony that is at work here, for he draws on his cigar and looks rather stern. 'It can hardly be to a young lady's taste. If you will permit me, Mrs Rochester, I will happily keep company with your ward, here on the forecastle deck, while this unseemly business takes place.'

Edward is like a bear, waking from hibernation. 'My daughter cannot oblige you, Captain Sharp. I shall need her eyes to describe the scene.'

My husband does not mean to rebuke me, I feel sure, but I cannot help remembering how I was once his eyes, and I lose track of the conversation as remorse takes me to task. Surely this at least is a loving service that I can now restore? It was not something that I ever consciously intended to withhold – but while the world was drab and colourless to me, what was there to relate? 'By all accounts there will be more than enough going on for two pairs of eyes' I manage at last.

At three o'clock we are solemnly escorted to our seats amidships. Most of the sails have been reefed to slow the ship's progress – a wise move, as few of the sailors will be on watch – but without their shade and the cooling effect of our onward motion, it is stiflingly hot. A sail has been slung from the yards and filled with water, stained bright green. To one side stands a kind of ramshackle throne, all stuck about with shells and pieces of coral. Then from below decks we hear the sound of a horn – it turns out to be a conch-shell, – and a half-naked figure climbs into view, his lower limbs swaddled in a scaly fishtail, complete with fins. He wears a massive golden wig, which on closer examination turns out to be composed of curly shavings from the carpenter's shop, and his shoulders are draped with strands of frayed rope and canvas, like sea-weed. As he brandishes his trident the din is augmented by heart-felt roars from the shellbacks (a term I learn from Captain Benwick) denoting those who have undergone this ceremony on previous voyages. As I strive to convey the scene to Edward, I ponder how odd it is that a spectacle so queer should mark my return to a once familiar duty. 'Pollywogs!' I hear myself bawl in his ear. 'That is the name for the initiates!'

'There's Harry!' Emily is perched on a crate beside Adèle: two pretty young women in the flower of their youth. Adèle is dark haired and pale complexioned, while Emily is a perfect specimen of that kind of beauty we like to associate with an English dairy-maid, buxom and rosy. The two of them could be a tableau of artless gaiety, as they wave at the gaggle of pollywogs who are awaiting their ducking. Edward's valet is wearing no more than his drawers, and even that garment has slipped a little below his navel. While it is true that his fellow pollywogs are also bare-chested and barelegged, there is something about Harry that makes his near-nakedness seem if not indecent then at least faintly dangerous.

'Did I hear Harry's name?' asks Edward at my side.

I hesitate to describe his impact – for indeed there is a stir around him that suggests that his striking physique is the object of some jocular comment. 'He is among the pollywogs, waiting to be shaved' I say. 'Another grotesque figure is mixing a huge bowl of soap-suds. And then I suppose they will be tipped into the green bath. I fear we shall all be splashed.'

'No matter. We shall dry in a trice.' I hear that little grunt of the sardonic laughter that used to be such a familiar aspect of our conversation. He is stretched out basking in a low chair, and I wonder whether the heat stirs any memories of his time in Jamaica.

Now Adèle is attempting to describe the scene, but she is blushing and giggling too much to be intelligible. Perhaps I should wag a finger in reproof, but somehow the languorous, heated air has affected me too; we have left disapproval behind, in colder climes. I have not worn stockings since we entered the tropics. I glance at the Bishop and his lady, who are whispering head to head. His hand is on her knee and I wonder if he knows yet that he is to be a father. Suddenly I too crave some loving touch, but when I reach for my husband's hand, I find that all his attention is with his daughter.

'Now it is Harry's turn to be shaved! And see how Emily is blushing!'

Indeed she is – her rosebud cheeks are now in full flower. My husband leans towards me. 'This I must hear.'

'The barber's assistants have hold of him and he is pretending to struggle.' There is a sudden cheer and a mighty splash as our man heaves his assailant into the green bath – now awash with dollops of shaving-foam.

'So, what was that? Come, Jane – do not let me miss the excitement!'

It is not only decorum which holds me back. I am not sure of the words. 'By the look of him, Harry has been exercising quite strenuously.'

'With the dumb-bells, so he tells me. He must have a fine set of muscles.'

His arms and shoulders shine like polished bronze as he is thrown into the tub. 'I think he must be very popular among the sailors, for they are holding his arms aloft as if he has won a fight.' Shrill whistles and a great bellow of applause seem to confirm my guess, but I do not attempt to describe how the drenching has rendered Harry's thin drawers near-transparent, and how they cling to his thighs. A line of thick black hair snakes down his torso. I glance at our young ladies. Adèle has her face buried in her hands, though her spread fingers suggest she is peeking; Emily is staring eagerly, her neck and bosom as red as her cheeks.

'A wedding may be needed' I whisper to Edward as the hubbub dies down. 'Emily is quite madly in love.'

He grunts. 'We have a Bishop on board.'

'Better still – let St John officiate, when we reach our destination!' I speak without thinking – and see my husband stiffen. The afternoon has brought back a little of our old closeness and now I have re-introduced our difference. Suddenly I have had enough of the crude pantomime in front of us. I close my eyes and conjure a modest, white-washed chapel, shaded by swaying palms. I see a choir, with brown faces; and I see my cousin in his starched surplice, with the sunlight making a halo of his golden hair.

**This evening, we dine in state, on curried goat.** Towards midnight I excuse myself and make my way towards my usual vantage point. Every trace of the afternoon's festivities has been tidied away, but as I cross the deck, sounds of conviviality rise from below. At the prow, however, all that is behind my back, driven out of hearing by the onward sweep of our passage. We have hoisted full sail once more, and the ship swoops and rises like some great bird breasting the currents of the air. Above, in a velvet sky dusted with stars, a full moon sails, and her light silvers the sleek, curling wave cut by our bow. I lift my head and gaze full in her face, wondering if she has a message for me tonight – but it is not she who speaks.

'Mrs Rochester. I hope I do not disturb your reverie.' It is Bishop Fisher. The small red glow of his pipe is the only colour in this moon-washed seascape.

In truth he does disturb me, but that I can hardly admit. 'Captain Benwick's dinner-table is a miracle of ingenuity, but a little cramped.'

'And when the whole of heaven is above us –.' He gestures with his pipe and as a few sparks drift through the air, I see him follow their passage and stamp on one that lands on a coil of rope. In my perch, I tower above him, and to remove that awkwardness I begin to clamber down. He takes me by the arm and together we move a few steps to a more sheltered section of the rail.

'I believe my wife has told you that we are to have a child.'

For a moment the beauty of the night is scored by pain and I want to walk away; but he stops me. 'Alice wants to thank you for the kindness you showed her, though she fears she may have distressed you.'

'Not at all' I say. It is what I am used to saying: the most efficient way of curtailing a conversation which would be more painful the more it is prolonged.

Again, he detains me. 'But I am sure it did. The thoughtless happiness of others can only reawaken your pain. It is something you must have endured many times.'

'Almost constantly.' I had no intention of responding with anything more than a further platitude, but his directness prompts me to speak the truth.

It is some time before he speaks again. 'You seem to have gained in spirits as our voyage has progressed, and yet – forgive me if I am impertinent – you sometimes seem uncomfortable with our conversations.'

I cannot quite bring myself to tell the truth – that I am disappointed in a Bishop who does not burn with the same ardour for his task that had possessed St John in the weeks before his embarkation, all those years ago. 'It is I who have more reason to fear my impertinence. But yes, I am somewhat confused by your interest in the heathen religions you have been called to oppose. I had expected to hear more fervent condemnation.' Perhaps it is the moon's unblinking eye, and the vastness of the waters that surround our tiny craft, but I find myself sounding more forthright than I had intended.

'*Called* to oppose?' He sighs. 'Mrs Rochester – it is not God's voice that orders me to India, but the Prime Minister's. That is not to say that I go unwillingly, or that I have any doubt that this is what God wants for me. But too much of a zeal for conversion would disqualify me from an appointment that is as much political as it is spiritual. Neither the government nor the East India Company is yet entirely convinced of the wisdom of allowing missionaries to operate among the native people.'

I think of the cruel set-backs and opposition that St John once hinted at in the letters we used to receive. 'I must confess that I am disappointed. I cannot believe that anyone would allow mere expediency to stand in the path of such unquestionable benefits to millions of hapless souls. Do you not earnestly desire to see every last heathen brought into the fold?'

'Profoundly. But it must be the work of time and patience. I wish to discover for myself something of the country and its people before deciding how to begin.'

'But does not the scale of the need demand urgent remedy? From what I have read –'

He interrupts me. 'We have all *read*, Mrs Rochester – but what do we really know? You have doubtless read of gods with a dozen arms who tear the heads off innocent babes, of virgins surrendered to the lusts of venal priests, of widows forced to succumb to the flames of their husbands' pyres – and you have no doubt responded with a generous subscription to a missionary society.'

This rouses me. 'I have a cousin – a dear cousin – who has devoted his life – his health – to the cause.'

'And no doubt his ambitions have been frustrated by the present incumbent. You will not expect me to criticise the man whose shoes I am to step into, but my predecessor's dilemma has been intractable – and I, God help me! – am sent to try and repair something of the damage that has been laid at his feet. Those are my instructions, Mrs Rochester, and I must reconcile them with the commands I hear from heaven.'

His candour subdues me. 'I must thank you for taking me into your confidence – and I will confess that my actions have been prompted as much by feeling as by knowledge. I would be sincerely grateful to learn more.'

'I should be glad to earn your trust. But not tonight, I think.'

He nods and raises a hand, and I see that the rest of our party has left the Captain's cabin and is come to join us. A servant carries more of the long-necked bottles. But I am in no mood for further conversation and busy myself with Tug. We have brought from Ferndean an ancient twist of rope, which he likes to tussle with. Back there it was Edward's custom to hurl the thing as far as he could – and this is what Tug expects now, for he backs off and crouches, back legs braced, ready to tear off in pursuit. What the poor creature cannot grasp is that if his toy was thrown with any gusto, it would land in the sea – and I fear that Tug in his longing for a good run would all too likely follow it overboard. Perhaps it was selfish to bring him. There are doubtless at least as many dangers ahead for him as there are for us, but to Edward he is invaluable. Though Captain Benwick runs a tight and tidy ship, Tug helps him avoid the many obstacles that lie about the decks. What we did not anticipate however is the reaction of some members of the crew. I remember the lascar who was ordered to carry Tug on board at Lisbon, stripping himself afterwards because he considered himself defiled – and I think of how the Bishop has cautioned me to be wary of my ignorance.

**I have told Emily** that I have no need of her tonight. Seldom have I been more aware of the virtues of thrift than on this voyage, when my washed-out old muslins are far more comfortable than Adèle's spanking new wardrobe can possibly be. But as I undress I discover how much the impact of Mrs Fisher's news still lingers. Like the after-effect of some fearful accident that was narrowly avoided, my nerves are still taut, my senses over-alert. When Edward enters the cabin he takes the brush from my hand and lifts my hair off my shoulders, teasing out the wind's tangles with long, firm strokes. The tension in my limbs begins to ease, and as the ship rises and falls, rises and falls, and her timbers groan softly, I feel his dear, familiar lips on my neck – and the unfamiliar rasp of the beard he has allowed to grow since Lisbon, reminding me that all is changed. Though it rends my very heart-strings I turn my face away from his kisses.

'Jane, Jane! What is this?' he implores. 'Today you seemed so much restored I felt reason to hope.' He folds me in his arms once more and attempts to pull my head towards him, but I dare not permit it. Then he would kiss my lips: no.

'Jane, Jane!' he calls again – in such an accent of bitter sadness it thrills along every nerve. 'I am your husband! Do you not love me?'

I cannot help myself. 'I *do* love you, but... I cannot let you come to my bed.'

'Do you find me repulsive, Jane? Has the company of so many fine fellows on this ship finally brought home to you how hideous I am?'

I could almost laugh, so far is he from the truth, and an instinct to reassure him impels me to take his wounded face between my hands. 'How foolish you are! You are as fine a man as when I first set eyes on you!'

His hands steal around my waist. 'You did not think me handsome then, if I remember.'

It needs but a moment of such tender recollection to have me yielding again, and when his lips seek mine, I soften and respond with an unthinking eagerness to his embrace. Strong hands slide down the length of my back and pull me close. With nothing but our thin night-clothes between us I long to give in while at the very same moment I am urgently reminded of why I must break off. 'Mr Rochester – you must release me. I cannot.'

'But why, Jane? Why?' His voice is hoarse with anguish.

'Everything is changed about me. I must change too.'

He grabs my wrist. 'I think you are still in love with your cousin.' I am struck rigid with shock – unable to imagine how he might have misinterpreted what urges me on. Enough moonlight is penetrating our cabin for me to see the look of a man who could in an instant plunge headlong into violence.

'You intend to give yourself to him.'

'Only my service. Not my body. How can you think such a thing?'

'Because you refuse *me*. I am your husband, Jane.'

Suddenly the floodgates open and my tears gush forth. I do not remember when I last wept. Dimly, I hear a terrible groan, then Edward's arms encircle me and I sob helplessly on his breast. 'I cannot' I gulp. 'I am afraid.'

He strokes my back until I am calm again, then wets a cloth and tenderly washes my face. 'Let us go back on deck' he whispers. 'We can talk more freely under the moon.'

We make our way towards our secluded spot. Though I must guide him, my legs are weak and I need to lean upon his arm. The sailors' hubbub is stilled now, and I do not think we shall be disturbed. He settles me in a chair and sits at my side, holding my hand.

'My Jane – afraid? My Jane, who has faced so much? We can turn back at the Cape –'

I stop him there – perhaps because I do not want to hear the sudden note of hope in his tone. 'I am afraid of your love.'

He is silent for a moment. 'My love – or its consequences?'

I nod, forgetting that he cannot see. 'Its consequences' I manage at last.

He stands up at that, and moves towards the ship's rail, holding out his hand to find it. I think he will make out the moon's broad pathway. 'Jane' he continues at last, his voice hardly more than a whisper, 'there can hardly be a man alive who does not curse the consequences of his love when he sees his wife in the agonies of childbirth – and vow that he will live a monk's life thereafter. But nature has ways of making us forget – as you yourself have said of your own pangs.'

'It is not the birth of more children that I fear.' My voice sounds hollow to me. 'It is their deaths.'

'But why? You are young still. Surely to God we shall not be afflicted a second time.'

'But how can we be sure? My own death would be nothing to me. Indeed, I could think that I have undertaken this voyage to meet it. But to bring another life into the world, knowing that it might die before me – that I cannot do.' Even as I speak these words, the misery they arouse in me longs for the very comfort I am rejecting, but Edward remains at a distance. I crave my darling's love in every fibre of my being, and yet I know that if I were to yield to the promptings of my blood rapture would be overwhelmed by terror at the very moment of union.

'You are punishing me, Jane.'

Do I hear a tinge of threat in his voice? Is that what makes me suddenly on fire? 'It is *I* who have been punished, for choosing a life of satisfaction and ease. And you are using guilt to undermine my strongest instincts.' Now, heaven help me, I know I am leading us into waters deeper and more treacherous than the ocean beneath our keel.

'But what of *my* strongest instincts, Jane? Do you think I am too old for passion? Why must you deprive us both of a love in which you once exulted? Jane, I am not a gentle-tempered man…I am not long enduring.'

Now I tremble, because the veil is being torn from the threat. He will take a mistress. That is what happens to unprincipled Englishmen, far from the restraints of home. Helpless, I do what human beings do when they are instinctively driven to extremity – I look up to the heavens for aid. But the moon has turned stern and even hostile. A sullen cloud blurs her features. She is the goddess of tides and storms – and of the currents and rhythms that ebb and flow in her creatures. 'God help me!' I cry as I flee back to our cabin.

I hear my husband's voice over a rising wind. 'I will win you back, Jane! I will have you again!'

# CHAPTER 7

**He grips the rail** so hard that pain shoots up into his shoulder. Beneath his feet something has shifted. The ship, that for days has ploughed on with a steady, upright motion, has begun to twist and writhe a little, as if some new force beneath the surface is trying to alter its course. There is a subtle difference too in the orchestration of creaks, groans and dim rumblings that constantly accompany the vessel's slap-slap-slap against the waves – a new strain through the shrouds, irregular rustlings among the spread of canvas. He finds himself needing his lost hand, to help him balance, and shifts his feet to stay upright.

He listens. Those rhythms, of sail and timber, wind and water, have become so familiar that he hardly hears them. But tonight he is newly alert. Some repeating patterns identify themselves: the rasp of a rope over straining canvas; a knotted cable tapping; something grinding in its socket, one way and the other, one way and the other.

And then he becomes aware of two repeating notes, no louder than the rest. Just a squeak and a thump, a squeak and a thump. Nothing alarming, nothing as unfamiliar as that thin keening which has begun to stir among the topsails. Squeak-thump, squeak-thump – he knows it, but cannot identify it. 'Tug!' he calls. 'Tug! Up, boy!' The rhythm has got into his head and will not leave unless he tracks it down. Tug staggers to his feet, unsteady on the now perceptibly heaving deck, and sets off on his usual circuit. The noise persists, close at hand, then far off, but unidentifiable – until suddenly it comes to him: Ferndean. The old nursery at Ferndean. He squats, lowers his head between his knees, tries to breathe deeply. The dog whimpers, nuzzles his neck. With a groan, Rochester lowers his backside to the deck, and clutches the eager, baffled animal to his chest.

Ferndean. The day before departure. A truce of sorts with his wife, who was upstairs with Adèle. He has hidden himself away to avoid the clamour of Cousin Diana's arrival, with her brood. They are to occupy the house while Diana's husband supervises the rebuilding of Thornfield. Once again he hears their children chattering and clattering up the stairs, heading as usual for the nursery, to greet his own – Ted and Maria, and baby Helen, gurgling on her nurse-maid's lap.

But that room has been silent for more than two long years. Even the maids a-dusting talk there only in the softest of whispers.

He is calmer now that he has matched that relentless squeak-thump to a memory. Did the emptiness of the room suddenly bring home to those visiting children the loss that the house had suffered? They fell silent when they reached its door. George was old enough to remember his cousin Ted, whom he had hero-worshipped, as small boys will. Rochester imagines Dottie and Lottie, finding in its cradle the doll they had begged to hold, and wondering who now they need to ask before they dare touch its bland china face. Even the little lad stayed silent, whose name he can't remember, born in the same month as baby Helen. As grief swamps him, a wave strikes a-midships. Spray spatters around him, and when he buries his wet face in Tug's warm fur, the salt water might be mingling with a tear.

The noise is louder now. That ancient rocking horse. Ted had loved its battered paint, its scanty mane and much-mended harness; the uneven squeak and thud which defied all attempts at repair. But it was the creak of a floorboard that first broke the silence. Diana's littlest – because the footsteps had the stolid, uneven rhythm of a child still not quite confident in his balance. Then another movement, and another – quiet, tentative sounds, almost furtive, as if the children were testing what permission they had to be in that place – and still they spoke not a word until one of them climbed onto the rocking horse, and all the familiar sounds of children at play returned to that haunted room: the toddler clamouring to be allowed to join in whatever his sister was playing with; her voice appealing to her sister, to take charge of the toddler; plus a tin drum falling to the floor and the clatter of dominoes being emptied from their box, and over it all the squeak-thump, squeak-thump of the rocking horse.

Then Adèle calling: *What weather shall we have at the Cape, Mama? What wraps should I take for the voyage?*

Interrupted then, interrupted now, he finds Tug whimpering and butting his neck. He claps the dog on the rump, trying to pretend this is just one of their usual tussles. While he still does not understand what is driving Jane to India, that moment outside the nursery was when he perfectly understood why she could no longer bear to stay at Ferndean. On that at least they are as one. But he longs for the comfort of his wife's body, and sobs, unashamedly now, because he has only the dog. Tug, puzzled, embarrassed perhaps, tries to wriggle away. With a last gulp, Rochester pushes himself to his feet. Though the squeak and thump on the ship has been lost in a growing racket as the storm closes in, its echo lingers in his head. Suddenly, Tug wants to play. He grabs for the leash, but the dog is away. He hollers after him. In this weather – he yells again, hears a frantic bark. 'Where the devil is the brute?' he mutters, beginning to feel his way aft.

As he reaches the top of the companionway, he hears another sound nearby and stops – reluctant to call what is probably a half-drunk sailor to his assistance, but also unwilling to trust his footing to the ladder in seas that are now far from calm. A series of deep grunts is coming from a patch of dense shadow below him. Then the ship rolls, the impassive moon penetrates the darkness beneath, and the shapes he makes out and the sounds he is hearing combine into an unambiguous vignette. Two men – one bent over a barrel. The moonlight gleams on his naked back, jerking as he is strenuously buggered. This is the sight that has Tug barking.

At that moment he hears a whistle, a cry of *All hands on deck!* A dim square of light appears as a hatch crashes open and sailors begins to swarm up the ladders. Another shaft of moonlight falls on the pair below just as they break apart, the prone fellow tugging up his breeches as he flees, while the other stands his ground. There is something familiar in the shape of him as he turns to greet the mustering crew, but it is not until a few moments later, when most of the sailors are gone aloft that he hears the familiar sound of Tug's eager yelps and knows that the same man has charge of his dog. His servant, Harry.

**The storm is not especially dangerous,** but it keeps the passengers below decks for three days and their confined quarters are stifling. The small cabin that has been made over for their use is no bigger than a pantry at Ferndean. As if every one of them has become a giant, demanding an excessive share of this narrow space, their characteristics seem to become exaggerated. Just when he feels that he and his wife might benefit from some distance between them, high winds and waves that swamp the decks force them together.

She volunteers to read aloud. The bishop has produced *The Bride of Lammermoor* – 'A treat I was saving for those days when I shall long for a cold blast of the Highlands' – but the lamps (which add to the heat) swing so wildly that she can hardly make out the page. What adds to his irritation is that Harry is now become the hero of the hour. It is he who gallantly braves the slippery planks and driving spray to fetch little comforts that help while away the tedium – a pack of cards or a jug of tea from the galley. Mrs Fisher calls him a treasure. Her own servants are prostrated by sea-sickness, but Harry is cheerfulness itself – as well he might be, thinks his master. Particularly trying are the little hints that his wife and Mrs Fisher bandy about, of the man's good looks, and what a fine match he will make *for someone*. Rochester is sorely tempted to shock them all with the truth of the matter.

'I have been reading the *Gita Govinda*' says Bishop Fisher when the day's ration of Scott is finished. 'The song of the herdsman. The poet compares the embrace of Krishna and his consort with just the sort of weather we are presently enduring – lightning and black clouds.'

'Is Krishna the blue one?' asks Adèle. 'With eight arms?'

'Blue, yes' says the Bishop. 'But as to arms, that seems to vary according to the god's immediate needs.'

'A monstrous religion' says Captain Sharp. 'They say it has three hundred million gods.'

'You should have no difficulty explaining the doctrine of the trinity, Bishop. A mere three avatars of the godhead must be child's play to a Hindu.' He speaks more to rouse his wife than to provoke the Bishop, but she seems out of reach.

'You may have a point, Rochester' says the Bishop, keen for another round in their joust. 'Though I suspect you think that Our Lord Himself cuts rather a pale figure in comparison with either Krishna or Rama.'

'I have indeed felt that the New Testament could benefit from a bevy of *gopis*' Rochester replies. 'And your cherubim and seraphim are no match for *gandharvas* and *apsaras*.'

'What *are* you talking about, Papa?' Adèle is easily bored. 'What are all these strange creatures?'

'So few among three hundred million' says Captain Sharp. Rochester can hear the curled lip.

'*Truth is one: the wise call it by different names*' says the Bishop mildly. 'A *soupçon* of Sanskrit wisdom for you, Captain. Modern reformers in Calcutta have made a convincing case for Hinduism's essential monotheism: its myriad gods expressing diverse aspects of the creator.'

'I think you will find that the supposedly ancient text they produced as evidence has been proved a forgery.' This is the Captain again. 'And – I am sorry to say this, Bishop – was not an English missionary party to the plot?'

'*Plot?*' The Bishop leans over. 'You see, Mrs Rochester. This is my point. How easily even the best-intentioned intervention turns to muddle and resentment.'

Rochester hears his wife rouse herself at last. 'But how can we stand idly by, when women are burned to death on their husbands' funeral pyres?'

'Far from it, Mrs Rochester!' The Captain is quick off the mark. 'We do not stand idly by. Permission is required of a British magistrate. It cannot take place without an official witness. I can assure you that the practice is thoroughly regulated and recorded.'

'But is that not worse?' The Bishop's lady interrupts.

He is relieved when Adèle calls out. 'There goes my work-basket again! When the ship corkscrews like this one does not know what will slide about next!' Some fuss ensues, and when the conversation resumes, Mrs Fisher has deftly changed the subject. 'I am impressed by their female deities, though I cannot always remember who belongs with whom. None of the religions of the book offer much scope for the feminine principle. Now, where are my scissors?'

The ship takes another dive. 'Under the table. Here you are, ma'am. But it is precisely the degradation of the Hindoo woman that justifies the extension of our rule.' This man Sharp is like Tug with a bone, thinks Rochester. 'Child marriage, polygamy, purdah and sati – to say nothing of abominable customs which I cannot bring myself to mention when ladies are present –'Mrs Fisher interrupts. 'Is it not curious that men think women unfit to hear what most concerns their sex?' She sighs. 'But you are right, Captain, up to a point. These are practices which every Christian must abhor and hope to see abolished – by education and enlightenment.'

'But why not by law? That would be quicker.'

'By enforcement, you mean. I agree with my husband.

Reformation cannot be imposed. It must proceed from an improved understanding.'

These opinions seem to devour the limited supply of air – as if two armies are skirmishing in a china-cupboard.

**The seas are still choppy** when tedium and vexation begin to tempt the passengers out into the air, though the space that is their substitute for a drawing room continues unusable. Each time the ship slices into an oncoming wave the deck is awash. Tug, who has been restrained in his kennel, greets his master joyfully but the scope for exercise is even more limited than usual, and they must confine themselves to circling the quarterdeck. The master is as much in need of exertion as his dog.

He has heard it said that there is nothing quite like the threat of death for reviving appetites. But perhaps the storm was not perilous enough. His wife remains impassive, though every night of this damned voyage and twice a night since the storm he heard the Bishop merrily rogering his good lady in the neighbouring cabin. It has driven him mad – especially when some miscalculation in the couple's position has driven someone's body against the partition – thud, thud, thud – until he must gnash his teeth in frustration and silently relieve himself in the only fashion available.

He had half-forgotten what it is to be thwarted. He should have remembered the stony will with which Jane refused him after Bertha came to light. At first, after the children, even he could understand her reluctance to look for comfort in their bed – God knows, he was for a time unmanned himself – and though in that respect his spirits have recovered more readily than hers, he has been patient. But a man can only stand so much – and now he feels quite cruelly deceived. There have been unmistakeable signs that this voyage – this desperate remedy – is doing her good: she grows daily more talkative – even to the point of energetic debate, which she always used to relish; she has resumed her old habit of describing what he cannot see; she has sat close and held his hand – and palpably responded to his caresses – so dear Christ, why will she not allow him to take her? Could she not even allow those less than total forms of love which would not endanger her – better than nothing, even though they have always agreed that such satisfaction was imperfect? And would not a child restore her to her senses? A terrible urge to have her by force is boiling up in his head, his chest and his loins – an urge which his better nature can barely subdue. Only distaste holds him back – and vanity: he has always prided himself on the readiness of his women. Distaste, pride – and potential embarrassment: those thin cabin walls. How in God's name does he find himself with a lusty Bishop mere inches from his bedside?

After a dull dinner, he lingers outside. The clouds that have covered the sky for the past few days are beginning to break up, and an intermittent moon shines patchily on the heaving seas. Landward, a sulphurous lightning still flickers: he can faintly make out the boiling underside of the retreating storm-clouds. It is exhaustingly hot and his thin linen shirt clings to his back. When he hears a woman sobbing in the shadows nearby, his first instinct is to ignore her. He knows it is neither his wife nor his daughter: they are both earnestly rehearsing the rights of women with Mrs Fisher – though where they find the energy, God alone knows. It must be Emily – love-sick, no doubt. It would be a kindness to quash her foolish hopes – though how the poor chit still entertains any hope in the teeth of her beloved Harry's neglect is quite beyond him. Not for the first time he reflects on how hard it is to deflect a woman from something she has set her mind on. Like Tug at his feet, growling and snuffling over his favourite toy as he chews it to pieces.

A lull in the wind allows Emily's unrestrained sobs to be heard more clearly. Lord, what if she throws herself over-board? He hesitates, but Tug is before him, scooting across the wet planking towards someone he expects will pet him. There is no choice but to follow, though he curses the dog when he nearly trips over an unseen hawser. An obliging moon shows him Emily's seated figure, laughing through her sniffles as she buries her face in an eager Tug's fur. The dog's tail thumps on the deck.

'Come, come! Why these sobs? What ails you, child?' He sits down beside her, hoping that the rattle of the sails disguises his lack of much sincerity.

'Tis nothing, sir' she gulps, though the moon reflects the streaks of her tears.

Tug, guilty for having deserted his master, nudges his hand with a wet nose. 'You are missing your mother and father, perhaps. But we shall reach the Cape in a few days – this storm has pushed us on. The Captain says that even so, letters may well have over-taken us on a faster ship. You can write to them yourself – tell them how bravely you endured the tempest.'

She sniffs deeply. 'My mother will ask after Harry – and I do not know how I will answer her!' She gives in to a helpless wail.

He leans forward to bestow an avuncular pat on her shoulder. 'You can tell her that he seemed fighting fit, the day we crossed the line.' *Coward* he accuses himself. 'And that Miss Adèle has nothing but praise for how well you have starched her petticoats in these cramped conditions – and how she values your company.'

Emily seizes hold of his hand and grips it tightly. 'Oh sir, do not think the worse of me, for I do so love Miss Adèle, but how is it that *she* can have Captain Sharp at her feet, when she cares not one jot for him, while *I* – who love Harry dearer than my life – cannot even coax a smile out of him? Am I not as pretty as she?'

'Of course you are.' He tries – in vain – to pull his hand away. 'As pretty as a picture.' Not that a blind man's opinion counts for much, he thinks. He has a general impression of plump, healthy rosiness bursting out of a pale muslin frock. 'Now, why don't you dry your tears?'

She sniffs obediently and bends forward to lift her skirt towards her eyes.

'If you will only let go of my hand, I will find you a handkerchief. We can't have that pretty face all drabbled and wan.' Startled, he hears in his voice an echo of tones he fears he will never have occasion to use again – and he finds that she has responded as his dead daughter might have done, by holding up her face – a pale, round disc in front of him, as if she were a child of the moon.

Bemused, faintly horrified, he spits on his folded handkerchief, and gently dabs her cheeks. He can feel her breath on his face – sweet, wholesome. Somehow, he knows that her eyes are closed, and that she has put up her lips for a goodnight kiss. He bends, finds her mouth with his own, hears her gasp, feels her lips soften and part, tastes the slick of her tongue.

At his feet, Tug growls suddenly and scuttles backwards. Now he has his arms round the girl, his hand pulls her buttocks towards him, claws at her skirts. And she is as eager as he is. Her tongue, sleek and muscular as a trout, wrestles with his own; her heaving breasts strain at his chest. He pushes her down and she pulls him on top of her, spreading her legs beneath him. Panting heavily, he lifts his head for air, then plunges his face deep into her neck – where he comes to his senses.

He staggers to his feet, appalled but painfully aware of what his restraint has cost him. The dog seems to want to congratulate him, jumping up and licking his face – quite contrary to his training. 'Down, sir!' he barks, thinking ruefully that at least settling the dog has given him a moment to think what to do next. There is only one thing for it. 'I must apologise. I was carried away.'

'So was I, sir.' He thanks God that there is no hint of a sob in her voice, but then she continues, in a whisper. 'I don't know what came over me. But I would if you want to, Sir.'

'Are you a virgin?' He asks almost without thinking, more to berate himself for the crime he has only just avoided than out of any curiosity – though at the same time he notes that if she is new to the game, she is unusually adept.

'Yes sir. I was saving myself for Harry.' Now the sobs are close again.

'You would have waited for a long time. Harry takes no pleasure in aught a woman has to offer.' The brutality of this is restorative, as a cold bath would be.

'I think I know that sir. I think I have known for some time.'

He admires her bravery. 'There are other fish in the sea, Emily. Shoals of em! Men who will love you and cherish you as you deserve.' *And revel in that sweet, keen flesh* he adds to himself.

She sighs. 'I know, sir. So Miss Adèle tells me. But I have ambitions, sir. I would like to do well for myself.'

It is safe to sit down again beside her, he decides. He is very grateful that she is not making a fuss. 'And you deserve to, Emily.' Perhaps he can risk a little humour. 'Who do you have in your sights? Not Captain Sharp?'

She shudders. 'Pah! Even if I liked him, he would not look at me. He's only got eyes for Miss Adèle, for all she scorns him. Servants is invisible to the likes of him.'

He is mighty pleased to hear this of his daughter, but his immediate need is to re-establish a more proper relationship with her maid. '*Are* invisible, Emily. Not *is*. So was Harry the height of your ambition?'

'My mother used to say he will go far, that one. Ha! As far as India. Will you dismiss him, sir?' She is suddenly alarmed.

'You still have a soft spot for the rascal? No, I shan't dismiss him, as long as he is discreet. But come now, tell me what made you like him?' Though his lust is ebbing, there is always something piquant in the company of an artless young girl.

'He looks like you, sir.'

This is preposterous. 'How can that be? Harry has all his faculties

– all his limbs. He is young and strong.' Then something sinks in – something he must correct. 'And – even granted a faint resemblance, for Harry is of my build, and dark like me – how could that have made you like Harry?'

'Because I love you, sir. Because I have always loved you, since first I began to have an idea of what it is to love – as a woman loves a man. But you was married to Mrs Rochester.'

He has heard such admissions before, though not always with the tremor that he detects in this young woman's voice. 'Yes, married. Poor child! But Emily, I am thirty years older than you. I am disfigured. My character is far from spotless. I am selfish, demanding – you would not love me if you knew me. Even if I were not married.'

'I know, sir. But I cannot help it. I am drawn to you for all your faults – and despite the difference in our station.'

'Then you are as blind as I, my child. I would not make you happy.'

'But I would make *you* happy, sir.'

He forces himself to be honest. 'For a while you would. I could have my way with you here, on the ship. Two minutes in a dark corner against a bulwark. At the Cape I might contrive to come to your room for half an hour. In India God knows what arrangements I might manage to make – but all in secret, all lies – and I should tire of it very soon. And so would you, child – for that is what you should be to me. I would give you pleasure – God knows, I have the skill – but not security. I should buy you trinkets that you would not be able to wear freely – and one day you would sell them. And as you yourself have reminded me, I have a *wife.'*

'I do not forget, sir. But you and she –'

She stops, and something in her silence rouses his anger. 'Yes? What were you about to say?' She remains silent. 'Come girl, spit it out.' He knows what he is inviting, knows also that he wants her to speak because her words will add weight to his sense of himself as a man wronged.

'Only that – you and Mrs Rochester are not – do not – that you are no longer in perfect harmony, sir.'

Her stammered words are too mild to bring about the full effect he wants, but they irritate nevertheless. A gentleman does not allow his disagreements to be visible to anyone – let alone his servants. 'You speak of Ferndean? No doubt you heard raised voices. I will admit that I doubted the wisdom of this voyage, but nothing else would satisfy my wife. Her mind, her spirits – have not recovered from our loss.' He despises himself for alluding to the children and hurries on. 'But you will have seen how much restored she is. This storm has fretted everyone's temper, but the skies are clearing again.' The moon has reappeared and he can see the girl draw herself upright and lift her face to its beams. When he hears her breathe deeply, he seems to see the rise of her breasts.

'I do not think she understands your needs, sir.' This in a whisper that he might not have heard but for a sudden vagary in the wind. He would rebuke her for her impertinence, were it not for how vividly he remembers the taste of her tongue. And she is right, of course. Jane does not understand his needs. There is no cause to wonder how the girl has come to know the state of affairs: she changes their sheets, lauders their linen. And some part of his need she may indeed understand, for that keen young body unmistakably longs for a lover's embrace. A shudder runs through the ship as the crest of some last relic of the storm passes beneath them, and the deck tilts as her bows sink towards the trough.

'She has her own needs. You say you have ambitions, Emily. So does my wife.'

'She has *you!* What more can she want?'

*That our children should still be with us.* 'To do some good in the world. To be useful. Love isn't everything.' He feels avuncular now, would pat her hand but fears what would follow. 'You are still very young, Emily – and I am not quite old enough to have entirely forgotten how vexing it is to be told that one day you will feel differently; but some men – and yes, some women too – long for action. They cannot be content merely to be at the whim of their circumstances, but must take the helm – much as Captain Benwick has steered us through this storm. My wife is such a woman. Always has been. The captain of her ship.' He is conscious of how pompous he sounds.

'Captain Benwick says all we women should keep below decks, lest we should slip.' She sounds puzzled – as well she might.

He has a sudden vision of a rain-lashed Jane, gripping the wheel. Despite her charms, this girl is none too bright and he is beginning to be tired of her. 'It is very late. You should try to sleep.'

She stretches and yawns. 'But it is so very hot below. And Mrs Fisher's maid snores so very loud.' When he says nothing she sighs ostentatiously, as if to remind him of what he has declined – and sure enough he catches the far from unpleasant scent of her sweat as she gathers herself together. 'Shall I give you my arm, sir? The ladders are very slippery.'

'Tug will take care of me. You may leave me alone.'

'I will not speak of this to Mrs Rochester, sir.'

This is vulgar – a parlour-maid's cheap reminder of her sole advantage. He wonders now how he was ever tempted. 'Goodnight Emily.' Tug rouses himself as she moves away, but he calls him to heel. The girl's footsteps are uneven as she tries to keep her balance against the ship's motion.

But for a familiar residual ache, the relief he feels is oddly akin to how spent he would have felt, had events taken a different direction. Intercourse, however, might have been followed by sleep; instead he is wide awake – and bad tempered. What he cannot understand is why so many women – even sensible women – have been so willing to throw themselves at his feet. Conquest has always come easily – even the little resistance he has ever encountered has been, he suspects, merely for form's sake. The sole exception is his wife – she alone refused to succumb, and that despite the fact that of all the women in his life, she alone has sincerely loved him.

And for the first time he asks himself why. The others – at worse pretenders, at best deluded – were seduced by his wealth, his looks and even his notorious reputation – but none of these things would ever have appealed to Jane. He remembers how stubbornly she opposed his wish to pour the family jewels in her lap. She liked my rudeness better than flattery, he thinks; she overlooked my shaky principles and forgave my cruelty. If any man were to treat Adèle as heartlessly as he once tormented Jane with the prospect of a marriage to Blanche Ingram, he would seek out an assassin.

*What in heaven's name do I have to recommend me?* he asks himself. He had served neither his country in war, nor God in His church. He had no distinction in the law or letters. She claimed that she loved him because he did not treat her as governesses are wont to be treated. Was it really as little as that? He braces himself more securely between the rail and some invisible strand of the rigging as the deck tilts beneath his feet. The wind has driven the clouds away from the moon for an interval, and overhead he can make out the pale, taut curves of the topsails, let down again now that the gale has spent the worst of its fury. There was a storm that midsummer night at Thornfield, when she promised to be his wife – a storm that crowned his exultation as she clung close to his side. He remembers how slender her shoulders felt when he unwrapped her drenched shawl, how he dried her soaked hair – and how her wet skirts clung to his legs as he kissed her warm tender lips again and again and again. Three times he knocked at her door, and three times he would have swept her off her feet. He smiles a little bitterly when he recollects how quaint and unfamiliar at that time were the scruples that held him back and how he demanded her utmost trust without ever taking her into his confidence. Yes, he was intrigued by her independent spirit, but condescendingly, *de haut en bas*. Not because of his lineage – from some sins he can surely exonerate himself – but most certainly because of an unquestioned conviction about those rights bestowed by his sex. Rights which nature, history and custom have endorsed. But if he were a woman, would he be drawn to someone like himself?

And yet she was – and if tonight's experience is a true indicator, other women still might be too. This is the kind of thinking best soothed with a good cigar. He nudges the dog with his foot. 'Up boy! Fetch Harry!' Tug barks and skitters away across the deck. Rochester hears his uneven course as the dog slides backward when the ship rolls, then struggles for purchase as she rights herself again. He must instruct Harry to make doubly sure that there are no gaps in the gunwales that the poor brute might slip through – though he can hear from Tug's barking that he has safely found his quarry. What sport is the dog interrupting? he wonders. Well, he is not inclined to begrudge the fellow – providing he brings him his smoke.

**Tug is out of the boat** before the keel scrapes the sand, chasing the braying penguins up and down the beach. Carriages are waiting. The Bishop and Mrs Fisher are to stay with the Governor of the Cape. Mr Rochester and his family will lodge close by. There are letters from home to be read, though as they were written a bare two weeks after their departure, they contain little news. Captain Fitzjames writes that the new house is going according to plan.

That night, after dinner, the Governor takes him and the Bishop aside. The cholera has spread from Calcutta. Already it has reached Madras.

His wife sits at her mirror, brushing her hair, tugging through the knots. 'They say, hundreds have died.' Then, when she says nothing, 'We might turn for Jamaica –' He cannot see her eyes, but knows they are fastened on him, through the mirror.

# CHAPTER 8

**It is only after he has held his new-born daughter** in his arms that St John Rivers writes at last to his cousin Jane. Never has he known happiness like this, and yet he feels as exhausted and drained as the woman he calls his wife – as if a complete new self has been tugged and wrung out of him.

But he cannot write about his marriage or this child. The fuss and speculation that the simple facts would arouse among his recipients are repugnant, and any more extensive account is beyond him. He would like every soul on earth and every angel in heaven to join his loud hosannas, but though he might rely on the generous hearts of his kin, he knows that there are those who would not unstintingly rejoice to learn of his relationship with a native woman, while some further instinct makes him want to hide the birth, as if even the mildest forms of disapproval might be harmful.

He is also still able to command enough good sense to know that any immoderate out-pouring of joy to a woman who has lost her own children could only cause pain. If he had written sooner, his present task might be easier; but when he first heard of her calamity, he had been no more than a castaway, struggling to build some kind of shelter out of the wreckage of his ambitions – and still bitterly aware of how makeshift and shabby his contrivances must seem in comparison with the grandeur of his hopes. Now he is certain that all that has happened to him was necessary. If he had not been broken into pieces he could never have been reassembled so adroitly. Formerly he would have striven to quench his exultation. The old St

John looked on joy as a kind of idolatry – a sinful disregard of the woe that is every fallen creature's lot. The new man allows himself to rejoice. It is hard to feel humble when the perfect rightness of his life is telling him how minutely God attends to the best interests of his creation. This at least is something it should be possible to convey.

*God's purpose is to teach us His will, even if we do not understand it,* he writes, conscious that such words represent only the thinnest abstract of his feelings. He pushes back his chair, takes a long drink of water and stares at the star-smudged heavens. Perhaps activity will set his pen going. He crosses the grass to the schoolroom, empty at this hour of the night, to find that someone has already prepared for the morning's lessons. The primers are stacked on the teacher's desk and the blackboard has been cleaned. But though he has the place to himself, the children seem to have left their shadows behind, and the echo of their voices. The air holds some faint vibration, as if they had run out to play just moments before. He closes his eyes for a moment and is in another school, far away, with the children of Morton bent over their slates and Jane at the blackboard showing them how to shape their letters. Then he knows what he will write.

*I have reflected of late on the village school that you kept at Morton – employment that I first thought was too humble for a lady of your accomplishments; but I watched with admiration as you proved the truth of the poet's dictum:* who sweeps a room as for Thy laws, makes that and the action fine. *You are still young, Cousin, and though you grieve, do not let your God-given talent for educating the young in the paths of righteousness be hidden under the bushel of despair. Be sure that our Father has work for you to do, even if He has not yet revealed the way.*

This is the old self writing; a voice that his cousin will recognise. When he writes her name on the skimpy package, it is as if the last rope that bound him to the wharf has been cast off, and an eager current has seized his craft.

**When he sees the sealed letter still lying on his desk next morning,** he is inclined to tear it up. By the time it reaches its destination, it will be three years and more since the deaths at Ferndean and whatever words he sends into the void will not suit the circumstances they eventually meet. Jane may herself be dead – or rejoicing in another child. What could be more natural? Suddenly an overwhelming emotion weakens his limbs; he sinks to his chair with the letter gripped tight in his hands and gives way to unstoppable tears.

Shocked by this loss of control, he tries to order his thoughts. His tears have blurred the address on his letter. For a moment he is disgusted by the inadequacies of what he has written, but insufficient as it is, this is the only letter he can write, and it must take its chances with whatever circumstances will be there to receive it. He rewrites the address and then, quite unable any longer to keep away from the next room where his wife and child are sleeping, he pads barefoot along the veranda, avoiding the boards that creak. It is still very early: not a sound from the kitchen; none of the children are stirring in the dormitory and even the crows still sound drowsy. But as he approaches, he hears the murmur of women's voices and the splash of water. Asha is helping his wife to bathe. He wonders if she will subject herself to some special form of puja, yet while he very earnestly hopes that she will not want to seclude herself, he recognises a sacredness in these moments, even a need for some brief ceremonial separation, to mark off the great difference between time then and time as it is now to be. Then he hears that the two women are laughing, and though the sound is reassuring it also deepens his sense of a mystery from which he must forever be excluded. And this is right too – that he should be reminded of how utterly distinct is a man from a woman, and each person from any other. The child that has been born to him is as much a part of him as his heart's core, yet he has known from his first glimpse of her smeared little body that she is as separate and different from him as a total stranger. The miracle is that love, like a spark of electricity, can cross that great divide.

All of his new thoughts and feelings are fascinating to him. He contemplates them with almost as much wonder as he examined his newborn baby's fingernails. Just a few minutes ago he was impatient to reach his wife's side; now he is perfectly at peace and could wait here forever, as certain of the joy to come in the nearby room as he is of the joy in heaven. He has never until now felt so at one with nature – and yet he feels that all nature's familiar laws have been upended. Even time and distance seemed to buckle as he wrote his letter. But these are not the only fixed principles to have been altered. His daughter's coming seems to have reversed the findings of Copernicus; the sun revolves around him – an absurdity that seems to him like an inkling of the laughter Martin Luther hoped to find in heaven. Then the creak of a floorboard restores him to his senses. Asha has finished her work.

Her smile is as condescending as a pat on the head. It is just six months since she became a mother herself. *Now you know* she seems to be saying and of course he forgives her because it is true: he has been admitted to the world's great secret society. What she actually says is 'What will you call her, sahib? She is very beautiful.'

He has not thought of a name. The child seems too all-engrossing to be defined by a single word. He mutters something vague and pretends not to notice the blood-stains on the sheet she is carrying away.

When Asha has disappeared, he stands silently for a moment at the door of their room, absorbing the tableau within. Jaya, on a white sheet, leans against white pillows, wearing a loose muslin robe. The baby, swaddled in a breech clout, kicks in her arms. Besides her feet stretches her son Jivaj. The boy's face is propped in his hands and he gazes at his new half-sister with the same unclouded adoration that St John feels in his heart. Their brown skin is the sole colour in the picture, muted by the swags of muslin that protect them from insects. Like some drawing from antiquity, the draperies are sketched with the lightest of pencils while their faces, hands and feet are dusted with a rich, earthy pigment: the Virgin and Child, with Jivaj as the young Baptist – the saint he himself was named for.

Perhaps it is the intensity of his emotion that makes her aware of him, for she looks up and smiles, then pats the space beside her. Jivaj wriggles aside as he finds his way through the draperies. *I must do something for Jivaj* he thinks; *adopt the boy.* He would like to gather the whole world in his embrace.

Jaya holds the baby towards him. 'Your daughter. Take her. Like this.'

The weight of the child's head in his hand astonishes him, and its perfect fit. This is what a hand was made for. When the little body squirms and kicks, Jaya laughs at his panic and shows him how to hold her close to the wall of his chest. Jivaj reaches out his index finger and strokes his sister's instep, drawing back with a crow of delight as the tiny foot curls and kicks again.

'What shall we call her?' St John asks.

'Your mother's name? I do not know it. Your sisters'?'

*Diana? Mary? Or Jane?* He looks down at the small caramel-brown face, still creased from its birth. Drinks in the twin crescents of her closed eyes, with their clumped lashes, the dainty curve and splay of her small nose, the working mouth – and the heartrending glimpse of her toothless gums, her rose-petal tongue. Then he looks up and meets his wife's dark eyes. 'Parvati' he says.

**Some months later,** beyond the time when his letter might have reached England, and when Parvati is cutting her first tooth, a visitor arrives.

'Elephant! Elephant!' yells Jivaj, running ahead of a gaggle of boys who have been swimming in the river.

St John leaves his accounts and makes his way to the small rocky elevation that overlooks the lane leading up from the road. The mango trees have put on leaf since the monsoon, and their dark, dense foliage bristles with new orange-pink shoots, so that he cannot at first make out what might be approaching. Then he hears the jingle of harness and catches a flash of scarlet. Behind a couple of mounted outriders, a handsomely caparisoned elephant is plodding uphill. A single figure sits in the howdah behind the mahout, but the shade of a bobbing umbrella prevents him seeing whom it might be. Six more armed guards follow on horseback, and another elephant brings up the rear of the procession, this one a pack animal, laden with bundles. A sudden glimpse of the leading elephant's forehead reveals an elaborate painted design, including a stylized eye. St John lets out his breath in relief; this is not a visitation from any of his Christian brethren.

He hurries back to the compound to shoo the children to a stretch of the verandah where they can watch but not get in the way, then stands ready to welcome the visitors to his domain, suddenly conscious that he is not an impressive figure. He cannot remember when he last felt a collar round his neck or wore shoes on his feet. But his buildings and his grounds are well-maintained; all the surviving children thrive and he is on good terms with the local villages.

As soon as the leading elephant breasts the rise, he recognises his visitor: the Dewan – tutor, adviser and first minister to the still youthful Maharaja. A man he respects, and to whom he is profoundly indebted. Though it was a share of a bequest to his cousin that allowed St John to acquire his land, the processes involved would have been endlessly cumbersome and expensive if the Dewan had not taken an interest in him. And now he may even owe his life to the medicines supplied by the compact figure now dismounting from his kneeling elephant. For a second he is aware that his scars are being scrutinised, but a brisk though almost imperceptible nod tells him that the minister is satisfied with his physician's skill.

'Rivers! My friend! How do you do?' He holds out his right hand.

St John has been bowing his head respectfully over his steepled fingers. It is a long time since he has shaken a man by the hand, and he has forgotten that the Dewan likes to amuse himself by imitating the British to the point of parody whenever an appropriate opportunity presents itself. 'This is an honour' he says, sensing the energies of a larger world in the man's firm grip. 'Let me find you some refreshment. What do your men need? And your animals?'

Soon the Dewan is settled in St John's study, and the children are leading the unloaded animals and their men down towards the river. He fetches a basin of water and a towel himself. There is no point in pretending he keeps any state. Few of even the grandest British establishments could ever come close to the magnificence of the courts his visitor has known. 'Will you eat with us?' he asks. 'Simple fare will be ready within the hour. A chicken will take a little longer.'

The Dewan waves away the chicken. 'My dear fellow. I am a simple man.' This is not true. The sun strikes a flare of crimson from the huge cabochon ruby on his little finger, though in other respects he is indeed quite plainly dressed for a man of his eminence. St John stands back and observes him as he rinses his hands and dabs his face and head. The Dewan has removed his turban and his still luxuriant hair is plastered to his scalp. St John suspects he may have dyed it, but otherwise there is little sign of vanity about him. He must be around sixty years old, short and dapper. He wears baggy white breeches, tight at the ankle and a little dusty from the road. His coat, buttoned to the throat, is a fine piece of tailoring, but its buttons are plain silver and the silk is unadorned save for a narrow belt of embossed leather that sits just below his small paunch.

He tosses the towel aside, not so simple that he does not expect a servant will be at hand to pick it up. 'I am on holiday' he announces. 'I have – in part – retired from the Maharaja's service and I am travelling for my own amusement.' He beams, mischievously.

St John retrieves the towel from the floor. 'You will be much missed I am sure. Is the old Queen still advising His Highness?' The Maharaja came to the throne as a child the age Jivaj is now.

The Dewan gestures vaguely. 'She busies herself with her music and good deeds. His Highness is turned twenty now, quite old enough to manage his own affairs – though perhaps he relies on the Resident just a little too much. The departure of Colonel Morrison is very much regretted.'

'An honest man – or so I have heard.' St John remembers his meeting with the naked sadhu – the Colonel's paymaster. It is strange to be talking of such worldly matters; these are topics he hardly thinks of these days. 'I wonder he did not live out his time here, as a private citizen.' He imagines the blasts of a Scottish winter, after the Colonel's forty years on the Deccan.

The Dewan shrugs. 'He is a soldier. He obeys orders. But you are right. An honest man – who spoke as he found. And if that was not what his masters wanted him to find, nevertheless he spoke.'

'I live a secluded life here. I am unfamiliar with the details.'

'You British grow fat on details. You eat details like a pigeon eats corn. With no war to be fought, the Colonel was asked to record the incidence of crime. Infanticide, suttee, ghaut murders, dacoity.' The Dewan pauses. 'Shall we say the list was selective? You know the kind of thing.'

'So not pilfering, disorderly conduct, rape –'

'Nothing a red coat might get up to. Precisely. He found that the presence of a large army led to wealth for some, poverty for many. Certain wrongdoings follow.' The Dewan raises his eyebrows as if to say *that much is obvious.*

St John taps the account book on his desk. 'The market price for our produce rises every year and I pay my labourers accordingly.'

'But you are a model farmer, Rivers! I hope you will take me on a tour of your estate.'

*A farmer?* he thinks. Is it forgotten that he came as a priest, with a duty to the poor? Is it friendly interest or polite espionage that has brought the Dewan to his gates? Probably a mixture of the two. After all, he is himself one of the endlessly curious Minister's experiments; he will want to inspect the results. 'Shall we go now? There is time before our food is served.'

The Dewan is already on his feet and St John finds himself following rather than leading his guest towards the fields. Here is a man who is a stranger to doubts, uncertainties or misgivings, a man who instinctively takes the lead and expects that his foot will find the right path. As he follows, St John remembers their first meeting. So accustomed was he to frustrations among his own kind, he had only expected worse from a stranger. Puffed up with the righteous fury that had propelled him out of Madras, he had steeled himself for a tedious interrogation at the hands of a pettifogging court functionary and had even assumed that his petition was being examined by an exalted figure like the Dewan because of a general deference to his race. Only later had he come to realise that it was his oddity that had attracted the Dewan's attention. An Englishman determined to shun the company of his compatriots was a rare bird, and in his own way the Dewan was as avid a collector of interesting specimens as the notorious Mrs Porter with all her curiosities.

Now the Dewan stops to survey the patchwork of fields on the slopes below and St John moves to his side. The prospect is gratifying: neat rows of healthy green, divided by tidy paths, protected by upright slabs of stone and barricades of thorns and cactus. A scattering of industrious labourers are bent to their tasks.

'O fortunatos nimium' declaims the Dewan. 'Sua si bona norint, agricolas! quibus ipsa, procul discordibus armis, fundit humo facilem victum iustissima tellus!'

St John suspects that this has been prepared for the occasion, though he knows that the Dewan is as good a Latin scholar as he ever was himself; but this must be corrected. 'Humo *facilem* victum? No, there is nothing easy about the produce of this soil. Come, let me demonstrate!' And he leads the way down the slope towards the orderly spikes of his onion crop. This time the Dewan obediently follows.

Crouching by the bed, St John folds back one of the stalks, and invites the Dewan to look closely into the enfolded crevices. 'What do you see? A perfect, healthy plant!' The Dewan may claim to be a simple man, but he is likely to be aware that an infestation has devastated onion and garlic crops across the region. St John explains how the larvae attack the bulb, how the leaves wilt and yellow.

'And is it your prayers that have singled out your plants for salvation? As Moses' God spared the children of Israel from the ten plagues of Egypt?'

St John suspects he is being teased. 'Not prayer but science!' Then he corrects himself. 'Prayer *and* science.'

'Science and *prayer*' repeats the Dewan piously. 'Science is a gift from the gods.' What he wants to hear about is the science.

Even as he describes how he drenched the soil with a solution of ground neem seeds, St John knows that this is what the Dewan came for. He has discovered that the Englishman has been able to take a healthy crop to market, where scarcity has multiplied the price. It irks him that the Dewan might suspect him of keeping his knowledge to himself, for commercial advantage. 'This was not my discovery' he continues. 'I read of it in a paper sent from Bombay, but I was unsure of how to prepare the seed, and when to apply it. Now that its efficacy seems proven, I will gladly share with other farmers what I have done.' What he does not confide is that it was Asha who first alerted him to the neem drench. Not that her own mother's onions had owed their lustre to its properties; the seeds were beyond her means. But she had heard of the remedy.

The Dewan is still peering closely at the onion. 'Nor was this discovery made in Bombay' he says thoughtfully. 'It has been widely used by our farmers for centuries. But your application is more methodical.' He straightens himself with a grunt. 'We should plant more neem' he continues and his eyes sweep the mountain-side as if looking for a suitable site. 'My hakim tells me that a bolus of neem oil can deter conception.'

St John finds himself blushing and a little enraged. Surely there is only one proper way of deterring conception; fewer infants would be left at his gateway if more of his neighbours were able to contain themselves.

The Dewan continues. 'Did you know that the Company wants to purchase nearby land to clear, and grow tea?'

'I have read something of their experiments in Assam.' St John's peace of mind is being disturbed on all sides. There are some changes that he would not welcome to these hills – and yet is he not himself an instrument of progress? A small figure waving from the gate interrupts his thoughts – Jivaj, sent to announce that the midday meal is ready. 'I usually eat with my pupils. Would you like to join us or shall I have them serve you privately in my study? I'm afraid we are rather short of space.'

'But I see you are building' says the Dewan as they retrace their steps. 'For your growing family, I assume. How is the child?'

Is there anything this man does not know?

Before St John can say anything, the Dewan continues. 'I should like to meet your wife, if you will allow. Or have you become too much of a Hindoo? Do you keep her in purdah?'

'Not at all.' His irritation is near the surface now. 'My wife enjoys the same freedoms as any Englishwoman.'

They find her standing at the entrance to the school-room, now rearranged for the meal. She is wearing not her finest sari, which would be modest indeed by the standards of the court, but she has changed from her workaday attire into a blue muslin and threaded her plait with jasmine. St John is calmed not just by her comeliness, but because of how perfectly she has judged her appearance. One of the many delights of their marriage has been these mild surprises, when without any sign of agitation, she quietly makes a sound decision while he is wracked by confusion. The Dewan leans towards him. 'You have chosen well, my friend.' He is eyeing Jaya with an undisguised approval which she wisely chooses to ignore.

The Englishman in St John bridles. 'My wife is my helpmeet' he replies, a little frostily.

'And beautiful as well as useful.'

For a moment St John wishes that his wife's face were veiled.


**Their guest announces that he must take a nap,** and retires to the couch in his host's study. The carpenters are happy to retire to a patch of shade and drowse away an hour or two so that the Dewan can doze undisturbed by their hammering. St John takes the opportunity to inspect their progress. Adjoining his two rooms he has had an extensive platform constructed. Here will be his private quarters, including a broad veranda overlooking the curving river. Though this afternoon is hot and still, the spot is cooled by the breeze rising from the water, just as he had hoped. For a few moments he allows himself to imagine his wife, at ease in the lamplight after the day's work, and children – a vague number – playing around her feet.

A cough announces one of the Dewan's escort. 'Sirr – sirr. Cap'n O'Reilly at yor sarvice, sirr. If I could have a worrd wi' ye.'

The man is not a sepoy, though his skin is burnt brown and his moustaches are as black and glossy as any rajput warrior. 'What can I do for you, Captain?'

The horses have been fed and watered, the men are rested, the pack elephant has been re-loaded and the Dewan's mount is ready for the howdah. If they do not leave within the hour, they will not reach a safe camp-site by nightfall. 'Would you be so good as to rouse his Lordship, sirr? Seein' as how it isn't my place.'

'I'm not sure it is my place either, but very well.' He finds the Dewan lying on his back with his hands folded atop his small paunch. When he taps the man's shoulder the black eyes snap open and he grins like a child who expects some treat. 'Sir, your men tell me it is time to leave. I'm sorry to wake you.'

The Dewan closes his eyes again. 'Tell them we will camp here for the night. And do not worry, my friend. We have ample provisions. It will be my turn to feast you.' Though his eyes remain closed, he raises his eyebrows and smiles; then his face sags into repose.

Captain O'Reilly shakes his head. 'There's no shiftin' the ole gent when his mind is made up. I larnt that the day we set out. But don't you worry y'rself. We'll be no trouble.'

St John leads the man away to discuss what is practical. Then for an hour and more, St John and all his household watch as a military encampment is erected in front of them – a procedure conducted in near silence, so as not to wake the sleeping Dewan. The horses are tethered, their hay-nets slung between bamboo poles. A jingle of chains brightens the hushed air for a while as the elephants are chained, front foot to back leg, but that is the sole sharp sound. Asha with her little one on her lap sits among the awestruck girls on the veranda steps while Kamil patrols the boys, who are bursting with the excitement of it all. Suddenly Jaya hands Parvati to her father. Jivaj is among the troops. His mother starts after him, then stops, turns to her husband and holds out her hands in a wry, helpless gesture. Perhaps soldiering is in the boy's blood, St John reflects: he is after all the natural son of a military man. This thought reminds him that he has made no headway with his plans to adopt the child. What has held him back is his reluctance to engage with his own kind, but now it comes to him that maybe something could be contrived under native law. He will ask the Dewan for advice. He bounces his daughter, fretful and dribbling after her nap. *Elephant* he whispers, and *horses. See the nice horses.* He holds her close, but his words are stiff.

The Dewan's pavilion is now being constructed. Two soldiers stagger across the grass carrying a sagging bale between them. As they untie the last cords a pool of yellow silk spills forth, glowing like molten gold in the lowering sunlight. Another bale disgorges panels of crimson felt embroidered with mirrors that flash and dazzle as they are hoisted over the plain canvas walls and roof of the tent. Glossy carpets are unrolled, a large camp bed is assembled and covered with a velvet sheet; a gilded screen is unfolded and ivory rods slotted together to form a wash stand. A brass bowl and ewer appear, as if by magic.

**Emerging from much plainer** bathing arrangements, St John finds his wife brushing his broadcloth coat, though in the almirah is a brand-new kurta-pajama that would be far more comfortable. A sharp inhalation announces her disapproval. He looks at her, baffled.

She frowns at him, impatient with a pupil who will not learn his lesson. Annoyed now, he shakes out the folded kurta. She brandishes the near-threadbare black coat. When the Dewan's man-servant comes to summon him into his master's presence, St John realises that once more his wife's instinct has been correct. The Dewan has given up all pretense of being a simple man. The star of some order glitters on the breast of his brocade coat, and the aigrette that adorns his turban includes another massive ruby. Beside this, in native attire, St John could only look like a petitioner; in his rusty clerical black he at least represents an alternative principle.

The meal, served outside on a carpet by torchlight, is exquisite, ceremonious. Far and wide, all who hear of these royal favours will understand that the Dewan's patronage is not just a mark of esteem, but a demonstration of his power. How will the story go in the cantonment at Mysore, or among the Bishop's people in Madras? He puts a hand over the goblet which the Dewan's servant is about to refill. 'Forgive me. I have become unused to wine.' He suspects that few of his compatriots have ever had a chance to become used to wine as fine as this.

'I was surprised to discover a fellow countryman in charge of your escort' he resumes. 'Though Captain O'Reilly is from Ireland, and I am from the northern parts of England.'

'A useful chap' says the Dewan. 'Assigned to my use with the Resident's compliments.' He pauses. 'A spy, of course. Though I pretend not to know it. My visit here will doubtless figure in his reports.'

And are *you* not spying on me? thinks St John. 'Surely all the man will have to report is that you take a close interest in horticultural advances?'

'Pah!' The Dewan waves for a water-pipe. 'Shall we smoke? It is a game, my dear chap. We are at peace. The unpleasantness is long behind us. Your army now takes its pleasure hunting in our mountains and measuring our ruins.'

St John declines the pipe but he would be glad of something to calm his returning unease. It is the army that Pisgah supplies with its produce. 'Surely the presence of troops is to His Highness's advantage? If there were to be any threat to his sovereignty. Or might they not be deployed to suppress those crimes that Colonel Morrison discovered?'

'As you know, my friend, the Company does not interfere with the customs of the country.'

St John knows only too well. This is why his Bishop feels able to forbid those like himself who would bring the Gospel to the heathen. 'Perhaps my countrymen expect that once these evils have been pointed out, his highness – who is an enlightened man – will take steps to eradicate them.' *My countrymen* sounds odd in his mouth. Not for many years has he been more conscious of how displaced he is. 'The practice of female infanticide, for example –'

'I left his highness translating *Othello* into Kannada' interrupts the Dewan – and then, perhaps to disguise any possible judgement in his words, he beams. 'I tell him that his next wife should be an Englishwoman.'

St John recollects that the young rani died recently, of a fever, he thinks. But now there is a whiff of something like ribaldry in the air and he does not want the Dewan asking after his wife.

**In his own room at last, St John finds Jaya** with Parvati at her breast. The love that rises in his throat is the more painful because his troubled state has not eased. At last Jaya covers herself and lowers the sleeping child into her cradle. 'Another newborn was left at the gate' she says.

St John sinks onto the bed with an angry groan. 'A girl, no doubt.'

Jaya kneels on the bed behind him and begins to massage his shoulders. 'The child is very weak.'

He rouses himself, wishing this was not a cause of relief. 'I should baptize her.'

Jaya pushes him back. 'Poonam will call you if need be.'

And Poonam has become expert in such matters, he concedes. 'I saw how Jivaj was interested in the soldiers.'

'I do not like it. I do not want him to be a soldier.' Her voice is sharp.

But what will be open to the boy? he thinks. A half-caste and a bastard. He has forgotten to ask the Dewan about adoption. He reaches for Jaya's hand and kisses her fingers. She slides her arms down his chest and presses herself against his back. He can feel the outline of her milk-tender breasts through his coat. He eases her away and strips it off – a button bursts from his breeches as he wrestles free of them. Already she is on her back, hoisting her draperies aside. The damp stains on her bodice gleam in the lamplight. His last thought before the completion of their embrace is that she is as troubled by this visit as he is.

**Parvati wakes him before dawn** and he carries the pungent little bundle to his still drowsy wife. She yawns, turns on her side, and slips her nipple into the baby's eagerly working mouth. Though in public she is as decorous and dutiful as any vicar of Morton might wish, in their most private moments she can be as indolent as a cat in sunshine. Now the sight of her bare arm limp across the pillow, the sag of her breast on the rumpled sheet and the idle, sleepy manner in which she strokes Parvati's curled feet is a picture that he finds faintly shocking – and deeply compelling. He wants to lie down at her back, to cup her belly and part her buttocks so that he can slide into her as effortlessly as she has taken the baby to her breast – but a sudden noise from the compound alerts him. He pulls on his breeches and steps onto the verandah.

Already the camp is half dismantled. Only the Dewan's pavilion still stands intact, its curtains closed, like some casket hiding a secret. The business proceeds in near silence, as before. Some of the older boys have already emerged to watch, while others are peering out of the dormitory windows. It could be some time before the effects of this visit are dispelled. He looks for Jivaj, does not see him at first – and then spots him among the horses, trotting along at the side of Captain O'Reilly, whose coat glows like a red coal in the first rays of the rising sun. Alarmed, annoyed, he is about to step out when he sees Poonam hurrying towards him. The foundling has weakened.

There is clearly no time for the Lord's prayer, let alone the baptismal collects. The infant is already flaccid; her dark skin has a purplish tinge and she seems strangely elongated. He holds the small body close to his face and thinks he detects the faintest of breaths. 'Name this child.'

'Phoolan' says Poonam. She holds up a small brass basin of water.

*Phoolan.* A flower. He dips his fingers in the water and makes the sign of the cross on the child's forehead. 'Phoolan. I baptize thee in the name of the Father, the Son, and the Holy Ghost.'

'Amen' says Poonam. The child makes not a sound. Her swaddling clothes are now her shroud. This will be the third abandoned girl-child he has buried since his own daughter was born. Two more have survived. As St John makes his way back to his own quarters, his anger is gathering again – an anger that contends with something like panic. He tries to order his thoughts. Infanticide is commonplace. God knows, it was not unknown at Morton – a child starved in the womb, born to a peasant nigh-on starving whose crop has failed or who is in thrall to an exorbitant landlord. And now he has provided a benign alternative to stopping that unwanted mouth: *leave the child with the sahib.* But his resources are not bottomless. He came as a missionary – has been turned into a farmer and is fast becoming a nursemaid. How can he alone absorb all the sins and misfortunes of his hapless, benighted neighbours?

This milling rage has visited him less often since his marriage. He resents its reappearance now and is glad to see that the Dewan's elephant seems just as impatient for the party to be on the move. The great beast sways and flaps its ears, rootling with its trunk and flinging clods of earth over its shoulders. But still the crimson pavilion remains undisturbed. Then he hears clack-clack-clack – Bhanu's rattle – and sees the boy running to confront the restless elephant. The mahout yells, warning him to keep back, but Bhanu is still advancing, doing the job that he knows best. How can he be expected to understand that an animal which must be scared away from the fields can be tolerated in the compound? Suddenly St John is alarmed. Bhanu knows that elephants are dangerous. His rattle summons help, but now no help is coming. Nor is this elephant retreating, though Bhanu is yelling and whirling his rattle ever more furiously as he heads towards it. The beast raises its trunk and bellows, but before St John can reach the boy one of the soldiers seizes the lad round the waist, claps a hand over his mouth, and drags him off. Bhanu kicks and breaks free, yelling more loudly than ever until another soldier pinions him to the ground and cuffs him hard about the ears. It is Captain O'Reilly.

St John grabs the man's arm. 'Let the boy go!'

Bhanu's face is blubbered and his shirt is torn. The soldiers are laughing.

'Leave him to me! Get back to your men.' St John makes no attempt to keep his voice down. If the elephant has not woken the Dewan, he will rouse him himself. God knows how this will affect the boy. His one small talent so cruelly misunderstood. It is time for this charade to be over. He is panting with fury when Asha, still only half-dressed, dashes from somewhere and folds her brother in her arms.

At last there are signs of activity around the Dewan's tent. Deeply agitated, St John returns to his rooms to prepare for the day ahead, but even Parvati, burping happily on her mother's shoulder, cannot command his full attention. Never before has he been so aware of how frail is what he has built.

Kamil has mustered the children for a ceremonial farewell, but St John's thoughts are still elsewhere as the girls scatter marigold petals and the boys cheer – until his attention is recaptured by Jivaj, who has fallen in behind the escort with a cane at his shoulder, like a musket. Well, he must find some other way of safeguarding the boy; he cannot become more beholden to the Dewan than he is already. When he turns back to the compound, the only record of the visit is a few circles of ash and piles of yellow dung.

# CHAPTER 9

**There are still no letters** from England among the mail that Kamil brings back from Mysore, though he calculates that his letter to Jane should have reached her many months since. Anything sent to him before that arrived in England would have been addressed to the church offices in Madras, where the Archdeacon will let it lie. He is not anxious for news, and even regrets writing himself, not for the inadequacy of the message, but for fear that it will oblige him re-start a correspondence which it would have been better to abandon. Yet Jane has come into his thoughts quite frequently of late, as the trickle of abandoned babies becomes more like a stream – girls, for the most part, though two boys are also slipped through his night-time patrols. It was the last of Jane's money that paid for the timber to build the new rooms he intended for his family's use, now become a nursery. Even if prices hold up, it will be a good while before he can afford the materials for further extensions. A more immediate problem is the shortage of servants. Both Asha and his own wife have their hands full and Poonam now needs nearly as much care as one of the infants.

'There are women in the villages' says Jaya. 'And with their wages, fewer babies will come to us.'

But none of the women in the surrounding hills is a Christian, and while St John employs Hindoos in the fields and his kitchen, he cannot bring himself to hire heathens to look after the children. Then an outbreak of sickness sweeps through the school room. It is not the cholera, thank God: their isolation has protected them from the disease that is creeping along the Eastern coast; but it leaves the affected children listless and all who care for them exhausted.

'We must have help' Jaya insists.

He has vowed that he will not be any more obliged to the Dewan, but there might be a respectable widow in the cantonment. 'I will ask Kamil to make enquiries when he next goes to Mysore.' Not once since the day when the cartwheel broke has he himself ventured more than a few miles along the highway. It has been Kamil whom he has sent to deal with the world beyond his own small patch. His wife's look tells him that this is not enough and his own pulse seems to accuse him of timidity. 'I will go with him, of course.'

They set out the next day. The dust and traffic of the road are unpleasant, but nothing worse; any man with his infirmities would want to avoid the din and the jolting. Kamil is young and naturally he enjoys getting out once in a while, to drive a tidy cart with a fine bullock, but as they leave the hills behind them, St John begins to feel ill at ease.

There is nothing threatening or unfamiliar about the scene. The same vehicles are travelling the road, the same unending stream of people trudge or stride or dawdle in both directions under the arching branches of the same squat trees, but his heart is thumping wildly. Deliberately he straightens, pulls himself together and scans the scene, consciously noting the pattern shaved into a passing camel's hindquarters, the huge turban that sits on top of its starveling wearer like the head of a pin, a glossy black cockerel stretching its wings in a bamboo crate. But just as on the day when the cartwheel broke he feels as if he is gazing through some strange impenetrable substance that allows him to see but not to connect; and – worse – as if his thoughts were being snatched out of his grasp, so that the more he tries to identify the feelings that possess him, the faster they fly from his reach. Then he could blame his panic on fever, but he has no fever now. It seems impossible that Kamil and the rest of the world should be unaware of his turmoil. He should reach out, touch the man, ask for water, but he is powerless to move.

Eventually he feels able to take stock of his surroundings again. The road is level at this point in the journey; ahead and behind it stretches, bordered by the orderly trees. Beyond its verges lies a flat yellow-brown landscape, dabbed with wispy scrub, that recedes mile after mile until it becomes indistinguishable from an indeterminate pale sky – and as he thinks of those vast unchanging distances rolling on beyond what any man could ever hold in his sight, a wave of sheer terror crashes over him, as if it is that unreachable horizon that has sucked his shapeless thoughts out of his skull. The solid world seems to be fleeing his grasp, whirled by some invisible maelstrom that is ripping his heart from his chest yet does not stir so much as a leaf. He grabs the edge of his seat, digging his nails deep into the wood, as if only pain can supply some source to the nameless terror that possesses him.

How long the spasm lasts, he does not know, but a load of hay that he half-noticed approaching has now passed by. He remains silent for the rest of the day's journey, brooding on what has happened. From time to time he becomes conscious of Kamil's concern, but he can do nothing to deflect it. When they reach the village where they are to lodge for the night, he goes to his bed without eating.

**Though shaken,** he is rested when they set out next morning, and the remainder of the journey is safely accomplished. As they find themselves enfolded by the city's crowds and bustle, he feels a vague anxiety begin to gather strength, but gradually it subsides without any kind of crisis, and when they eventually reach the cantonment, the orderliness of the lines seems reassuring. Every brick is perfectly aligned, every guy-rope taut, every marker-stone is whitewashed, and yet the unexceptional normality of the place is troubling, as if he has come to measure what is valid by an altered set of rules. He attends to the routine business in a daze, telling himself how pleased he is to have proof of Kamil's competence, yet troubled to know that without him, he could no longer cope with the simplest aspects of Pisgah's transactions. Safely at Pisgah he could in a trice deduct the price of ten sacks of rice from his load of carrots; here, in the cantonment, his brain seems incapable. I am distracted by more pressing matters, he pretends; I have merely got out of the habit. He sends Kamil to the canteen to negotiate what they should prepare to supply in the months ahead.

'Thirsty work' says the Quartermaster. 'You must be parched after your journey, Reverend.'

'Touch of the sun, I fear' he says, following the man into his office – a compact, leathery fellow hardened and preserved by twenty years of India, who shouts for a bearer.

'Try this' he orders, tipping a few drops of bitters into a tumbler of what looks like neat gin, and St John obeys, distractedly reflecting that as his symptoms already resemble the effects of strong drink, somehow the Quartermaster's tipple might put him right again.

The man squints at him. 'Have you seen the Chaplain?'

'I suppose he is the man I should consult.' But it is likely that the last the Chaplain heard of him was the letter announcing his plan to marry, and he does not want to have to give an account of what has happened since. 'Though you might be just as useful.' He explains his problem. 'I am averse to employing any native woman who is not a Christian. While it was never my intention to take in orphans of such a tender age, the one advantage is that infant minds are still a blank sheet. There are no heathen influences to be eradicated.'

The Quartermaster nods sagely. 'Unfeelin' bastards the lot of 'em – beggin' your pardon, Reverend. Not a drop of kindness in the whole race. But I do know of a woman who just might suit.'

It is hardly worth trying to persuade this man that compulsion and necessity rather than inborn cruelty might be the spur to infanticide. 'You do? What are her circumstances?'

There is a long pause while the man gathers his thoughts. 'She lost her man a while back – and then her babby was born dead.' He pauses, starts again. 'An Irishwoman. Catholic – but I suppose that's near enough.'

St John nods. He can hardly ask for more.

The woman is a picture of modest respectability, tidy and demure. Her apron is spotless. 'What is your name?'

'Dolores O'Reilly, if you please, sarr. But they call me Dolly.'

Because he is sitting in the shadows, she does not at first notice his scarred face; then, after a brief but unconcealed flicker of repugnance, she holds his gaze steadily. A soldier's woman, he thinks, used to injury; it must be years since he last encountered eyes as blue as his own. 'I met a Captain O'Reilly a few months ago. He was escorting the Dewan. Was that your husband?'

She nods and a single tear spills onto her white cheek.

The man who thrashed Bhanu. In every other respect she seems promising. 'And then I believe you lost your child.'

'The babby came early, sarr. The day my husband died. It was God's will.'

He is impressed by her emotional restraint. 'And have you other children?' Surely she is a little old for a first-born?

'No sir. Captain O'Reilly was my second husband. He found me a widow after my first was killed.'

'You have known misfortune. I am sorry. But let me explain what your duties would be.' Within an hour, she is ready with her bundle. She rides in the back of the cart, perched on a rice sack, spruce as a parlour-maid and visibly triumphant.

He suffers no recurrence of whatever affected him on the outward journey to Mysore, but never has he been so pleased to see the roofs of Pisgah again.

**Dolly is not best pleased to find herself sharing her quarters** with a native woman and an idiot boy. It seems that Bhanu has crept back to Poonam's room. ''Tis downright indecent' she insists. 'The lad is near fully grown.'

Poonam makes a show of her frailty. She needs the boy to fetch and carry. And so St John has the carpenter partition a section of the nursery for Mrs O'Reilly's private use: a room with a screened-off porch where she can take her rest of an evening and enjoy the view over the river that he had planned to enjoy with his wife. But he needs to correct her attitudes. 'We are all equal in the eyes of our maker.'

She fixes her blue eyes on his. 'But some of us has more sense than others, and is harder working.'

She brings to her task something of the late Captain O'Reilly's talent for order. Already she has set about marshalling the older girls to assist her. By breakfast time she has the babies ready for parade. Relieved of her more humdrum responsibilities, Jaya now has more time for teaching and for training Asha, who will soon be competent to teach the four and five-year-olds their letters and numbers. Yet while St John has reasons enough to feel pleased with his choice, he still feels vaguely uncomfortable. He suspects that Mrs O'Reilly finds clever ways of conveying her racial superiority that are invisible to her master but could be painful to her master's wife, but he does nothing. 'Army ways' is the closest Jaya comes to any complaint.

Kamil's young wife is soon devoted to the newcomer. Asha comes when Dolly calls; she rubs her feet in the evening. The servant class quite naturally accepts hierarchical distinctions, St John believes; it is only those whose means do not match their birth who feel the differences of rank – like his sisters, who for years endured the indignity of a governess's lot. What forces him to rouse himself is seeing Bhanu burrow his face in Poonam's lap as Mrs O'Reilly looms over the pair of them.

She is far readier to be blunt than he is. 'You can't afford to have two useless mouths about the place.'

He would like to tell her that Bhanu had his uses until her own late husband gave the boy a thrashing for trying to scare off the Dewan's elephant, but he is even more wary of her tears than of her insubordination. 'It is our Christian duty to take care of those who cannot fend for themselves.'

She is unimpressed. 'That old woman spends all her time on one lubberly boy. I have half-a-dozen babbies to take care of.'

'With some help, Mrs O'Reilly. And you are paid a salary. Poonam receives nothing beyond her keep.'

The blue eyes do not blink. She knows that though he might dismiss her, he would be lost without her.

Angry with himself for not being more firm, he sets off for the river. Poonam in the strictest terms has not earned her keep for some time, but Pisgah would be poorer without her. He thinks of the boys and their headlong games once lessons are finished for the day. If Poonam is crossing the compound in their path, they will halt and let her pass safely. The girls will thread her needle without prompting. She teaches them kindness far more effectively than any of his homilies. But some of the older lads are already fascinated by Dolly O'Reilly's blue eyes – including Jaya's boy Jivaj. She winks at him and calls him 'my little soldier'.

He has walked some distance without being aware of his surroundings and finds himself in a dense stretch of forest. A sudden rustle in the undergrowth halts him in his tracks, but though he peers closely into the tangled green he can see nothing to alarm him. And yet he is alarmed. The same formless dread that overwhelmed him on the road to Mysore is seeping into the margins of his consciousness – a dread out of all proportion to his anxieties over what is – after all – no more than a trivial problem with his servants. But the more he tries to convince himself, the more this other fear swells in the background of his mind, as if welling thunder-clouds were building on the horizon too fast to run for cover. He turns, and breaks into a limping run.

**There is no time to bathe before prayers.** Unshaven and grimy, he stands before two rows of shining children, all neat as a new pin. His wife and baby sit to one side with Poonam and Bhanu; Kamil and Asha are on the other with their toddler. He had feared at first that Mrs O'Reilly would be unwilling to join in, but she says the prayers and sings the hymns, perhaps because the simple forms of worship at Pisgah no longer bear much resemblance to the Book of Common Prayer, or perhaps because she is not a very punctilious Catholic – though she continues to cross herself. 'Old habits' she explains, and catching his eye now she pulls a regretful face and flaps her hand to signal that the gesture was unintentional, and that she meant no harm. But St John has caught sight of another movement. Under the veil that Asha has drawn across her face and bosom, she too is making the sign of the cross. Irritation flares up in him again. He has explained to the children that a Protestant's relationship with God does not need these showy, theatrical gestures, but he did not think there was any need to say these things to Asha. He must ask Kamil to have a word with her later.

He bathes while the rest of his household are at supper. The troubling mental spasm that attacked him on his walk has taken his appetite and he would gladly sink into bed, except that he has that morning asked Kamil to come to him once the day's business is concluded. The healthy profits of a season ago have dwindled to something that is not yet a deficit, but which could be soon, given their rising expenditure.

'We need more land' says Kamil. Several acres of good growing land are currently available on the other side of the river. He would like to invest his own savings in return for a portion of Pisgah's income and a formal share in its responsibilities. St John can see that the proposals which the young man has prepared are sound. Here, set out in neat rows of figures, is the sum that will be needed to pay the additional labourers, and a sensible calculation of what should be set aside to cover their risks. But he cannot rid himself of that glimpse of this man's wife, and her ignorant papist gesture. In vain he tries to focus on the evident wisdom of Kamil's plan, as the same turbulent, nameless dread which now seems to hinder all his actions begins to threaten him again.

'We would have to get a boat' is all he can manage. 'I will think about it.' He pushes Kamil's orderly papers away from him, and the young man retreats, baffled and hurt. St John tries to tell himself that his hesitation is not a sign of mistrust, but his conscience is far from clear. Asha's surreptitious gesture might be a symptom of incipient disloyalty. With his head in his hands he tries to reassure himself. A new division of responsibility is nothing to regret. If he is no longer obliged to spend so much of his time on the mundane, he will be free to concentrate on the spiritual aspects of his mission. But he cannot allow himself to turn a blind eye to anything that threatens his authority.

As he walks along the veranda, he is trying to suppress any acknowledgment of how muddled is his thinking. How can it be that his once radiant ambitions are so be-fogged? Irritation and self-disgust have possessed him by the time he taps on Kamil's door. Surprised and still cautious, the young man prepares to step outside – and in that instant St John glimpses something that horrifies him. Propped on a table is a cheap print of the Virgin, draped in tinsel and marigolds, with an oil-lamp and incense burning in front of it. He sees it for just a second, in the near darkness of a dimly-lit room, but there is no mistaking. Muttering he knows not what, he retreats, leaving a puzzled Kamil staring after him.

It is anger now that accounts for his thumping heart, anger that prevents him from ordering his thoughts, anger that makes him feel he is losing control. And Mrs O'Reilly needs to see his wrath. He has been moderate and mealy-mouthed for too long.

There is still a light burning in her room – the room that should have been his.

'Why Reverend!' she says. 'Whatever's the matter? Hush now, you don't want to be waking the babies.'

How can a man convey how furious he is in a whisper?

'Did you think I'd be trying to convert the poor girl?' she asks, when at last she understands what he is trying to say. 'Sure, I wouldn't know how.' Those blue eyes are laughing at him.

'But you gave her that picture – that image?'

'You believe in the holy mother of God yourself, do you not?'

'We do not pray to her.' He has spotted a small plaster statuette in the corner of the room: a blue-robed Mary, but no tinsel, no marigolds.

'But where's the harm? A pretty picture, a few beads –'

'*Beads?*'

Now she looks a little shifty. 'An old rosary. She saw mine.' Then she squares her jaw. 'You know Reverend, there's not a lot of colour in your faith. That young woman grew up with heathen idols. With incense and garlands an' stuff. You can't be grudging her a few beads.'

'The faith I teach is of the spirit. The true believer needs neither the intercession of saints nor the assistance of trinkets to reach our God. Asha is a simple village woman. I must ask you not to make it any harder for her to understand these things.'

The contrition he leaves behind him is plainly insincere, but so is his promise that he will talk to Asha himself. The residue of his unspent anger sits in his chest like the discomfort following an over-rich meal, and he knows he will not be relieved of it by admonishing a timid young woman who shrinks at the slightest sign of his displeasure. He finds his wife sitting cross-legged on the veranda, sewing by lamplight. She is clad in the shapeless white gown she wears to bed, with a thin shawl over her shoulders. Has she ever craved beads? He remembers that his sisters could never bring themselves to sell their mother's garnet brooch, even when necessity kept them short of coals.

**Another visitor arrives:** a visitor far less welcome than the Dewan. A troop of cavalry comes smartly to a halt under his trees and a tall, gaunt European dismounts from a handsome grey. The Reverend Simeon Brackenbury, Archdeacon of Madras, is even more pinched-looking than St John remembers, though he can tell from his old enemy's unsmiling appraisal that he too is being measured against the man he was. Only a near invisible spasm of distaste tells him that his scars have been noted, and when nothing is said he assumes that news of his accident must have circulated long ago.

'Brackenbury.' The syllables feel odd in his mouth.

'Rivers.'

They do not shake hands. The cavalry, ramrod backed, stare straight ahead; only their horses shift and flick their tails against the flies that buzz around them.

This must be some tour of inspection. He will show the Archdeacon the nursery and dare him to still maintain that this country has no need of missions. 'May I offer you some refreshment? I can order my cook to prepare a chicken.'

Brackenbury's laugh is a bark. 'A single chicken? To feed all these men?'

Ruefully St John acknowledges that half a dozen fowls will now die to save his face. 'And do you need fodder?' He tries not to sound bitter.

Fortunately, the troop has provisions for its horses, which only need to be led to the river. But he can hardly expect the Bishop's envoy to strip under the pump like his men, and so he leaves him in his study to wash off the dust of the road while he gives the cook his instructions. When he returns, he is convinced that Brackenbury has taken the opportunity to pry. As the silence between them lengthens, he begins to suspect that something more than their mutual antipathy is holding his old adversary in check.

At last the Archdeacon clears his throat. 'Since your arrival in this country, you have been aware that neither the Bishop nor myself is prepared to sanction your mission. Our church is the church of our state; its King is the head of the church, and when the government decrees that we should not interfere in the customs of the country, there can be no room for disagreement.'

A small shoot of something like glee tells St John that there has been some change in this official policy.

The Archdeacon sighs and his mouth works for a moment while he considers how to proceed. 'Personally, I am of the view that beyond a little education – in our language, book-keeping and stuff – we should leave the Hindoos' preposterous beliefs to the Being who has endured their offences for so long. It is for Him to reform the Hindoos when He sees fit. And it is surely proof of God's almost infinite patience with sinners that He has allowed such idolatrous nonsense to continue unchecked for so long.' His tone is sour enough to curdle milk.

Again, St John says nothing.

'I said God's *almost* infinite patience' Brackenbury continues. 'But perhaps one drugged widow too many has been roasted alive; one excess traveller garrotted in the name of Kali; one last hapless virgin sacrificed to the lusts of their lascivious priests. For God, it seems, has lost His patience at last.'

This is the kind of witty sneering that sends a *frisson* round the more worldly members of the Madras congregation, and St John is as disgusted by it now as he was at first. Only now a defensive note colours the Archdeacon's cynicism. 'Please go on' he says, sensing that the man is beginning to squirm.

Brackenbury straightens himself abruptly and leans forward, pale eyes glaring. 'Oh, do not think you will be exonerated, my friend! The tide may have turned, but your wreckage will not be salvaged.'

'Am I to take it that the government has changed its mind?' St John is suddenly flushed with power, as if the Holy Spirit has alighted upon his shoulder. 'And has the Bishop?'

'The present Bishop remains of the opinion that the prime duty of the Anglican church in India must be the care of those born into the faith.' The Archdeacon's lip curls. 'God knows, there are enough sinners among them – especially with the increasing numbers of troops.'

St John presses on. 'But the government no longer agrees.'

'The government has forgotten Vellore – and so, I think, have you. Half the garrison was murdered there because the sepoys supposed that their religion had been insulted. The government has given in to untravelled sentimentalists and scandalised old maids at home, and it will have reason to regret its indulgence in due course.'

'Nevertheless, the Bishop is now at odds with his masters in London.'

The Archdeacon's gaunt features are now scarlet with fury. As he pushes himself to his feet his chair topples behind him. 'I have come here to inform you that the Bishop has been replaced. Dr Fisher will arrive in Bombay shortly. He plans to spend several months traveling overland to Calcutta, to judge for himself the state of the native peoples. Though he is known to be of the evangelical persuasion, he is expected to be cautious. Do not suppose that he will approve of your feeble rebellion, Rivers.'

'Am I to be part of this grand tour? I should be delighted to show his grace what I have achieved single-handedly – and to share with him my thoughts on how much more could be done with the co-operation and support of those who are supposed to be my brethren.'

The Archdeacon's smile bodes worse than his fury. 'You can be sure that you will figure prominently in the mercifully short list of nuisances he will find waiting for him. Whether he chooses to include a visit to your premises will be his grace's decision.'

Now it is St John's turn to feel his anger mounting. 'And you intend to do this without having seen with your own eyes what I have done? Shame on you, Brackenbury. Is such an abstract account likely to find favour with a Bishop who likes to judge for himself?'

The Archdeacon spreads his long fingers. 'But yours is a private, unofficial enterprise. There is no requirement that I should trouble to inspect it. I came here only to inform you that the Bishop whose authority you flout is to be replaced by a man of your own persuasion – a man under whom you might have found preferment, had you but had the patience to wait in obedience. But I must admit to some curiosity about how you have spent your benefactress's donation.'

Biting his lip, St John leads the way to the school room. 'Do you wish to catechise the pupils?'

The Archdeacon pulls a face. 'Please spare me.' All the children's eyes swivel in his direction and they start to get to their feet. 'Do continue your lessons!' He sounds benevolent, but the pupils are now self-conscious under his gaze.

Kamil is teaching the older boys the principles of the lever. On the other side of the room, Jaya is showing the girls how to record household expenditure. She catches his eye – and with some shame he discovers that he does not wish to disclose their relationship.

'They seem very tidy' comments the Archdeacon when one of the boys correctly calculates where the fulcrum must be to lift a hundred-weight. 'And quite clean. And you teach in English, I note. Of that I can approve. Teaching the useful arts in English is the only way to make these people sufficiently like ourselves to respect our good intentions and serve us well.'

'Few of these children have any original language in common. Nor do my staff. In what other language could we raise the foundlings?'

'Quite so. The foundlings? You take in foundlings?'

St John is now heading for the nursery. Mrs O'Reilly, flustered by the sudden arrival, bobs a curtsy.

'And this lady is Mrs Rivers, I take it? I recollect some correspondence about your forthcoming marriage. I suppose the chaplain at Mysore performed the ceremony?'

'O lord, sir, I'm not Mrs Rivers! Mrs Rivers is not –'

St John manages to interrupt her. 'Mrs O'Reilly was formerly a nursemaid in the garrison. Here, she takes care of the infants.'

'So many' murmurs the Archdeacon, scanning the cots. 'I fear that the local peasants have cunningly taken advantage of you, Rivers. I wonder you can afford to feed so many mouths.'

'My land is profitable enough to support us all. Perhaps you would like to inspect the crops.'

The smile that is turned on him does not match the cold of the Archdeacon's eyes. 'Really, I am no farmer.' He steps to the window and looks down at the fields below. 'And have you attempted to convert those fellows I see toiling among your cabbages? Perhaps if they were Christians, they would not be quite so prone to saddle you with their unwanted daughters.' Then, without waiting for a response. 'The horses are returning from the river. My men will be hungry. Shall we go back to your quarters?'

He hurries ahead, hoping to warn Jaya that he does not want to expose her to this man, but she is supervising the re-arrangement of the school-room for the meal, and before he can reach her, the Archdeacon has caught up. 'Be so good as to set up a table for me, in the shade, if you will. And have one of your servants keep the flies off.'

The horses are tethered beneath the trees; the air will be thick with flies. 'I think you would be most comfortable if we return to my study. Kamil will bring our food.' Now he is even less inclined to leave his guest alone; the man is far too crafty, his eyes too sharp to be trusted.

The Archdeacon pointedly recites a Latin grace far too elaborate for the meal that is placed in front of them on St John's cleared desk. Then Parvati begins to wail. Unbeknown to him, Jaya must have laid the child in her cot for a nap.

The Archdeacon looks amused. 'Have the foundlings overflowed into your study, Rivers? Should you not summon the Irish nursemaid?'

But it is Jaya who comes hurrying along the veranda. The Archdeacon raises his eyebrows. His enquiring smile is deadly.

'My daughter.' St John's face is stiff.

'And her amah. A comely creature.'

'My wife.'

The eyebrows remain raised, but the smile disappears. 'Your *wife*?'

'My wife.'

The Archdeacon stares at him. 'I see. And where would I find the record of this union? I am sure the Chaplain at Mysore would have informed me of such an irregular proceeding.'

'The ceremony was conducted according to the rites of the Anglican church.' And so it was, but St John cannot bring himself to reveal that the officiant was the same man who has just carried away the Archdeacon's chicken bones. Kamil has no official status; no banns have been read; no register signed.

The Archdeacon coughs delicately. 'Your refusal to elaborate speaks volumes, Rivers. I shall draw the obvious conclusions.'

'In the eyes of God, Jaya is my wife.'

'But in the eyes – and indeed the courts – of this world, she is no more than your harlot.'

He is on his feet; his hand is raised.

'Strike me and I will have my soldiers put you under arrest.'

With a shudder St John manages to bring his rage under control. 'You have delivered your news. I have fed you and your men, and your horses have been watered. Now you must leave my house.' Beyond the curtained archway that leads to his bedroom, he can hear Jaya trying to hush a whimpering Parvati. It appalls him not just that she should have heard herself so vilely insulted, but that she should have witnessed both his murderous impulse and how impotent he is.

With insolent slowness the Archdeacon takes a leisurely drink of water, wipes his mouth and gets to his feet. 'You came here to convert the heathen, I believe. But it is you that is turned. You have been corrupted by the sensual indolence that is this country's curse.' He picks up his hat. 'I bid you good day.'

Still breathing rapidly, St John follows him out of the room. The horses stand under the trees, stamping impatiently, and a few of the soldiers are sprawled on the grass in their shirt-sleeves, smoking their pipes, but the rest are nowhere to be seen. St John enjoys a moment of petty satisfaction as the Archdeacon stares helplessly around him. The loungers shuffle untidily to their feet. One points in the general direction of the kitchen and at the same time a few sudden whoops and cheers come from the same quarter. Visibly furious now, the Archdeacon heads off to round up his escort.

St John runs after him as best he can, ignoring the pain in his wasted leg and determined at last to be master in his own house. Past the screen of bushes, a dreadful sight greets him. A circle of redcoats is enthusiastically battering something at their feet, egging one-another on with loud oaths.

"Smash the beggar's 'ead in! Evil varmint! He's escaping – stamp on 'is tail!'

One has his musket raised above his head and pounds with the stock. Another is slashing with a spade. They are kicking, stamping, jeering in a murderous frenzy, while at the edge of the mêlée two burly fellows hold a cowering Mrs O'Reilly in a rough embrace – and she is shrieking her head off.

The Archdeacon seems paralysed. St John pushes him aside. 'Stop this, in God's name! Stop, you barbarians!'

But one of the men grabs him by the arm. 'Step away, sir. We ain't finished with the bugger. 'E could still be dangerous.'

Are they beating his cook? He struggles to get free. 'What do you mean, *dangerous*? How dare you set upon him!' He strikes out and manages to land a feeble punch, but the soldier has his wrists in an iron grip.

'No need to get hysterical, sir. You're settin' the lady a bad example.'

Somehow, he manages to break away and pushes into the circle just as its fury subsides and the men fall back; and there at his feet, bloody and lifeless in the dust, lies a snake.

A silence has fallen – except for Mrs O'Reilly's shrieks, which rise even more shrilly now that she can see it. 'Holy mother-of-God! Look at the nasty thing! To think we was livin' with that among us!'

He sees one of the soldiers give her waist an extra squeeze. 'You'll sleep easy in your bed tonight, my darling.' She has lived in army camps for years, he thinks. She has put them up to this.

One of the men has stabbed the corpse with his bayonet, and now he attempts to hoist it skyward. It slithers from his blade and thuds to the ground in a heap. The sight of its pale belly fills St John with a moment's unbearable sadness, but before he can gather himself to intervene other men are jubilantly prodding the tangle.

'Blighter were pinchin' your eggs, Reverend' says one of them, but behind the coarse laughter St John can hear his cook moaning. Pushing the crowd aside, he enters the hut and finds the man crouched by the hearth, holding his sides and rocking back and forth.

'Are you hurt? By God, if these men have hurt you —'

The cook points angrily. What was only a modest, clay-brick shrine has been shattered, and behind where it stood is a black and gaping hole. Fragments of marigold petals have been trampled into the earth, and the saucer has been smashed. A faint trace of bluish-white milk still clings to some of the fragments. St John puts a hand to the cook's shoulder. What has been desecrated is not so much the shrine, but his peace — his small acreage of imperfect but still precious order. A sensible man would be relieved that a mortal danger which he has not fully appreciated has been removed before anyone could be hurt; a father must surely shiver when he thinks of what small bare feet might have trodden upon. But St John can think only that something undefinable has been lost, and that he cannot put it right again.


**That night, when he retires** to his rooms, he finds his wife weeping as he has never seen her weep before. The more he begs to be told what is wrong, the more uncontrollably she weeps. When at last her grief subsides, he fetches water and a cloth, and bathes her face; but still she cannot tell him what has caused her tears. He thinks — hopes — prays that he understands her trouble, but he can no more put his understanding into words than she can, and a nameless something drifts in the air between them. She clings to him, but her caresses are as unavailing as he knows his own to be. Grief seem to have left invisible bruises on her every limb, adding a fear to his touch, as if the brush of his lips or his fingers might reawaken her pain. Once, briefly, their content was boundless, a blessing he carried with him day and night, in the fields, among the hills, at work and at prayer. Now it can only be sought here, in this room, in this bed, in the small circle of each other's arms which he fears is no more than a hiding-place.

When Kamil returns from market the next day with the news that the Archdeacon was struck down as he reached Mysore and died within hours, he keeps the tidings to himself until his household is settled for the night. Jaya hears the news in silence. There have been no more tears, but she is still strangely withdrawn. Tentatively, he caresses her cheek. She seizes his hand, pressing it hard, as if she would like to print it on her face forever. He pulls back a little to read her expression but the lamp is weak and, in any case, her other hand is behind his neck, pulling him towards her. She gnaws at his lips as if she were starving and when they topple onto their bed in an ugly heap their coupling is clumsy and brutal. His climax leaves him dismayed, aghast.

He wakes to find that he is alone. Then he sees a small light burning in the next room. She is standing by Parvati's crib, watching the sleeping child. The lamp lights up her face from beneath, transforming it into a mask of something solemn and unknown. Half fearful, he stretches a hand towards her. When at last she returns to their bed, she takes it, but he can tell nothing from her dry touch. Whatever fires were consuming her earlier have ebbed away, leaving a woman who seems like a stranger.

Her first cry, deep in the night, is no shock. This, he already knows, is inevitable. When he leans over her, she pushes him away, twisted in agony. He is almost calm as he lights more lamps from the lamp that burns beside their bed. The face that was so glassily serene a few hours before is clenched with pain; her arms grip her belly. She opens her eyes and tries to speak. 'Parvati – take her to Poonam.' Her words turn into a desperate gasp as she struggles against a fresh spasm.

He hesitates only long enough to kiss her brow, drinking in the rankness of her sweat as if he could welcome the poison that is wracking her body. Then, for an endless instant, he stands over Parvati's crib, knowing that the sleep he is about to wake her from will never be so untroubled again. She stirs and stretches as he slides his hands under her warm little body, and whimpers sleepily as he presses her head to his shoulder. When for a third time he pauses, it is at her mother's bedside. He makes to hold the child towards her, but Jaya, mouth clamped against a scream, shakes her head with a terrible fierceness and points him towards the door. He nods, shuddering with the tears he must hold back, and turns away knowing that the eyes that are boring through his spine are looking into the face of eternity.

What element he moves in, he does not know; yet while he is a stranger, he finds his way as readily as if he had inhabited this place his whole life long. And with his occupation comes a strange authority. He has only to raise a hand and Poonam's fear is quietened. With a simple nod she settles the child in her own bed and he makes his way back to his wife somehow certain that he can consecrate himself entirely to her service in what time remains to them. He does not pray for her recovery but only that his ministrations can express the infinity of his love. And this at least is granted: in the dreadful hours which follow, the well of tenderness never fails him.

He finds her panting feebly. Her hair is clogged with vomit and their white sheets are soaked in a thin yellow excrement, but never has he caressed her with more love than now as he sponges her limbs and changes her bedding. He tries to moisten her lips and rinse her mouth, but she cannot swallow without retching and he sets the cup aside. For a few precious minutes he is able to sit at her side, to hold her hand and smooth her forehead. The hairs of her eyebrows still spring after his fingers have traced their curve, but the fine bones of her hand seem more prominent, as if her skeleton were readying itself. Her eyelashes flutter as she manages to look into his eyes, but when she attempts to form some word, she gags on a flood of vomit and her bowels give way again. Someone – he knows not whom – has brought fresh water to his door, and once again he bathes her reeking body, cleansing its deepest crevices with a compassion unshadowed by any disgust. But soon the tide is unstoppable and she is too exhausted even to let him lift her arms. She gulps sporadically and with every gulp more liquid seeps from her blackened mouth; her belly convulses as more fluids drench the already puddled sheets. Now her face has lost its familiar outlines. The dearly loved flesh of her cheeks has caved in and he can see the shape of her teeth and the bones of her eye-sockets beneath a wrinkled pall of skin. As he gazes at the pitiful spectre before him, her beauty seems to hover just beyond his vision, like her immanent ghost. Only the faintest pressure from her fingers tells him that she has any sense of the love that is flooding from his heart as unquenchably as the life that is draining from hers.

Outside this room, he is dimly aware that some subdued form of normality is taking its course. So far it seems that the contagion has not spread – a blessing for which he will give thanks to God, when his concentration can be spared. And now the calm that has come unbidden to his aid and continues to sustain him seems to have extended its mercies. Jaya's convulsions and retchings have ceased at last, and though he cannot delude himself about the quiet that now possesses her, he is glad that her suffering is over, even though he knows that his own has yet to begin. He would welcome death without a murmur, but he feels strangely certain that it will be denied to him for a while yet, and for a moment as he holds his wife's still warm hand and watches the barely discernible rise and fall of her chest he wonders what work his God can still have in store for him.

Parvati, he supposes. He remembers the night of her birth, and how he was overwhelmed with love and responsibility; but for now, it is as if those feelings have stepped aside, allowing him to love his wife exclusively in her last hours. But she, he knows, must be reassured. There will be no peace till then. He leans close and pushes her sodden hair away from her ear. 'I will take care of Parvati' he whispers. 'And of Jivaj. All the love that we have shared I will devote to them and I will not die without taking care of their future.'

A movement beneath his hand tells him that she is trying to speak, but no sound comes. He dips his fingers in the pitcher of water that stands at the bedside and dabs her parched lips. As the tip of her tongue reaches for his finger-ends a scalding flash of memory seems likely to rip the heart out of his body: *this tongue, these lips.* His jaw trembles and for the first time his eyes flood. He leans closer so that his tears fall on her face, and with them he anoints her mouth.

She lingers quietly for a few hours. Poonam brings Parvati and Jivaj to the door of the room, where they stand in silence. As the daylight dwindles, she speaks at last. 'I leave you all to God.'

'His will be done.' His words are more broken than hers, but deep within him he feels a surge of something that might almost be a transcendent joy. Like an old friend, half-forgotten, faith has rejoined him. He inhales the sourness of her final breath like a yeast.

# CHAPTER 10

**After weeks at sea,** it is the stench of Bombay that first strikes Rochester's senses. A stench no worse than the stink of London, but exotically different. Tug strains at his leash. It will take two strong arms to haul a dog with this brew in his nostrils. Not that the ship itself can be sweet. Salt, tar, sweat and excrement, grilled under a merciless sun; add tallow, fusty linen and vomit, stale pickles and animal droppings. It is only because they have lived with it for so long that they are unaware of how foul they must smell, but what he cannot ignore is the lice which are infesting all the seams of his garments. Every crevice of his body itches like the very devil.

He can make out little of the harbour except that other shipping is moored close by. The decks are piled with bales ready to be loaded onto the lighter which is bumping against the hull. He thinks how thrilled his boy would have been.

'A splendid sight!' says the Bishop, coming up behind him. 'Which your wife has no doubt described to you.'

'Already she thinks that India will tax her arts.'

'I fear India will tax far more than our powers of description' says the Bishop with a sigh. 'The cholera has not reached Bombay, but it is spreading towards the Western Ghats. I have persuaded my wife that in her condition she should move to the hills at Poona to await her confinement. By then, God willing, the epidemic will be over, and she and our child can sail on to join me.'

'I imagine Mrs Fisher will not like you going on alone, in danger.'

'No indeed. But I shall put myself in the hands of the Lord.'

'We have put ourselves into the hands of a Parsee fellow. Captain Benwick's recommendation. He is to find us lodgings.' His wife is impatient to get on, but his daughter understandably craves some gaiety after being cooped up for so long and his dog needs exercise.

**There is no news of your brother** *and I fear that any reply to the enquiries I sent ahead of us may have been directed to Ferndean. Even if news has reached you, it cannot now catch up with us before we head south – my head swims with these loops and arabesques in the passage of time! But there is no word here of any calamity, and so my hopes have revived. My dream is that I might contrive a meeting between St John and Bishop Fisher. One hour of my cousin's eloquence would persuade him to abandon his last misgivings in regard of our missions, of that I am sure.*

*I am quite ashamed to be living in such opulence but it is expected of us. There are no inns in Bombay suitable for the accommodation of ladies, and when I inquired of Mr Chatterjee whether more modest lodgings were not available, he appeared quite shocked. So, for a while I must make do with more rooms than I can count – and a proportionate army of servants, of which but a very few speak even a dozen words of English. My command of Hindoostanee is tried to the limit and beyond – those texts which I once studied with your dear brother were not altogether apt for domestic management!*

*Our garden is as lavish as our house, but a degree of riot that is vulgar in one's furniture is no extravagance in nature. Our lawns – where peacocks stroll – are bordered with hibiscus and oleander; our carriageways lined with beds of white hedychium and frangipani trees. Last night as we took the evening air under a full moon, the scent was quite intoxicating.*

*You must not think I have been distracted from my object when I confess that we are presently almost gay. It will hardly surprise you to learn that I am a grave disappointment to those ladies who long to know what is the fashion in London. But where I am lacking, Adèle supplies the want. No prisoner after years of confinement would gulp down fresh air and sunshine as eagerly as she fell on the treasures of the chauk, and as all our clothes must be sent to the laundry when we arrived, even I had to allow the absolute necessity of a new dress for the Governor's Ball.*

**Whenever have circumstances more propitiously combined,** to favour the seducer? The lady is flushed with neither too little nor too much wine; her conversation has been admired as much as her dress – and she is moreover his wife, so she has no grounds to protest her virtue. A full and naked moon silvers the faint sweat of her rising bosom as she inhales the scented air.

He hardly needs her guiding hand as they stroll the paths of raked white sand. She leans against him, and through the sliding silk of her gown he feels the brush of her haunch. Ahead of them some tiny fragment of mica flashes for a moment, piercing the cloud of his vision. A roaming moth flies so close he can hear the pulse of its wings.

As they reach the steps to the house, she halts. 'Do you wish to take another turn?' he asks, hearing the hoarseness in his voice. There is a bed at hand – a broad white bed, draped in muslin like a cupid's downy cloud. Beneath the windows, cones of incense will be smouldering in silver caskets, scenting the darkness.

She nods – he can hear the tinkle of her earrings. 'The house is so stuffy. Let me call Harry if you wish to go in.'

The dog runs to greet him. He stumbles on the steps, bellowing for a cigar.


**I dream of my northern moors**. Grey clouds scud across a wind-torn sky. It must be winter because the stalks of heather that scratch my ankles as I pass are bare and brown. The summer's bracken lies sodden and decayed. Ice rimes the edges of a peaty black pool. I am alone, and lost, and yet as I stride on, I am not altogether dismayed. The wind that stings my face and strikes through my thin clothes is forging my resolve.


**Where does a man go for a whore in this town?** A query that a gentleman in his predicament might put to his valet, but Harry will hardly answer. Only Adèle can soothe him. She can wheedle as charmingly as her French mother and he can deny her nothing. But there is an element of spite in his indulgence: he is mocking the austere path that his wife has preferred. She claims to have letters to write. 'Adèle is all the company you need in the bazaar' she says.

Of course, he expects to be cheated, but not grievously enough to spoil the pleasures of these teeming lanes where the stink of dung mingles with the scent of cloves and sandalwood. There is something piquant about chaperoning a virgin in this dark arcanum of roguery. Now that Adèle's wardrobe is replenished, she turns her talents to furnishings. 'For the drawing-room at the new house, Papa. We could not buy half so fine at home for the same price.' She sits on a small throne while brown men in white pyjamas pile yards of gleaming silk around her feet. Their colours affect him like strong drink. Amongst the muted tones of his native landscape, contrast and vivacity have been lost to his eye. During all the weeks at sea it was nigh-on impossible to distinguish between sea and sky, or sail and cloud. Now he exults in vermillion and emerald, turquoise and amethyst, saffron and lime.

A sumptuous crimson is poured out before her. 'I fear this would fade' she says to the protesting vendor. *Where does a woman acquire this expertise?* he wonders, thinking that yes, all this must fade, under an English sky. 'Did we not have crimson curtains in the old house? Thornfield?'

'Oh *Papa!*' His daughter's sigh is youth's eternal protest against the hopeless tastes of age. 'The new Thornfield will be quite different.' Now she is pointing. 'That one. The ivory damask. And the eau de nil stripe.' Her selection is to be brought to the house at Mazagon. 'It is for Mama to choose' she explains. 'She will be mistress of the new Thornfield.'

Will she? It seems beyond imagining.


**'How gorgeous you will be'** croons Alice. 'Oh, feel this silk, Bishop!' This sultry climate is very relaxing – dangerously so, I suspect; it would be easy to succumb to languor and extravagance. I settle on a heavy matte fabric, the colour of an English corn-field, to get the business over.

'And now that Mrs Rochester's drawing room curtains have been selected, let us give ourselves up to pleasure!' The Bishop is in the same high humour as his wife. 'I have agreed to abandon my correspondence for the afternoon and submit to a picnic.'

It seems that the amiable Mr Chatterjee has arranged it all. It is he who has procured the Bishop's fine mount. 'I must get used to the fellow' says the Bishop, 'and he to me, before we set out on our travels.'

'You are to come with the ladies in the barouche' says his wife to my husband. 'Mr Chatterjee will explain the points of interest as we pass, and dear Jane can describe the scenery.'

Soon we are five miles from the thronged lanes that surround the fort and the handsome mansions we pass are separated by stands of fine timber. 'Really, the prospect is quite like Torquay' I say, rousing myself to my task. 'These glades, those fine bold rocks, the handsome woodlands – and the sea below.' At first, I feel as if my gift has failed, but as I gaze around, the stranger elements in the scene begin to stir me. 'The trees! Never have I seen such trees! So tall, so airy! Their grace seems to belie their immense height. The trunk is smooth and unblemished for thirty feet or more. Then level, well-disposed branches begin to spread themselves, each one sufficiently distant from the other to allow the passage of sunlight, which sparkles on a million shimmering leaves.' I come to a halt, embarrassed by my own exuberance and feel Mrs Fisher's searching gaze upon me.

When Adèle jumps down to take her father's arm at our next halt, she detains me for a moment. 'My dear. I feel all is not well with you. If a friendly ear can be of use –'

I should protest. Instead I give her a hurried nod and follow our party down a narrow path. We round a bend, and there in front of us stands what I know immediately to be the fabled banyan tree. Its extent must be two or more acres, and its huge branches appear to be propped by knotted grey columns, like some strange pagan temple. But as I try to begin my description, I see that it will not be needed. Tug is scrambling over its huge sprawled buttresses. His master, struggling to keep his footing, can sense their extent and character far more vividly through his own exertions than any words of mine can convey. When the dog stops to investigate some particularly intriguing smell, Edward can gauge the massive dimensions of the central trunk, and how it is fluted and latticed with creeping vines. Then Adèle takes his arm and leads him through the arcades where pendant roots couple its limbs to the ground; she guides his hand to the dangling, rope-like tendrils that have yet to find the soil.

I am making my own solitary circuit, from the other direction, when I come across a small shrine, tucked in a hollow between two gnarled outcrops. A roughly hewn slab, tilted by the roots that have pushed up beneath it, leans over a stone cylinder with a rounded top that has been daubed with scarlet paint. The demonic image carved on the slab's surface has been partly obscured by time and dank black lichens, but it has been visited recently. A limp garland hangs over one corner and a mess of cooked rice grains has been left at its foot. The surface of the knee-high pillar seems to be sticky. I shudder, and would have passed on quickly, but suddenly Tug comes bounding over the roots, tail in the air and nose to the ground. Adèle runs up and grabs his leash just as he starts to hoist his leg.

'Naughty, naughty dog! Papa! Come see what mama has found!'

Mr Chatterjee bounds to the fore. 'The god Siva' he explains. 'See the trident, and his three eyes. He is the destroyer. See the skulls round his throne.'

Adèle makes a little *moue* of distaste. 'But what is the significance of *this*?' She points to the pillar. 'I have seen women pouring milk over similar objects in the bazaar.'

Mr Chatterjee seems eager to explain, when the Bishop hastily interjects. 'It is a symbol of the creative principle, regularly employed by the ancients. That such an emblem is universally associated with the destroyer, implies that destruction is only another name for regeneration.'

Adèle stares at the object with a puzzled frown. 'A horrid, nasty thing' she says, and gives it a little kick.

My husband stifles a brief laugh as the Bishop and his wife exchange an amused glance. She wags a finger at him. 'Naughty dog!' she whispers, and I feel the heat rise in my face.

But there is no denying that the creative principle has been continuously at work among the luxuriant verdure that surrounds us, as our guide leads us along a jungle path. Every plant we pass is bursting with recent growth: bronze-tinged buds swell on leather-leaved evergreens; young tendrils grope to embrace the nearest vine whilst among the palms, spears of the liveliest green seem ready to unfurl at the slightest touch. From a branch above us hangs a cloud of yellow orchids, like a bright swarm of bees. But there are ruins among this extravagant, rapacious foliage: a few shattered steps; a collapsed archway, half-hidden by serpentine lianas; a small dome cracked open by an eager sapling. The destroyer is here too.

Suddenly we emerge from the shadows of the forest to find ourselves on a broad terrace of broken pink flagstones. The steep steps leading to a rectangle of weed-scummed water have crumbled in places, but a group of devotees have found their way down. A woman standing waist-deep in magenta robes has opened a dark circle around herself as she pours the green water over her black locks. Once again, our over-eager Tug has to be restrained. Mr Chatterjee invites the ladies to rest and enjoy the view while he takes the gentlemen to inspect some unusual carvings. He assures Edward that he will be able to make out some remarkable details by touch alone.

Mrs Fisher sighs as she settles herself on a fallen column. 'I fear that the indefatigable Mr Chatterjee does not quite understand the implications of my husband's pectoral cross. He has arranged for us to attend a nautch. Do say you will come, Jane, so that we may blush together.'

'I confess that is not a spectacle I should wish to describe; my husband will be able to make out very little for himself.'

My companion is observing the bathers. 'The Bishop says that when their wet draperies mould themselves to their figures like that, he is reminded of the caryatids at Athens.'

**The young woman in the carriage beside him** is flushed and perspiring. He catches the musk of her body as she fans her hot neck, hears how her breathing is not yet quite calm and her voice is still thick. This is his daughter, preening herself after another orgy of shopping. Coal-scuttles and fire-irons of brass, lacquer finger-plates and ivory doorknobs, silver sconces and crystal chandeliers – a shipload of shining stuff for a future he cannot foresee. He remembers the years when he returned to the old Thornfield only to be reminded that the delusions of endless travelling were preferable to the bitter truths of home. But though he can pass the hours pleasantly enough in his daughter's company, no amount of delirious spending will ever be enough for him to lose himself entirely. He questions how any man can live chaste in this country as their laden carriage skirts a line of women selling vegetables. Tomatoes, from the colour, and something green. Sitting cross-legged – he can tell from their outline – or squatting with their knees around their ears. He glimpses a blurred brown arm, a glimmer of bare midriff, the gleam of a brass anklet. No wonder they keep all their best specimens safe indoors.

Then suddenly Adèle shrieks. He hears an answering mutter break out all around them. 'What is it? What is the matter? Tell me, child!'

She gasps, sighs, buries her face in his shoulder and hugs him hard. 'It was nothing. Something –'

'Are you hurt? Did someone touch you? Or say something? For God's sake –' The stir around them seems to be growing. Is this a riot?

She is pulling herself together. 'It was nothing, Papa. Something nasty – Now where is my fan? I've dropped my fan.' She bends, seems to be searching around her feet.

'What do you mean? If someone – If something? Did you see something?'

She shudders. 'It was nothing. I don't want to think about it.' She has found her fan and is wielding it furiously. 'There is nothing we can do.'

If there was a hubbub, they have left it behind. 'Are you sure you are unharmed?' He feels very inadequate.

She pats his knee. 'Yes, Papa. It was silly of me to cry out like that.'

Perhaps Jane will get it out of her when they are safely back at the house. Because whatever upset her, it was not nothing. He wonders how much more of this country he will never see.


**I am playing patience in the drawing room** when my husband returns with Adèle. They say they are late because they stopped to buy me another shawl for tonight's occasion: a *soirée* at the house of a wealthy Hindoo. We are to be entertained by the dreaded nautch-girls. I am already dressed in the same dress I wore at the Governor's ball. It is the colour of an old rose that has been pressed between the pages of a bible. The quite unnecessary new shawl is a loud cerise. Although she does not try to curb her father's extravagance, Adèle usually manages to impose her own more subtle tastes. Something has happened. Poor Edward sees only the brightest colours, the shiniest trinkets, without her to guide him.

But whatever delayed them, there is no time to investigate now. As she heads for her dressing room, I hear Adèle calling her orders to Emily. 'The primrose taffeta with the gold stripe. And the new gold slippers! What *is* to be done with my hair? This climate does make one frizz so!' Nothing wrong with her there.

Her hair is still wet when Edward hands his glittering daughter into the carriage. 'You must take my shawl' I insist.

'Oh maman! How you fret! It is at least as warm tonight as a midsummer noon in England.'

Maybe so. But after the steamy alleys of the bazaar, she will feel the breeze along the bay.


**'I was at first surprised to see so many ladies present'** says Mrs Fisher as he escorts her into dinner. 'But they are here to safeguard their husbands.'

He has already concluded that there is little chance of encountering some willing matron left idle whilst her husband toils up-country – but tells himself that the afternoon's unresolved mystery has left him in a sour mood.

Mrs Fisher gives one of her heavy sighs – almost a groan. 'I fear that we shall be part of the entertainment. Everyone will want to see if the Bishop is scandalised.'

'I think the Bishop will take it in his stride.' Her husband was unabashed by some fulsome carvings the other day. He remembers the imprint of a granite nipple on his palm.

The oil-lamps that flicker in every niche are making the room unbearably hot. All along the table he can hear fans rattling. Adèle's light laughter rises above the din. Whatever upset her this afternoon, does not seem to be troubling her now. As usual, a crowd of eager young gallants is panting around her. 'How do you find the local fare?' he enquires. Much conversation is beyond him tonight.

At last they adjourn to a garden lined with flaming torches. The scent of jasmine is overwhelming, and the breeze – now a keen wind – is blowing clouds of heavily perfumed smoke from bundles of incense that are keeping the insects at bay. A little way off an invisible group of musicians is playing – a rippling, plaintive sound half lost under a chorus of coughs.

Then a woman begins to sing. She must be seated among the musicians because he cannot make out any distinct outline. He hears titters and barely suppressed groans from his compatriots. Not that he understands or even likes these strange discordant notes so much better himself, but he welcomes the song's harshness, the lack of simpering and prettiness too familiar from a lifetime of after-dinner recitals.

'What do the words mean?' hisses the Bishop's lady.

'Roses, nightingales, tears – that sort of thing' says the Bishop vaguely.

As the song subsides to its close, he hears his wife moan faintly. Something of the young Jane still survives – a woman whose very soul once throbbed at the merest touch of a feather. But when a brand-new sound bursts out of the shadows – like the shrill crunching of a hundred sleigh-bells – he hears her sharp intake of breath. Here are the notorious – the infamous – nautch-girls. He senses his wife bracing herself. Something of the governess has never left her either.

The dancers' perfume precedes them, wafted by their swirling veils. A staccato drumbeat matches the slap of bare feet on the marble pavement. Torchlight picks out the gleam of precious metals, the flash of jewels, and the sheen of gauze. His fogged sight blurs outlines and colours. The dancers' hissing skirts are edged with gold, tracing a skein that seems to linger in the smoky air as they circle and dip. Beaded fringes patter with their pirouettes, bangles cascade and clink, their filigree crowns tinkle and gleam – and continually, under these sweet and dainty notes, he absorbs the steady clashing of their ankle-bells and the drum-note of their naked feet. But what he cannot see is the warm lustre of their flesh.

Even after the dancers have left the stage, and polite applause has given way to a buzz of semi-scandalised amusement, the rhythm of their dance continues to throb in his head. The Bishop is declaring that he has known English parlour-maids far less modest in their general demeanour whilst his daughter is rhapsodising about embroideries. His wife and Mrs Fisher seem to be of the opinion that is only the sturdy principles of women like themselves that prevent the men of Britain from treating their whole sex as ornamental playthings. Close by, some burly dame whispers 'Did you *see?*' Surly now, and keen to be away from his countrymen and their excited wives, he calls for a cigar, turns his back on the lights and heads for the darkness – the shadows where a blind man for once has the advantage. It is not often that he is oppressed by his handicaps, but tonight his blindness shames him. He feels like a schoolboy who has been shielded from some indecency in a museum – and yet at the same time he is consumed by a burdensome arousal. Everything seems to be conspiring with his wife to remind him of how he is deprived. It is impossible to continue like this and retain his health.

But it is Adèle who collapses. She seems to miss her footing as she steps down from the carriage, stumbles and falls in a faint. Jane sinks to her knees and tries to raise her head. For a moment he is paralysed. All he can see is a litter of pale silk sprawled in the pathway. Then he is staggering up the steps with his child in his arms, fearful that she will slip from his imperfect grasp. Her head lolls against his chest, then falls away as if her neck were broken.

Emily bursts out of nowhere and rushes to support her. Together they manage to reach a couch. Jane sweeps the piled-up cushions to the floor. A dozen servants hover at the edge of the scene. Harry rides off to find a doctor, and while they wait sharp salts are held to Adèle's nose, eau de cologne dabbed on her temples; the backs of her hands are slapped and the soles of her feet. But she remains profoundly unconscious, beyond the reach of any stimulus. Only the faintest pulse tells them that she is still alive. Desperately they try to reassure each other: her limbs only seem to be getting colder because the night is cooling. Emily brings blankets. When he lifts his daughter's shoulders to wrap her in its folds, she flops like a discarded rag doll.

And still they wait. His wife is silent as a stone. In the background he knows that Emily is struggling to keep her sobs unheard. He longs to stride the room, to curse, to strike a man or break the furniture, but he does not want to make any noise that might prevent him from hearing the slightest whimper.

It is Jane who breaks the silence at last. 'I should not have let her go out with her hair wet.'

'But the night was warm.' He remembers well enough thinking that it was strangely cool, but he knows that this is unimportant. 'I should have made sure that we came back in good time.' What has begun is a familiar antiphony in which each of them will assume some guilt they can offer up as a sacrifice, as if by taking on the blame they could appease the furies.

'I knew that room was too hot.'

'We should have left after dinner.'

*We should never have come to this accursed place.* The thought comes but he holds it back; it was he who insisted that Adèle should accompany them. Jane would have had the poor child cloistered with Cousin Mary at the parsonage.

'I think her colour may be improving.'

He cannot speak of it, but this too is familiar. For hours and days at Ferndean they fed each other such crumbs of hope and even believed them, though their own observations gave them no such reassurance. He sinks to his knees and leans close, his lips against his child's ear. But the warmth that he feels as he whispers her name is only his own breath, stirring her hair. Dull dread gives way to a keen stab of fear, but he keeps it to himself, as once he kept to himself symptoms of his boy's sickness that he hoped his wife had not discovered – even though he knew that her sharp eyes must already have noticed other symptoms that she was keeping from him.

Already there is an emptiness in the room. His daughter's eagerness, her vitality, her artless affection and her girlish silliness seem to have been sucked out of the air, leaving only a vacuum. They sit in numbed silence. To stir, to sigh, even to breathe seems like an affront to that motionless body until a sudden shout and the crunch of gravel announce the doctor's arrival – a plump, busy figure who makes straight for the patient. 'The young lady's stockings must be removed so that I can examine her extremities.'

Emily is already unwinding the blankets, ripping away the primrose taffeta with its golden stripe, stripping her white legs.

Someone must ask. 'Is it the cholera?'

'No, no! There is no cholera here. Even in the south, the epidemic is waning.' The doctor calls for more lamps. 'A scorpion – snakebite – might have induced this sudden collapse.'

'But surely she would have cried out.' His wife is beside the doctor, poring over his daughter's legs. He thinks of that shriek in the market place.

'A scorpion will hide in a shoe or the folds of a shawl. A krait can wrap itself round a door-knob.' The man pushes himself to his feet with a grunt. 'But I can find no sign of a puncture.'

'Then what must be done?'

'Bleeding will be our best course – to draw the force of circulation away from the internal organs which must be the seat of the malady.'

He stands close, fuming and helpless, while the cushions are retrieved and Adèle is propped upright. The lamplight catches a bright steel blade, and then the scarlet gush of her blood. A stain spreads across her lap, but still she remains unconscious. The doctor calls for her to be turned and her bodice unlaced. Cups are heated over a blue flame and applied to her back. He can make out the row of purple bruises when they are pried off.

'You see!' The doctor is now triumphant. 'The debilitating agents are being drawn to the surface!'

Rochester can think of nothing but the violation of that perfect young body, but then – at last – she stirs. A faint gasp, as if she were surprised. Instantly everything changes.

'Stand back!' orders the doctor as both Rochester and his wife try to come close. 'The patient needs air.'

Both are now motionless, waiting for another sign. Jane whispers at last. 'This time I am not mistaken. She has more colour in her cheeks.'

Soon he can see it too, all too clearly. This is not the healthy blush of youth but the hectic hue of fever. Her throat, her chest and shoulders are all aflame. Now she cries out again, a high, breathless shriek. 'Oh maman! Sauve moi! J'ai peur, j'ai peur!'

'Is the young lady by chance a foreigner?' asks the doctor, but before he can be answered Rochester sees the form of his tattered, bloodstained child shudder and convulse, and from his wife he hears an awful, trembling moan that he would have given his life not to have heard again.

But this is not the end. The flesh that was clammy now burns; the limbs that were so weak she now flings from side to side as if she wished to be rid of them. He had imagined nothing could be worse than her terrible silence; now her shrieks and gibbers seem to flay him alive. Jane is on her knees at the couch, struggling to prevent his darling girl – his firstborn – his last child – from throwing herself to the floor in her delirium.

'If she can only be restrained, we can bleed her again' says the doctor. 'The capillaries are still overloaded.'

Wearily he becomes aware that the sun has risen hours ago. Harry taps his arm. Messages have been left. He follows his servant into the hall, has him read them out. The Governor expresses his concern. The Bishop and Mrs Fisher are praying. Mr Chatterjee asks if there is some service he can render. He shakes his head. It is impossible to believe that any kind of life is continuing. Surely the whole world must have stopped in its tracks.

'Take some tea, sir' says Harry. 'You need to keep up your strength.'

The morning wears on and gradually Adèle's convulsions subside, though he fears that it is exhaustion rather than any recovery that has produced this semblance of calm. 'My darling girl' he whispers.

'Cher papa. Mon très cher papa.' She is struggling to say more. 'Dites a maman que je regrette beaucoup...'

'Il n'y est rien à regretter, ma pauvre petite. Calme-toi, je t'en prie.'

'Mais ma jolie robe est salie du sang! Maman sera fachée. Et mes belles chaussures! Ou sont mes chaussures d'or?' She is shaking helplessly again. 'Elles sont perdues.'

Surely only a girl with life ahead of her would fret about her slippers? The first hope expands in his chest. 'Mais maman ne s'inquiètes jamais les vêtements, comme tu sais, cherie.' But the *maman* who would be angry because her daughter's dress is stained with blood, is not Jane. It is Céline.

**It is some days before I feel calm enough to write to Diana and Mary.** There is little point in harrying those at home with an account of a catastrophe that has been safely averted and so I record Adèle's illness and her recovery in only the barest outline: *When I tell you that her chief complaint is that her hair – which had to be cut – is still 'a fright', you will know that she is herself once more.* No point in describing those dreadful hours when the unutterable darkness of supreme loss threatened to engulf us once more. They are mothers. They will feel the shadow of Death's sooty wing brush past for an instant, and shudder.

And there is more good news to convey. Among the copious reports awaiting the Bishop he has found no word of my cousin's fate. Alice tells me that there are still many papers yet to be read (her husband prefers to be out and about, to see for himself) but that if there were any news of St John's demise, it would surely have been brought to his attention. 'If he was a thorn in the flesh of our predecessors, they would have rejoiced to be rid of him' she says.

I get up from my desk and step on to the veranda. Across the grass in a patch of deep shade Adèle reclines in a hammock, reading with Emily beside her. Of course we must remain here in Mazagon until she has regained her strength, but the doctor has recommended further convalescence at a hill station, with more wholesome air. Three months, he says! I know that any difference a further delay will make is in God's hands, but I am impatient to be on the move, especially now that I have new reasons to think that St John must be alive. It would be heartless to feel that in any sense Adèle is holding me back, but I am beginning to think that I could be heading South – on my own. This very morning, I have spoken to Mr Chatterjee, citing the famous Mrs Porter as a lady who travelled the length and breadth of India without her husband.

The girls have spotted me, and Adèle gives a drowsy wave. Much more of this heat and even my own purpose might be blunted. She needs brisk mountain air, not the swampy vapours of the coast. We all do. If I go ahead, Edward can follow with her, once she is completely well. Within a few weeks I might discover the truth – and if – God forbid! – I find that St John is dead, then I can return to their hill station without them needing to travel south at all.

The murmur of Adèle's voice creeps across the baking lawn, and though I cannot make out her words they reinforce my conviction that my further journey is not for her. It is not only frailty that should prevent her, but her temperament. Her delirium was a heaven-sent reminder that she is Céline's daughter, not mine. And was it not her eagerness to wear a new dress that brought on the fever? She and St John will never suit. Her sweet, affectionate nature would count for little with him.

What now occurs to me is that she might travel to Poona, where Mrs Fisher is to await her confinement – precisely that change of air which the doctor proposed! Alice will be a reliable chaperone and glad of a familiar companion. Emily can stay with them as well – I have no need of a maid. Edward can come with me if he must. So convinced am I of how much this prospect will appeal that I set out across the shadeless lawn. Before I am halfway towards that picture of maiden innocence, a trick of the air carries Adèle's words to my ears with perfect clarity:

*'Yamen! Receive me undefiled' she said*
*And seized a torch, and fired the bridal bed!*

Both girls collapse in a fit of silly giggles. Well, that confirms the matter: Adèle is not made for the solemn task that lies ahead of me. I even have to wonder whether she is not a little too frivolous to be company for a Bishop's wife? But I tell myself that a taste for sensational reading is hardly conclusive evidence of a tainted inheritance, and that Alice will provide just the kind of moral guidance that Adèle clearly needs.

When inspiration possesses us, how rapidly do good sense and reason rush to lend their support!

# CHAPTER 11

**With every bone-jarring stride** of his elephant the conviction becomes stronger. If all the sultry promptings of the Orient (to say nothing of his own relentless efforts) cannot melt his wife's stony heart, then hope must be abandoned. He has heard that a brush with the grim reaper can be enough to enflame a stone, but even his daughter's near death was not enough send her back into his arms. A sudden shaft of sunlight emerges from the thunderous clouds that darken the skies every afternoon, defining her upright silhouette atop the swaying beast ahead. He will see out this enterprise, but once he has bid farewell to India, he will set about establishing a convenient mistress. Then he remembers his cursed Jamaican inheritance. Setting his affairs in order there is part of the bargain he struck with his wife. For her India, for him the Indies. But his wife consented very unwillingly – and he is far from eager to re-visit the scenes of his disastrous marriage. If he relinquishes Jamaica, would she be more likely to tolerate a discreet liaison? Really, it is the only rational course of action.

They have left the city and its hordes behind them and are now three days along the road to Poona, among mountain scenery of such blatant grandeur that even a half-blind man must be impressed by its sublimity. At present their path is climbing a narrow ridge that divides two blue chasms. On the far side of the valley on his left, a notch in the horizon and a long, perpendicular streak of brightness informs him of a waterfall, but it is the steady din rising from the fathomless gloom below which tells him of its magnitude.

A sudden clatter of stones interrupts his thoughts. Bishop Fisher and his horse have not yet quite settled who is master, and the Bishop has several times dismounted where the track is especially precipitous. He is leading the beast now. 'You may be glad of your blindness' he calls, rather breathlessly, 'when there is nothing but a thousand feet of air between you and eternity. The ladies have all covered their eyes.' But the thrill Rochester detects in his tones is that of excitement, rather than fear; the Bishop is not regretting the mild landscapes of his English parish. Perhaps when they reach Poona he will arrange a mount for himself. There will be a few days while they see the ladies settle in and the climate at this altitude is agreeably stimulating.

Up ahead, he hears Tug barking eagerly. Yesterday the dog nearly fell from a cliff edge, chasing a covey of quails.

**The enthusiastic welcome we receive** at the garrison strengthens my belief that it would be far more sensible for me to travel on alone. I had not taken sufficient account of the toll Adèle's illness took on her father until I saw how Poona instantly revived his spirits, and now that the occasion draws closer, I cannot pretend to imagine that meeting St John will be easy for him. In the meantime, it is good to see Adèle in full bloom again, thoroughly revived by the admiration that greets her on every side. But though she turned all heads at the impromptu ball that was arranged to greet us, I am glad to see that she singles out none of her partners for an undue share of attention.

'Do you think she has grown more thoughtful since her illness?' Edward asks.

'I do, but it is your watchful presence that most effectively deters any over-importunate suitor.'

'Any young blood who sees as little female company as these fellows will no doubt be calculating what a blind man is likely to miss.'

But a blind man *at hand* must still be effective, whereas even the clearest-sighted father will be powerless to prevent mischief if he is hundreds of miles away. It is not only for Adèle's sake best that I should go on by myself. In our life together Edward has seldom had the opportunity to spend much time in the society of men, and he finds the company of the more seasoned officers highly agreeable. Nor is he alone in that. Even my own heart beats a little faster when I think of the perils these gallant men have braved to defend our interests. And as for Harry! I caught him just yesterday staring after the troops on the parade ground. Perhaps it is his valet rather than his daughter that Edward will lose to the army.

**Mrs Fisher invites him to breakfast while the rest of their party** and God knows how many eager blades have ridden out from the fort to watch the sunrise.

'*Armed with Thy word and Truth's bright sword, Thy name upon our standard, Lord.* My husband's new hymn.' Alice Fisher waves off the servant and pours tea herself. 'I think this is how you like it. Now we are comfortable, I have a confession to make.'

'Nothing demanding much penance, I suspect.'

'No indeed. I have – quite simply – persuaded Adèle to stay here with me until after my confinement. Then – all being well – we should rendezvous with the Bishop and you and your wife in – well, some convenient spot. Your splendid Mr Chatterjee can arrange everything. With your permission of course. Your wife has already consented in principle. Indeed, she is thrilled at the prospect of my husband meeting her cousin and what might be done for him.' At this point Mrs Fisher sounds a little bashful. 'I have warned her that what that might be, remains to be seen.'

'We do not even know if the fellow is still alive.'

'There has been no mention of his death in all the papers that greeted us in Bombay. But you have said nothing of my proposal to kidnap dear Adèle.'

He is thinking that he would like to stay in Poona himself. The climate and the company suit him. Mr Chatterjee has found him a fine mount. He can see why Adèle would prefer to stay. She probably views the prospect of meeting her step-mother's old clerical *beau* with no more relish than himself, while here she basks in the admiration of the regiment. Mrs Fisher is a sensible woman, but his own presence would provide a double protection against any foolish entanglements. His wife hardly seems to need him.

But what kind of man would let a woman travel on her own – especially when her intention is to meet the fellow who is in some sense his rival? Such folly would make him the laughing-stock of Poona. Besides, the gossip would say that he is keeping company with the Bishop's lady – who is blooming with each passing day. She too is to be abandoned by her spouse. The thought is surprisingly intriguing.

He arrives back at his own quarters to find that the party from the fort has returned before him. The Bishop takes him aside. 'In case I do not get another chance, Rochester, I want you to know what a comfort it is, that your daughter is to keep Mrs Fisher company. You will miss her sorely – though you will have your wife. I shall envy you on my own journey. Spare a thought for me sometimes, in my lonely tent!'

There has been some conspiracy of the ladies here. While he was happy enough to go along with Mrs Fisher, he is suddenly irritated. He has not explicitly given his consent to this arrangement. Well, if his wife feels entitled to part him from his daughter without so much as a word, there must be consequences: that secret cottage at Thornfield; buxom Emily's eager tongue; cuckolding the bishop. He shakes his head to clear these half-bidden thoughts as the self-same bishop remounts and takes off in a rush and a clatter. Jane is climbing the steps to their porch. 'Is the Bishop's mount answering to the reins any more willingly?' He is not surprised to find her hand is sliding under his arm. Jane is not the woman to wheedle, but he suspects she is about to account for her scheming.

'He told me how glad he is, that Adèle will be here with his wife.'

So she is certain that the matter is settled. He says nothing, to force her to explain herself further.

This pause is lengthy. 'Edward, – dearest – we must not underestimate how daunting all this is for Adèle. Yes, she is recovered, but – dearest – do not start at my words –'

He knows what she is going to say. 'You ask that I should remain with her?'

She falls on his breast. 'I hardly dared hope that you would agree. Oh Edward!'

He does not agree – but he is tempted. What rubs is her obvious longing to be alone and on her way. The mansion at Mazagon with its over-attentive servants, Adèle's dutiful affection, the solicitude of friends – even her husband's futile devotion – she clearly longs to be rid of. Besides, he is jealous. He knows the irony of it, in a man determined to take a mistress, but there must be a difference. Really, there is something almost brazen in his wife's eagerness to be reunited with her former suitor. 'But I do not agree. You cannot know what you are thinking, Jane. I cannot allow a wife of mine to face the dangers of such a journey on her own.'

'But what dangers? The winds at this time of year are moderate, so the seas will be calm; in the south the roads are good, the country is at peace, and you will recall the doctor saying that the cholera is

abated. Captain Sharp tells me that an escort can easily be arranged
–'

'Captain Sharp? I thought we had seen the last of that
opinionated young –'

'He is just today returned from the country. Some unrest among
the hill-tribes, I believe.'

Now, his only urge is to cross her. 'You did not tell him of your
preposterous scheme?'

'No, no dear! Come, you are agitated. Let us sit down.'

He shakes free of her hand and heads for the door, barking his
shin on a low table as he goes. The Captain's return is another good
reason to stay in Poona and guard his daughter. 'Harry! Fetch Tug! I
am in need of exercise.'

**He is still in a vile mood** when he arrives at the mess that evening.
Lamplight strikes gleams from the regimental silver and the mirrored
inlay that decorates some parts of the panelled walls and roof. 'These
buildings got knocked about a bit during the siege' Colonel Meikle
explains. 'But we salvaged some relics of the old Mughal style.' A
native servant is charging his glass for a toast. Suppressing that unrest
among the hill-tribes has raised Captain Sharp to the rank of Major.

Rochester rouses himself a little, though he is confident that once
the conversation has been set going, it will need only the semblance of
his attention. 'I recently had the honour of meeting your erstwhile
commander in Bombay. Tell me, Colonel, would I be correct in
thinking that a habit of self-deprecation made light of what was in
truth a remarkable victory?'

It is enough. He hears of the Peishwa's cunning, and the
overwhelming numbers of the Mahratta cavalry swarming over the
brown hills; of how the Colonel's own regiment, the Old Toughs –
the only European corps within reach – marched seventy-odd miles
across the ghauts with but a single halt, entered the British lines with
band playing and colours flying; and not a straggler dropped behind.

'The native regiments were coming up on our flank from
Dapoorie' intones the Colonel. Rochester senses that his audience of
young officers has heard all this many times before, though they are as
eager and attentive as if they were ignorant of the outcome. 'That
was the moment for treachery!' He turns for a moment to his guest
and lowers his voice. 'Our spies had told us that the Peishwa had tried
to turn our sepoys against us. Bribes, threats – that sort of thing.'

Then he resumes his narrative. 'But not a man wavered, though before the junction was complete a horde of Mahratta cavalry poured down upon them, dashed through the opening left between the two lines, enveloped either flank of the little army, and attacked the European regiment in the rear!'

And so it goes on, till long past midnight. Though his attention frequently drifts away, he finds himself more than a little envious of men who can not only tell such tales of themselves but seem to live entirely unvexed by doubts or questions. When some young officer appears to assume that his own injuries are the scars of some campaign, he is for a moment tempted not to correct him. The hour is late, much drink has been taken and the general din could easily account for such a harmless misunderstanding, but he catches the sound of Captain – no, *Major* – Sharp's laughter nearby and is obliged to set the record straight. 'My injuries were sustained in a fire. I have never had the good fortune to serve my country under arms.'

Then, to his very considerable surprise, the new Major joins in. 'Mr Rochester is too self-effacing. He was wounded trying to save the life of his first wife.'

A silence spreads around him as a rage grows within. 'I do not care to speak of it' he mutters – and finds, to his relief, that he could have said nothing more effective. He is among men who will boast without restraint of their regiment's derring-do, but blush like a virgin if their own gallantry is singled out. The conversation resumes with a general murmur of approval, leaving him to wonder quite how much Major Sharp knows of his history. Very likely he has discovered Adèle's parentage – well, that should keep her safe from his attentions.

Eventually the Colonel walks him home. 'My dog is almost useless in this country' he admits. 'There is too much to distract him.'

The Colonel gives a bark of laughter. 'Rather like some of my young men. Your daughter is in great demand. A product of your first marriage, I take it?'

In some far-fetched way she is, he thinks – and merely grunts an assent.

'My wife is curious. You hardly needed to bring such a charming young lady all this way to find her a husband?'

So his family has been the subject of general speculation. 'I brought her to put a distance between her and a certain presumptuous young architect. I confess that I had not reckoned our journey would bring us to a garrison.'

The Colonel chuckles. ''Out of the skillet – eh? But my wife will set her right. There are few women suited to following the flag.'

Rochester's impression of the Colonel's lady is of a buxom, weather-beaten type, with as many tall tales as her husband's officers. 'May I offer you a last cigar, Colonel?' They have reached his quarters. A servant is summoned and they settle on the veranda. 'Did you meet your wife in India?'

'In Peshawar.' Another slew of reminiscences is underway. 'I was all over the place during the war with Boney.'

He is close to dozing when a name rouses him: *Spanish Town* – where he married Bertha. Instantly he is alert and calculating. It seems that the Colonel was in Jamaica as a young lieutenant during his own days in that hell-hole. Their paths may have crossed – and worse: Bertha had a particularly keen appetite for a man in uniform. He listens, but he does not intervene.

'Can't say I cared for the place' says the Colonel. 'Of course, there was money to be made. Fortunes! But dirty money. Blood-stained money. Give me India any day, say I.'

Here is a chance to turn the conversation towards safer subjects. 'And are there not fortunes to be made in India? That is certainly the common understanding, in Britain.'

The Colonel grunts ruefully. 'Not in the army. A company box-wallah can still put by a tidy sum, but not an army man.' The Colonel grinds out his cigar and leans forward, suddenly confidential. 'Look out for your daughter, my good fellow. A pretty girl with a handsome dowry is like a Spanish galleon to a buccaneer.'

**He passes a near-sleepless night** and still has a splitting headache when Adèle knocks on his door at first light. 'Come for a ride, Papa! It is such a beautiful morning and I shall not have the pleasure of your company much longer.' Tug's claws slip and skitter on the pathway as he races ahead.

She has something to confide, he can tell; and he dreads hearing that already she has fallen in love. He instructs the groom to lead them to a view-point that he has heard the colonel's lady commending, in the faint hope that if he can remind her how wide the world is, and how much of her future still lies ahead, she might still be deterred from an over-hasty choice. But as in dense shade they plod along a narrow gully beside an intermittent brook, he remembers how recently this girl has been reminded of how easily her life might be cut short. He can hardly blame her if she wants to snatch every rosebud within reach. The track begins to zig-zag steeply upward. 'Can you see the rocks, Papa?' she calls out, panting a little as she tugs at the reins. 'Some are as big as a house!'

Yes, he can make out the rocks – tomato red, in full sunshine – and the shadow of Tug, scrambling among them, quite oblivious to the possibility of basking snakes. A yell brings the reluctant dog to heel. Jane would have identified the ferns growing among them, he thinks, for surely there must be ferns: he can hear the trickle of water. She would have likened each rock's profile to some fabled beast. But it is his daughter that his heart yearns for – another child he nearly lost; a child he will lose to a husband before too long – and he longs to stay close to her.

They emerge on the lip of a barren plateau. Even he can see that a plain of yellow-pink grit stretches for miles. A range of lofty blue mountains borders the view to west, north and south; the nearest loom large and dark enough to be visible to him, though he suspects that endless folds extend far beyond what he can see before they merge with the over-arching blue of the sky. He hears her coming up behind him. 'Well, my dear one, does the prospect match your expectations? Is it truly sublime?' He is teasing.

She says nothing for a moment, then 'It is awful.' Her voice is trembling slightly. 'The immensity of it.'

He holds out his hand, hoping that nothing more profound than her romantic sensibility has been disturbed. His mount shifts and he tugs the reins again. 'More awful than Glencoe?' This before India has been Adèle's *ne plus ultra* of horrid mountain scenery.

But she is not to be amused. 'You do not understand, Papa!' Now there is an unmistakable sob in her voice.

He dismounts and signals the groom to take the horse to a distance. 'Come, child. Here is a rock that I think is as big as a bench. Come and sit beside me.' He whistles for Tug, who settles at their feet.

What she tells him is not a complete surprise. Last night, over cards, Mrs Meikle – the Colonel's forthright lady – had questions to ask. Petting Tug and playing with his ears seems to allow Adèle to speak of matters which they have seldom openly referred to, though her voice sounds particularly small in the immensity all around. 'Mama was quite wonderful. She said I am *my husband's second wife*. But no more.'

What she means is that Jane diverted impertinent questions about her step-daughter's parentage, not with a downright lie, but a convenient truth. Good of her, yet it still disgusts him that respectable society should prefer his child to be the daughter of a mad wife, rather than a French mistress. But he doubts if this defense will hold for long. He has always tried to protect Adèle from the consequences of her illegitimate birth, but now – in a garrison: the worst possible setting – she seems to have become fully aware of her social disadvantage. Anger begins to boil in his breast. This at least is something that might have been left at home in England. There he had always known that unless his daughter caught the eye of a saint, her suitors were only likely to overlook the taint of her birth if the size of her dowry were sufficient to draw its poison. Now that she is his sole heir, the stakes are even higher. He suspects that every impoverished officer is calculating what hefty subsidy could be asked to relieve him of such damaged goods.

'You must tell me if anyone has said anything more to hurt you, my child.' *I will have any such fellow whipped*, he thinks.

'No' she says, rather flatly. 'But I have been thinking a great deal since I was ill.' Suddenly she leans closer. He knows she is staring into his face and that whatever she asks must be answered with unswerving truthfulness. 'Papa, when I was sick, I thought *maman* was in the room – my real mama, I mean. In France. Can that be possible?'

His heart is cracking. 'It was a feverish dream. A nightmare. And that is all behind us.'

'But it is not. It will always be with me.'

How can he pretend otherwise? 'Yes, it will. But it is only a small part of your history – and you are not to blame for it.'

'That is not how the world sees it.'

'The portion of the world which does not understand that the blame is all mine should be beneath your notice' he cries, all too aware that here he has lost his grip on reality. He peers around, as if some miraculous improvement in his vision might lend him a new insight, but all he can see is the endless yellow dust.

'No' she says firmly, 'it is the portion I must be most aware of, for they are the people who can hurt me most. It is a very large portion.'

She is trying to sound wry for his sake. He thinks for a minute. 'Alas, you are right. But though I could have hoped that you would never learn such a bitter truth, I am glad that you have acknowledged it. It will be your armour, child.'

'That is what Mrs Fisher says.'

'You have spoken to her?' This startles him.

'Mama says her ideas are very advanced. I need some advanced ideas – and she is very kind.'

'And have you told mama herself – Jane – of your anxieties? In all that counts, she is your true mama.'

A barely discernible movement suggests that she is shaking her head. 'Mama is too worried about her cousin. And – and – I do not think she likes to talk about *maman*.'

That is true. He finds a ball in his pocket and hurls it across the yellow sand. Tug hares after it.

'I have spoken only to Mrs Fisher and to Emily. And now to you.'

'To Emily? And what does she say, pray?'

Is that a giggle? 'She says that Captain Sharp is far too superior to want to marry a bastard' – she hesitates only slightly at the word – 'and that now he has found out about me he will stop his pestering. I have no secrets from Emily, nor she from me.'

'*Major* Sharp' he corrects; 'he is even more superior now.' Tug drops the slobbered ball in his hand and he throws again, covering thoughts of a secret that he hopes to God Emily has kept to herself, though at the same time he is admitting a huge, unexpected relief. Here surely is a sign that his daughter is capable of taking care of her own best interests. It is a shock to discover that his little girl has grown up so suddenly and in other circumstances he might be saddened by what has awakened her, but now it is hugely reassuring. Yet what a wrench it will be, to abandon the company of a pretty young woman who has just acquired this slight tang of salt.

The sun has risen beyond the point when they should have returned to the shade. Her complexion will suffer if they do not seek shelter immediately. 'Before we go – that afternoon in the bazaar – before you were – ?'

She interrupts before he can finish. 'Whatever are you talking about, Papa?' And before he can answer, she is hitching her skirt, ready to mount.

He yells for his dog and the groom and envies the man who puts her up. He would give the world to have two hands to cup her foot. But at least when they reach their bungalow she can rely on his shoulder. She springs to the ground and he pulls her close.

'Dearest Papa! Don't worry about me.' She turns his head and whispers in his ear. 'I shall never love anyone as much as I love you.'

He can smell the sun on her skin, the dust in her hair, and he knows he should tell her she will change her mind, but what he says is quite different. 'Remember that you are at least the equal of every man and woman on this earth. My daughter is fit to marry a prince!'


**It is the custom** to ride out in carriages to see the sun set beyond the ghats. I am about to fetch my bonnet to go with our friends when Alice takes my arm and leads me aside.

'Jane, my dear. Do not be alarmed, but the Bishop has news of your cousin which I think you will want to hear straight away. I will take care of Adèle, while you and your husband stay behind.'

After all this time! I feel I shall faint, and it is half in a dream that I hear myself saying that I will hear this news alone. 'Adèle will be alarmed if neither of us accompanies her. I will of course inform my husband later.' I choose to ignore the slight question in her look as I see her to the door where Edward is handing Adèle into the Bishop's carriage. Two or three officers are already trotting up to greet them.

When I return to my sitting room, I find it infested with servants.

'I took the liberty of ordering tea' says the Bishop, and I think *he fears that I will need sustenance.*

Not for the first time I regret the absence of one sensible English parlourmaid, who would have brought in a tray and had done with it. Instead I must wait impatiently while a lace cloth is spread, a silver spirit lamp is lit, and an endless procession of dainties – none of which I shall eat – is brought to the table. We cannot even be left to pour our own tea. A turbanned servant for each of us hovers behind our chairs, and when I at last convey that we wish to be left to ourselves, they look hurt and abashed, as if I had found fault with them.

'I am not used to such state' I confess.

'My wife is already determined that our own establishment will be less – shall I say – *oriental*.' But he is a kind man. He knows how eager I am for his news. 'Mrs Rochester. Let me tell you first of all that when the report I have was written, your cousin was alive and apparently in tolerable health.' He pauses. 'That was some weeks ago, but I have no reason to suspect any change in his circumstances.'

My heart is beating faster and I know the colour is rising in my face, but my relief is mingled with apprehension. If the Bishop's news is wholly good, why is he so anxious for my well-being?

'Let me explain how I came by my information' he continues. 'As you will appreciate, my predecessor has prepared various extensive reports, some of which were waiting for me on my arrival in Bombay. Men of the cloth are seldom given to brevity.'

He is trying to calm me, but the effect is to tighten my nerves.

'Mrs Rochester. You know that that I do not share my predecessor's reservations about missionary activities. So, you will perhaps appreciate that when I discovered that a separate item on an unauthorized mission in the Madras presidency was still to follow, I was glad to have left Bombay before its arrival. However, I have underestimated the efficiency of the in-country mail. The document was forwarded to the garrison here and delivered to me this morning.'

I cannot understand why he is prefacing the news I crave with this rigmarole, and my impatience prompts something like rudeness. 'Bishop Fisher. I am a woman who has borne blows far worse than any you can have for me. I am grateful for your consideration, but do not hold back whatever it is you fear will distress me.'

'Very well. In brief, your cousin refused to accept the authority of his Bishop. There were quarrels, and Mr Rivers left Madras. He has subsequently acquired land in the foothills of the Western ranges where he has set up some kind of school and orphanage. He refuses any contact with the clerical establishment.'

'But this is good news, not bad!' I cannot help myself. 'We had some inkling of a disagreement and of my cousin's disappointment. But how noble of him to defy an authority that would bind his zeal in chains! Surely, Bishop, an evangelist like yourself must applaud his courage! He has chosen to obey the commands of his Saviour, not the timid prescriptions of the Church.' I am on my feet.

He rises to meet me. 'But Mrs Rochester –'

I will not be stopped. 'And to found a school! An orphanage! In this country where so few receive the benefits of an education and so very many orphans are abandoned – if not worse! I have been a teacher myself, Bishop Fisher, and I tell you it is a worthy calling!' As I speak, I can feel my courage revive within me. I was right to make this journey. There is work for me here.

He puts a hand on my arm. 'All that may be true. I confess I have some sympathy for a rebel myself, and though I will reserve judgement a while longer, I fear that my predecessor has not served our faith well. But please sit down, Mrs Rochester. There is more I must tell you.'

I sit, somewhat placated, though I am hardly able to contain my exuberance. Oh, how I regret this detour to Poona! My soul longs to be at sea again, heading south!

The Bishop sighs. 'Once again, I think it is best to be brief. Your cousin has taken a native mistress. She is a woman of ill-repute, formerly the mistress of an army officer, by whom she has a bastard son. Now she has a second child. Your cousin's bastard. I am sorry.'

The blood drains from my limbs. 'I cannot believe this. It cannot be true. What evidence can there be? You say that he has no contact with his own kind. This must be rumour! Where there is prejudice, malice abounds –'

He cuts me off. 'There is evidence. I have a detailed account from the Bishop's delegate, the Archdeacon of Madras, compiled the very day he paid a visit to your cousin just a few short weeks ago.'

'A report written by a man who was at odds with my cousin before he approached this task!'

'Your point is valid, I am happy to admit. But, Mrs Rochester, you should know that the Archdeacon fell sick and died, barely a day after signing this document. We cannot now examine him to test how he may have misjudged what he saw, and I have no reason to doubt the veracity of the facts he cites.'

I think of Adèle, imagining in her delirium that she was in France, with her mother. 'Perhaps the Archdeacon had fever. The fevered mind will sometimes vent our secret wishes.'

He closes his eyes and shakes his head. 'Believe me, I have given some thought to the possibility you refer to. But this report is not the product of a disordered mind. The Archdeacon writes that he ascertained the truth from the only other European in your cousin's establishment – a woman who had been resident in the garrison at Fort St George at the time of the previous liaison.'

'May I see the report?' Despite the heat, I feel as if I am encased in a hard, cold shell that prevents me absorbing what I have heard.

'You may. I have it with me.' He pats the pocket of his coat. 'But I fear it will only distress you more. Its language will cause you pain.'

I want to say that I would welcome pain; that now I feel only numb. The Bishop has been blunt, but only a sharp instrument can penetrate my armoured breast.

'Come, you have received a shock, I know. Let me help you to some fresh tea.'

I drink, and gradually feel myself calmer, though I cannot yet tell what this news has done to me. 'You have been very kind' I manage to say at last. 'I cannot think that I should have borne this, had I heard it from anyone else.'

'Now you must try to understand it.'

'I do not know what you mean.'

'Will you continue your journey?'

'I do not know.'

He is silent for a while. Unidentifiable thoughts whirl in my brain, like a flock of exhausted birds that long to land; the farmer's gun keeps them aloft. 'I do not think I can go back' I say at last. 'Perhaps I will die here.'

He smiles. 'I do not take you for a quitter, Jane. Yes, go on. But in the right spirit.'

'In charity? Not in judgement.' I am still trying to discover how I feel.

'Your cousin may need you.'

'Need me? No, I think not! He has a mistress.' Where does this vehemence come from? I blush and shudder.

'There are other needs' says the Bishop gently. 'And remember, he believes he has been rejected by his own kind. He is alone and far from home. It is not uncommon for a man to find solace where he can.'

'But St John is an ordained priest!'

'Forgive me, Mrs Rochester, these are delicate matters – have you any reason to think your cousin was vowed to a celibate life?'

I shake my head.

The Bishop nods. 'Indeed, there is evidence that he intended to marry. For my own part, I could not recommend any man to the mission field who does not have a wife. I could not have accepted my own present responsibilities had not providence arranged that Alice was at last free to marry me. Only with such a helpmeet –'

There is no holding back. 'Intended to *marry*? What *evidence* do you speak of?'

Now he can no more ignore my agitation than I can disguise it. 'Pray calm yourself, Mrs Rochester. Perhaps more tea?' I shake my head. 'Very well. I will find the passage in the report.' From his pocket he produces a sheaf of papers, tied with a black ribbon. As he sorts through the closely-written pages I try to compose myself, but the wait seems interminable.

At last he finds the place. 'Ah, here we are! *My office had previously received from Mr Rivers a letter intimating his intention to marry, though he supplied no details and so of course no banns were ever published. When I reminded him of this fact, he flew into a rage and declared that he was now married 'in the eyes of God'.* He puts the papers aside. 'No doubt the letter referred to will be filed at Fort St George.'

'But is there nothing more? Who was his intended bride? What happened to prevent this marriage?'

'I know nothing more. We can only conjecture. Perhaps she died before it could take place. You yourself have too many reasons to know how swiftly death can frustrate our hopes. It seems unlikely that the lady in question was from the society he had repudiated in Madras. Perhaps she was connected with the residency in Mysore.' He hesitates for a moment. 'But my wife's livelier imagination has suggested another possible explanation of this mystery which – just possibly – you may be able to confirm.'

'You have discussed this with Alice?'

'Forgive me, Mrs Rochester. Perhaps I have presumed too far. But I anticipated that once you had absorbed this news, you might be in need of a woman's sympathy.'

'Perhaps. Thank you. You know how I value Mrs Fisher's good sense.' But how can I confide in Alice when I am unable to confide in my own heart?

'You will want to speak to your husband first, of course.'

To Edward? What shall I say to Edward? I clutch at the nearest straw. 'You said that Alice has imagined some possibility?'

The Bishop seems to think I am over the worst. He smiles. 'You women have a knack for these insights!' Now he is leaning back in his chair, tapping the knees of his breeches. 'You cannot have failed to notice that there is a shortage of eligible young ladies in this country. But what is a man to do if he cannot find a mate among the available supply? His thoughts turn to those he left behind – to a sister's friend, perhaps; a lady whose own choices have become – shall we say? – somewhat circumscribed –'

'Rosamond Oliver' I say. It is quite involuntary.

The Bishop raises an eyebrow. 'You concur with my wife? There is a lady –'

Again, I interrupt. 'I cannot tell. I heard of no such thing. But yes, there is a lady. I know that my cousin was once powerfully drawn to her, and that she loved him too.' Uncomfortable now, I come to a halt.

'But something came between them. A father's needs, perhaps, as in my own instance?'

Was it I who came between them? No, that was not quite the case. I consider my reply carefully. 'Her father approved the match. But St John believed that Miss Oliver was unsuited to the rigours of a missionary's calling and that he must look elsewhere for a wife.' I get up and go to the window. The glare has left the parade ground and the sunset party will soon be returning. Behind me, I am aware that the Bishop is watching me keenly. Gathering myself together, I return to the tea-table. 'There is still hot water, if you wish?' He shakes his head. I fill my own cup. 'Miss Oliver is now a widow. Lady Granby. Her marriage was a sad affair. She is now as sober and as earnest as any missionary could wish.' I can hear something in my voice which I hasten to correct. 'But all this is no more than speculation. It may be that my cousin heard of this change in her circumstances, and his hopes revived. But I have no knowledge of how that might have come about.'

'And even were our speculations to be correct, it seems that your cousin's hopes were disappointed. Perhaps the lady did not wish to trust her health to this climate.' He sighs. 'I am a romantic soul. My wife tells me that I am sometimes too inclined to be fanciful for my own good. But this at least seems clear: following the frustration of his hopes to marry, Mr Rivers has' – he hesitates – 'fallen into temptation. Regrettably, the situation is not unknown. Perhaps it is inevitable, given the scarcity of suitable partners – though I have to admit that I am disappointed to find such an instance among the clergy. But a man of the cloth is still a man. I think you will understand that, Mrs Rochester.'

I know temptation; that is for sure. 'Does the report contain any further information regarding –'. Now it is my turn to hesitate. 'His consort?'

'Mrs Rochester, I warned you that the report would distress you. I do not know the woman's name, but that can hardly matter. She is a servant, but – God knows – too many in our own society are seduced by their masters. That was certainly this woman's fate, and though this is not in the report, it is perhaps to your cousin's credit that he took her in, together with her first child, when her seducer had abandoned the poor creature to her fate.' He sighs. 'I fear that the supply of fallen women may be as bottomless as the pool of orphans.'

I am too deep in my own thoughts to respond.

'There is more, I fear. Though a record of her baptism is believed to exist, it seemed that she wilfully persisted in her heathen practices: among them, she habitually made offerings to – a snake.'

Perhaps this should matter, but it hardly needs to figure in the story I must prepare for my husband. I dread that the carriages will return before I have composed myself.

**It is late before** he at last finds himself alone with his wife. Her abstraction throughout the evening he puts down to further scheming. If she knew how much he would prefer to stay behind with his daughter! Duty and propriety oblige him to accompany his wife but he can see little chance of any pleasure in the journey ahead. 'So what news did the good Bishop have to impart?'

She speaks at last. 'News that has rocked me to my very core.'

A sudden hope springs. 'Is he dead? Has all this journey been in vain? Good God.' Instantly he regrets words which reveal feelings better kept unspoken – but which she hardly seems to notice.

'No, not dead. His death would be simple in comparison.'

Her narrative is shame-faced and rambling. By the end, her voice is breaking. What she feels seems more like disappointment than outrage, but how can he expect to fathom another's mind, when he cannot sound his own? In all that years that St John's venerable presence has haunted the verge of his marriage, this is the first time he has ever felt a glimmer of fellow-feeling. A bitter laugh escapes him. He feels her staring at him, open-mouthed, aghast.

'Forgive me' he says. 'It tickles me to discover that my rival has feet of clay.' What succeeds is relief. The secret of her cousin's silence has been revealed. Further travel would be pointless. Indeed, the blessed St John will hardly want to be discovered. He pictures the austere character he has always imagined now luxuriating in some lush seraglio and laughs again. But his amusement turns to anger when his wife makes plain that she is determined to press on.

'The report which the Bishop received was written in malice. I must discover the truth for myself.'

'The truth? That there was enough of the man in your sainted kinsman to succumb to the flesh?'

'The woman's character may be less blemished than we have been led to believe. They may be married.' She pauses, then steps away. 'There is really no reason for you to come with me. You can stay here. With Adèle.'

This nonsense again! 'Jane, Jane! Do you not see that it is now doubly unthinkable to let you proceed on your own? How your reputation would be damaged? The man is a reprobate.' Besides, his curiosity has been roused. He must see this fallen idol for himself.

# CHAPTER 12

**What do I expect?** Not what I find. We leave our modest escort to make their camp by the river, close to the village named in the Archdeacon's report. *Vidyalay kahan hai?* I call to the most intelligent-looking man I spot among the throng in the market-place. I do not know the words for mission or orphanage. Whether or not he understands me, I suppose it must seem likely that we are in search of a fellow countryman, and we are pointed along the road, riding the last mile or so with only Harry to accompany us.

I fear that we shall not be greeted kindly. We have travelled as swiftly as any messenger could, so my cousin has received no warning of our arrival. I am also fearful of my husband's reactions to what we find. I wish – oh, how I wish! – that he had stayed behind! The close quarters of the ship that took us to Cochin forced us to be outwardly civil, but now as we ride in silence up a steep narrow lane, over-arched with massive, leather-leafed trees, the politeness of a gentleman is more than I dare to hope for. The noise of the village traffic dwindles to nothing, replaced with only the noise of our steeds and the humming of insects as they gorge on the decaying mangoes that litter the verges.

Then suddenly a lumpish native boy, turning a large rattle, is careering down the track towards us. Behind him staggers a frail old woman, thin grey witch-locks streaming behind her. She grabs the boy just as he is about to collide with Harry's horse and gazes up at us in blank-faced wonderment. A long strand of spittle runs from her charge's open mouth. It is a scene from some asylum. *'Pisgah kahan hai?'* I call in alarm; *'Angrez kahan hai?'*

My scraps of Hindoostanee are unlikely to be understood here, but perhaps the old woman catches something, for she draws the idiot boy aside and points wordlessly up the hill. Dread is turning into blank dismay as we emerge into an oval of shabby, leaf-thatched buildings, surrounding a worn stretch of grass. A small gang of scrawny, rough-looking lads is advancing to meet us. One of them – bolder than the rest – runs up to my husband's stirrup and scans him frankly. It is a hot day and Edward has removed his coat. The hook that he uses when riding is clearly visible, and he has covered his more sensitive eye with a patch to protect it from the dust of the road.

'Are you a soldier?' asks the boy. 'Did you fight in a battle?'

I have become used to the accents which make sing-song out of even perfect English. Before anyone can respond, our attention is caught by a shout, and a strange figure comes limping and stumbling across the grass towards us – a tall, emaciated man, with a wasted leg. Barefoot, he wears a short, kilt-like garment of rough homespun and a billowing collarless shirt. Even before I recognise my cousin, my mind is telling me that I must reverse every last expectation. This man's skin is yellowed by many fevers, he is near bald, and what sparse locks remain are snow-white. His cheeks are hollow, as if he has lost many teeth, and his eyes are sunk deep beneath a line-scored brow. So fleshless is his jaw and neck that his head seems to be hoisted on a scaffolding of poles. Only when he halts and pulls the boy to his side do I see that his face and scalp, one forearm and that wasted leg are sheathed with the familiar slick scars of a burning. The sight strikes to my bones.

Behind me I hear Harry mutter 'Good God' and sense my husband's unveiled curiosity turn to alarm as he picks up how shocked we are by whatever it is we are seeing. For a long moment I stare and the spectre stares back at me.

'Jane Eyre. Can it be you?'

Among a welter of indefinable feelings, I can at least register something profoundly shocking in being immediately recognizable after so many years, when he is so changed – as if, after all, the sufferings that I have known fall way short of what a human being can endure and still survive. This man, once as finely chiselled as a young Greek god, is now a ruin. In a trance I murmur 'Yes, it is I – Jane Eyre. I have found you out' – and hear my husband's intake of breath behind me.

The spectre seizes my hand, and though its grasp is as dry and bony as a bundle of sticks, its warmth brings me to my senses. 'But I am Jane Rochester now, and have been for many years. This gentleman is my husband.' Then, to my surprise, Edward holds out his hand. Whatever he is thinking, he seems to have registered that the reactions he has prepared do not suit what is happening. Suddenly baffled and embarrassed, I look around. The boy that St John is holding close to his side is staring up at us, while behind him, all around, more silent children have gathered. I take another, less suspicious, look at my surroundings. Three fine trees shade the centre of the compound. Their extensive roots have broken through the ground, providing snug niches and perches for further boys and girls scattered across the scene. Some are playing familiar games with jacks, tops or marbles – though they have all looked up to stare at the strangers. Tug retreats to his master's side, grumbling quietly, as if he has not made up his mind, and the boldest boy ventures to pat him. I hand my reins to Harry and jump to the ground.

St John calls to the boy. 'Jivaj! Take care!' He explains. 'The boy is a child I am keen to adopt.'

This must be the officer's love-child, from Fort St George. St John cannot know what we have already learned about him. Edward seems more composed than I am. 'The dog will not harm him. But he is excited by crowds. Keep back the rest of your brood.'

For the first time, St John smiles and I catch in those dull hooded eyes a faint flash of their old fire. 'My pupils. I have just one child I can call my own.' He pauses. 'She has taught me how grievous your loss has been.'

So, he knows of our great misfortune. Once, I would have demanded why such news was not enough to break the silence that has called me here. 'You are married?' I had certainly not intended that this should be the first question I ask.

'My wife is dead.' At these flat words the boy – Jivaj – rushes to St John's side and buries his face in his flank. 'Forgive him. It is a recent loss and he takes it hard.' They rock together for a moment or two.

'I am sorry. I did not know.' And I do not know what to think. I had not expected to feel the pity that is rising in my breast.

'How could you know? I have cut myself off from my former life.'

A trace of bitterness, even hostility, is beginning to well up in his words when we are interrupted by the sound of a bell. The children stream across the grass towards the buildings leaving us rather awkwardly alone – Edward, Harry and myself, travelled-stained and weary, our horses and the dog, this scarecrow who should be our host, and a lanky brown boy who is now trying to wriggle out of his grasp.

We are saved by another brown person who announces himself as Kamil, and calls us to eat. He too speaks our language very competently. Still bemused, we tether our horses, tie Tug to a convenient root and follow him, but midway across the grass St John leaves us and trudges towards a gate that divides the range of buildings. Kamil turns to us before we enter the school room. 'My sister died at noon. He will spend this time by her grave.'

'Your sister died too? Was this the cholera?'

He shrugs. 'Only my sister died. And the Archdeacon. But that was not here.'

'So when did my cousin's –' I do not know what word to use.

'Sin-junsah'b's wife was my sister Jaya.'

Of course I have known since Bishop Fisher told me that the woman in question was a native. But that her own brother should consent to the arrangement! 'Mr Kamil. A few short weeks ago I did not know of your sister's existence. Or any of this.' I gaze around. Already I am seeing how very much needs to be done. 'It was the late Archdeacon's report that partially enlightened me.'

Mr Kamil's gaze shifts. 'The Archdeacon was no friend to Sin-junsah'b. And he insulted my sister.'

'How was that?' I am beginning to sense that whatever the truth, it is a delicate thing which might easily be damaged if I set about uncovering it too eagerly.

The man cannot look at me. 'He said that she – that she was not his wife.' Then suddenly he raises his head. 'But *I* married them. *I* heard their vows.'

'But are you ordained?'

'No. It is not allowed. But Sin-jun calls me his curate.'

My husband interrupts. 'Do not badger the poor chap. There will be time later.' He leans closer and whispers. 'If I'm not mistaken, a ship's captain can conduct a wedding. So why not this fellow?' He straightens up. 'You speak our language very well, Mr Kamil.'

'It is my language now. And since Sin-jun lost interest in his books, I have studied when I can.'

St John lose interest in his books? That surely can be put right. I am tempted to tell this solemn and godly young man that a new Bishop is come, who has more advanced ideas, but while I am trying to recall Bishop Fisher's views on the ordination of native converts, Edward takes over the conversation. 'You seem like a sensible chap,

Kamil. Why do we not take advantage of Mr Rivers's absence to hear your account of this place? How many acres do you farm?'

Like the well-born Englishman that he is, Edward can quickly take command of even the most outlandish situation.


**This fellow Kamil seems honest enough**, though how competent he is remains to be seen. Few of the natives seem to have much staying power. Rochester can see enough to know that this lame, witless dotard is not at all the lusty nabob he had in mind, and whatever his wife imagined, she must be disappointed too, though she is too proud to admit it. Of course, she pities the poor wretch, and will doubtless want to stay close by his side till the end, but that will not take long by the sound of it and then they can be off.

Still, he is curious – and tired of being a brute. They eat in the schoolroom, where a supple young woman is ladling food onto a square of banana leaf. Bangles chink on her wrist – Kamil's wife; fortunate man. The ancient, nervous crone and her idiot boy are somewhere around, and there is a determined little Irishwoman, but what their parts are in the story, God alone knows. Though so much here is a mystery, it has its familiar aspects. He sat at a desk very like this when he was a boy – and when he accompanied his wife on her inspections of the village school at Ferndean.

Perhaps she is remembering the same scene, because she is catechizing the children about the potatoes they have been eating. 'Is this vegetable native to your country?'

A girl babbles the answer. 'The potato was brought from the Americas to Ireland by Sir Walter Raleigh, where it is now the principal food of the poor.'

'Which English monarch was then on the throne?'

'Good Queen Bess, fifteen-fifty-seven to sixteen hundred and three' they all chant in unison.

'Very good. Now, who introduced this useful tuber to India?'

A silence falls. He smiles to himself as he remembers just such desperate moments when he overheard his wife coaxing an answer from their little ones.

Then a timid voice ventures *Was it Sinjun-sahib?*

She hesitates for a moment. 'His real name is Mr Rivers. Well, I doubt it was Mr Rivers personally, but certainly some European' – she laughs, and he thinks she will be fit in well here; this is what she does best. He could scoop up Adèle – return to the new house – find a mistress. Blanche Ingram, married now, would still be willing. With an effort he gets to his feet. His cramped seat must have weakened his legs. 'Come, Harry! I must see to the dog. I will leave you to your interrogation, Jane.'

Tug, tethered to a tree-root, nearly strangles himself as he leaps up to greet him. A clatter and a sudden wetness about his knee tell him that he has kicked over a bowl of water.

'It must have been the lad who fetched it' says Harry. 'Not many of these natives have much of a fondness for the dog.' He belches noisily. 'Beg pardon. Shall we take a walk sir? The local grub is inclined to be indigestible.'

He is struggling with Tug's leash. 'Confound this knot!'

'Let me sir.' Tug bounds free, circles and returns. Harry leads the way. 'This is the gate, sir. Mr Kamil says we should look out for elephants if we go as far as the river.'

It is not until they are clear of the compound that he asks his question. 'Tell me, Harry: this missionary fellow – that we've travelled all these months to find out – is he right in the head? From what I could make out, he seems to be in a bad way.'

'It's shocking what this country does to a man who won't look out for himself.'

Harry has been exercising even more vigorously since his spell at the garrison in Poona. 'You saw no signs of illness – the smallpox, perhaps?' There is an obscurity here; the air needs clearing.

'Careful, sir. The path is rough.'

'You have not answered my question. There is an answer, I think.'

'Well, sir, it's very strange and I hardly like to mention it, but he is burnt, sir. He has been in a fire.'

He stumbles for a moment. A cane would have been useful. 'So he is as ugly as me?'

Harry laughs. 'Oh no, sir! You are much the better looking! I wonder the children aren't frightened of him.'

'Poor fellow. How did he come by his injuries, do you think?'

'Oh, have a heart sir! We have barely been here two hours!'

'You mean that you will find out by nightfall. Are we to stay here, by the way, or do we return to our camp?'

'The Irishwoman seems like a promising source of what's what around here, sir. And we are to stay at Pisgah if we wish. Mr Kamil thinks that his master will get used to our presence.'

'Or hardly notice it. I think Sinjun-sahib lives in a world of his own. He is not much of a host.'

'Unexpected guests can disturb the household routine, sir.'

They are on level ground now, among a patchwork of what seem to be well-tended fields. 'I shall need you to be my eyes, Harry. My wife is otherwise occupied.'

Suddenly Harry is rushing ahead, yelling for the dog. He returns, dragging a stinking Tug by the collar. 'Rolling, sir. Bad dog! Phwaugh! You won't need anyone to be your nose, sir.'

'No, indeed. Is that elephant, do you think?'

Harry is no agriculturalist, but he describes the state of the fields adequately enough. A rudimentary exchange with a couple of labourers confirms that the crops are healthy and the yields satisfactory. 'And how would you assess the state of the place generally?'

'I'd say that the fields are better maintained than the buildings, sir. The place needs money.'

Well, the donation he is inclined to leave behind should patch things up. 'As I thought. Are we close to the river yet? Throw a stick for the dog, to rinse off the stink.'

'We'll walk a bit further, sir. Someone is watering his horses.'

There is a sudden uproar ahead – barking, whinnying, a boy's shouts of alarm. 'What is happening? Is Tug in trouble again?'

'They are our horses, sir!' yells Harry. 'They must have been stolen!'

A bay horse charges past, nearly knocking him off the path. He lunges for its bridle and misses, but it pulls up a few paces on and stands there, nervously snorting. It seems to be his wife's gelding. 'What an earth is happening?'

Harry returns, dragging a small figure with him. Something tells Rochester that this is the missionary's boy. 'Jivaj? Is that you?'

'Let me go! I am not doing bad things. The horses were thirsty!'

'And no one but you had the sense to look after them? Well done, lad. Only three is too many for one boy to handle. You should have got some help.'

Harry is leading the gelding back towards them. 'Can you take his reins sir? So, what have you done with their saddles, you young varmint?'

'Leave the boy, Harry, he meant well. Where did you learn to handle horses, Jivaj? Does Sinjun-sahib keep a horse?'

'Only a bullock. The soldiers have horses.' Tug is fussing around him. 'Your dog smells of shit.'

Who supplied him with that ornament to his English vocabulary?

Such a lad must be a fish out of water in this pious retreat. 'Yes, he does. And have you ridden a horse? Would you like to ride this one?'

Harry gives the boy a leg up and hands the reins to his master. 'I'll see to the others, sir, and give this fellow a scrubbing. The poxy mongrel ain't fit for polite company.'

Jivaj is shy of speech but otherwise fearless. Rochester warms to the lad, but is glad of his silence. It is a long time since he has spoken to a child and the instinct, so thoroughly suppressed, seems lost to him. But as they reach the top of the slope Tug comes pounding after them. Just in front of the gelding the dog gathers himself and gives a mighty shake. River water flies in all directions. The horse takes a step backwards and sneezes; Rochester loses his grip on the reins, stumbles and falls over the dog. Jivaj laughs – and suddenly a memory explodes like a blow to the chest. Himself, with Ted on his pony, and a younger Tug bedaubed with horse-shit. And Ted's peals of glee at his father's improper language.

He is still trembling when he leads Jivaj through the gate. His wife, recognisable from the shape of her skirt, is sitting in the shade on one of the tree roots. Tug dashes towards her. 'Look out! He's wet!'

She gets to her feet rather awkwardly. Even from a distance he can tell that she has a child in her arms.


**What is it that has defeated my cousin?** Sickness, loss and this merciless climate will slacken the resolve of an ordinary mortal, but the St John Rivers who once bent the force of his will upon me, would only have been strengthened by such adversaries. Mrs O'Reilly is of the opinion that he has spent too long among the natives, and though I do not care to encourage her speculations I fear that his moral purpose has been sapped by the general passivity that is so well-known in this land.

'You must not think that you have failed' I exhort him. 'Your hour is about to come.' I tell him of Bishop Fisher's intention to reverse his predecessor's lamentable strictures.

'Something of the sort is what Archdeacon Brackenbury came to tell me, the day before my wife died' he replies; 'that the new Bishop is inclined to be more amenable to the missionary's calling.'

That word *wife* still perturbs me in ways that I do not wholly understand, but though I like to think I am forthright, I have as yet been unable to bring myself to ascertain whether the woman he calls his wife was in fact no better than his mistress.

We are sitting in the room he calls his study, though it contains precious few works of scholarship, all gnawed by insects or stained with mould. It is late afternoon, the hour before prayers and the evening meal, and in the days that have passed since our arrival St John and I have fallen into the habit of spending this time together, though he has little to say and even I am often at a loss for words. Lying and evasion have always been abhorrent to me, and to return to England with such a question unresolved is unthinkable. I could not present an adequate account of their brother's life to Diana and Mary were I not in possession of the truth. Any irregularity would dismay them and sully his reputation among the circles that remember him, but my own conscience would be too much troubled if I allowed any evasion or ambiguity to be falsely interpreted. And deep in my heart I also know that not the least of my concerns is that Edward would know I was dissembling. It would amuse him to see the woman whose scruples once barred her from becoming his mistress now turned hypocrite.

But save for this hour when I sit with my cousin, he deep in silent thought, me with a pile of mending, practical matters distract me from these intransigent concerns. Give any sensible woman some worthwhile work and she will very likely discover that the abstractions which have plagued her have put themselves in order. God knows there is plenty to busy ourselves with here: Edward is instructing Mr Kamil in sound English principles of managing an estate – and teaching young Jivaj to ride – while Harry has become a drill instructor! As for myself, I am a teacher once again. Though St John conscientiously takes his classes in the morning, his spirits fail him later in the day; and while Mr Kamil is very willing, his duties about the farm often keep him from the classroom. He tells me that since Jaya's death, the girls' education has been grievously lacking.

Our reverie is interrupted by Asha, Mr Kamil's wife, bringing a freshly bathed and fed Parvati to her father, whose immediate reanimation at the sight of his child has been the main source of my conviction that he can – that he must – be roused from his lethargy. It shocked me at first that St John should have chosen a heathen name for his daughter, but the child herself is enchanting. She is at that age when a little one first seems to become conscious of how much there is to learn. Her father carries her shoulder-high onto the veranda to enjoy the evening air, and she pats his thin, scarred cheek with her tiny brown hand: *Bapa, bapa. Ball* I say to her and *bird* – pointing at the crows that are gathering to roost in the trees, and I remind myself that I must talk to Mr Kamil about what toys might be purchased in Mysore to stimulate this keen little mind. When she spots Tug racing across the grass ahead of Edward and her half-brother, she wriggles with excitement, nearly throwing herself out of her father's arms. St John has his children, I think. Why should he despair?

The whole household (save the smallest infants) gathers every evening for a simple service of prayers and hymns. Tonight, St John resumes the office. 'You see?' I whisper to Mr Kamil. 'Already there is an improvement. Let us hear no more talk of dying.' Afterwards we all share a plain but ample supper. From my own early days at school I know that no child can be expected to thrive without adequate nourishment and I have told Cook that we must keep more chickens and introduce more milk and goat meat to the diet. Edward has introduced his own improvements too: the adults among us now sit on full-sized chairs.

**It is two months now,** and the fellow shows no sign of dying. In another few weeks, Sinjun-sahib will be back to his old self and they can leave him to it. His wife relishes being queen-bee of this small hive, even though she is not entirely reconciled to the irregularities of her cousin's *ménage*. He reminds her that their stay here cannot be allowed to last (there is Adèle to consider, the new house at Thornfield – and that cursed business in the Indies) yet for the moment he finds himself surprisingly contented. For the first time on this wild goose chase he can be useful himself. Kamil has been too much cowed by piety and deference, but he is a handy chap, and right now he is checking the list of building materials they are to purchase in Mysore. Rochester congratulates himself on his decision to spend his money while he is here rather than leaving it behind him, like a tip.

Jivaj has begged for a holiday. He travels in the cart with his uncle while Rochester and his man ride alongside. He will enjoy the lad's company less self-consciously without his wife's eyes upon him. The more he allows himself to be reminded of Ted, the more danger there is of his half-healed wounds bleeding afresh; but the risk is his alone, he will bear it and take the consequences. Jivaj has long since lost his shyness, but though the lad's incessant excitement reminds Rochester that children come with their own *longueurs*, not once does he wish that he had left the boy behind.

Letters from Ferndean and from Poona are awaiting him at the garrison headquarters, and an invitation. 'A private audience' reads Harry. 'With a native gentleman as far as I can make out.'

'The Dewan' Kamil explains. 'He is a good friend to Sinjin-sahib.'

'How the devil did he know I was here?'

'The Dewan knows everything' says Kamil.

Some kind of major-domo is waiting to welcome them. Rochester explains the boy: 'Sinjun-sahib's ward'. Jivaj's silence and the uncharacteristic caution of his movements are a far more eloquent response to their surroundings than Harry's awe-struck, useless exclamations: *Would you look at the size of that!* He gauges the opulence of the palace from its echoing spaces, the scented breezes, the constant tinkling of water. Tug's claws clatter across polished marble or patter across soft rugs.

'The paintings in this chamber are very fine' intones the major-domo in heavily accented English. 'Here, see the Lord Krishna, playing music with the gopis.' Rochester can make out very little. The entire surface of every room is embossed, gilded, stuccoed, carved, inlaid with mirrors, encrusted with gems. Like a thirsty traveller, he longs for a whitewashed wall. When they finally emerge into a vast, arcaded courtyard the impact of heat on plain stone is as reviving as a cold bath.

The dog, who has been as subdued as his master while they trudged through the state apartments, now pulls free and runs ahead, barking. With a yell, Harry lunges after him, Jivaj at his heels. From somewhere inside the walls comes a monstrous high-pitched bellow and a sudden eruption of shouts. He races across the cobbles, sliding and stumbling as he goes; sheer momentum keeps him from falling. Then Tug careers into his legs and brings him to the ground. The dog is whimpering with fear, licking his face in relief, cringing with panic and shock.

Harry runs up, panting. 'One of the brutes kicked out. I only just managed to grab him before he was flattened.' He hauls Tug to his feet and cuffs his muzzle. 'Stupid animal. Take on something your own size next time.'

Rochester brushes himself down. Then an icy hand grabs his heart. 'The boy. Where is the boy? Jivaj!' There is still shouting in the arcade. 'Here, Harry, hold the damn dog.'

The sudden gloom blots what little sight he has. He grabs at the wall to steady himself, cursing his fate, and strains to make sense of his surroundings. The smell of straw and dung tells him he is in a stable, while the reverberating echoes give him some idea of its vast extent. The line of tethered elephants stretches way beyond the limits of his vision but he can hear that they are trampling restlessly in their chains. Their shrill bellows reduce to a puny squeaking the yells of those who are trying to subdue them. All this he knows in an instant, but there is no sign of the boy. With a pounding heart he heads for where the shouting seems most frantic, ahead of him in the shadows. When a small figure jumps down from a straw-bale to grab his arm, relief floods through his tightened chest: he has forgotten what emotion can do to a man. The child ought to be rebuked for running into trouble, but he wants only to gather that small body to his breast, and when he discovers that Jivaj is quite oblivious to both the danger he has been in and the feelings he has unleashed, he is close to weeping.

The boy prattles cheerfully as he leads Rochester closer to the heart of the din. 'He is the Raja's elephant. The biggest!'

The size of the beast appalls him. Through his shoes he feels the ground shuddering as it sways from foot to foot while the light jingling of its chains suggests something far too dainty to restrain such power. When one of the mahouts urges the boy to come to its head what revisits him is a sensation half-forgotten: that mingled anxiety and pride when a child takes a venture. Familiar too is the judgement he makes as he automatically follows the boy, close enough to haul him out of harm's way, but far enough to protect his confidence. A glimpse of what must be the beast's massive curled trunk raised above the boy's head and he is for a moment once again the father of a son.


**Much brushing and sponging** is necessary before Harry is even half-way satisfied with his master's appearance that evening. He is wearing one of Harry's shirts.

'We came to purchase timber, not dine in a palace' he grumbles. 'And what about you? Are you respectable? You will be with me?' The thought of some ignorant, over-attentive native servant helping him with his food has him shrink.

'I won't leave your side, sir.' He makes a final adjustment to his master's cravat, stands back and holds up a lamp to check the effect.

'Good God, man? What are you wearing?' In the brighter light, Harry's silhouette is visible: a long coat, some kind of pantaloons.

'You have my only clean shirt, sir. I bought this in the bazaar.'

'Did you, by Jove. You will cut quite a dash at the new house, if we ever get home.'

A torchlit procession escorts him to meet the Dewan. Rochester, gloomily expecting that he will have to eat with his fingers, sitting cross-legged on the floor, is immediately relieved by the familiar gleam of candlelight on a polished table-top. His host's manner and his command of English are equally polished. The natural superiority he takes for granted in any encounter with a native will be hard to maintain in this man's company.

'So Mrs Rochester has found her cousin. That is most remarkable! Most English ladies would be too timid, I think.'

'Timid is a word unknown to my wife. And since we lost our children to an epidemic diphtheria, most risks have lost their power to hold us back.' He cannot understand why he is talking so freely to a stranger, almost as if he were drunk.

After the plain fare of Pisgah, the Dewan's subtle banquet sets his senses reeling. 'All cut up and no bones, sir' Harry whispers as another bowl is set before him. The suspicion that every dish has been prepared with his handicaps in mind unnerves him further; he would almost rather be wrestling with a beef chop.

'And how do you find my friend Rivers?' the Dewan inquires. 'Do you think he will live?'

'There is no doubt that he has taken his bereavement hard. But my wife is determined he will pull through. The new Bishop is much more favourably disposed to the work of missionaries.' But it is time he took the initiative. 'I would be interested to hear your view of the matter.'

'The British government must not expect that a handful of missionaries can overturn the traditions of centuries. Do not forget, Mr Rochester, that even though the teachings of Jesus were brought to these shores by one of His own disciples, few chose to hear them. Perhaps the very poor will be persuaded: outcastes – such as Mr Rivers' own servants. I have no objection to that. But what is to be feared is your rulers' intolerance: whilst few of them keep their religion's commandments, they expect our people to respect no laws but theirs. A missionary may think he is the instrument of his God; in fact, he is the tool of his government.'

By now he has drunk just enough of the Dewan's excellent wine to welcome an argument. 'So, you think St John Rivers is merely an unwitting agent?'

'No doubt we are all unwitting agents of some higher power. Rivers interests me. He chose his own path. Those that come after him – and they will come now like locusts – will have little more success, but they will allow your government to say *We have offered these people salvation. If they are too stupid to welcome such a gift, we will have to impose it. It is for their good, not ours.*'

'You think my government so cynical, then?'

'My dear Rochester – I have been a governor myself; I deal with men who are your government's representatives in all but name.'

He concedes the point. 'You say Rivers interests you.'

'Like many men who are known for their cunning, I am intrigued by a man who is too brave to know what he is doing. I like Rivers. I am pleased that he recovered from his injuries and found some happiness. But I have observed him as an experiment. I wanted to study how the introduction to our society of a previously unknown element would affect those who are touched by it.'

'The results I have seen include a well-run farm, employment for labourers and servants under a conscientious master, a sound education for children who would otherwise have been kept in ignorance – and life itself for infants who would otherwise have been left to die.' He is surprised to find himself speaking up for Rivers's achievement. His own words make Pisgah sound admirable, even enviable. 'As far as religion goes, he has had little impact, I suppose. The locals remain steadfastly heathen. But he is a good man. He has done good.'

'I will forgive you that word *heathen*. But do you not see what is happening? Landlords can raise their rent with impunity if Rivers will take in the children starved by their demands. You say that our people are too passive, but who is making them more so?'

His wife believes that Rivers himself is too passive, but he sets that side. 'So, what are your own people doing? You have the power, you have the wealth – .' As he hears his voice rising Harry touches his shoulder and hisses in his ear.

'Keep it calm, sir. The fellow by the door has a bloody big dagger.'

The Dewan must be sharp of hearing, for he laughs. 'You seem to be the only servant still awake. Pour more wine and join in. There are no despots here. Take a seat and tell us your views.'

He mutters 'Sit if you like, Harry. You've been standing long enough.' A silence falls.

Harry says 'We're all different, aren't we? I don't see why we can't live alongside each other, not interfering – mingling, like.'

'Ah! An idealist!' The Dewan laughs benignly. 'As a young man, I fought in a bitter war. When I first heard of Rivers, I thought here is a man who will seek to persuade, not to force. A man whose creed tells him to love his fellow creatures. Let us see if he can live comfortably among us.' He laughs again. 'I did not think it would take him so long to find a wife. A man cannot expect to sleep in a lonely bed – would you not agree, Mr Rochester?'

He grunts, not for the first time thinking that the Dewan understands him too well.

'There was a time when it seemed we might rub along together. Your people learned our languages, respected our laws and admired our poetry. They wore our comfortable clothes, ate our food and married our women – several women, some of them. They did not seek to change us. But they grew greedy. They brought armies. The war you will have heard of at Poona will not be the last.'

He interrupts. 'But Rivers has no army. Nor friends among his own kind.'

'Precisely: just one lone man, but his small actions have had their consequences – which will sink his good intentions. He cannot cope with what he has set in motion.'

That damned oriental fatalism, he thinks. Even in this worldly-wise man. 'Surely all that is needed is a little extra effort. I have the means and the knowledge to get the farm back on its feet. My wife has plans to save the school. The manager – a man you would consider an outcaste – has sound instincts. I am training him up to the task. We shall leave behind us a thriving concern.' He has today sent off Jane's letter for Alice Fisher, asking her to find more teachers for Pisgah.

'No doubt you will. But how long will it thrive? It will not be a native plant. The soil may not suit. You flourish by feeding an army which your countrymen have introduced.' The Dewan gets to his feet a little unsteadily. Harry rushes to support him. 'Thank you. I have enjoyed our conversation and I hope we may resume it soon. His highness will want to meet you, I am sure. He is a great admirer of your country. My own views are more clouded: old men naturally think that the best can only be behind them.'

Back in their own rooms, Harry helps him to prepare for the night. 'Plenty to think about there, sir. Another time we'll bring a better shirt.'

'If there is another time.' But he would like to return. He has an argument to win.

He is nearly asleep when a sound rouses him. 'Harry!' he calls. 'Harry!' There is no response. The heavy curtains which are all that guard his threshold are being cautiously parted – he hears the faint clink and hiss as the rings slide along the pole. 'Harry!' Then he sees a small light, and above it the pale oval of a golden face. Her perfume reaches his nostrils and he hears her bare feet suck the marble floor. The Dewan has sent him what he knows he needs.

Almost instantly his body repeats what his mind has already told him: he is sorely tempted. But very much to his regret another part of his brain intervenes. He will argue with the Dewan but he will not be obliged to him. He sends her away and spends a sleepless night regretting how old he has grown.

# CHAPTER 13

**Alice Fisher's latest letter** contains news of the widow of an American missionary who ran a school near Bijapur. Their government has no qualms about missions. She could be with us in weeks. I pass the letter outlining her history to St John, who gives it barely a glance.

'I have heard of her husband: I modelled my own school on what I knew of his.'

It troubles me that he still seems so indifferent to the future. Parvati is on his lap, and he can think of nothing else. But after we are gone – and I must be realistic – this American woman could in time become his daughter's governess. How can I rouse him from this fatal apathy?

Adèle's letter I read only to Edward when we are sitting on our broad terrace, where after dark we can benefit from a faint breath of air rising from the river. Fat, clumsy insects drone round our sole lamp. Her best news is that all being well (she means after Mrs Fisher's confinement) their party will travel to Cochin to meet the Bishop. From there to here is but a short journey across the mountains!

'When does Mrs Fisher expect to be confined? Surely she will not want to travel until her lying in is complete?'

I calculate the date. 'She will be eager to see her husband. Three months after the birth and I am sure she will be raring to set sail. How good it will be to show the Bishop all we have done here!' Time enough surely to hurry along St John's recovery and reignite his purpose. If I can show Bishop Fisher an example of how Christian faith and works have flourished here despite the hostility of his misguided predecessor, then perhaps I have not lived in vain. And yet instead of comfort, this thought stirs the pain that months of daily work have only dimmed. To God, perhaps, my children were a fair price to pay for this small advance in his purpose. To me – I am glad when Edward's voice cuts off the torrent of my thoughts.

'Adèle will find us very dull when she comes.'

I turn to the next portion of her letter, which seems at first to consist of nothing more than ridings out, suppers and balls and new frocks, so that we are both silenced for a while after I have finished. 'Perhaps there are some hints that she finds the incessant attention somewhat tiring?'

'And has the incessant attention been reported to Colonel Meikle? Such puppies deserve a hiding.'

'She would not wish her hosts to think she does not appreciate their hospitality. But listen. There have been good effects. She writes that she has been glad to seek relief in books and study. *Dear Alice has drawn my attention to Miss Wollstonecraft's observation that soldiers are no better than the very idlest of our sex, being particularly attentive to their persons, fond of dancing, crowded rooms, adventures and gallantry.*'

Edward pushes himself out of his low seat and strides to the rail. I see it trembling slightly in the power of his grip. The heat is enough to inflame even the mildest temper and though it is too dark to see his expression, I know that frown. 'Edward! Dearest! Can you not hear that she is exasperated with the whole sex? If she was ever inclined to fancy a scarlet coat, Alice has rather cunningly brought her to her senses. A little longer in the company of noodles will only help her to value the sound principles that govern our lives here.'

'She must leave at once. It was folly to let her stay. That teacher at Bijapur would be a reliable escort.'

'Edward, dearest! Think. What ingratitude to Alice, that we should snatch away her companion at the very moment of her confinement! Be patient. The time will pass quickly enough – and it will only make Adèle more glad to escape in due course.'

'I do not agree. A baby on the scene will rid her of her wits. All women are the same at such a time. She will think of nothing but how she must have one of her own – and the first villain that spots his opportunity will carry her off.'

His words are unconsidered. He does not mean to stir the pain I try to suppress. 'If that is the case, there are babies enough here to dote upon.'

'And another garrison but a day's ride distant!'

'Mysore's royal court is thoroughly enlightened – or so you tell me.' Edward's visits there have done much to reconcile him to the length of our stay – though it is not so enlightened that it extends its invitations to a woman. We have seemed recently to be so much more comfortable with one another but now we are on the verge of quarrelling. Before I can fully calm my feelings, a sudden stirring in the shadows alerts me. It is Mrs O'Reilly.

She feigns a pretty confusion. 'O sarr! O madam. What was I thinking? This was my room once, until you came. Old habits, you know! I must have been distracted.'


**Hardly a week passes without him taking to the road**, to deliver and pick up mail, to order more building materials, supplies for the class-room, crates of chickens, wine and cigars – and books from the Dewan's library. English gold goes a long way here and seldom has Rochester been more aware of the benefits of a substantial income. Several cartloads of new furniture and decent linens have trundled up the lane; a range has been installed in the kitchen. Another bullock has been purchased to cope with the loads. At first he spends gingerly on comforts, thinking that his wife may think it unsuitable to introduce any luxury to a mission, but soon she is adding to his lists – aprons, toys, bees-wax and scrubbing-brushes. Women and their nests. They will fly this nest soon, but he is glad to see these instincts reviving. It bodes well for the new Thornfield. A handsomely carved chair with an ingenious contraption to hoist his feet is installed to face the sunset; add a good cigar to keep off the insects and an idle man can be very content.

Not that he is idle for many hours of the day. New dormitories have been built and quarters for the new teachers are taking shape. He has encouraged Kamil's investment in a few additional acres, and there neem trees have been planted, thorny hedges installed and the first new crops sown. Then another parcel of land is for sale, bordering the Pisgah fields up-river, and he is keen to buy. Kamil says the price is too high. If Rochester buys too readily, others will want to sell.

'And what is wrong with that? We might own the whole valley in due course.'

After a lull, first one, then another and within weeks a third new-born is found at their gates. Perhaps the local population at first suspected that the new English régime would be less accommodating, but once one baby is admitted, further arrivals are inevitable. Harry is dispatched to buy weapons and train a nightly patrol. Of course, he does not intend that anyone should be shot; but they need to be warned. English bounty has limits.

Dutifully, he tries at first to consult Rivers on every decision, but the missionary declares himself glad to leave material concerns to others. So Rochester finds himself taking charge. His handicaps have curbed for too long those automatic priorities which are due to a man such as himself, and there is considerable satisfaction in being so readily acknowledged as the effective master of Pisgah. Kamil may grumble a little, for form's sake, but the man needs to understand that it is not his place to make the decisions which Rivers has abandoned. If the missionary does not pull himself together, it may be necessary to appoint a manager to take over when he and his wife leave – as they must in due course. Already Alice Fisher at Poona has identified a likely candidate – a capable fellow, looking for an opening, who does not want to return to England after his retirement from the army because he is married to a native woman. When he writes to Colonel Meikle – and he must ask him to dress down the hotheads who have plagued his daughter – he will ask him to vouch for the man's good character and the native wife's honesty.

His own wife continues to argue that a girl who may have been annoyed by too much attention at Poona, will certainly be bored by too little at Pisgah. He himself concedes that providing amusements for Adèle would only delay the completion of their task. He suspects that Jane does not relish the thought of introducing such a fashionable young lady to her high-minded cousin. His own efforts to warm to the man have been in vain and he has long since reverted to mere courtesy in their occasional dealings. For the life of him he can detect no trace of the ardent spirit she once found so compelling. Increasingly he asks himself whether it is not only his health and enthusiasm that she is striving to restore, but the paragon she admired in her youth. He suspects that were some accident to befall himself (and this heat alone might carry a man off in a trice) she would stay and marry the fellow.

He eavesdrops shamelessly on their nightly conversations, claiming – quite justifiably – that the stretch of veranda close to St John's quarters is the coolest spot at that hour of day. Others have long since discovered the same. Old Poonam lies prone, with her arms flung above her head, while the idiot boy rubs her feet. Mrs O'Reilly sprawls in a low chair. Perhaps she thinks he cannot make out that her legs are spread flagrantly wide, and her skirts hoisted almost to her knees.

What his wife is too well-mannered ever to raise in these sessions, is the question which he knows obsesses her: whether her cousin and his daughter's mother were ever properly married. It matters not a jot to him, nor should it to any person of sense, but he has to acknowledge that his own history has made her sensitive to a question which she is too much of a lady to ask outright. Instead, he hears her report on the day's activities in nursery and classroom. One of the infants is especially fractious; maybe no more than teething. She has ordered new books from Calcutta for the older girls because nothing that is suitable can be obtained in Mysore. Rochester idly wonders what will happen to this motley batch of youngsters, reared in a language none of them was born to, drilled in what will make them useful to their foreign masters and fed a drab religion. St John's replies are more difficult to make out, but he can hear that they are brief. Just as he has let the management of his land fall to his cousin's husband, so he has allowed the conduct of his school to be taken over by his cousin herself.

Her reports completed, Jane asks after the children's spiritual welfare and perhaps finds a hint of something closer to enthusiasm in St John's replies, but really the only unmistakeable warmth he ever hears from the man is addressed to his baby daughter. Rochester smiles as he hears his wife attempting to teach her cousin the sweet and foolish language that parents use to address their infant offspring, but St John is too halting, too austere. He can recite the psalms to his baby daughter, but he cannot bring himself to call her petal... butterfly...chicken. The names they called baby Helen. In another life.

He pushes the little ghost away. Really, during this one hour every evening his wife and the missionary might as well be married already. If he saddled up and rode away tonight for Poona, she would hardly miss him. If he cannot be a husband, he can still be a father – Adèle squealing with surprise and delight as he rides into the cantonment, flinging herself into his arms, her lithe young body pressed against his dusty, battered limbs. Is this impossible?

Of course it is. Though Jane might dream of staying here forever, she is married to himself: to remain as the unchaperoned companion to a widower would be scandalous – especially if she manages to restore him to health. The thought of what the local gossips would make of this has him chuckling – though what constitutes a scandal when there is not a single Englishwoman within a day's ride is a puzzle. It is too hot for coherent thought, and hours of supervising the carpenters has left him smugly weary, but the thought of a scandal worms under his skin. God knows, he has stirred enough gossip in his time – enjoyed the notoriety. But there would be no pleasure in the gossip that would greet him in Poona, if he were to arrive there without his wife. From where he is now, at Pisgah, St John's transgressions look like nothing more than the familiar story of a lonely man and a handy maidservant, but at Poona the tale will have become more richly coloured – the houri and the renegade priest. To leave his wife in the company of a libidinous rebel – even for the short time it would take to fetch his daughter – would have his own reputation instantly unmanned. No, it is impossible. He must stay until Adèle arrives with the Bishop and his lady. Then they can leave.

Until that time, he will continue his now regular rides with Harry to Mysore for a fine meal and an evening's conversation with the Dewan, always returning with a fresh hoard of books and periodicals. The Prince often joins them – an earnest, under-occupied young widower whose extravagant admiration for everything British includes a wish to see the Pisgah school's benefits more widely extended.

'Nothing could bring greater advantage to the sons of our court officials than to receive a sound British education' he says.

Rochester declines to mention some aspects of his own British education that the Prince might not find so admirable. 'Don't forget, your highness, that Rivers is a missionary. Conversion is his main purpose. I doubt that he would be willing to abandon the elements of religious instruction.'

'All faiths are in the end one' the Prince declares blithely.


**How very narrow is the distance** between intrusion and concern, and how difficult it is to judge! That my cousin, like my husband, has been scarred by fire, seems so palpably a hint of the Divine plan that there must be more to learn. St John knows of course how Edward was burned. He heard the news before he left for India.

'The kitchen' he says when I ask him outright. 'Such accidents are regrettably common here.'

Despite several attempts, I cannot induce him to say more. Though I suspect that – like Edward – his scars are a consequence of some heroic act, my curiosity is obliged to console itself with admiration for his reticence. It cannot be that Jaya died of the same fire. Her death preceded our arrival by only a few weeks; his scars are older. Nor did she die in childbirth; Parvati was trying her first words when we arrived. But St John will say nothing of the manner of her death, and neither will Mr Kamil, when I at length bring myself to enquire. 'Was it the cholera?'

Is he nodding, or shaking his head? At any rate, he is silent.

'Like your master, my husband has been terribly burned, but we had the advantage of the finest doctors in England. I am surprised that my cousin was able to recover, in so remote a place as this.'

Mr Kamil does not often look at me directly, but for once he addresses me full on. 'The Dewan sent the Prince's own physician – a man who has been *haj* many times –'

'A mussulman?' I shudder to think of what treatments St John may have suffered. 'Could you not have sent to Fort St George?' Such lack of initiative! At Madras there would surely be a physician to the Company, possessed of all the latest science, like the doctor in Bombay who treated Adèle.

He looks away. 'Sinjunsahib does not wish for any contact with the people there.'

'And was the *hakeem* consulted when Jaya fell sick?'

Now he looks sullen. 'Sinjunsahib does not care to talk about her death.' He pauses for a long while and I am about to prompt him when he looks at me again. 'It took only a day.'

A few days later, one of the babies is sickly. I find Mrs O'Reilly preparing a mustard poultice. 'If that doesn't work, a dose of Godfrey's Cordial should do the trick.' She winks at me. 'Himself does not approve of the laudanum for little'uns, but we don't like to lose 'em, do we?'

'No, indeed.' I have been told that Mrs O'Reilly's own infant died at birth, but I do not care for her attempts to draw me out. 'Tell me, how many of the infants that are brought to Pisgah survive?'

'More than would if they stayed with their own kind, I reckon. But there's a fair number of little crosses in the graveyard.'

'Did the recent cholera reach you here?'

She gives me a sharp enquiring glance, then swiftly crosses herself.

'Lord a' mercy. Imagine.' She sweeps her hand over the cots and shudders, and I imagine the contagion, bounding from cot to cot, like fire across a drought-parched heath. She wipes the infant's forehead with a wrung-out cloth, then sinks into a chair without asking my permission, wipes her own face with the same cloth and tosses it into a nearby basin full of water. Gathering a corner of her apron, she fans her face. 'It come close, mind. Very close. Many died at Madras.'

I sense that there is more to tell – and that she wants me to ask. Though I say nothing, I draw up a stool and put the back of my hand to the child's cheek, dry and as hot as the newspaper we might use to draw a fire up the chimney in England.

Mrs O'Reilly shakes her head. 'The cholera, that's different.' She thinks I am too delicate to hear it described.

'You have seen it?'

She looks full upon me. 'No. But something like's what carried her off. His missus. He wouldn't let no-one nurse her.'

'But surely it cannot travel through the air. Did any stranger come here, from Madras?' I now know there is some difference between the truth and the the Archdeacon's report. In her artless fashion, Mrs O'Reilly may shed more light.

'The soldiers came. Them that killed the snake. And a man –'

I cut her off. 'Soldiers? To kill a snake?'

'The one she gave milk to. Like it was a pet.'

*She persisted in her heathen practices.* I remember Bishop Fisher, reading the report – and I remember, back in England, staring horrified at images of heathen temples where drugged serpents writhed among the naked feet of their devotees. Was such the woman whom my cousin calls wife?

Mrs O'Reilly must have glimpsed my thoughts because she chortles, and leaning over she pats my hand. 'Lor, don't take on so! In most respects she was a decent Christian woman, none more so! And many much less.' She is becoming uncomfortably confiding. 'But they never quite understand, do they? There's always something not quite the thing.'

I cannot allow her to talk like this, but neither can I let this rest. Diana and Mary will not be persuaded by a story half-discovered. I must try to find another way of looking into my cousin's heart.

**The clouds build up under cover of darkness,** so that the first sign of what is to come is a sudden, violent wind that shakes their bed-chamber, followed moments later by a fusillade of hailstones. His wife is already dressing. 'The children! They will be terrified! I must go to them.'

Thunder cracks like great rocks splitting. Muddled by the tumult, he drags on his breeches and follows her into the storm. The lightning is so intense and continuous that he is able to see aspects of his surroundings which are normally invisible to him – how small and frail their clearing is amidst the mountains and the wind-lashed trees. But although some of the littlest ones are whimpering, those children old enough to understand how the seasons turn are greeting the storm like a long-awaited treat. He can make out Jivaj, arms outstretched, blissfully embracing the stream of water that cascades over him from the roof. Sodden girls are squealing with delight as they push each other on the swings that hang from the branches of the three great trees.

Rochester lowers himself to the veranda steps and lets the rain beat down on his unprotected head. The whole firmament shudders as flash after flash rips through the night. The din pounds all thought to smithereens until even the most exuberant children are subdued. He peers into the shadows, looking for his boy among the squatting figures now huddled along the veranda – and cannot find him.

'Jivaj! Jivaj!' he shouts – but the thunder swallows his call. When he tries to haul himself to his feet, the weight of his drenched garments drags like a new infirmity. Then a sudden clumsy blow to the back of his knees fells him, and he sprawls helplessly across the rain-slicked planks. A warm tongue lollops his cheek, a snout nuzzles at his throat: a soaked and frantic Tug is upon him. With an oath, he manages to right himself. He grabs the dog by the scruff of its neck and hauls him close. The poor beast's convulsions knock against his own ribs.

Jivaj is squatting beside them, panting. 'He was frightened.'

It is shame that chills him. He has let a child see to his dog. 'And the horses?'

'Harry is with them. He said, take the dog.'

He wants to pull the boy to his other side and holds out his arm. But he has misjudged. The lad is excited; it would be babyish, to be comforted. He struggles to get up, needing the boy's shoulder to lean on. 'Look after Tug for me, there's a good fellow. I must find –' He nearly says *your mother*.

But their rooms are empty and stuffier than before. As he wrestles to be rid of his sodden nightshirt, he berates himself. The affection of an eager lad, a good dog, the mild intellectual stimulation provided by the Dewan and his Prince, all these, plus a modicum of honest toil and bestowing his wisdom on Kamil – these are the consolations of a pensioner. It shocks him to think how long it is since he wanted more than sleep from his bed. Naked now, he kicks his soaked clothes aside and towels his hair. Outside, lightning turns the still drumming deluge into an impenetrable white curtain, which traps the room's sweltering air. He is as wet with sweat as with rain. Even if he could find dry garments, they would be soused as he pulled them on. He stares into the storm. A flash – a flare – a shuddering blast of light deprives him for long moments of what sight he has, and as he stands in utter darkness the thunder shakes him like an engine that must grind his very bones. But as the vestiges of his sight return, the fear that he acknowledges is not of the storm, or of death – but of failure. What he has glimpsed in that blackness is vacant wastes of inconclusion, of nothing resolved, of a life merely sloping into oblivion. With the stump of his arm he rubs furiously at the insect bites that ring his waist.

**Among the playthings** I have asked Edward to bring back from Mysore is a paint box – not exclusively for the children's benefit, I must confess. Like many women, I neglected my so-called accomplishments once I was married, though with better excuses than most, because to paint when my husband's sight was too poor either to appreciate or to correct my work would be a distressing reminder of his loss. I hardly sketched my children lest it caused him pain. Instead I have tried my best to paint the world for him in words. But now for some weeks I have been preparing my small talent to draw St John out of his shell.

At first I looked to baby Parvati for some trace of her father as he used to be. Resemblances in a child so young are always fleeting. Both my little girls had the look of their father, though I could hardly say how Helen's baby features matched his craggy and grizzled countenance. Parvati is so animated when she is awake that she seems to change by the hour, so I try to capture her while she sleeps. There is nothing adamantine in her rounded lips and dimpled cheeks, but perhaps in her nose and the angle of her jaw there is something of the youthful St John. Or perhaps I see only what I wish had not been lost. What is more certain is the strong likeness between Mr Kamil and the boy Jivaj; the child is after all his sister's son. And gradually I come to see the same features in Parvati.

There is a tenderness in sketching that binds the artist to the subject. As I copy the fan of her eyelashes and the pout of her lip the plain wooden room dissolves, the scent of rain-scalded dust fades and the relentless chorus of night's insects dims. The babe and I are almost as alone together as if she were at my breast, and though when I bend over her, I could say that I was gauging the precise angles of her nose, I find myself inhaling the sweet mealy fragrance of her scalp.

I show St John my sketches of his daughter. 'I think Diana and Mary will see their brother in her.'

'As I was, perhaps; not as I am now. But it is her mother I see in her.'

'Parvati resembles her half-brother too. And Mr Kamil. Were he and his sister alike?'

'I did not see it before her death – now I can see her in both.' He pauses for a moment. 'But then I see her in everything. In the air – in water – in the soil.'

He has never spoken so freely before, but I hold back and continue with my experiment. Jivaj is more difficult to capture because he will not stand still, but I manage a reasonable likeness of him perched on Edward's horse, and now I have a paint box, I can add colour to my outlines. He looks like a little soldier.

'And this too you will send to Diana and Mary?'

'I think they will be put in mind of their own boy, George – riding our Ted's pony. Though perhaps he has grown too big for it by now.' As I coax his feelings into the open, I find myself releasing some of my own.

'I mean to adopt the boy' he says. 'In all that matters he is as much my child as Parvati. But I have neglected the formal business.'

'But that can easily be arranged' I cry – too eagerly, though I blunder on. 'Mr Rochester can arrange for a notary next time he goes to Mysore.' Too late, I bite my lip as I see his face cloud over. I am so caught up in everything that needs to be done that I am inclined to forget that there is a dangerous border, dividing what is useful from interference.

Within a day of the storm, we are dry again. In two, the rain is merely a memory. For a while I content myself with sketching the buildings and the surrounding countryside. Until recently I have been too busy to notice the beauty of this place, but now that a steady routine has been established, I have a little leisure for the broad river with its sandbanks, the vast and mysterious forest, the patchwork of irregular fields among the foothills and the sublime blue pinnacles soaring above. Though my skills are slight, the steady concentration of my eye seems to slow my heart and brain, and an exquisite peace steals over me when I paint the thistledown mist that lingers among the upper branches of the great trees in the morning, and the evening sunlight that streaks the lofty crags with fire.

My Indian sketches grows as voluminous as the famous Mrs Porter's: Poonam with a brown baby on her lap; Mrs O'Reilly rocking a crib with her foot; the girls bent over their slates and the lads at their drill with Harry – even Bhanu with his rattle. I take particular care over a portrait of Mr Kamil with his wife and their toddler. Asha is too shy to enjoy being looked at for long, though she likes how well I capture her bangles and the jewel she wears in her nose. But she is not my main interest. Her husband's features I accentuate a little where they seem most to resemble Jaya's children and as I work, I detect more likenesses in their little boy as well – he and Parvati are cousins. With my heart in my mouth, I show the family group to St John. 'It is a good likeness' is all he says. 'You have captured Kamil's modesty as well as his competence.'

So, I am on the right tracks! At night, despite the heat, I gather a dozen lamps around me and begin my work in earnest. On a sheet of fine card-board I draw a careful outline of a woman's face. Her eyes, her chin, her breadth of brow and her hairline are all features that my living sitters have in common. Her hair I can guess – and besides, what man ever notices how a woman's hair is dressed? Her nose I model on Jivaj: Parvati's is not yet fully formed, Kamil's too masculine. I take his brows too, and decide that I can obscure the unknown line of my subject's jaw with a fold of her veil. It is the work of several evenings before I feel able to shade off her drapery, add a final touch of carmine to her lip and deepen the shadow of her lash. But I have made her too pale. Fearful of spoiling my efforts, I carefully load my brush. Like her brother, she must have had the dark skin of the South, not the paler hue that her children have inherited from their English fathers. I have not forgotten Mrs O'Reilly's mention of the snake, but any hint of the heathen in my portrait would be fatal to my enterprise. I want to break down St John's guard.

But first I must test whether I have captured her likeness. Mr Kamil and Asha are too ready to flatter me; Jivaj might be distressed and Poonam's old eyes are not up to the task.

'That's her alright' says Mrs O'Reilly. 'When she was younger.'

'You knew her before she was married to my cousin?' Does my voice catch on that word *married*?

'She was well known at Fort St George.'

There is an emphasis here that I do not like but I present St John with my handiwork at our usual quiet hour. He gazes at it in silence for so long that I begin to fear I have offended him.

'Forgive me' I say at last. 'I know too well how hard it is to speak of those we have lost. But for your sisters' sake as well as mine, can you not tell me a little about her?'

The burns on his face gleam like polished marble, but at last a faint smile softens his stony expression. Then a tear drops on the edge of the image and the paint begins to dissolve. He blots it with a thumb wrapped in a fold of his kurta. 'It would be a pity to spoil your efforts, Jane.'

He takes the portrait closer to the light and stares at it for what seems an age. When at last he turns, his face is suffused with the passionate animation that I remember so well from long ago and have never once seen here. 'You have tricked me again, Jane Eyre. Do you not remember how I spilled the secrets of my heart to you in your cottage at Morton, when you showed me the picture of the woman I loved then?'

I move to his side and see in the portrait I have painted the faint ghost of another woman: the glossy hair, the blooming cheek, the bright, eager lips of Rosamond Oliver. Miss Oliver's skin was never so brown, nor her eyes so dark – and yet there she is.

He sets the square of card aside. 'You have made her too gorgeous, Jane. Jaya was a poor woman, who had known much hardship and sorrow.'

Was she plain, like me? 'Her children are exquisite.'

'I do not mean to say she was not comely, but you have painted a lady. Jaya was wise and thoughtful, but she was not educated.'

Now that I have burst the seal on his soul, I do not want the spring to dry up. 'I should like to have known her.'

'There was much about her that I did not know myself. She expressed herself in her actions, not in words.' He shakes his head wryly. 'You would not have found much to talk about, Jane.'

'O, come now! Women will always find common ground. She spoke some English, I suppose?' He pushes back his chair and I fear I have annoyed him. 'I mean that I hope we could have been friends.'

'You have pieced together her physical likeness, Jane. But what she was to me I will not – cannot – tell you. She was my wife, the mother of my child. When I asked – no, demanded' (and he smiles slightly) 'that you would marry me, all those years ago, I did not know what love for a fellow creature could be.' A hand on my shoulder prevents me from breaking away. 'Hear me, Jane. I speak as one whose joy would know no bounds if but the edge of his beloved's shadow crossed his path for an instant. But only my own ending will re-unite us.'

Why is it that I feel not just rejected, but corrected, like a thoughtless child? Again, I turn to leave, but he calls me back. 'Do not think I have failed to appreciate all that you are doing here, Jane. You and your husband. I believed him to be a reprobate. Here he has been an instrument of God.'

I cannot help it. I laugh.

St John smiles himself. 'Huh! Did I not tell you, years ago, that you were born to do God's work?' He is holding out my painting. 'Take this home with you. It will be an ornament to your portfolio. Here, damp and insects will devour it.'

Reluctantly, I accept the slip of card. If I were to give it a name, it would be *Portrait of an Unknown Indian Woman*.

**The heat begins to build again.** Every day dawns with a sickly yellow light. Towards noon the air boils with sulphur-streams, then rises beyond the mountains in dense, livid heaps which rumble and threaten, but refuse to release the relief that everyone longs for. Heat clamps itself greedily across the landscape and not even darkness brings any respite.

He throws off his sodden sheet and whistles for Tug. The poor brute is suffering as much as he is, but needs exercise. He would head for the river-bank in the hope of a breeze, but Harry has reported that a tiger made a kill there last night, and though the vultures have disappeared beyond the purple clouds, there are likely to be jackals scrapping over the remains. If the dog's mood is like his own, he will want to join in – and the wild beasts will turn on him. So they must keep to the compound where not a breath of wind is stirring.

Within moments Tug is fussing over a hidden figure. 'Get off, you daft bugger. It's too hot for your slobbery kisses.' Dolores O'Reilly is taking the air. She smells pleasantly damp. ''Tis fortunate the night's dark and you're half blind, sarr. I'm down to me shift.'

'Are you, indeed.' He is down to his nightshirt himself.

'If you pour a little water over yourself, like this' – he hears water dribbling – 'it cools you down nicely, for a moment or two. Would you like me to do you, sarr?'

Would he? 'I fear it would put the dog in a frenzy. He misses his swim.' He should move on, but he stays – and hears the slap of damp drapery on soft flesh.

'Ah – that's better. Do you not feel the heat sir?'

He does. 'More rains must come soon.'

She gives a little moan. 'Oh, to be up among those mountain-tops! Or on a ship at sea.' Suddenly, she is very close; he can smell her hair – like a wet dog, or a fox: disturbing. 'For the love of God, when you go, take me with you, sir. I can't stand it here a moment longer.'

He is in no doubt about how she would repay him. 'Are you not happy here? Mr Rivers is a fair employer, I think.'

She leans even closer, to whisper in his ear. 'I've had my fill of brown faces and heathen ways. This is no place for a good Christian woman.'

*Good?* He laughs. 'But you are among good Christians here.'

She laughs herself, and slaps the wet fabric that drapes her. He hears her flesh wobble. 'Too good. You know what I mean.'

He does. A shimmer of distant lightning shows him her head thrown back, the droplets in her unbound hair and the column of water she is pouring inside her shift. A thumb is hooking the fabric free of the channel between her ample breasts. She is a little too buxom, a little too squat, but a woman so ready to give her own body pleasure would surely be generous and skilful with another. A trickle of water crosses the planks between them and touches his bare foot.

'Shall I do you, sarr?' It's a whisper now. He takes a step deeper into the shadows and she follows. 'Bend your neck, sarr.'

She holds the front of his head steady while she slowly pours a ladle of water over the back of his neck. It runs down his spine, between his shoulder blades, and parts at his waist. The fabric of his night-shirt absorbs most, so that only the smallest trickle crosses his haunch and follows the line of his belly down to his groin. It is enough. This is no virgin, like Emily. Mrs O'Reilly is a woman who knows what she is doing. And if her price is a passage to England, why not? He allows her to empty a second ladle over his shoulders – time enough for thought to become the enemy of impulse. How would he explain to his wife why they should carry a children's nursemaid to England? Well, he will simply give the woman the cash she needs to buy her own passage.

But from across the compound the thin wail of a fractious baby brings him to his senses. He and Mrs O'Reilly will not be the only ones awake tonight.

'Thank you' he says courteously, holding out his hand for the ladle. 'I will fend for myself, now. It is a useful trick, but the water is stored here in case of fire. It shouldn't be wasted.' It is petty, to rebuke her with such misplaced self-righteousness, but he suddenly has no taste for squalor.

Or perhaps it is just too hot. Yet he remembers Jamaica, and Bertha − and the sweaty delirium before the madness.


**The Bishop's wife is safely delivered of a daughter.** The news reaches us with remarkable swiftness, coming not from Alice herself or Adèle, but from the Dewan at Mysore. Edward says that where there are soldiers, there will be spies who travel fast, but beyond my anxieties for the perils which my dear friend has endured, I am faintly troubled that an Indian ruler should make this news his business. It is a week later that a fuller account reaches us from Adèle. It seems that Alice's pangs came early and sudden, while the two ladies had driven into the mountains to seek some relief from the scorching heat of the cantonment. Adèle dispatched the groom to fetch help, but the event moved too speedily for him to return with assistance before the child was born. Edward falls silent when I read this passage, and it is some time before I feel able to resume her narrative. The child is thriving, but Alice herself succumbed to a fever, and could bear no one but Adèle and Emily to attend to her most private needs. I think of the girl who in the throes of her own fever, fretted that her golden shoes were lost. But the letter ends happily: the fever abated, the child is to be called after me, and Adèle is her godmother.

We do not speak of what she has written. It is a few days before Edward refers to it. 'I suppose we cannot expect the party from Poona to come south until Mrs Fisher is fully recovered and the monsoon is done with: there will be storms at sea and the mountains will be dangerous.' I think I nod. Though the rains hold off, they must come, and the end will then be in sight. And since we must leave, I must consider what is ahead. For weeks now the satisfaction of my work here has been rubbing sorely against the bargain we struck − that once we had discovered St John's fate, we would set sail for the Indies, to settle Edward's inheritance there before returning to the new house. Countless regrets will echo my footsteps on its polished floors, rebuking me for the work I have abandoned here.

But St John expects us to leave, and I do not think that my husband has for one moment thought we might stay. That has been my dream, a secret that I have hardly revealed to myself. Here I can be useful; and if either ambition or necessity demand it, I have the aptitude, the means and the connections to achieve more. Here are children who need the loving care that I have still to give. Here is nature at her most glorious and bountiful. My breathing quickens as I succumb to a fantasy I have already forbidden myself, of a life in this place. Here, here, the restlessness that is in my nature might be assuaged. The dangers I can easily dismiss – wild beasts and intemperate weather are nothing to a woman who has lost her children. I force myself to consider what I should regret: Diana and Mary, for sure – but here is no shortage of objects for my love. My elegance and ease? Not a jot.

How easily hard practicalities can be resolved when our plans are only day-dreams. I tell myself that the pleasures my husband has found at Pisgah are enough to make him as contented here as I could be: the Dewan's friendship, the exercise of his tutelary influence, the cigar he relishes every evening as we look back at the day's tasks completed. But in truth I am not convinced. There is a restlessness in his nature too. How much longer can it be before impatience calls him home? And what of Adèle? He will want her settled.

My consolation must be the improvements I have left behind me.

**Still the rains do not come.** Each night the thick, still air is riven with shrieks from the dwindling river. Leopards and tigers have become so bold that the children cannot be allowed outside the compound.

Each night he prowls the veranda, as restless as a wild animal himself. Often, he encounters Mrs O'Reilly, though her presence is seldom more than a shift in the shadows or the rattle of a fan. Tonight, she speaks. 'Surely the rain must come tonight – do you not think so, sarr?'

The rain, or something else. Would her ample body give as much relief as a drenching? Lightning flickers constantly among the mountain peaks. 'It must come soon' he mutters, and calls his dog.

'Goodnight sarr' she calls softly. Then 'Down boy! Down!'

He suspects that she often slips the dog a tidbit, under the table, to make a friend. 'Tug! Heel!'

'Let me fill his bowl, sarr. The poor creature must be dreadful parched.' Water slops; Tug laps.

There is no moving on until the dog has finished. 'Thank you' he says, then nothing. Crickets screech; thunder growls and grumbles, a long way off,

'Would you care for a drink yourself?' – she is moving towards him – 'Sarr?'

Then he hears the tread of another figure approaching.

'Is something the matter, Mrs O'Reilly? Are the children restless?' It is Rivers.

'Just taking a breath of air, sarr – if you can call it air.' She disappears into the shadows.

'Can't sleep?' On previous nights the only indication that Rivers might be awake has been a small light in his study; of the man himself, not a sign.

'I am glad to have found you. There are matters I am anxious to discuss before you leave.'

'But that is not to be for some weeks – unless you have reason to wish us gone?' Suddenly a chance to be on the move refreshes him like a dash of cool water.

Rivers ignores him and leads the way to his quarters. Tug flops in the doorway.

'Please sit – and continue to smoke your cigar. It helps to keep off the insects.' There is the merest trace of warmth in his voice – as much as Rochester has ever heard from him. 'I have documents that I want to give into your keeping. They will, I am aware, be illegible to you, so I must ask you to trust my account of their contents.'

'Of course.'

'One is a record of my marriage. Yes, I am conscious that its legality is of concern to Jane; she will want to reassure my sisters. For myself, I am utterly certain of its moral validity. But for the world, here is a record which may be entered into the parish register at Morton. The ceremony may have been irregular, but Kamil has made a thorough study of the matter, and he believes that it was as sound as any wedding conducted at sea. It is not essential that the officiant be an ordained priest.'

'That is of no concern to me – but yes, Jane will be reassured.' He pauses. 'Why must these matters be settled at this moment?' St John ignores his question. 'Mrs Fisher and my daughter will not leave

Poona until the monsoon here is over – and no-one needs to be reminded that it has not yet started.' Surely the heat alone is enough to account for their present inaction? 'The plan – which is long agreed – is that the Bishop will meet them in Cochin, where the welcome is likely to be prolonged. The Cochin court will put out all its flags and I gather from the Dewan that our own prince will be joining them with an impressive number of elephants. Only after that will they turn their faces towards the mountains – and us.'

St John continues as if he has not spoken. 'Over the last months, your wife's many services to my small establishment have been of great benefit. And you have been most generous in meeting our material requirements. Because of you, Pisgah has some hope of a future. I believe you were both sent here by Our Lord, to do His work on earth.'

Such familiarity with the deity's intentions makes Rochester uneasy. What sent him here was his wife's headstrong nature and the need to distract her from their grief. Yet St John's formality warns him not to be frivolous. And then it comes.

'I would like you to witness the terms of my will. Kamil will be my heir. I am leaving Pisgah in its entirety to him. It was your wife's money that enabled me to settle here originally, so naturally I would prefer to have your consent – though my mind will not be changed if you withhold it – and I would like you to act as my executor.'

His first reaction is relief. If Jane had been the heir, she would want to be here when the time came, to take charge of Pisgah herself. Possibly forever. Then other thoughts rush in. Jane *should* be the heir – not because of her money but because it cannot be wise to give command of the enterprise to a native. Yet why should he care? All this is for the future. They will be long gone. He peers through the lamp's meagre, smoky light, wishing he could better make out St John's looks. The man is not dying – Jane assures him on this – or likely to die soon. His voice sounds steady enough. Then another thought strikes him. 'But your children! Your daughter – and Jivaj! Kamil may be an excellent fellow, but to leave your son and daughter unprovided for – good God, man, are you mad?'

'I believe I am of sound mind. Kamil is more kin to Jivaj than I am; Parvati is his sister's son. I have complete trust in him.'

'But Kamil has a son of his own! And if my wife is not mistaken, another child on the way! If Pisgah flourishes, then no doubt he will be generous. But if it founders, what will happen to your children? You are a fool, Rivers. No, you must make specific provisions for their

welfare before I can put my name to your proposals.' The stifling air
of the room remains undisturbed, as if his anger is making no impact.
He steadies himself then speaks again. 'You may be struck down at
any moment, or you may have years left in you yet, but whether we
are still here or long gone, when you die your children must come to
us — to Thornfield. I will leave here the means specifically for that
purpose. We will make a home for them. And should we not outlive
you, I will provide so that your sisters can take them in.'

There has been no deliberation. This has come upon him in an
instant, and entire. Half-stunned, Rochester rises and moves towards
the veranda — not in hope of more air, but of a larger space. Tug,
expectant, rouses himself and licks his master's hand. 'I have money
in the Indies which I neither need nor want. It shall be settled on your
children. But why wait? If you are so indifferent to their fate, let us
take them to England now — to a home where they will want for
nothing. There they will not lack a father's love!'

A silence follows. Not a little dazed by his own impetuosity, he
hears Rivers push back his chair and braces himself for some
retaliation — for surely no man who is a man could stand to hear
himself accused like that? And Rivers's tone has indeed changed —
but not as he has anticipated.

'Come, take my hand. You have passed my test. Do not ever for a
single moment imagine that I do not love my daughter and my wife's
son as steadfastly as you have loved your own. That is why I have to
be sure that when I die, I shall be consigning them to someone who
will care for them as I do. That Jane would care for them dutifully I
was sure I could rely on, but to set my heart at rest I also needed
proof of your affection.'

Regret mingles with Rochester's relief. For a moment he has
imagined a miraculous, immediate resolution — leaving tomorrow,
Jivaj riding beside him, Jane with the baby — but now he has
committed himself to an outcome that he may not live to enjoy.
Rivers might live for years. He thinks of a decade hence, of a young
man and his half-sister, alighting from his carriage at the door of
Thornfield when all the hopeful impulses which are driving him now
have long since faded. But he has spoken. He has given his word. He
tries to recall exactly what he has promised. All he can be certain of is
the urgency of his need to be a father once more. Passion has forced
his feelings to the surface, but now that they have been exposed, they
do not need to be repeated. Men do not talk to each other of such
things; nor can a gentleman correct or modify avowals made in the

heat of a moment, no matter how they may look when cooler thoughts prevail. When he has composed himself, he speaks carefully. 'You have my word, Rivers. I shall stand guardian for your children and I will put in trust for them my Caribbean properties. Tomorrow I shall go to Mysore where I will have a notary draw up the documents.'

'As you wish. I have no more doubts of your sincerity. I know Jane will as always want to do what is right, but I will confess that I previously thought you were only amusing yourself here – playing the Nabob.'

The man seems abstracted, as if the essence of the matter is done with, and he has no time for its details. Their conversation has shifted. 'At least allow that I did not attempt to grow rich from Pisgah. Although at first I may have wished no more than to make my time here of interest to myself, I have come to know what I hope is an honest satisfaction.'

Rivers cuts him off. 'Mr Rochester. None of us knows what he does here. I came determined to be a saviour of souls. Now I think that too often I have caused damage which I can never repair. The consequences of our presence belong to a future we cannot know.' He stands up abruptly, as if he wishes to cut short his own words.

A chance flash of lightning, closer now, allows Rochester to see his outstretched hand. He reaches out and is surprised to find that what he grasps is the rough, gnarled hand of a labourer. For a moment, he feels the other's grip tighten, and then they part.

He lets Tug lead him back to his room, but lies awake for many hours. Jane is breathing steadily – sleeping the sleep of one who always wants to do what is right. How will she greet the news? What will he tell her? Now he longs to be away – but he cannot leave the children. Not the boy. Might they stay longer? Might they stay forever? Pisgah could be expanded – rooms built for Adèle. Staying would make Jane happy. And if Jane were happy...Suddenly he thinks of Rivers. Jane will restore his health. She has done so much already. The man he encountered tonight is surely well on the mend. And when that happens, which man will his wife choose?

Horrified, he wrestles his thoughts to what he can cope with. The West Indian money is nothing. He will be glad to have it put to good use. It will be more than enough to fund a good regiment for Jivaj when the time comes. The lad is not cut out to be a farmer, let alone a parson. And the girl child – there will be a sad gap when Adèle leaves him, as she must, very soon...His thoughts circle and thrash. It is monstrous to hope that Rivers will not prolong his stay in this world, but the man must have been weakened by so many years in this climate. Jane seems to thrive here, but she is still young. Young enough for children. But she has seen how easily children die here. He must get her home. To Thornfield...

He wakes grudgingly when Kamil pounds on his door in the clammy dawn. St John Rivers has died in his sleep.

# CHAPTER 14

**No Bishop, no Alice, no Adèle;** no Harry, no Emily – and no Captain Sharp. By good chance, the ship that brought us to Bombay is now carrying us westwards, to the Cape and then Brazil. There we will leave the estimable Captain Benwick – the sole relic of our outward journey – and embark for Jamaica. God knows how long it will be till the fresh winds of Europe waft us homeward. We have left much behind, but with us are the two dear children that my cousin bequeathed to us – and Mrs O'Reilly.

That lady's services more than pay for her passage, and leave me ample time to write the letters I have barely had time for since St John left us. Yet writing to Diana and Mary comes hard. My promise to them was that I would discover what happened to their brother, yet I suspect that what I can tell them will be a partial account, and that much of the story will remain forever locked in my heart.

*Edward was delighted to receive Captain Fitzpayne's account of the new Thornfield's completion, and your raptures over the silks and ornaments that dear Adèle chose in the bazaars of Bombay cheered us both with the thought that something of her will be part of Thornfield still. We carry with us Parvati and Jiwaj who have already done so much to heal our hearts, and the satisfaction of having built on the foundation which St John created at Pisgah, despite so much adversity.*

*Before we left, our dear friend Bishop Fisher told us that on his travels he had encountered some among the native people (few as yet, but increasingly respected) who are bent on reform. He has real hopes that many of the hideous practices of a deluded religion will soon be proscribed. That prudent caution which has prevented our people interfering with the customs of the country (no matter how heinous) will not be so necessary once its own natives have attained a higher kind of understanding. At Pisgah we had our own experience of how enlightenment is spreading among those rulers who are not too vain and self-absorbed to benefit from our more advanced learning, and it is gratifying to think that in some small way we too have contributed to the country's progress. But these are topics for the library and the fireside at Thornfield and you will be hungry for more news that the bare bones I have supplied in previous letters.*

**The scramble of claws across the deck t**ells me that Edward is approaching our cabin. 'Come Jane, there will be time enough for scribbling.' He speaks softly; the boards that separate us from where the children sleep are thin. True as always to his name, Tug hauls us towards my familiar perch. 'This dog smells home.'

'Impossible!' And yet who knows? There is an eagerness like Hope personified about the beast. Edward fastens his leash to a convenient point in the rigging and reaches for my hand. It is not entirely because the space is so narrow that we must stand so close.

No one is near us. There is no reason to whisper, but Mrs O'Reilly tends to appear from nowhere. She seems to think that without Harry, Edward needs her support. 'Where is Dolly? Has she been offering you her arm again?'

'I left her amidships taking a tot with the bosun.'

'When we reach England, we must find her more suitable employment. I cannot think that she and Mrs Fairfax will rub along.'

'But Mrs Fairfax approves of the new curtains, you say. So she is not averse to all our Indian baggage.'

'Mrs O'Reilly should go to Ireland. There are garrisons there, which will suit her well. And perhaps Mrs O'Gall at Bitternutt Lodge with her five daughters is still in need of a governess?'

How strange it is, to be teasing like this. I had thought the habit was lost forever.

***The fatal news*** *of your dear brother's death was, I hope, softened by my reassurances that he died strong in faith, respected by all who knew his work and eager to be united with the woman he called his wife – the woman who was indeed his wife. One of Bishop Fisher's first actions on reaching Pisgah was to examine the documents concerning the ceremony which Mr Kamil conducted and declare them valid. There can be no doubts about the legality of Parvati's parentage, and* *what the gossips of our acquaintance may wish to construe as an exotic concubinage was as respectable as the biddies of Morton could wish for their vicar. It is a pity that the formal adoption of Jivaj could not have been accomplished before St John's death, but Edward and I expect to take that upon ourselves when we reach England. Naturally, there will be difficulties: the colour of the children's skin will always be a badge of their origins, but with our connections (both in England and now in India!) and a sound education for both, we are quite undaunted. All the same, I would be grateful if you could – in some small ways – prepare the Thornfield household for their arrival.*

As the last of India drops below the horizon, I find myself oddly reluctant to continue my letter. What I was on the voyage out, when I spent so many hours facing the horizons of the unknown – that woman is gone. Not for a moment have I forgotten our Ted, or his bright-eyed sister and baby Helen. While we have been away from England, time and distance have tumbled my memories, but now, as we turn towards home, they come back to me, steady and grave. Those children will visit the new house, and rooms they never knew. Edward and I can talk of them now, and we do not always weep.

Of this there is little need to write. Of Jivaj and Parvati, one must hope that their wounds do not bleed for very long: it is not in the order of things that children should forever mourn their parents.

What I cannot bring myself to write of at all, is the immediate consequences of my cousin's will. At first, I was overjoyed when Edward revealed St John's wishes. God's plan for me was clear at last: to be the mother of his children, though never my cousin's wife. Then, when Mr Kamil wailed that he cared little for the property and everything for his sister's offspring, I was inclined to share Edward's misgivings: it was unwise of St John to entrust his legacy to his native subordinate. I urged that we should remain in India, to exercise some supervision. In the will (which I pored over) I could find no explicit instruction that the children must go to England, only that we were to be their guardians. At that, Edward and I were in danger of quarrelling once more, until he assured me that England was plainly spoken of in their midnight interview, and it must be our sacred duty to carry out a dying man's last wishes.

I can hear my husband's voice now, discussing with Captain Benwick whether Jivaj should be prepared for the army or the navy. Naturally Captain Benwick favours the navy, though I fear cousin Diana's husband would not agree. But for his employment at the new Thornfield, the peace has not been kind to Captain Fitzpayne. How soon into our voyage have my thoughts turned homeward – but memories of Mr Kamil pull me back. How stubbornly he argued that his sister had not wished her son to become a British soldier, when there can be no doubt that the boy has a taste for it: a British soldier's blood runs in his veins. Who knows, the boy might one day return to India in a position of command. But when I said as much, Mr Kamil turned petulant and disagreeable.

Revisiting those scenes is almost unbearable. It saddens me that we did not leave our Indian friends entirely happy with all we had done for them. Where we might have expected some expression of gratitude, the whole household instead united in a parade of unfettered grief that left Edward and myself stunned and embarrassed by its excess. When Poonam prostrated herself and pawed at my feet, I could hardly bring myself to stoop and console her. 'You will still have your idiot boy' I reminded her – the boy with his rattle. Mr Kamil's wife – Asha – was the worst. When our paths crossed, she would snatch up her own child and hide – as if she suspected I might have designs on her baby!

Suddenly the cabin is too cramped. The strain of those weeks between St John's death and our reunion with Adèle and the Fishers drives me from my desk to seek the air. Our ship is in full sail; the canvas swells and huffs before the wind and the passing waves clatter beneath our keel. Under an awning, Parvati wriggles on Mrs O'Reilly's lap and I can hear Captain Benwick explaining to Jivaj the use of the sextant.

Edward's voice cuts into my thoughts. 'Benwick thinks we will easily find a ship at either the Cape or Brazil that would take us to Jamaica.'

'But I thought that was abandoned.' I can hear the tremble in my voice. 'We are taking the children to Thornfield – as St John wished.'

'That Jamaican legacy is on my conscience, Jane. I promised Rivers that I would turn that cursed inheritance into these children's future wealth. God knows what is happening with no reliable fellow to manage it.'

I look at my husband. His bulk stands between me and the westering sun so that I see only a featureless silhouette. His expression is unreadable. Even of those we love most, there is so much we cannot know. Does Jamaica and what happened there haunt him, as India and St John haunted me? My own conscience is telling me that if this is what Edward wants, then I must consent – as he consented to my wish for India.

But the *children* – how instantly I abandoned all thoughts of staying, once I was sure of what St John willed for those little ones! Affection had already wound them to our hearts; obligation now binds us with hoops of steel. *Jamaica is not what St John wanted* is the protest rising in my breast. I see danger, contamination, but I know my fears are not enough.

'You are unhappy, Jane. I am as anxious as you to return to Thornfield, but –'

I interrupt him. 'The new house is complete. Captain Fitzpayne will be looking for further employment. Can we not send him to the Indies? Is he not that reliable fellow you are in need of?'

In full view of the deck he plants a smacking kiss on my lips. 'The man has been to the ends of the earth – he has survived a world-wide war. Would Diana wish to accompany him, do you think? I will pay him handsomely. Their children might come to us – God knows we shall have rooms enough – and they would be company for Jivaj and the little one…'

He is running on and I am asking myself what perils will my moment of thoughtless inspiration visit upon my blameless cousin and her husband? We cannot always come safely to harbour. But there is no retracting. Once Edward has seized upon a notion, there is no letting go.

I pick up my pen. *Parvati is too young to understand her losses, but for many days after her father's death she would sit on my lap, gazing pitiably all around her, looking for what was gone forever. Every night her plaintive keening near broke my heart, and I took her into my bed to try and comfort her.*

Shall I think of a new name for her? Parvati is too strange for English tongues. Jivaj might become George. This evening as I was settling him in his bunk, he asked me whether his mother and 'Papa Sinjin' will still watch over him from heaven, when we reach England. Papa Sinjin, whom we buried with his wife the evening of his death. I looked down into the grave where that marble column lay in its snowy shroud and saw uncovered the edge of Jaya's winding sheet, now stained the warm, rich red of the soil – the only glimpse of her that I shall ever have, this side of eternity.

*We heard of our dear Adèle's safe arrival in Cochin with Mrs Fisher and her baby just before the monsoon rains came at last. Christianity of a sort is well established in the city, and the Bishop, who managed to join them before the roads became impassable, was welcomed with much ceremonial. Meanwhile at Pisgah we contended with washing that never dried, mildew and mould sprouting on every surface, roofs leaking, chalk crumbling and school-books falling apart. But still crops had to be harvested and taken to market and more urgently than before, now that our departure was in sight, building had to continue.*

Again I come to a halt. When a new chapter in one's life is about to begin, one is impatient for the preceding phase to be ended. In truth, those final weeks at Pisgah were clouded by more than the black skies of the monsoon. I grieved for my cousin, but I was eager to begin the work of mothering his children – and this was marred by the continuing, silent tussle with the mournful Kamil and his family. Their resentment crept through all our doings, like the mildew.

I scribble a few paragraphs about the patchy news which crossed the mountains from Cochin. Some of dear Adèle's breathless missives must have been lost in the mud, but we made out that our own Prince, whose interest in our religion had prompted him to join the festivities, was likewise marooned by the weather. That eagerness for our modern ideas, which Edward had so often reported, frequently brought him into company with the Bishop and his party.

**We are at the Cape** and Captain Benwick has intercepted letters from home that were heading for India, sent when Diana and Mary knew that their brother was alive but not that he is now dead. My letter, written from Poona when I knew only the Archdeacon's account, had said nothing of Jaya and her history, nothing of Parvati, nor of Jivaj. When they wrote, they did not yet know that these children are now ours. I had written again, when I was more confident of the truth, but I have still not told the whole story. I said nothing of Jaya's snake, nor of her early history. Though I am confident of Diana and Mary's charity, there are others who would eagerly blacken her ghost. 'Replies to further letters from us in India may be on their way.'

'Then they will be lost. We are heading in the other direction.'

'Will it matter?' I shall be glad when this topsy-turvy arrangement of time and distance is put right.

And suddenly we are melancholy, despite the sunny garden, and I know that Edward is thinking of his daughter. That is more news which those at home do not know. My hand is on his knee. 'The Prince has promised that they will visit. It is not so rare these days.'

'Ships still founder.'

'She has Emily, to remind her of home. And Harry too. But I confess I am not looking forward to breaking the news to Emily's mother.'

'Bessie may have wind of it before we arrive. Emily came to me for help with her spelling before we left.'

So typically kind of him. I raise my hand to his face. 'Now that we too have given a child we love to a foreign country, perhaps Mr Kamil and his wife will feel that some balance has been restored – that while some sorrow is unavoidable, securing the future for his sister's children must be our main concern.' Jivaj and Tug are grappling with the frayed rope-end which has been the dog's companion since we last saw London's river. At Thornfield we shall make a young Englishman of the boy, before he must go away to school.

Edward raises his eyes towards the great slab of mountain and I think that what he makes out is another landmark that our journey has put between us and his darling Adèle, in her kingdom below a range of blue mountains. I have not told Edward how his daughter confided in me on the eve of her marriage. There are some things that women speak of only among themselves – and then only rarely. As the child of a courtesan she was doubtless from infancy vaguely aware of matters that would normally be known only to a daughter of the farmyard. Mrs Fisher's ordeal had terrified her. As the nearest thing to her mother it was my duty to explain that beyond some trifling pain on her wedding night, she would soon learn to welcome the sweetness of her marriage bed, though in truth I felt at a loss: I have glimpsed statues and paintings which suggest that the customs of India may be very different from even the boudoirs of Paris. But there is so much I could not – cannot – say. I heard myself reciting what every woman is obliged to believe: that the joys of motherhood more than reward the agonies of childbirth, but I do not think I can have provided much reassurance, for in truth at that moment I could only remember that the joys my own children had given made their loss more unendurable. So much that begins in joy and hope ends in unforeseen catastrophe. But a young woman in love listens with only half an ear and I like to think that the promptings of nature made good for her what was lacking from my counsel.

Edward's familiar grunt brings me back to the present. 'Yes, she is happy. And not just because all the chauks of India, the souks of Constantinople and the boutiques of Paris are now hers to command. India has sobered her. She will be eager to discharge the responsibilities that belong to her high position.' He laughs again – this time a little bitterly. 'A station she could never have gained in England.'

*Of course, our eventual reunion was joyful* – *how could it be otherwise? Old friends to rediscover, a new baby and a newly grown-up Adèle. My only sorrow was that they were too late to know dear St John, but the delay had given us the opportunity to present Pisgah at its very best. The Bishop told me that it was on the Ghats at Benares that he came fully to realise 'the daunting enormity of the task ahead' and I cannot help feeling glad that at Pisgah he found a small but sure beginning.*

*After examining Mr Kamil closely he pronounced himself perfectly satisfied with the soundness of his understanding, and with due though modest ceremony he was installed as the official chaplain. How St John would have rejoiced! It is pleasant to think of how tidy we have left everything behind us.*

This may come to be what I believe, but as I write it seems to me that the Bishop's approval only inflated Mr Kamil's self-importance. The spiritual aspects of Pisgah were now his to command, and by his way of thinking, this included the welfare of his sister's children, so his plaints renewed. When the Prince requested a visit to Pisgah we hoped that putting on a show might distract him.

*Native celebrations being somewhat prone to muddle, we feared the worse; but the Prince was very gracious, and endured the pupils' recitations with far more good humour than Lady Ingram at a Ferndean bazaar. I shall have to trust to memory when I work up the hasty sketches which were all I had time for at the scene, but I remember Edward saying that our dear Adèle seemed like a princess herself as she inspected the girls' needlework. Nor shall I ever forget our moonlit banquet under the three great trees. On a whim, I fetched Parvati from her cradle, and though I know that she will not remember how that golden pavilion gleamed in the torchlight, I like to think that something of the scene reflected in her fathomless brown eyes will remain with her forever as it will with me.*

*As I would say to the Bishop later, the author of* Waverley *himself could hardly have imagined what followed. It was very late, and we were sitting alone on our veranda, enjoying the night air and reflecting on the day's success, when Harry – somewhat mystified – came to inform us that the Prince craved a moment of our time. Edward thought it must be about the school – the Prince had previously expressed an interest in providing an English education for the sons of his ministers. Of course we quickly made ourselves available – though in truth we were too weary for much earnest discussion – and were beyond amazement when we discovered that the Prince had come to ask for Adèle's hand in marriage!*

*Really, the episode was not without its comedy. The poor dear man would not rest until he could be certain that Edward would hear his suit sympathetically. Of course, we hardly needed to ask after his means, there was no question of fortune-hunting, but other enquiries were essential. He assured us that it was not just Adèle's beauty but her modern ideas that had captivated him; not only will she bind our two countries together, but she will help him in his great work of reform. In the end, Edward's only provisos were that the Prince should confine himself to a single wife and leave instructions forbidding Adèle to immolate herself in the event of his death. I will confess that I anticipate some pleasure in being able to remind Lady Ingram that our daughter is the Rani of Mysore.*

What I do not describe is Edward's grief. I woke in the darkest part of the night to find he had left our bed and was on our veranda once more, staring over the invisible river. The small rush-light I carried revealed a glint of the tears that brimmed in his poor wounded eyes. I tried to console him. 'We knew she must be married soon. Remember that this is not Captain Smart – nor the Edinburgh architect. The Prince loves and admires her for herself, not for her fortune.'

'But to be so far away.' Suddenly he turned, to face me fully. 'Shall we not stay, Jane? Make a new home for ourselves, here in India?'

How I would have welcomed this, just a few months before. Now I have to remind him that returning to England was part of his promise to a dying man. And I think we were both reassured when we saw the Prince and Adèle together the following morning. Their love was unmistakeable, while His Highness's respect and admiration for his future bride promises well for his country's future. Adèle will be a beacon for Indian womanhood.

*Subdued elegance seems to be a concept quite foreign to the general Indian sensibility, and though I am told that the wedding was modest by princely standards, my meagre powers of description will quickly be exhausted when I attempt to give an account of it. Fifty elephants in the procession! Even Scott's powers would be tested, the Bishop surmised. He remained in Mysore just long enough to conduct the marriage ceremony – a brief moment of sacred calm among all the gaudy riot for which I shall always be profoundly grateful. And then – before the day was out – he and Mrs Fisher left for Madras, where urgent business awaited him.*

**I cannot write what followed that night**, though it glows in my memory like the ruby pinned to the Prince's turban. But now that we plan to continue with Captain Benwick to London, instead of disembarking at Brazil, no letter can reach Thornfield much before us, so there is no urgency about it.

For several days the wild ocean has formed all our horizons; we have seen no land, no birds, but now, late in the afternoon, the look-out's cry calls us all to the side. It is Jivaj's keen young eyes that have spotted what to me is no more than a tiny irregularity where sea meets sky. 'A whaler' he shouts, and looks up at Edward with a face full of adventure, and though I know there is little that my husband can see, a spark of the boy's eagerness kindles the father in him, and I remember how he was with Ted, when Tug was just a puppy.

I beckon Mrs O'Reilly and Parvati is transferred to my arms. 'How can you tell that it is a whaler?'

He answers with that emphatic patience which boys use to explain what mothers cannot understand. 'Her sails are furled. And you can see the fire where they are boiling the blubber.'

Yes, I can make out the faintest glint of red.

'Tush, boy' Edward chides him. 'You have been yarning with the sailors.' And he pulls the child towards him.

Jivaj squirms, peering upwards. 'They are hoisting a signal.'

For the next hour Edward and I exchange our impressions of the lad's excitement, sometimes aloud, sometimes by the smallest gesture. 'See the pretty colours!' I urge Parvati, who laughs and wriggles as a series of flags is hauled jerkily up the mast.

'They are sending a boat!' cries Jivaj. 'How fast they row! They are chasing a whale!'

'More likely coming to give us mail or take on provisions.' Edward's arm is round my waist.

'That man – he is blue!' This as the lighter draws close to our side. 'Why is he blue, *Bapa*?'

'I cannot see, my lad. Ask your mama.'

Before I can explain that the man is tattooed – a South Sea islander, no doubt – Jivaj suddenly gasps, awe-struck. His voice sinks to a whisper. 'It is the Lord Krishna! My mother told us stories of Lord Krishna and the gopis.'

My heart seems to miss a beat as my husband's arm tightens around me. 'Do you remember, Jane, on the voyage out, Adèle asking the Bishop to explain the blue one?'

Here is another child I must share with the ghost of an alien mother. I have brought with us my sketch of Jaya, to hang in the new house. I think of the ruins of the old Hall, left standing to indulge Adèle's romantic yearnings, and wonder if they can be dismantled now.

Jivaj is tugging at my sleeve. 'Mrs O'Reilly says it is tattoos. Can he be tattooed *all over*?'

'Very like' I say, laughing now. Certainly, all the parts that can be seen.

'Come, Jane' whispers my husband, close to my ear.

We dine late. The children are hard to settle and I think Mrs O'Reilly has been tippling. While Edward takes a last cigar with Captain Benwick I try to resume my letter, but my efforts convey little of the enthusiasm which will be needed for the work I have in mind.

*If my previous scribbles have reached you, you will at least know that I intend to use all the advantages of Mr Rochester's position and his fortune to support from England the good work of the Bishop and Mrs Fisher. Dear Mary – your husband was a good friend to St John – warn him to expect my attentions! But I have to confess that I quail a little when I think of what must be undone before there can be any progress. India has been painted in the blackest colours by those who think that outrage and indignation will prompt larger donations to their cause. Our Jivaj and Parvati must not grow up seeing the country of their birth so cruelly represented. Those who dwell on the manifold indignities which the women of India may suffer should reflect on how their own female compatriots are often situated. I have known no more than a corner of it; I have been sheltered and privileged. But I have seen signs of better things to come and we must make it our business to tell a story of hope.*

**I read this passage to my husband the following morning.** 'Jane' he says carefully. 'You should write a novel.'

'That is what Adèle says. She has an insatiable appetite for romance. But I want your opinion.'

He hesitates and I conclude that I must have expressed myself even less adequately than I imagined. Every morning when there is not too much activity among the sailors, we circulate the decks for an hour. We complete another circuit before he answers. 'The night before he died, Rivers admitted that he did not know what he was doing at Pisgah. I forget the phrase. All I can be sure of is that we are inextricably bound to the country.'

'The children we take with us and the dear ones we leave behind.'

'Yes, the children. Whom we love as if they were our own – but they are not. We think of making an Englishman of Jivaj – of re-naming him George – but are we right?'

'George is Diana's boy's name. It could be confusing.' But he means more than that. 'Yet men of distinction – men trusted by the government – are saying that our future in India depends on making its people more like us.'

Something is troubling him. I glance around the empty ocean, wondering if he has sensed a storm in the offing.

'And who is the Englishman should be the model? I am not fit. Not the boy's father – that scoundrel.' He hesitates for a moment. 'Jane, I received a letter at the Cape. I could at least make out enough to suspect a military origin, so I asked Captain Benwick to read it to me. It is from Porter.'

'Porter? Mrs Porter's husband? What could he want with us?' But I know before it is explained. 'Do you still not know how much these shoulders can bear?'

He strokes my cheek with his knuckles. 'The man is a blackguard. But Jivaj is his son.'

'He has never shown the slightest interest in the boy!' The sky is still blue, the sea is calm, but suddenly the breeze is cold as polar ice.

'Pah! He accuses me of abduction. But I cannot think that he wants the child. He writes of *recompense*. That is, money.'

'Then give it him!'

He shakes his head. 'Gladly. Except there is no ending is such a business. He would be forever demanding more.'

I look beyond him. Under our awning, Jivaj is studying with rule and protractor. He bites his lip as he measures an angle. 'You cannot lose the boy. *We* cannot lose him. Surely the intrepid Mrs Porter would never consent to take on her husband's –' But she relishes notoriety. An Indian bastard might be as essential to her cabinet of curiosities as a stuffed cobra.

'Nor shall we lose him. But we may have to go to law. It is very much for the best that Fitzpayne should take on the business in the Indies.'

He speaks as if this is a settled matter. The sky is unsullied, the bulging sails are steady and the prow dips and rises with the regularity of a clock, yet a profound melancholy has begun to affect me, and the sensation is so keen that it brings back to me another moment when joy was suddenly chastened by more sombre reflections. 'Do you remember the evening of Adèle's wedding?' I hush him before he can respond. 'I mean the elephants' stable.'

Though the night's festivities continued around us there came a point when I longed for quiet. We left the marble colonnades behind and let Tug lead us. There is a value in silence that is all the more poignant when there is merriment in the distance.

'If I am not mistaken, this courtyard is where the dog got the fright of his life' said my husband. 'I am surprised he should be so eager to return.'

A deep arcade ran around three sides of the space, and the few lanterns seemed more to cast shadows than shed light. The howdahs in which we and the other guests had ridden that afternoon were lined up on the cobbles, waiting to be stored like half-dismantled items of furniture in some vast attic. I could sense rather than see the huge beasts rocking and swaying in their stalls.

I asked what had happened. Now it is hard to remember that for many months at Pisgah we had confided almost nothing of our feelings to one another. And is it not strange, how our most profound understandings may come to us unexpectedly, and in such incongruous surroundings? A palace was at hand, and yet it was with the stink of the stables in my nostrils that I discovered how cunningly my feet had been set on the way of renewal. As if in a trance I heard Edward describe his moment of terror, when he imagined that Jivaj might be among the elephants, and like a lightning bolt it struck me that St John's children had already completed that task with which all children are entrusted at their birth – to make us fearful for them.

Like an enemy stealthily creeping up on the fortress of my heart, love had won the siege. Surreptitiously I had been made a mother again, and Edward a father to St John's children – and unawares, while that love grew, we took on love's great price. I heard my husband say 'How Maria would have loved today' and it came to me that for the first time we were exchanging our thoughts about the lives our children might have lived.

'She had something of Adèle's taste for finery.' I could not see Edward's face but I thought that like me he might be smiling.


**As the present afternoon** wears towards sunset, we begin the routines of a day's ending – the children's supper, bathing, fresh night-clothes stiff from the sun and the southern wind. Edward reviews the day's progress with Captain Benwick. Mrs O'Reilly's chatter blurs but does not quite subdue my anxiety. Sickness took our children. It would have taken Adèle, as it cut short the days of my cousin's wife. And now there is another enemy. Is Jivaj now to be snatched from us by the cold hand of the law? Truly, the price of maternal joy is perpetual worry.

Our evening meal passes like a jumbled dream of riddles that neither man nor woman will resolve this side of Judgement Day. Dimly I perceive that Captain Benwick is happier at sea than at home with a wife he married too hastily. How fortunate I have been, that unlike many of my sex I too have been able to temper my unhappiness with activity and even – I must admit to it – adventure. The moon is near full tonight as it was the night of Adèle's wedding and once the table is cleared we leave the Captain to his calculations and let Tug lead us to the prow, where I stare down at the curling, moon-lit wave below, with my husband's arm around my shoulders. Perhaps later, a little later, in that blest interval between ecstasy and sleep, when our souls are most nearly one, I will try to sort out my thoughts. But for a moment I am very content to linger – and recall more sweet memories of that evening at the palace.

Perhaps it was thirst that drew Tug to a small, secluded garden, where water bubbled gently in a wide marble basin. When Edward slipped his leash, he drank deeply, then looked appealingly towards us, waiting for a ball to be thrown, or for some other excuse that would allow him to plunge in. A tiny frog disturbing a lily pad was all that he needed – and I too needed just one small signal that I might unleash all my pent-up longings. Yet I was consumed with a more than virginal shyness. My cousin's death and his wishes for the children had over-ridden the sharpest of our differences, but I had begun to fear that the companionable ease we had recently found was no better than a kind of truce. That garden had been designed to caress all the senses. Languid springs trembled amid the swelling lotus buds; heat captured in its shady nooks sucked perfume from garlands of roses and jasmine – and we strolled on, arm in arm, like contented pensioners exercising our pet.

An alabaster lamp allowed me to study my husband's profile – and see how grey his hair had become. Am I too late? I asked myself. Has age overtaken us? I remembered the chair he had made for himself at Pisgah, where he would sit at sunset and smoke his cigar, and I thought he is reconciled to a life without passion; he has embraced an evening calm.

I smile to myself now as I remember those fears, and settle myself deeper into his arms. He has always been a master of delay. Well, I too know that pleasure will be sweeter for a little waiting.

There was a broad marble bench in front of a shadowy pavilion. 'Shall we sit awhile and watch the moonlight reflected in the water?' I asked. I remember how my voice was shaking.

'Poor dear!' he murmured. 'Are your feet hurting? You must be in dire need of sleep after the day we have had.' He patted my hand.

Somewhere in the palace, blossoms were being strewn on the silken covers of a bridal bed. I looked up at the moon and implored her help, but she pulled a skein of cloud across her face and disappeared from view. Almost frantic, I clapped my other hand atop of his, trapping it between mine. 'Dearest!' I croaked.

He sighed. 'So, we are to lose Harry too. I must confess I was unaware of how the Dewan had come to rely on him. I shall miss the fellow. But it will be good for Adèle to have another familiar face at hand.'

'Bessie will think that her daughter stays to be with Harry. It puzzles me that they have not reached an understanding before now.' Disappointment was turning my limbs to lead as our discourse took this humdrum turn.

'Oh, Emily has understood for a long time. She knows that Harry's affections tend otherwise. He is the Dewan's swain now.'

Something began to dawn on me, but before my imagination dared to give it form, I was inwardly wailing *Are all to know love tonight, save me?* Instead I said 'How will you manage without him on the voyage? We must look for another servant, I suppose.'

'My wants are simple nowadays. And Mrs O'Reilly assures me that she can supply them. I have promised to pay for her passage in return for her help with the children – and some other minor services.' He pulled his hand away from mine and patted his pockets. 'I have a cigar about me somewhere. Help me to light it, will you Jane?'

Somehow, I managed the task, though as I gazed at that dear scarred face in the circle of flame-light, my mind was racing. *Mrs O'Reilly? Minor services?* What could he mean? I was on my feet now and moving away so that he should not be conscious of my distress. Tug shook himself and licked my hand, hoping that his walk was to continue. Perhaps it was this movement that roused a bird from its night-time perch among the foliage, because with a flutter of wings it flew into the open, then settled on the topmost branch of a flowering tree and began to sing. I raised my face to the dark sky, hoping to find a breeze that would cool the fever still running in my blood, and saw the moon throw back her veil. Now! she insisted: I can do no more! In an instant I took in all before me: the white flowers sprinkling the shadowed lawn, the sharp blade of a fish's fin cutting through the silvered waters, the bulbul's throbbing song. 'Mr Rochester! Put out that damned cigar!'

In another instant the cigar was in the lotus pool, I was in his arms – and Tug (roused no doubt by my tone of command) was leaping around us. Poor dog – we had to push him away as we

showered kisses on each other's mouth, face, throat, neck, hands –
'Forgive me, Jane' he groaned in between kisses. 'I had to be sure.'

'Nothing surer' I panted.

I think I was tearing at his beautiful new shirt. Really, I blush to
think of it now, weeks later, when passion has steadied and I no longer
need to fear that love is lost forever. I close my eyes so that the sound
of the Atlantic waves below us will cool my thoughts. 'Do you
remember the marble pavilion?' I whisper, turning in his embrace to
look up at him.

He frowns – that frown which still dissolves my sinews. 'Pavilion?
Pavilion? I am an old man, and my memory is failing. You will have to
remind me.'

'Of this' I say. 'And this. Is your memory stirring – with this?'

'It is coming back' he says. 'Remind me again.'

'Do you remember how we fumbled, as we tried to tie Tug to that
bench?' I know that the dog will be roused by the sound of his name
and sure enough he tries to thrust his nose between us.

'Damn dog' grumbles my husband. 'Never knows when he's not
wanted.'

'We could leave him with the bosun and Mrs O'Reilly.'

The decks are awash with moonlight as we make our way to our
cabin. Beneath our feet the ship moves steadily on. There is one last
thing to be done before we give ourselves up to the welcoming
darkness. Carefully, so as not to make a sound, I raise the latch. The
faint glow from a swaddled lantern outlines two white-covered forms.
Among all the familiar rhythms of the living ship and the passing
ocean, I hear their steady breathing.

'Is all well, Jane?'

'Yes, my dearest. The children are safely sleeping.'

I turn towards the door and a moment of sadness closes my throat
as I move to take my husband's hand. But before I can reach him, he
holds up a listening finger. 'Hush – the babe –'

But it is not Parvati who whimpers. Jivaj has shifted in his sleep
and the light catches a tear escaping those dark lashes that I tried to
copy in his mother's portrait. I smooth his forehead. 'No fever.'

'Thank God.'

The lad blinks, stretches a little and curls himself round his pillow.
Do I hear him call Mama? Perhaps – but that is not me. He is old
enough never to forget the woman I never knew, whose image, marked
with St John's tears, hangs by his bedside, framed in ivory, ready for

Thornfield. But what will his memories mean in what lies ahead? His movements and perhaps our presence have disturbed little Parvati too. She frowns and yawns and her tiny white teeth reflect the lamplight. She faces the future with hardly more than my sketches to tell her where she came from – and as I straighten her bedding and tuck her in more securely for some reason I recall one of the last pages in my album, no more than a hasty scribble on the day we left, of the idiot boy sitting cross-legged by St John's grave, staring across the river to the distant hills.